WHITE WINGS
WEEPING

Praise for Lesley Davis

"*Pale Wings Protecting* is a provocative paranormal mystery; it's an otherworldly thriller couched inside a tale of budding romance. The novel contains an absorbing narrative, full of thrilling revelations, that skillfully leads the reader into the uncanny dimensions of the supernatural."—*Lambda Literary*

Pale Wings Protecting "was just a delicious delight with so many levels of intrigue on the case level and the personal level. Plus, the celestial and diabolical beings were incredibly intriguing…I was riveted from beginning to end and I certainly will look forward to additional books by Lesley Davis. By all means, give this story a total once-over!" —*Rainbow Book Reviews*

Dark Wings Descending "is an intriguing story that presents a vision of life after death many will find challenging. It also gives the reader some wonderful sex scenes, humor, and a great read!"—Reviewer RLynne

"*Playing Passion's Game* is a delightful read with lots of twists, turns, and good laughs. Davis has provided a varied and interesting supportive cast. Those who enjoy computer games will recognize some familiar scenes, and those new to the topic get to learn about a whole new world."—*Just About Write*

By the Author

Truth Behind the Mask

Playing Passion's Game

Playing in Shadow

Starstruck

Raging at the Stars

The Wings Series

Dark Wings Descending

Pale Wings Protecting

White Wings Weeping

Visit us at www.boldstrokesbooks.com

WHITE WINGS WEEPING

by
Lesley Davis

2018

ISBN 13: 978-1-63555-191-4

This Trade Paperback Original Is Published By
Bold Strokes Books, Inc.
P.O. Box 249
Valley Falls, NY 12185

First Edition: May 2018

Credits
Editor: Cindy Cresap
Production Design: Stacia Seaman
Cover Design by Sheri (hindsightgraphics@gmail.com)

Acknowledgments

Thanks always to Radclyffe for granting me such a marvelous publishing platform to launch these stories from.

Thank you times infinity, Cindy Cresap, for your editing prowess, your encouragement, and that sly sense of humor that makes me think you were wasted not being a Brit.

Thanks to Sandy Lowe and to everyone at Bold Strokes Books.

Many thanks, Sheri, for such a seriously striking cover that was exactly what I wanted to have capture this story's essence. You totally rock!

Huge thanks to my friends and readers whose marvelous support truly keeps me writing: Jane Morrison and Jacky Morrison Hart, Pam Goodwin (Thank you for walking by my side, sword at the ready. You, my friend, were truly heaven sent.) and Gina Paroline, Kim Palmer-Bell, Cheryl Hunter and Anne Hunter, Kerry Pfadenhauer (especially for the times we spend on the PS4 talking about my characters and their journeys while playing and somehow still gaining XP in our respective games! Game on, fellow Reaper!).

And to you, Cindy Pfannenstiel, I keep my promise from all those many years ago. Way before Rafe and Ashley were even thought of, "this" was always meant to be a part of their story. Finally, I get to run amok on your home soil just like I said I would and exactly how I said I would! *evil chuckle* Thank you for you invaluable help on this story in so many ways. X

Keep fighting those demons no matter what form they take in your life.

Stay strong, reach out, and hold firm.

You are not alone.

Chapter One

"Kieran? Kieran Lee? Can you open your eyes for me, please?"
Whiteness. A burning brightness that seared through her
eyelids with a painful intensity. That was what Kieran registered as she
regained consciousness. She could hear a voice calling her name. They
weren't going to leave her alone anytime soon either, judging by their
tenacity and the increase in volume.

Kieran felt something on her skin, prodding, poking at her. The
sharp sting of a needle being inserted brought her ever closer to being
awake. She grunted at the pain and willed herself to reach out and slap
away whoever was intent on disturbing her. Her body didn't cooperate
with her mind, though. It felt sluggish and weighed down.

Why couldn't they just leave her alone? All she wanted was to
drift away and sleep.

"Kieran, open your eyes."

A different tone this time. Deeper, a touch harsher. The tone of an
exasperated mother trying to get her child out of bed and up for school.
A distant memory surfaced, and she could almost hear her mother's
voice calling to her from downstairs, "Get up now before I come drag
you out!" Irritation always colored her mother's voice because Kieran
was still huddled beneath her sheets, pleading for just five more minutes.

Kieran paid no attention to this voice either. She didn't have to
listen to anyone anymore.

"Kieran, do you know where you are?"

Please, lady, just shut up. Kieran groaned in exasperation, then
gasped as her eyelids were lifted up and an even brighter light was

shone into her eyes. Kieran fought against the hold on her head as she tried to shut her eyes against the intrusion. The light mercifully went away, and it was then she became aware of the monotonous sound of machines beeping out a steady rhythm beside her. The noise was too loud. Each blip and beep rang along her nerves and set them further on edge. Kieran blinked her eyes clear to take in her surroundings. The whiteness faded, leaving behind the reality Kieran had hoped not to see.

The pale cream walls of the hospital room were clean and stark under the bright fluorescent lights that shone above her. She couldn't mistake the faint odor of a pungent disinfectant that permeated the room. There was a harsh soap powder scent from the starched sheets underneath her and the faint fruity smell of sweat from whoever was beside her. A woman dressed in wrinkled hospital scrubs stood by the bed, checking on a tube fixed to an IV drip. So that was what they'd stuck in her. Kieran flexed her hand, feeling the uncomfortable tightness of the needle lodged in her flesh.

Damn it. I don't need whatever drugs you're pumping into me to be any more disassociated from life than I already am.

"Kieran, do you know where you are?" Dr. Reynolds, according to the name tag on her chest, leaned over to peer into Kieran's face.

"Trapped someplace between heaven and hell." Kieran's voice sounded tired and scratchy even to her own ears. Her chest hurt and her eyes felt rubbed raw. She tried to move, but for some reason, she was restricted. Kieran tested the limit of the thick bands that fastened her wrists to the bed rail. "What the hell?" She tugged against the restraints a little harder. Panic began to set in; Kieran did not like being tied down.

"You're in the St. Louis University Hospital. Do you know why you are here?" Dr. Reynolds was writing something on the chart she held in her hands.

Still trying to get free, Kieran closed her eyes again as realization sunk in. She was hooked up to drips, the beep of the machines was her heart being monitored, and she was restrained on the bed like a fugitive.

I failed again. Defeat weighed heavy on her soul.

"You were found washed up on the bank of the Mississippi River. Can you tell me what you were doing earlier tonight? Witnesses said they saw you climbing on the Eads Bridge."

Kieran sighed and opened her eyes once more, resigned to her fate. She stared up at the ceiling.

Suicide. I was attempting suicide.

Kieran didn't say the words out loud, but she could tell the doctor already knew that fact judging by the look on her face. Kieran couldn't meet the woman's eyes. She turned her face away from the pity she could feel directed her way.

Don't give me that look, lady. You can't possibly understand my motives and needs or why the hell I tried to die. I can't believe I screwed this up again. Trying to kill myself is proving harder than it looks. Next time I need to add more rocks to my pockets. Or maybe find a taller bridge. Seek out deeper water perhaps? A trip to Niagara Falls might just be my ticket out of here.

"You're going to have to talk to someone sometime. We can't let you just walk out of here now that you've coughed up all the river water out of your lungs."

Kieran sighed. That explained why her chest hurt so much. She had a vague recollection of throwing up most of the Mississippi after someone had applied CPR. She'd much rather talk to them about reviving her when she hadn't asked to be saved than deal with another goddamn shrink. *Yeah, yeah, sure, bring on another professional to join the long list of specialists I've been seen by already.* No one understood her predicament. No one would understand why jumping from a bridge to drown herself was far more suitable than living. She felt the harsh bite of the restraints clamped on her wrists, holding her down. Yet another piece of her control taken from her. No one would ever understand the nightmare she was in. It had made the depths of the water seem incredibly inviting.

Tears stung at her already sore eyes. *I just want it to stop, just for a while. Or even eternity. I'm past caring now. I can't live like this.* She stared at the ceiling. *And yet, I can't seem to die either.*

Five serious desperate attempts to kill herself in the past twelve months had all resulted in the same pointless outcome—Kieran left very much alive while medical professionals questioned her sanity and found her perfectly lucid.

If I was crazy enough to believe in such a thing as a guardian angel, then I'd start to wonder why he can keep me out of death's grasp but can't stop the madness from swallowing me whole every time it begins. Where's his blessed protection then?

She was startled when a hand touched her shoulder. She tried to wriggle out from under it.

You don't want to touch me. I'm marked. Marked by something so evil that I can't even wash away my sins for it by drowning myself.

"Tomorrow is a new day," Dr. Reynolds said. "I'm sure things will look brighter."

Kieran stared at her, amazed by the triteness of the comment. *My dear deluded doctor. Things haven't looked brighter for the last year. There's no sunshine and daisies in my future. I've seen it all, and the path put before me is laid in brimstone and paved in the bones of the dead.*

And I'm so tired. I'm weary and heartsick and need for it all to just stop. The weight of this knowledge is burying me alive. Yet I can't seem to die and I'm trying so hard to embrace the sleep of the eternal.

"Kieran?"

Kieran turned her head away. She screwed her eyes up tight to try to shut out all the light and grant herself the blessed darkness she wished for.

Just leave me alone. I'm done for today. Because while you see skies filled with sunshine, I'm left smelling sulfur and tasting ashes on my tongue.

Dr. Merlo Blue hurried through the reception area of the Craven Hope Psychiatric Hospital and made a beeline for the reception desk. She flashed the young woman behind the desk an apologetic grin as she placed the Starbucks coffee in front of her.

"Yes, Claudia, I know I'm late. The coffee is hot, though, I promise. And so fresh I watched them squeeze the beans myself." Merlo leaned over the desk to sweep up her day's patient folders. She juggled them around in her arms, making certain to keep her own coffee from spilling. She caught Claudia rolling her eyes at her. "Hey! I saw that look. I'll have you know I kept perfect time yesterday. You can't expect perfection two days in a row. Besides, I still have plenty of time before my first patient if I go now before you start berating me." She winked at Claudia, who still hadn't uttered a single word, and headed toward the doors leading to the psychiatric wing.

She found her office and as always marveled at the gold writing that spelled out her name on the frosted glass. Carefully balancing her coffee cup on top of the files, and praying nothing would fall, Merlo retrieved her key from her pocket and unlocked the door. She put everything on her desk and took a quick gulp from her coffee. Merlo winced as it burned her tongue.

"Damn it! You'd think after this long I'd remember hot coffee burns." She gasped for air to try to cool her mouth and shrugged off her coat to hang it in the closet. She brushed her hair back from her neck where it tickled at her. It was longer than she usually wore it, falling somewhere mid-shoulder and curling at the ends. She quickly fashioned a chignon, then eyed herself critically in the mirror that she had secreted away on her closet door. The swept-up hairstyle made her look more professional, at least. Not that she needed the confirmation. Merlo was outstanding in her field. She was a psychiatrist who excelled in the use of psychotherapy in her sessions with amazing, sometimes even miraculous, results. She was proud of what she had accomplished in her career. She'd worked hard and it was paying off.

Merlo riffled through the folders to get an idea of what the day had in store for her. There were a few new additions to her caseload she had to read up on before she would meet them. She sighed as she ran her fingertips over the pile. So much anguish consigned to a few sheets of paper and a checklist of triggers. She'd lost count of how many people she'd seen. Their problems were wide and varied, but all had the same effect—making life a living nightmare for them. Her time was divided between those with serious mental issues that they had no control over and those who were burdened by the weight of the world and their own problems on top.

So many souls struggling to keep their heads above water while the anxieties of the world see fit to drag them under.

Merlo despaired sometimes at how fragile people were.

She took a more cautious mouthful of her coffee to fortify herself for the day ahead and settled herself into her chair. She reached for the first case file, but before she opened it, she offered up a prayer. It was something she did before every session. It calmed her mind for the tasks ahead.

Let me ease the troubled souls of your children. Let me provide them comfort and soothe away their pain. Help me stand beside them as they face their inner demons. Strengthen me to be their faithful guardian and to arm them for their fight. Guide my hand to direct them on their journey. Help them find peace as they face the trials in this life until they are bathed in your light in the next.

She picked up her first case and began to read the notes. Forewarned as to what her first patient was experiencing, Merlo picked up her phone to tell Claudia she was ready to begin.

The psychiatrist is in.

CHAPTER TWO

The group therapy room was just big enough to accommodate the ten people who were currently sitting in a circle in a resigned silence. Kieran wasn't a part of the group, but she'd been seeking some peace and quiet somewhere, anywhere, and had been in this room first. She was, as always, accompanied by an orderly who followed her around like a badly trained stalker.

She'd pulled up a chair so she could gaze out the window and try to ignore her surroundings. The orderly stood at attention beside her. She acknowledged that her incarceration at this new hospital was something she had to resign herself to for the time being. And that meant her every waking moment was being monitored and catalogued. She was rarely left alone for any length of time. A steady rotation of orderlies dogged her footsteps as she wandered the corridors of the unit.

Kieran hooked a foot around a spare chair and nudged it into the orderly's direction in the hopes he'd quit hovering and just sit down.

The sky was clear and blue. There was a small well-kept garden just outside the window that Kieran was watching a man work on. He was meticulously measuring out rows to plant whatever seeds he had kept in his hand. He'd plant something, move along a little, and plant something else, then go back to the first small mound he'd just patted down to dig the seed back out again and plant it somewhere else. He'd been keeping Kieran entertained for the last five minutes. She was curious as to his reasoning behind it. She wondered if he did it deliberately to lengthen his time spent in the sunshine alone instead of being cooped up with the rest of them inside.

Kieran had been moved to the Craven Hope Psychiatric Hospital once she'd been considered well enough to leave the University Hospital for one more suited to her mental needs. What Kieran needed was to get the hell out of this place so she could go about her business.

She sat in a comfortable sprawl, feigning a nonchalance she didn't feel. She was fighting the urge to cross her arms over her chest. She'd lost count of how many times she'd been lectured over the defensive posture giving away her reluctance to join in and speak to those in charge. Kieran had learned the hard way that, no matter whether she told the truth or not, no one listened to her. She'd learned to hold her tongue unless she was badgering them to let her sign herself out.

She'd been diagnosed with having everything under the sun wrong with her. Differences of opinion ranged from her being chronically depressed to being bipolar or schizophrenic. Someone had suggested she was displaying the signs of some hereditary mental illness that only now was manifesting itself. Then there were the accusations of being attention seeking, a fantasist, or just another woman driven to distraction by her hormones. Finally, the manic-depressive with suicidal tendencies label was stuck in her file.

Kieran was hospitalized for a while after each attempt on her life, but what she had claimed she experienced had no physical evidence anywhere but on her own psyche. She'd had tests for tumors and chemical imbalances. They had delved into her family history but the Lee family was deemed relatively sane. All except for Kieran. However, she wasn't psychotic enough to be kept on a psych ward, and the hospitals had more than enough people needing to use the space she was taking up. So they charged her a small fortune for antidepressants and deemed her fit to rejoin society. That led to Kieran signing herself out and traveling over to the next state, one where no one knew her or her medical history, where she could try to kill herself again.

And fail miserably, over and over and over again.

Though not for lack of trying. The five big attempts were the ones that had gained other people's attention and gotten her on the mental health radar. More elaborate attempts such as the one that saw her stepping in front of a train late one night. It had seemed a good idea at the time, but it was doomed to failure like everything else she tried. Kieran had been hit by a deer that had had the same idea. It had bounded onto the tracks with her, knocking Kieran clear of the train while it took the brunt of the impact. Kieran swore the animal just appeared straight out of thin air to head-butt her in the chest and send her flying head over heels into nearby bushes. Yet, when the police checked her story, there were no remnants of a deer smeared on the train or any remains left on the track. Then there was her jumping off a building only to be thrown onto a balcony partway down by freak gales that blew in out of nowhere. Kieran couldn't explain it and knew she just sounded crazy when she did. And she was considered crazy enough without the mysterious occurrences happening every time she tried to take her life.

Those events didn't even begin to take into account the numerous other attempts of her swallowing a multitude of pills, waking up puking her guts out, and being all too alive with just a headache for her pains.

For someone so desperate to end it all she was becoming a master at cheating death.

Her gaze drifted around the room and over the group congregated in a silent huddle. Kieran had gotten to know them all by sight if not by name in the week she'd been detained. There was the OCD housewife who was trying not to give in to her need to rearrange the literature that was scattered haphazardly on the small table behind them. There was the man who could hear voices and was holding an in-depth conversation under his breath with Elvis concerning the merits of "Hound Dog" over "Jailhouse Rock." Then there was the guy who seemed lost in his own little world. He was the one Kieran envied the most. He seemed so peaceful and serene in his distraction. She could only wish for that kind of tranquility in her own mind.

Movement and hushed whispers at the door drew Kieran's attention away from her musings. Someone new was standing in the doorway. She couldn't help but stare at the woman who was talking to one of the orderlies. She couldn't hear what they were discussing, yet Kieran couldn't take her eyes off her.

She looks like an angel.

She berated herself for that fanciful thought. *She's probably one of those white coats who just signs the medication forms and leaves you to your delusions in a drug-induced haze. I've met enough of those on my journey.*

Still, she was *very* attractive. The woman's hair was the palest blond Kieran had ever seen. So pale it was almost translucent. Not just light blond, or even white. It was like the first morning sunlight breaking through the confines of the dawn and blinding you with its purity. Her hair was up in a bun that was just begging for someone to run their hands through to free it. She had high cheekbones that lent her appearance a classical beauty of years gone by. It reminded Kieran of the old movies her mother used to watch. The black-and-white film captured the timeless elegance of the women of that era. This doctor looked like them—ageless, flawless, with a gentle curve to her chin like a young Natalie Wood. Her skin was honey toned, hinting at a Mediterranean background.

Kieran found her too beautiful to be real. She wasn't very tall, Kieran guessed around five foot four, two inches shorter than her own height. The white coat she wore did nothing to hide the feminine shape underneath it. She was wearing a pale blue blouse tucked into a navy blue skirt. It was standard office wear, but she carried it off with panache.

Kieran knew her own hospital sweats and T-shirt couldn't even begin to compete in the fashion comparison.

The doctor interacted with the orderly. Kieran noticed how she carried herself with an authoritative poise but always had a ready smile to curve her full lips.

There is no point in me crushing out on a doctor here. They've got to diagnose me as suicidal for the umpteenth time and start me on that old familiar course of therapy. I will be the model patient, say all the right things, and ace all the tests. I will do everything in my power to be seen as cured before they release me back out into the wild so I can try again. She's a distraction I can't afford to have.

Kieran looked back out across the garden and beyond. She was searching, longing for an escape from yet another institution that didn't understand why she was there in the first place.

I'm just another lunatic raving about the end of the world.

Her orderly got up and stepped away. His abrupt departure surprised Kieran since he and the others had been hard on her heels for days. She turned to see where he had gone and realized the doctor had beckoned him over. When Kieran looked, she found the woman staring back at her. Her gaze felt as if it were a caress. A physical touch that penetrated through to Kieran's very marrow. She saw the woman's eyes change. For a brief instance, the dark brown seemed to intensify in hue and turn amber. Now Kieran *knew* she was going crazy. The expression on the woman's face barely altered, but Kieran felt the wave of curiosity that radiated from her. She couldn't help herself; she smiled as if she'd heard the woman's silent greeting. It seemed to break whatever spell the woman was under. She blinked rapidly as if clearing her vision, then turned her attention back to the orderly as if nothing had just occurred between them.

But not before she looked in Kieran's direction one last time with a small frown marring her forehead as if she wasn't sure herself what had just taken place.

Unsettled, Kieran shifted in her seat. She rubbed at her cheek. She swore she could feel the ghostly touch of a hand that had just caressed her in farewell.

Maybe I am finally losing my mind. It was only a matter of time, after all.

She cast another look over to the door again, but the woman was gone. Kieran debated if she had even been real or something her mind had conjured up.

Maybe she had just been a figment of an imagination that had long since stopped being entirely under Kieran's control.

❖

Merlo didn't waste time getting back to her office. She rummaged through her files to seek out a specific patient. Each file had a photograph of the patient attached as per Merlo's instruction. She could recall faces so much better than names so always asked for this evidence to be included in her files. Merlo picked out the file she was after, the one pertaining to Kieran Lee.

The photo didn't do the woman she had just seen in the therapy room justice. Her records indicated that Kieran was twenty-nine years old. She had to admit she was surprised by that. To Merlo's eyes, Kieran exhibited the same youthful appearance that fascinated her in the actress Ellen Page. They both shared the same strong jawline and the slightly pointed chin that could have made Kieran just another eye-catching woman but instead gave her a distinctly tomboyish air that made her even more alluring. She had blond hair, though shades darker than Merlo's own. She wasn't sure what style Kieran had sported before because now her hair was just messy and unkempt as befit someone who hadn't had it cut for some time and didn't care. Merlo decided that she'd have to schedule at least a trim for Kieran if she was agreeable. She just wished that the jaded look that was all too clear on Kieran's face wasn't there to mar those good looks. The dark shadows under her eyes told their own story to Merlo as well. As did the haunted look she'd glimpsed hidden behind the carefully crafted look of Kieran's indifference.

But it was her smile that had captivated Merlo's attention the most. It had caused her to lose her train of thought while discussing appointment changes with the orderlies.

"She doesn't look like she belongs here, even though this file would suggest otherwise," Merlo muttered as she flipped through the paperwork and read what had brought Kieran under her care. She sent up a silent blessing for her personal aide, who always managed to find out more information than the patients' own medical records ever seemed to contain. It seemed this Kieran Lee had more to hide than most. Her file was pretty innocuous on its own, but the extra sheets Dina had snuck in told a different tale. Merlo checked her desktop calendar and spotted that Kieran was scheduled for their first meet and greet tomorrow morning at ten o'clock.

"She's housed in G wing as a Class A serious suicide risk." Merlo shook her head in disbelief. She hadn't sensed that at all in Kieran's demeanor. She hoped she'd be able to learn more from their meeting tomorrow. Maybe she'd get a better read from being up close and personal. She studied the photograph one more time.

"You don't strike me as a candidate for so many suicide attempts, and I've never been wrong before in my diagnoses." Merlo leaned back in her seat and began strategizing how to start the session tomorrow with this particular patient. She had a feeling Kieran Lee wasn't going to be very forthcoming in revealing her reasons for wanting off the planet. She'd just have to make sure Kieran could see Merlo was someone she could trust to share the reasons with.

And that was just the start. Then came the unraveling of the mind to search out the root cause of all the distress. She closed the file and settled in to call upon a meditative state. Only with a clear mind would she be able to work her way through the minefield of someone else's mind. Today's patients needed her focus to be on them before she attempted to decipher what secrets lay behind Kieran's tired eyes.

CHAPTER THREE

Breakfast in the hospital was a lively occasion at way too early an hour for Kieran. She chewed at her toast and sipped at the bitter coffee that didn't improve in taste no matter how much sugar she dissolved in it. When she was finished, Kieran found herself back in the care of an orderly. She was getting ready to wander along the corridors when he pointed her in another direction.

"You've got an appointment," he said, gesturing for her to follow him.

Kieran frowned and stopped where she stood. "I wasn't informed of anything," she said. She reminded herself to stick to the story that she'd slipped off the bridge by accident. All the people she'd seen at Craven Hope had heard her trot out the same lines. She had it down to a fine art now, and she knew she could be very persuasive when she was in her right mind. No one could disprove her story, and Kieran had wanted to get started on her campaign for release. The doctor assigned her case had been reluctant to let her go when there was obviously more behind her being brought in. Kieran knew her rational and reasonable behavior since recovering from a near-fatal drowning was confusing to the staff. They had no definitive proof that pointed toward a suicide attempt or that she'd try to do it again in the hospital. It all boiled down to her word against everyone else's, and Kieran wasn't admitting anything that would keep her in the hospital for a moment longer. They had safeguarded themselves by ferrying her to Craven Hope for "further observation," so now Kieran had to start her bid for freedom all over again.

She followed behind the orderly and was wondering what more lies she needed to come up with this time. The atmosphere of the building altered as she was taken to a different area away from the psychiatric wing. The offices that lined the corridor gave out a much more professional air than the clean yet clinical rooms on the hospital side of the building. Kieran began reading off the names on the glass panels, impressed by the multitude of letters after everyone's names.

I've fooled people with those qualifications before and I can do it again.

The door Kieran came to a stop at had a curious name emblazoned on the glass. Dr. Merlo Blue. Kieran read it again, testing the way it sounded. She could almost taste it on her tongue. Merlo was an unusual name. She wondered what kind of person was behind that name. Maybe an old man who would try to browbeat her into revealing why she'd stepped off the bridge that night. Or a woman, quiet voiced and nurturing, who'd try a different approach with the hopes Kieran would open up and spill her soul. Kieran wished them luck.

She waited while the orderly knocked on the door and popped his head inside to announce her. Kieran let her mind wander. She wondered how hard it would be to die of exposure in Nebraska at this time of year. June was a hot and sunny month most everywhere. Maybe she'd try Kansas and step in the path of a tornado. She was getting *that* desperate. She pondered these possibilities and more as she let the orderly lead her into the office, and he left her alone.

Kieran didn't look at the person she was brought in front of. Instead she took in the room that was as much a prison to her as her room on G wing was. The walls were tastefully decorated with patterned wallpaper, and the carpet beneath her feet felt thick. She bounced a little to try it. There were a few framed pieces of art on the wall, nothing too garish and nothing that would trigger anyone unless they had an aversion to seascapes. Kieran yearned to be out on the sea somewhere, watching the sunlight shimmer on the water, feeling the gentle rocking of the boat lulling her, and hoping for a whale to come and swallow her up.

Eventually, she turned to face the desk and froze when she saw who was behind it. Dr. Merlo Blue was the angel-like creature she'd seen in the therapy room. Close-up, she was even more captivating.

Kieran had a feeling this was not going to go as well as she had hoped. How could she state her case for sanity when confronted by someone whose eyes seemed to see right through her? Kieran feared she'd open her mouth and end up talking in tongues.

Merlo waved her toward the chair in front of the desk. Kieran lowered herself slowly into it because she had the horrible feeling she was about to spring a giant trap on herself. She shifted a little, trying to get comfortable. At least this time she'd have someone pretty to look at while she tried to charm her way out of the psych ward.

Merlo looked up from the file she'd been reading, but before she could open her mouth, Kieran interrupted.

"How about I save you some time and energy, Dr. Blue, and just say there's been a terrible misunderstanding. I fell off the bridge by accident, nothing more. I was using my phone to catch Pokémon using that app I'm sure you've heard all about. It's embarrassing to admit it, but I was this close to catching a Gyarados, that's a water Pokémon, when I got too close to the edge of the bridge and ended up in the water. I wasn't paying attention and got careless in my footing. It's so stupid to admit it and I feel like such a fool. So if you'd be so kind as to just sign me out, I can be on my way from here with what's left of my pride intact."

Merlo leaned forward in her chair, propped her elbows on her desk, and rested her chin on her hands. "So you weren't trying to kill yourself?" she asked.

Kieran smiled what she hoped was her best and most sincere smile. "Of course not. I have no reason to do that."

Merlo smiled back. The sight of it made Kieran's heart race just that little bit faster. *Please let her buy this excuse because I'm starting to run out of them.*

"So the previous four attempts were all just accidents too?"

Kieran felt her smile slip. She willed herself not to react any further. *How the hell does she know about those?*

Merlo tapped a finger on the file before her. "You're very adept at changing your name in each state you try to kill yourself in. I'm impressed at the lengths you go to disguise who you are so that nothing shows up under your real name. You never seem to carry much identification when you're found either, and it's never your own ID anyway. It works, too, because you're never in the hospitals long enough to be recognized as a repeat offender. The official record I have just shows this latest attempt and some rather inconclusive notes." She held up a separate pile of paperwork. "However, these say something different. I had to dig a little deeper with you, Kieran. I have ways of finding out the truth about what brings someone like you into my office." She sat back in her chair and considered Kieran for a moment. "This time you used your real name. I'm wondering why you did that."

It was a spur-of-the-moment thing; see a bridge, jump off it. I got careless. I was bound to slip up at some point, but I'd hoped if I did it would be too late to worry about it. Because this time I was supposed to get it right.

"I know this isn't the first time you've attempted suicide. You're obviously determined to do it because you keep trying." Merlo tapped her folder again. "But this doesn't tell me about the other attempts you've no doubt made away from prying eyes. Ones where you've woken up alone and realized, against your wishes, that you're still alive."

Merlo fixed Kieran with a look that was so solicitous Kieran *felt* it. It touched her like a warm hand alighting on chilled skin. It somehow penetrated all of Kieran's carefully erected walls. For a fleeting moment, she felt something rest upon her head, caressing her hair. The gentle touch of a loved one that said, "It's all right now; you're not alone. I'm here."

That feeling of peace relieved and terrified Kieran.

"Based on what I've read of your other attempts, and how you somehow manage to get discharged every time on some technicality or another, I think we're going to need to set some ground rules." Merlo picked up a sheet of paper to reread something. She looked at Kieran from over the top of the page, shook her head, and then continued. "Number one being don't lie to me. I'll know when you do, and it will just drag this out more for you in the end. And from what I'm reading, you don't like to stay anywhere for long. Don't make me have you committed just to hear your side of the tale when you're ready to tell it."

Kieran stared at her, speechless. No one had ever threatened her with that before. She looked at this Dr. Blue with new eyes. *So, not just a pretty face then. More like pretty ruthless.* Kieran wondered what other sources she had access to. *Damn it, and I worked so hard to fly under the hospitals' radars.* The pile of papers had been deliberately placed so that Kieran could see them. They were all her hospital records, filled in under all the false names she had used. *How in the hell did she get her hands on those?* It would have been impressive if it didn't screw up Kieran's plans to just walk out of this hospital.

"And yes, you could tell me what you think I want to hear and I could tick all the boxes you hope I will to expedite your time here, but what is the point? I am offering to help you. At least give me the chance to try."

Kieran wished it were that simple. She could keep silent and not cooperate, but she had a feeling that would just make things worse for herself. Or she could go along with everything Dr. Blue suggested and be the good little patient and fast-track her way out of there so she could disappear again. She just hoped Dr. Blue would fall for it like the others had before her.

"Kieran, in our sessions together I'm hoping you'll come to trust me enough to be able to tell me why you keep trying to kill yourself." Merlo rose from her chair and gestured for Kieran to join her on the more comfortable seating.

Kieran followed her without a word, still shaken by what had just transpired. She sat on the couch she was directed to and watched Merlo settle herself into an armchair opposite.

"For today, though, how about you tell me a little bit about yourself? Who you are, what you do."

Kieran's mind scrambled to find something, anything, she could answer with. She had no clue who she was anymore.

The real Kieran Lee hadn't been home since the madness had taken up residence inside her head.

CHAPTER FOUR

Merlo waited while Kieran seemed to stumble over the simple request. She smiled at her in encouragement.

"Imagine we're in another setting if that helps. Perhaps we're at a restaurant, just getting to know each other."

Kieran's brow crinkled. "Like speed dating?"

Merlo laughed. "Humor me." She slipped off her shoes and drew her legs up under her on the seat to look less professional. She had a feeling Kieran didn't react well with authority figures.

"Well then, let's see. I'm Kieran, but you already know that from your files. I'm a Scorpio. I love anything that involves pasta. I'm kind to small animals and I like to take long walks," she paused as Merlo watched her intently, "*off* short piers."

Merlo cocked her head at that. She decided to let it slide. "Do you have anyone that knows you're here? I noticed in your notes you have no one listed as your next of kin."

"Oh, are we at the 'are you married, single, or gay' part of our meet and greet now?"

Merlo was enjoying the facetious way Kieran answered her. She had known from the second she'd seen her that Kieran wasn't going to be someone who would just spill her guts and expose all her secrets in their sessions. Merlo had had all kinds of patients sitting opposite her. The silent, the morose, the murderous. She felt comfortable with them all, treated them with the same courtesy and with the confidence that, under her care, she could help them.

Kieran was hiding something, Merlo was certain of that. What was intriguing was how calm and lucid Kieran was, even after spending time interred at the previous hospital and now in this one. She seemed resigned to being there, saw it as just another step in her journey, and was intent on getting out. Yet she wasn't combative in her desire to leave. And, Merlo recognized, she'd had all her arguments lined up to impress on them that she shouldn't be there in the first place. She'd heard them all from the doctor Kieran had seen last. Accidents happened, but Merlo recognized these as desperate attempts to end a life. And she recognized the lies that were being used to cover up those facts. What she couldn't understand was why Kieran had to lie in the first place.

"So, you have no family or friends or a lover to inform where you are. At least, no one you want to have told."

Kieran shrugged. "My mom died years ago. It's just me now, and I don't have much baggage."

Merlo caught a double meaning in that statement. The police had gone to the motel room Kieran had been staying in and had found nothing more than a backpack with very little in it other than clothing. It was devoid of any kind of personal belongings.

She found this curious. Merlo had settled into a place that had been her home for years now. She surrounded herself with ornaments and paintings, delighting in every object that made her house a home. It gave her comfort. She wondered at the deliberate lack of anything that could bring comfort to Kieran as she skipped from state to state ready for the next attempt on her life.

"Is there a reason why you travel light?"

"Well, it's not like I can take it with me, is it?"

Merlo saw the look in Kieran's eye that flashed for just a second and then was gone. Grief. The anguished look of loss. Merlo wanted to chase that fleeting thread and tug on it some more to unravel all her secrets, but Kieran's face had hardened and she knew she'd have to wait.

"What's your profession?"

"Unemployed...or more truthfully, unemployable. It's hard to hold down a job when you've got another place you want to be more. It makes a full-time position undesirable, and when your employer asks why you want part-time..." Kieran smiled. There was an edge to it that Merlo found almost chilling. "Let's just say being truthful at interviews isn't recommended for those with *other* intentions."

"What were you before your priorities in life altered?"

"A lawyer."

Merlo wished she'd have made a wager with herself on that one. That explained the persuasive arguments for everything and the ease with which she'd talked herself out of all the previous hospitals. It also explained how she had the funds to travel around.

"When did everything start to change for you, Kieran?"

Kieran looked up from where she'd been tracing a line on her hospital sweats. "There we were having such a nice conversation over an imaginary fine wine and linguini and you had to go spoil it by bringing in reality." Kieran looked at her wrist as if she had a watch there. "I think this restaurant is about to close. Your next patient is due, no doubt. And I get to go back and watch the world go by while you try to uncover the psyche of some other poor bastard."

Her eyes drifted to the door, and Merlo looked over her shoulder to see the shadow of the orderly waiting to take Kieran back to the ward. This had been just a short preliminary meeting, but it surprised Merlo how quickly the time had passed.

"My ride's here," Kieran said.

"Maybe we can continue this in our next session. I have you scheduled for daily appointments for a while until we can get to the cause of your attempts."

Kieran looked surprised and then annoyed but managed to pass it off with a shrug. "Sure, I'm free tomorrow. Tuesdays are always empty on my calendar."

Merlo bit back her smile at Kieran's sarcasm and stood when Kieran did. For a moment, she swayed on her feet. Kieran reached out to steady Merlo, and they both froze as a jolt of *something* passed through them both.

"Wow," Kieran said. "And I thought that was just something writers used to emphasize their romantic tropes."

"It could just have been static electricity," Merlo said, trying not to get flustered, and busied herself getting her shoes back on. "The room is carpeted, after all."

"Well, take it from me, it was a whole lot kinder than electroconvulsive therapy."

Merlo froze at Kieran's throwaway comment. "You've been put through that?"

Kieran paused by the door, her hand poised on the handle. "Different doctor, different treatment. An electric current blasted through the brain to chase out my 'depression' seemed a good idea at the time. At least to him." She glanced over her shoulder at Merlo. "Obviously, it didn't work because here I am again, going through the same old routine, answering the same old questions."

"I won't have you put through those methods here, Kieran."

"But you'll still keep asking why."

"I'd like to know why you keep trying to end your life." Merlo took a tentative step forward. That triggered Kieran to open the door, effectively ending the session.

"I'll see you tomorrow, Dr. Blue. Maybe I'll have thought up a good enough answer by then that will satisfy your curiosity."

Merlo watched the two shadows move away from her door. She didn't know how long she stood there after Kieran left, but it was enough that Claudia had to buzz her intercom three times before Merlo answered.

"Yes, yes, send the next patient in." Merlo settled herself back behind her desk and tried to ready herself for the next person. Her mind just couldn't let go of Kieran, though. There was something about her that Merlo couldn't decipher yet. She wondered what tomorrow's session would entail and whether she should bring out the big guns so soon to see just what Kieran was hiding.

She smiled to herself. She had a few secrets of her own.

There were very few moments in the day that allowed Kieran to be left to her own devices. So when not being hovered over she always put the rare time to good use. They'd allowed her a calendar in her room. It was a single sheet displaying the months and the days on a poor quality photocopy. Kieran didn't care; she pored over it. It had been just over a week now, a week of sitting in Merlo's office every day for a near hour-long session, skirting and dancing around the truth. Kieran had been careful how much she revealed to Merlo. After all, she wanted to leave the hospital, not stay there indefinitely as a hopeless case.

Kieran had toyed with the idea of breaking into Merlo's office and stealing the incriminating files she had held over her head. If there was no proof of the other attempts, Kieran could then press her case for release, maybe even threaten to sue the hospital for falsifying documents to admit her under false pretenses. She'd been building her case on it in one of their sessions and had caught Merlo's eyes on her. Kieran had begun to wonder if Merlo could read minds because in that moment she'd felt exposed. *Seen.* It had been enough to shake her out of her breaking and entering fantasies.

She spent far too much time as it was daydreaming where the pretty doctor was concerned. Kieran found her immensely attractive. She wanted to run her hands through Merlo's hair to see if it was as soft as it appeared. Kieran was fascinated by the lilt of a faint accent that clung to Merlo's words. Kieran had to smile at herself. She hadn't been this smitten by anyone in years, and it just had to be her damned psychiatrist. *I'm cursed every way I look at my life.* But if she had to wage wits with someone, then Merlo was by far the most intellectual, attractive, and mysterious of them all.

She was also the one who could keep Kieran trapped in that damned hospital for longer than she wanted to be, and time was of the essence where Kieran's life was concerned. She called on her memory to remember the dates she had marked in the diary she used to carry with her. That was no doubt in storage along with her backpack.

She was thankful that, for all she'd gone through, her legal mind still fired on all cylinders. She had a good recall of the significant dates she needed. Kieran marked the dates off with small x's. She frowned when she saw how the days between the x's were getting significantly shorter.

It's happening more frequently. There's barely even a month between it now.

She ran her fingertip through the months, charting the progression and frequency. Something made her pause and recheck the last few months over again. She counted off the days up until today.

Oh God. I need to get out of here now. I can't afford to be in here any longer.

She was just about to hide the sheet when a voice in her ear startled her.

"What are you doing there? Marking off the days of your captivity?"

The orderly grinned down at her, his eyes alight with glee. He was getting off on how he'd startled her.

Kieran slipped the calendar inside the bedside table drawer. "No, I was keeping a record of my menstrual cycle." She got some measure of satisfaction in his grimace and the way he backed away from her.

"It's time for you to get your ass to the dining hall for your last meal before we lock you down for the night."

Kieran didn't dignify that with a reaction. The other orderlies more than made up for this guy's attitude. Besides, Kieran now had other matters to attend to. She managed to bump into him as they left her room. He gave her a disgusted look and shoved her away in front of him. Kieran kept her hands in her pockets and her head down as she made her way to have supper.

❖

The food was edible as always, but Kieran barely recognized what was on her plate. She just swallowed it down and wandered back to her room when she was done. She stuffed her pillow under the bedsheets and turned off the lights. In her pocket, she fingered the keys she'd slipped off the orderly's key ring. She sent a heartfelt thanks out to the gentleman she'd represented three times on pickpocketing charges. He had taught her a few tricks of his trade as a thank-you. They'd never been more useful than for what she had planned for tonight.

Kieran had watched the nightly routines of the staff ever since she'd been brought in. The patients were allowed to wander around, and even those like her who had orderlies shadowing them were granted some alone time after the last meal of the day. Kieran had noticed that the new orderly who had collected her wasn't as attentive as her usual ones.

She slipped out of her room and was soon off out of the ward thanks to the passkey she had in her possession. She headed toward the kitchen. She wasn't familiar with the layout of the hospital, but she figured that the kitchen had to have a delivery door. That would be her point of exit.

Voices drifted down the hallway, and Kieran ducked inside an employee locker room. She huddled in a corner out of sight of prying eyes. She watched as the day staff prepared to leave. They gathered their belongings and left in a flurry of loud voices and laughter. Kieran waited a while until she was sure the room was deserted, then she stepped out of the shadows. She pulled off her sweatshirt and slipped on a white jacket that someone had left hanging off their locker. She hoped she could pull off a professional air while swaggering through in her sweatpants.

She walked out the locker room and headed straight for the kitchen. She snagged a piece of fruit from a counter and popped it in her pocket for later. She slipped out the back door and was soon outside in the evening's fading sunshine.

"Now for the fun part," she muttered and pressed the key fob she had hidden in her sweatpants. A car alarm beeped and flashed its lights at her halfway down the parking lot. "This will teach you to learn some manners, young man," Kieran said, hastening to the car and opening it. The car reeked of expensive leather. "I'm going to steal your car and then my first stop will be the tackiest drive-through I can find." She rummaged through his cup holder, riffling through the change there. "I'll be sure to use all this money you have left for me too. I'm going to spill cola all over your upholstery as payback for you getting all up in my face and looking at me like I'm trash."

She stuck the key in the ignition.

"Where do you think you're going?"

Kieran almost gave herself whiplash as she swung her head around. Behind her sat a young woman with dark hair and equally dark eyes.

"What are you doing in my car?" Kieran went on the offensive, as it always seemed a good move and usually threw the other person off balance. She just wished she could calm the frantic pounding of her heart in her ears so she could hear the woman's reply.

"It's no more your car than it is mine. And I'm waiting for a friend."

Kieran stared at her incredulously. "Then wait someplace else. I'm leaving and I don't carpool with strangers." She was startled again when the passenger door flew open and another woman climbed in.

"You're just full of surprises, aren't you, Kieran Lee?" Merlo said, shifting in the seat to confront her.

Kieran made a grab for her door, but there was the sickening sound of the locks engaging. She still tugged at the door handle to no avail.

"Where were you going?" Merlo asked as if there was nothing wrong in finding one of her patients out of the secure wing, wearing a stolen jacket, and preparing to drive off in a stolen vehicle she'd somehow gotten the keys to.

"I can't stay here. I need to leave. You have no idea what's going on with me, and I can't be here when it happens again."

"What do you think is going to happen to you?" Merlo reached out to stop Kieran's hand as it was inching toward the key in the ignition.

"I don't think it, I *know* it. But I can't tell you because you'll think I'm crazy, and I can't afford to be locked up any more than I already am. You don't understand. I'm running out of time. You *have* to let me go."

"You know I can't do that."

Kieran caught sight of the security guards rushing out from the building. She clutched at Merlo's arm.

"Don't let them take me back. I can't go through this again and nobody here will be able to help me when I do. Please," Kieran begged her, "let me go. I need to take care of this myself."

The locks popped back up. Kieran didn't hesitate for a second. She burst out of the door as if the hounds of hell were at her heels. She sprinted toward the main gates, ignoring the shouts for her to stop. She could see the main road ahead; she just needed to keep going.

Kieran found herself tackled before she ever got to step one foot off the hospital grounds. The air was knocked out of her. For a moment, she almost smiled, hoping this would be her last breath taken as they held her down and crushed her into the ground. To Kieran's dismay, they pulled her onto her feet and restrained her. She could hear Merlo warning them not to hurt her, but they were too intent on holding Kieran immobile.

She was already zoning out so Kieran focused on the dark-haired woman who was now standing off to the side away from everyone else. She stared at her and the woman mouthed something. Kieran strained her eyes to read her lips.

You're going to be okay.

Dragged away as if she were a criminal, Kieran swiveled her head around to try to see if the woman had anything else to say, but when she managed a glance back, the woman was no longer there.

This is it. I'm on the last lap to insanity.

❖

Kieran was marched back into the hospital. Merlo was storming in behind her, ranting at the men over their rough handling of her. The white jacket was ripped off her and Kieran was shoved down hard on her bed.

"Do NOT restrain her!" Merlo said as one of the orderlies began reaching for the straps.

Dr. Henry Cragon walked into the room, making a grand entrance as usual that befit him being the head of medicine at Craven Hope. Everyone except Merlo stepped back. He held a lethal-looking syringe. He took his time attaching the small bottle of sedative to the needle. He measured off a large dosage.

Kieran looked to Merlo for help. "Don't let him drug me. It makes the nightmares worse," she pleaded.

Merlo squared up against Cragon. "She's not your patient, Dr. Cragon; she's mine. There's a note in her file about her reacting badly to medications."

Dr. Cragon squirted a fine spray of liquid from the needle. "So you say, but she's a flight risk, so I'm choosing to disregard it." He gestured for an orderly to hold Kieran down.

"I need to know why she attempted to escape tonight. I can't do that if you knock her out."

"You'll have plenty of time to talk it all over tomorrow in your office. For tonight I want to make sure she doesn't try to pull this stunt again." He jabbed the needle into Kieran's arm and pressed down on the plunger.

Kieran yelled out at the pain and the manhandling she was experiencing. She felt the hands holding her down leave her body, and then she didn't feel much of anything anymore.

With the show over, everyone left the room except for Merlo and Dr. Cragon.

"If you won't have her restrained, then you'll have to agree I've found a better way to keep her from disturbing the night staff."

Kieran hated his condescending tone. Especially when it was directed at Merlo.

"Don't think I won't be filing a complaint—"

"And it will fall on deaf ears, Dr. Blue. You may have been here a considerable length of time, but until you can walk an eighteen-hole course with our investors, then all your complaints are just seen as sour grapes because they picked my experience over your hocus-pocus way of dealing with these people."

There was a charged silence, then Kieran heard his distinctive shoes clicking on the flooring as he left the room.

"God, I hate that man," Merlo muttered.

"Just be thankful he didn't stick you with that needle. He's got a lousy bedside manner and a really mean jab." Kieran splayed across the pillow that was still hiding under the sheets. She didn't care. She couldn't keep her eyes open.

"Let me turn you over at least." Merlo rolled Kieran over onto her back.

Kieran stared blurrily up at the ceiling. "Dammit, Doc. You could have at least left me face down to suffocate in the sheets."

"Are you still hell-bent on dying, Kieran?"

Her concerned voice drifted over Kieran's ears like a soothing melody. "Interesting choice of words there, Dr. Blue." Kieran tried to keep her eyes open, but she was failing fast. "I just want peace because every time this happens it's more than I can bear."

"*What* happens?"

Kieran couldn't fight the drug any longer. Her head lolled to one side, and she squinted at Merlo hovering over her. The words slipped from her lips before she passed out.

"*He's* coming. I've seen him. He's big and fearsome and he's going to kill us all."

CHAPTER FIVE

Merlo had dealt with many different temperaments from her patients, but she had never had anyone who sat in her office sulking on her couch with the intensity Kieran Lee was displaying.

"You're lucky Maria's appointment after yours has been canceled because you've wasted your session with this childish silence." Merlo looked up from the notes she was writing. She'd had to do something to make sure the hour wasn't a complete waste of time for her. Kieran's eyes flared at her use of the word *childish*. Finally, after an hour of Merlo using wheedling, cajoling, threats, and entreaties, this one word brought Kieran's attention back into the room.

"You should have let me go. Instead you let Cragon shoot me up with enough knockout drops to fell a fucking elephant. I couldn't lift my spoon out of my cereal this morning and had to be almost carried into the dining hall as it was."

"Unfortunately, I have no say over what Dr. Cragon can do, as you saw. I have, however, lodged a formal complaint."

"Yeah, but from what I heard that will hold as much weight as my demanding to be released from here on my own recognizance."

Kieran lay sprawled out on the couch, looking boneless. The effects of the drugs from the night before hung heavy on her features and had left her lethargic. Merlo didn't allow patients to put their feet up on the couch, but Kieran had toed out of her slip-on sneakers and just sank down on the cushions as if they were the only thing to offer her respite.

"So, who was your friend that stalled me?" Kieran asked.

"Who are you talking about?"

"The dark-haired woman who was already in the back seat of the car with me when you got in. You couldn't miss her. She was all long-haired and lean, in an Angie Harmon kind of way."

"Oh." Merlo purposely didn't answer, but she was surprised and intrigued that, out of everything that had happened the previous night, Kieran remembered seeing Dina. "Who do *you* think she was?"

Kieran scoffed. "Oh, you are not adding me seeing her as another black mark against my already crappy state of mind. I saw her as clearly as I can see you. What is she? A friend of yours who somehow was in the one car I was going to drive out of here in? The kind of friend who could get in even though I had the only key for that car?" Kieran shook her head. "Try again, Doc. No one knew I was going to try to leave last night, and I kept out of sight of the archaic cameras that are dotted around the place. So how did she, by chance, manage to be in the same place as me, eh? It had to be her that tipped you off to where I was."

Merlo shrugged. "I have no idea, Kieran."

Kieran huffed. "Just what kind of *hocus pocus* do you deal in, Dr. Blue? Cragon seemed rather dismissive of it, but I'm wondering if it doesn't involve you being the good cop to his bad cop and making folk believe they are seeing other people when, in fact, you have a buddy of yours come in and play the spooky part."

Merlo shook her head, not liking that analogy at all. "I don't play any roles, Kieran. Dr. Cragon doesn't like the fact that I get better results from my psychotherapy than he does from medicating his patients. He's been dismissive of my role here from the start." She leaned forward in her seat. "But I promise I *can* help you. You just need to talk to me. What made you try to leave last night? You haven't attempted that before in any of your previous hospital stays."

"How can you know that?" Kieran stared at her suspiciously.

"I've told you—ways and means."

"You don't know anything about me. You probably think this is a form of depression with more than a hint of paranoia added." Kieran lowered her legs and leaned back against the couch. "I've known depression. It can be the uncontrollable need to cry for no reason whatsoever that makes watching commercials a nightmare. There're the mood swings that drive the people around you as crazy as you feel. That's followed by the fun states of lethargy, worthlessness, hopelessness. I've been there, done that, Doc. Sometimes it bleeds into the next step, that deep, dark, empty feeling of 'I don't care anymore.' Nothing touches you; your soul is just a vast, blank, empty wasteland. That's when you find yourself driving along and wondering who would care enough if you drove off the side of the road into a tree with just enough force to crush the car and you in it."

Kieran stared off at a fixed point in the room before continuing her train of thought.

"Who *would* care? Sometimes there's no one left to care at all. You've got no lover, because really, who stays with someone who can't commit to a relationship when they're too busy looking for the next opportunity to die? Relatives don't want the inconvenience of your depressed ass sleeping on their couch while they have their own problems to deal with. You've lost your job because no one wants to employ someone who's a sad little Eeyore in their office. So it's just you and this big black hole of the one feeling you have left." Kieran looked back at Merlo. "*Done.* You just feel *done.* It's like checking out of your body and hanging a sign saying *vacant.*"

Merlo stayed silent. There was no doubt it was the drugs that had loosened Kieran's tongue, but this was the longest Kieran had gone in expressing herself. Nothing short of an earthquake was stopping Merlo from hearing this. This rant could explain everything, and once Merlo had that, then she could start her work.

"I've had those feelings. They began once all *this* started. But what I feel now is nothing compared to that. My wanting to die isn't because I feel lonely or empty. It's because my whole life has been taken over by something else and I no longer exist." Kieran ran her hands over her face and looked at Merlo with haunted eyes.

"Can't you see, Doc? Truth be told, I'm dead already."

Merlo was finishing up her paperwork for the day and trying to get some order back into the files on her desk. Her day had been a wide and varied selection of mental health issues, but Merlo had found it impossible to keep her mind from wandering back to Kieran's session.

She shoved the last of her files aside and leaned back in her chair. She let her hair down, then ran her fingers through it and sighed at such a simple act feeling so good at the end of the day.

"You and your simple pleasures."

Merlo smiled as she heard Dina's voice from behind her. Dina leaned over the back of the chair and kissed the top of Merlo's head. She then ruffled Merlo's hair affectionately.

"Had a long day, my friend?" She moved around to perch on the edge of Merlo's desk.

"An unusual day that followed in the same intriguing vein as last night's excitement."

Dina nodded. "Ahh, yes, your blond Houdini with the death wish." Dina nudged Merlo's leg with her own to make her look up. "She saw me when I shouldn't have been seen."

Merlo nodded. "So you noted last night. This woman is an enigma." She chewed on her lip, knowing what she needed to do but reluctant to employ such a drastic measure where this patient was concerned. She also knew she had no other choice. "I think I need to bring out the big guns. She's only opening up so far, and I'm getting a strange sense of urgency around her. Whether she's due another episode or what, I can't say, but if I don't get to the cause of her wanting to die, then I think she might succeed before I have a chance to help. Or she'll succeed in an escape and I won't have the chance at all."

Dina shifted down from the table and crossed the room. "So you're going to have to force the issue. After researching her, I have to agree with your choice. There's something more going on there." She stopped in front of a painting on the wall and perused it with a critical eye. "Tell me again why you chose this piece to be your guide."

Merlo joined Dina at the painting, and they both just took in the scene.

"It's the painting with the most tranquil waters. After what I usually witness within its frame, seeing the tranquil setting return brings me some semblance of calm." She ran her hand over the canvas, and it shimmered. A flash of purple light rippled over the oil painting and disappeared into the elaborate frame.

"I'd ask to sit in on this particular session, but I don't think I'd remain unseen for long," Dina said. "I'll watch from a safe distance instead."

"There's another reason why I've chosen to use the painting so soon with this patient. There's something about Kieran that just doesn't fit right with this place." Merlo hesitated in telling Dina the whole truth.

She knew she would figure it out eventually. "And there's something else…it appears…well, I think there is…we…"

"Spit it out, Merlo, please. The suspense is killing me."

"We *connected*." She wasn't surprised when she saw Dina's mouth drop open. "I laughed it off to her as static, but in all honesty, Dina, my energy called to hers and she reached back."

"How intriguing. In that case, the sooner you put this piece of art to work, the better. If you're going to connect with a patient, of all things, then you're going to need to know how deep her neuroses go."

"She's obviously open to the more curious workings of the universe." At Dina's quizzical look, Merlo pointed out, "She saw *you*."

"Indeed." Dina draped an arm around Merlo's shoulders and hugged her close. "I wish you calm seas tomorrow, young Merlo. I fear you're going to need them."

Merlo leaned into her oldest friend and drew strength from her presence.

She had a feeling Kieran's next session was going to shine a very bright light on what spurred her to reach out for the eternal rest she so desperately sought.

Chapter Six

Kieran's appointment had been purposely arranged to be the last one on Merlo's schedule for the day. Merlo was well aware that using the painting in her work left her drained, so she was prepared to go straight home afterward to just relax and decompress.

The orderly escorted Kieran to her door just minutes after Merlo's previous patient had left. Merlo was surprised by how disheveled Kieran appeared. Her eyes were shadowed and red rimmed. She was also paler than Merlo had ever seen her. Before Merlo had a chance to comment, Kieran spoke.

"Are you really going to have me brought here every single day until I tell you something that will satisfy your curiosity? I don't see any of the others getting this treatment every day, and frankly, some could use it more than I can."

Merlo just gestured for Kieran to take her seat on the couch. "You're a special case, Kieran," she said as she settled herself in for the session, making sure she could see the painting clearly.

Kieran just shook her head at Merlo's answer. "If this keeps up people will think you're playing favorites."

A myriad of expressions played over Kieran's face. She seemed to be fighting something, be it pain or perhaps her emotions. "Did you sleep at all last night?"

"Yes. This time without the aid of a tranquilizer dart stuck in my arm. It wasn't much of a restful night. I felt like I had everyone but the mounted police taking residence outside my door, all to keep a watchful eye on me every time I moved. I understand they wanted to make sure I didn't abscond again, but opening my door every few minutes and turning on the light didn't make for a peaceful night's sleep." Kieran rubbed at her eyes. "It also made my needing the bathroom a vast social event since I was escorted there and back. It's not like I could make another escape climbing down a roll of toilet paper."

"You did bring this attention on yourself. What with your history and you deciding to escape within two weeks of being here."

Kieran shot her a dirty look as she slumped farther into the couch. She looked like she was hoping the cushions would swallow her up. "My *history*. No one was supposed to learn about that, and I made damn sure I snuck around the legalities to hide my identity. Yet somehow you managed to uncover it all with your," Kieran made air quotes, "*ways and means.*"

Merlo ignored the disgruntled look she was getting and changed the subject. "I thought we'd try something new today."

Kieran sighed. "You're wasting your time, Dr. Blue. You've heard more than enough from me."

Kieran wiped at her sweating forehead. Her breath was audible in the quiet room. There was a wheezing quality to it. Merlo was concerned to see Kieran laboring to breathe.

"Are you okay? Are you asthmatic?"

"No, no I'm not. I'm just…really hot. Could I have a glass of water, please?"

Merlo reached for the pitcher beside her and poured Kieran a glass. She refilled it again after Kieran gulped the whole thing in one go. "Kieran, you look terrible. Do you need to go back to your room?"

"No," Kieran said. "How sad is it that the time I have to spend with you is the one rare moment of peace I get from being under Big Brother's watchful eye."

"Are you saying that my asking questions isn't as intrusive?"

"You're trying to understand my motives, and even I can appreciate that's your job. The others are watching my every move so I don't make them look bad again. I'm sure if they could fit me in a straitjacket and leave me in a padded room, they would. But I don't deserve to be left like that, Dr. Blue."

"Do I have your word that you won't try again to escape?"

Kieran smiled. "I never make promises I can't keep. I've told you, I can't stay here. For my own safety, you need to sign me out, and that way I'll be out of everyone's hair. I have to deal with this by myself."

"But that's why you're here. To get you the help you obviously need."

Merlo was surprised when Kieran laughed. The sound was unexpected and bordering on manic. Kieran took another long drink from her glass.

"I hope you're paid by the hour and not by the curing of your patients because I'm beyond help, Doctor."

Kieran's hand was shaking when she placed the glass down on the small table by her side. The glass clattered on the hard wood surface. Kieran looked ill and was acting stranger than usual. Merlo wondered if it was due to the chemicals Cragon had pumped into Kieran's bloodstream to knock her out. If she was right, then it looked like Kieran might still be fighting off the long-lasting side effects. Merlo regretted not bringing Kieran's file from her desk so she could check what reactions to medication she was prone to exhibit. If she looked like this because of Cragon's mishandling, then Merlo would screw his ass to the wall for his negligence. Kieran was going through enough without the added reactions to medication that Merlo had specifically argued against. His way of dealing with patients was the polar opposite of Merlo's.

She looked up at the painting. Time to put into practice one of the many things Cragon had no idea existed in her treatment of the Craven Hope patients. She spared Kieran a last look and noted that she seemed a little calmer. She just hoped what she intended to do gave her more insight into what ailed Kieran Lee.

❖

The blinds were drawn and the lights dimmed just enough to let shadows deepen in the room. Merlo set the scene she required. She could feel Kieran's eyes on her the whole time.

"Your magic mojo requires mood lighting?"

Merlo sat back down. "What I require is for you to be relaxed."

"What if you turning down the lights had freaked me out?"

"I always check the files first so that nothing I do is a trigger for anyone. I was just going to double-check with you anyway. You've shown no sign of being afraid of the dark in your room, though."

"No, not when there's so much else to be afraid of."

Kieran uttered this under her breath, but Merlo had excellent hearing and caught every word. She stared at Kieran for a moment trying to figure her out. She was such a contradiction. Merlo smoothed her hands down her skirt and prepared herself for the task ahead.

"Just relax, Kieran," Merlo said. "Clear your mind of all thoughts and distractions."

"Done."

Merlo bit back a smile at Kieran's swift reply. "How about you give it a little longer just to be sure?" Merlo thumbed a switch she had in the palm of her hand and a spotlight illuminated the seascape.

"What is this? Art appreciation hour?" Kieran said. "You work in weird and wondrous ways, Dr. Blue."

Merlo adjusted the light a little more. It pulsed with a steady but subtle rhythm. She stole a glance at Kieran and noticed that she had quieted, captured by the mesmerizing beat of the light.

"I want you to focus on the painting, Kieran. Let your eyes trace across the water." Merlo knew the hypnotic pull the painting was imbued with. She watched with satisfaction as Kieran's full attention was where she needed it to be. "Just relax and let yourself drift upon the water. Feel the rocking of it as it cradles your body and holds you safe." She saw the moment Kieran slipped under the spell of the painting. Now Merlo could ask the questions Kieran would never answer. As for Kieran, she'd have no memory of what was transpiring. She'd return to the room feeling relaxed and refreshed.

"Kieran, why is it so important for you to commit suicide? Why are you so desperate to end your life?" She knew there'd be no spoken answer.

Kieran was going to *show* her.

The painting shimmered. For a moment, it looked as if the sea was getting choppy. The sky darkened as the seascape's oils began to melt and shift across the canvas. They smeared, and the vibrant colors were lost as they melded into one. Then, just as quickly, the paint separated and began to render a new scene. Merlo watched in fascination as the painting became something new, brought about by Kieran's mind.

Piece by piece, the scenery arranged itself to tell its story. Merlo was taken aback by what she was seeing. Usually, she watched a parade of cruel and sadistic family members or so-called loved ones shown in their true light. Fears and phobias left their mark while anger, abuse, and violence blackened the canvas after showing their root cause. Other problems played out in short blasts of colors and visions. Every mental disturbance had its own story to paint.

Kieran's scene was different. As the oils stopped shifting, a distinct rural scene was left hanging on the wall. An old-fashioned farmhouse sat in the middle of a vast, flat landscape. Pastures housed a herd of Hereford cattle all huddled together, grazing. There was a large metal stock tank nearby and a silver windmill that was turning in the breeze. Behind the pasture, endless fields of wheat and milo grew. Far in the distance, an oil well stood in silhouette against the blue sky. It looked like a giant locust bowing to the ground. The sky was a brilliant blue contrasting with the verdant green of the grass and the bright yellow of the sunflowers growing beside the house.

"Did you grow up on a farm, Kieran?" Merlo asked, fascinated by what the painting was displaying. It was so detailed it looked almost real. Merlo felt like she was looking through a window seeing out across the farm.

"No, born and bred in the city." Kieran's voice was a slow and measured tone.

Merlo stared at the painting in wonder and then noticed that it was altering very subtly. The sky was shifting into the pinks and oranges of a glorious sunset. The sky above sent curious streaks across the farm, and Merlo thought she could see cracks appearing in the farmhouse walls. As the sky darkened, it took on the tone of a deep, blood red. Merlo watched as the cows began to lose their shape. Their stocky forms grew gaunt and their bones began to protrude crudely beneath their skin. They withered away, starving to death in mere seconds, even though there was an abundance of green grass beneath their hooves. The rotting flesh slid off their bones in a liquefied grease until nothing but their skeletons stood in the field.

The farmhouse's attic crumbled and fell into the house below. The walls shuddered as the wood splintered and broke away from the frame. All that remained was the broken shell of a home. The earth around it cracked open, and the once proud sunflowers curled and rotted on their stems.

What on earth was this doing in Kieran's head? The sky darkened even more. Merlo could almost smell the unmistakable smell of fresh blood as the sky brought forth a torrent of red rain. The bloodied drops poured from the sky and covered the farmland. It washed over everything in its path like a plague. It scattered the bones of the cattle and washed them away. It filled what was left of the farmhouse until it burst through the broken walls and began to bleed through the cracks. Bloody tears wept from the broken windows. The farm was devastated, the land in ruins, and still the sky came down.

The blood welled up to the edge of the frame, and Merlo was shocked to watch as it spilled out to run down the walls. She had never seen that happen in all the times she had used the painting. She had seen enough. She quickly switched off the light, and the painting returned to the calm sea on a beautiful sunlit eve.

Kieran blinked a few times, then looked over at Merlo. "So? Are we going to do this or not?" She rubbed at her eyes. "I have to say, as pretty as that painting is, it does nothing for me, so you might want to try a different method of whatever it is you were trying to achieve."

Merlo swallowed hard against the bile that had risen in her throat. She could taste blood in her mouth. She poured a glass of water and drank it down to try to cleanse her palate of the awful taste. She desperately wanted to talk with Dina about what she'd just witnessed and was going to call a close to the session early when she noticed Kieran's movements. She was not reacting like her patients usually did after this kind of session. In fact, Kieran seemed to be struggling with something.

Merlo looked back at the painting, frightened that maybe it still held some hold over Kieran. The painting was benign.

What was happening to Kieran was not.

Kieran kept brushing her hand across her forehead and could feel how hot her skin was becoming. She wondered if the room was growing humid or if it was just her. She had the dreadful feeling she already knew the answer to that question. She had no clue what had just happened to her, but she knew she had lost time in the session and now something was wrong with her.

Unfortunately, Kieran was no stranger to that feeling.

An all-too-familiar taste began to crawl its way onto Kieran's tongue. She had to force herself not to gag as it filled her mouth with its putrid stench. The strength of its acrid taste made her teeth feel rotten and decayed. Kieran feared they'd fall out of her mouth if she dared utter one word. She couldn't keep her hand steady as she fumbled to pick up her glass to bring it to her now cracked and bleeding lips. She nearly choked on the tepid water as she guzzled it down. Kieran tried to wash away the taste of roasting flesh as she felt her tongue start to burn.

"Kieran? Are you okay?" Merlo asked as Kieran started panting for breath.

This is too soon. Kieran's thoughts were in a jumble as she tried not to panic. She recognized that these symptoms were always the precursor for the main event she had to endure. The bouts were getting closer and closer now. When they had first started, she'd had months to recover before the next episode hit. Now they were growing in frequency. But she'd never had one start up quite so quickly before now. Her last bout was just a few weeks ago, right before she'd tried once again to kill herself. This wasn't giving her room for recovery now. It was all happening too fast.

It had to stop.

They were right, she thought, staring mindlessly at the surrounding walls and wishing they would just tumble down upon her. There was no rest for the wicked.

"Kieran, can you tell me what's happening to you?" Merlo had shifted from her seat and was now kneeling beside Kieran's chair. She reached out a hand to touch Kieran's and gasped as if the contact burned her. She gave Kieran a quizzical look and withdrew, staring at her fingers as if searching for scorch marks.

"You wouldn't believe me if I told you," Kieran said, gasping for air and starting to lose her hold on the conversation.

"You'll find I am open to all possibilities in the world of mental health. And you are quite the mystery. For someone so desperate to die you must have a powerful guardian angel watching over you to have kept you so stubbornly alive."

Kieran snorted. "I don't believe in such things."

"Never underestimate that which you can't see. What's happening, Kieran? What are you feeling?"

The concern in her voice made Kieran answer with the truth. "I might not be the best company tomorrow."

"You don't want to keep the appointment?"

"I don't think I'll be *here* tomorrow."

"What happens tomorrow, Kieran?"

All hell breaks loose in my head.

CHAPTER SEVEN

Dawn had just broken across the horizon when the hospital called Merlo back on an emergency. She'd almost welcomed the call as an excuse to get up because she'd been tossing and turning all night. Her mind had been too busy wondering what had changed Kieran's demeanor right before her own eyes. She'd have had to be blind not to notice how Kieran's health seemed to deteriorate in a flash and how flushed she had gotten. Her skin had been hot to the touch too.

Merlo's mind had spun in circles all night trying to explain what had happened. She flexed her hands against the steering wheel. She could still feel the rawness of the burns on her fingertips. It felt like she'd pressed her flesh to red-hot coals, searing the flesh like steak on a griddle. Yet there was nothing visible on her skin to show the tenderness she could still feel. It was bizarre.

"And I know bizarre when I see it," Merlo said out loud. "And this patient is certainly edging that way."

Dina had been mystified too. She'd stayed with Merlo for over two hours before saying she had some research to conduct and that she'd be back with all she could find. Merlo had a feeling Dina had more of an inkling as to what had happened.

The night duty officer that had called had said Kieran had been agitated all night. She'd been quiet and unresponsive for the rest of the day after her meeting with Merlo. At bedtime, the orderlies had dragged Kieran out from under her bed and restrained her. That irritated Merlo more than her being woken up had. Kieran hadn't been combative or ranting according to the officer. She'd just been uncooperative and "not entirely there." They'd fastened her down in case this was another escape ploy in the making. Merlo didn't believe it was. She'd seen the condition Kieran was in when she'd left her office. She'd been in no state to make a run from the hospital again.

Merlo wondered whether she was finally going to see what Kieran had kept hidden from her. She wanted to know if the unnatural burning sensation was just one part of what made Kieran foster such suicidal tendencies. If Merlo still couldn't shake the heat from her fingertips, she wondered how on earth Kieran coped with it as the host.

I don't usually get to deal with actual physical manifestations of a mental issue. This is going to be a first, I can tell.

She made a mental note to call Dina in, just in case. It never hurt to have a second opinion on a patient, and Dina was a font of knowledge that Merlo exploited. It paid to have old friends who had higher friends still.

When Merlo arrived at the hospital, she didn't recognize the new girl at the desk as she ran past her, distractedly waving her name tag and heading toward the wards. An orderly was waiting for her outside Kieran's room. He looked a little frightened, and that piqued Merlo's interest even more.

"What happened?" She peered through the small window in the door. "Did she *really* need to be strapped down?"

The orderly shifted uncomfortably under her glare. "Dr. Cragon ordered it, Dr. Blue."

Merlo grunted in disgust. "Of course he did." *I bet he wasn't pulled from his bed to give the order either.*

Merlo pulled open the door and turned to stop the orderly from following at her heels.

"I'd rather see her alone, thank you." She couldn't miss the relief on his face. He still argued though.

"But Dr. Cragon said—"

"Well, I'm not Dr. Cragon, and I'm telling you I'll see to this patient while you tend to your other duties. We're understaffed as it is."

He nodded but hesitated in walking away. Merlo sighed at his hovering.

"She's strapped to the bed. If she's going to be psychotic I think I'll be more than safe. It's not like she can go anywhere." Merlo shut the door on him before walking over to the bed. What she saw unnerved her more than anything she'd ever witnessed before. She edged closer to look down on Kieran, who was awake and staring at the ceiling with a furious glare.

"Hey there, Kieran. Can you explain to me what's happening to you?"

Kieran was shaking. Her whole body was a mass of tremors that made the fastenings on her wrists jangle against the metal of the bed rails. It was an unceasing rhythm that was growing louder in the quiet of the room.

Merlo took another step forward and Kieran turned to look at her. Her eyes were wide and fevered. For a split second, Merlo thought she'd imagined they were aglow with an unearthly light. Merlo placed a comforting hand on Kieran's shoulder.

The trembling halted. Kieran looked first at the hand touching her and then looked at Merlo in obvious shock.

Merlo didn't know which of them was more surprised. Merlo couldn't believe the change in Kieran's face. The drawn, desperate look disappeared, and she felt she was looking down at the *real* Kieran. She looked years younger and her skin tone changed from sallow to a much healthier one.

"How did you do that?" Kieran's eyes were clear and bright as she stared at Merlo.

Merlo hesitated before she replied and slowly lifted her hand off Kieran.

The change was instantaneous. Kieran aged before Merlo's eyes and the shaking started again, more ferocious this time, as if Kieran was a rage barely contained. The heat that rose from Kieran's body was tangible. Merlo could feel herself begin to sweat as the temperature intensified in the room.

"What are you?" Merlo asked, watching as Kieran's face seemed to morph and change shape before going back to her normal features again. A low growl rumbled from deep within Kieran's chest. Her eyes began to roll back in her head. The whites of her eyes were turning a deep blood red. Fractured words began to spill from her lips, spoken so fast Merlo couldn't catch what was said.

Merlo laid her hand back down on Kieran's shoulder. The transformation was startling once more.

Kieran seemed to gasp for air as if she'd just resurfaced from under the sea and needed to refill her lungs. She fought against her bonds, scowling at them for holding her immobile. She craned her neck to be able to lay her cheek on top of Merlo's hand to keep it in place. "I don't know what you're doing, but please, hear me out before you take your hand away again. This is the clearest my mind has been in two years since this nightmare started. Please, I need to ask you to do something for me."

Kieran's striking eyes captivated Merlo. They beseeched with such yearning that Merlo knew she'd agree to anything Kieran asked of her. "What is it?"

Kieran smiled at her, a heart-stopping gorgeous smile. "Please kill me, because your touch is the one thing that's ever kept the madness at bay. I can't hold it back for much longer on my own, and I can't take this anymore. I can't keep seeing the horrors that the visions conjure up. Don't let the madness eat me alive, please." She took a steadying breath. "This is me at my most lucid. I'm sound of mind in this rare moment. Please, put me out of this misery. Don't let me fail again and let the evil consume me."

"Evil?"

"I don't want to see the visions I endure come to pass. There are dark forces gathering in faraway places. I've seen them. They're not human and they have no love for us. They're coming. There's a whole army led by one who preaches hate and violence. We won't have the weapons strong enough to fight back against what he has planned for us. He's not of this world."

Merlo stepped back from the bed, inadvertently severing the connection between them. Kieran's eyes appeared to blaze into flames. The fire engulfed Kieran's eyeballs, rendering her sightless before melting them away. All that remained were two dark empty sockets, blackened and burned to a cinder. A cruel parody of Kieran's face stared up at her. Her smile was no longer sweet. It was cold and not entirely human.

"What do you see, Kieran? What do you see when these visions come?"

In a voice too deep to be her own, Kieran's laughter was laced with pure evil.

"I bear witness to the glory of Hell unleashed on Earth."

CHAPTER EIGHT

Being put through to voice mail was the last thing Merlo wanted to do. She waited impatiently for the rambling message to play through and then spoke the second the beep sounded its tone.

"Dina! I need you at the hospital right now. It's Kieran and it's urgent." She looked down at Kieran on the bed. "Just get here as fast as you can." Merlo hesitated before she spoke one last time. "It's a weird one." Merlo ended the call and leaned over the bed to study Kieran.

You're never going to believe how weird.

Kieran was sleeping. It didn't look like a pleasant sleep. Kieran was in constant motion, twitching and shaking. Her face was back to normal, and Merlo could see her eyes moving under her eyelids. The low growl rumbling from her chest told Merlo this wasn't something psychotherapy could help.

The door opened behind her, but Merlo didn't need to turn around to see who it was.

"What took you so long?"

"I wasn't expecting to be called in for a consultation at the crack of dawn. I was otherwise engaged," Dina said.

"I wasn't expecting to be called in either, especially to come face-to-face with *this*." Merlo stepped back from the bed to switch places with Dina.

Dina stared down at Kieran before shooting Merlo a look. "You called me to see how cute she looks when she's asleep? Because, I admit, she looks like a total babe. I'm sure if you can look past the fact she's tied to her bed and has a thing about throwing herself off bridges, then I'm sure she's quite the catch." Dina leaned a little closer. "Though that rumbling noise might support the necessity of earplugs in bed."

An unearthly growl burst from Kieran. It startled Dina so much she leapt back a few steps.

"Oh my God." Dina held her hand to her heart. "Just when you'd think nothing could surprise you anymore." She took a few steadying breaths. "Honestly, Merlo, you could have warned me."

"I'd have thought the shaking and the rumbling might have given you a heads up this is something strange," Merlo said.

"She looks like she's spiking a wicked temperature."

Dina reached over to touch Kieran's face. Before she could connect, Kieran's eyes flew open. They were not her own again. Instead of white, Kieran's sclera was red and the pupils stretched and elongated. The irises were yellow. As both Merlo and Dina stared at her, Kieran's eyes began to smolder. They caught fire, and Dina drew her hand back for fear of getting burned. Garbled worlds tumbled from Kieran's mouth. Deep and grating, it was more the sound of a monster than the woman Merlo knew.

"What language is that?" Merlo asked, watching as Dina fished out her phone and angled it over Kieran's distorted face. She pressed record. After a few minutes, Kieran hushed, the fire went out in her eyes, and she went back to the twitching and shaking. Merlo had a horrible feeling Kieran wasn't sleeping. She didn't think Kieran was present at all. She recalled Kieran's comment in her session.

I don't think I'll be here tomorrow.

"She knew this was coming. That means it's happened before to her." Merlo realized the gravity of that. "Oh my God, what is she living with?"

"How long has she been like this?" Dina took a few photos of Kieran.

"Since we viewed the painting." Merlo worried this was all her fault. "Did I trigger this somehow?"

Dina shook her head. "No, honey, there is nothing you could have done to produce this kind of reaction. This is all about her." She lowered her phone and put it back in her pocket. "I'm afraid this isn't your usual type of patient that you can help. This is something entirely different." Dina looked at Merlo. "In my opinion? I'd say she's possessed."

"I'm afraid that's way out of my level of expertise."

"That's all right. I may know someone who can help her." Dina smiled. "Yes, I think I know *exactly* who can deal with this sort of thing."

Kieran's body jerked, startling both Merlo and Dina. Her body pulsed as if she were being shocked. Her back bowed and bent, lifting Kieran up and off the mattress. Then, just as swift as the thrashing had begun, it stopped. She flopped back down and began weakly tugging at the restraints again.

"What the hell is going on here?" Dina said.

Merlo edged closer to watch Kieran's face as it ran through a series of grimaces and snarls. The features barely resembled the Kieran Merlo had come to know. Merlo reached out but stopped a mere breath away from touching Kieran's head.

"I'm more interested in what's going on in *there*."

❖

Trapped.

Every damn thing in Kieran's life conspired to take away what little power over her own choices she had left. And this waking nightmare was the worst of it. Kieran screamed at the top of her lungs, but there was no sound that escaped. No sound, no mouth to open, no air to breathe. There was just the overwhelming fear that she couldn't do anything to save herself again or click her heels three times to get back home.

I have no home.

I'm a lost soul.

Kieran had long since moved out of her apartment and taken to the road. She was alone now, trapped in the endless cycle of a never-ending nightmare that tore her from reality and entombed her in…some*thing* else.

She screamed again, and in her mind it felt like she was struggling, but she had no form here. She was nothing more than a consciousness trapped in a phantom zone, pounding her nonexistent fists against the invisible cage that imprisoned her. Buried alive with no way to get free. She had no arms to wrap around herself for comfort. She had no clue if she was dead or alive. She just knew she existed. Kieran railed against the blackness to no avail. Surely death had to be a blessed relief to this eternal limbo? The straps that held her down in the psych ward were nothing compared to the restraints this emptiness pressed upon her.

She could feel *something*, a heavy weight that pressed down on her chest even though there was no body to feel it. A presence, a force, something inevitable weighing on her. It constantly drew her back to this same exact nightmarish place again and again to relive it ad nauseam until the madness seeped into her soul and poisoned her mind.

Just let me die, she screamed into the blackness, but the blackness remained as silent as always.

Kieran panicked. She always panicked. This was the all-encompassing terrorizing fear forced upon her every single time this *shift* occurred. Claustrophobia clawed at her nonexistent throat. She wished for the ability to pass out, wanting anything to grant her an escape from this damnable place. The silence ebbed and flowed like waves against a shoreline. It was either deathly silent or filled with noises that she had to strain to hear.

A fear of the dark was nothing compared to what she dreaded was about to step out of it. No one could hear her, no one could see her, and no one would ever find her here. A lost soul indeed.

She tried to breathe, but she had no lungs with which to take in air. Yet somehow she could feel the motions of air drawing in and pushed back out. Something was breathing and it wasn't her. A stench threatened to make her gag, but she wasn't smelling it. The blackness began to lighten, and Kieran's struggling began in earnest. She whimpered knowing what was coming. She'd been here before, countless times, and it never got any easier to see.

No, not again, please...

No one heard her over the roar of sound that pummeled her from all sides. A cacophony of anguished voices, howling and screaming, wailing in pain and anger. The noise deafened her. It was all the anguish of the world condensed into a megaton explosion of sound that rocked through her.

As light slipped in to bleed the blackness away, Kieran prayed for release. She wished to crawl as far away as possible into a corner of whatever was left of her mind to hunker down and hide. But the light was coming, and with the light came terrifying clarity.

As always, the scorching reds and oranges of the sky in flames made her feel as if her skin was peeling off, layer by layer. She could feel the intense heat and was rendered blind by what appeared to be a sun. The ball of molten plasma pulsed to an angry rhythm. The whole surface twisted and shifted as solar flares spewed forth from its surface. Back on the ground, decayed buildings littered the skyline. Whatever had been erected there had long since been destroyed. The remnants were broken, and jagged frames reached up beseechingly to a blood red sky. The horizon was row upon endless row of ruined towers, left in place like tombstones to mock the fallen.

She was moving across the littered wasteland. Kieran tried to close her mind to what she was walking upon. Bodies littered the ground, unrecognizable lumps of the recent dead, torn limb from limb. This was a battlefield, and whatever served as her eyes and ears here lived on it. She always came back to this exact spot and walked over the dead as if they were mere pebbles on the seashore.

She could hear a voice above all the noise. A powerful voice, preaching to his flock. She could see the figure of something very tall, covered in a flowing robe. The hood was up over his head, hiding his face from view. Huge black wings like those of a dragon rose from his back. They looked leathery and were tipped with thorns. He held a huge tome, opened to a page he appeared to be reading from. The language was foreign to Kieran, but the closer she got, the more began to filter through and be translated.

"And there will be a great scourge among those who dwell above. The true descendants will wage war for a final time and lay waste to all that live there. For we were cast down to the earth and then banished from its bounty. No longer will we reign in Hell. We shall reclaim our birthright. Cast off your damnation, my children, for I shall lead you to a land where violence already has dominion. Hatred and cruelty's seeds have already been sown and flourish in the soil there. It is ripe for our taking, and our servants will be plentiful. They will worship us or die. Either way, we are taking back what is rightfully ours."

The cheers rang out, but Kieran couldn't see where they were coming from. She had taken her place beside the instigator. All she saw was his immenseness in the filthy robe that swathed him.

He turned a little to face her, the hood still masking his features. "You'll soon be home, my son. Back where you were banished from. We'll take the war to those creatures on the earth and then…"

He cackled and the sound grated on Kieran's ears like nails down a chalkboard. "Then we take the fight further and bring down the very heavens themselves."

"We're going to kill the humans?"

Kieran recognized the voice; she heard it in her dreams.

"We're going to kill every last one of them. We will rid the world of the vermin horde and take it for ourselves." He turned back to the throng below to address them. "We shall bring forth the fires of hell upon the human race!"

Kieran's head spun with the deafening chants of "Kill the beasts! Kill the beasts!" She couldn't plug her ears to block it out. She watched as the figure turned to face her.

"We'll kill all the men first, then wipe out the children as a matter of course. Then, when the women realize they have no one left to fight for them, they will capitulate to our mastery and bow to our every need. We'll repopulate the earth in our image, and I shall rule as a god."

He tossed back the hood of his robe, and Kieran witnessed again the true face of evil that haunted her very existence. It was the reason why she tried so hard to kill herself. She stared into the face of Death itself.

Dying seemed the only blessed choice she had left to never have to witness his hideous face again.

❖

The horrendous sound of gagging drew Merlo and Dina back to Kieran's bedside.

"Oh my God, is she choking on her tongue?" Merlo tried to pry open Kieran's locked jaw. A thick plume of smoke escaped from Kieran's mouth when Merlo managed to ease her teeth apart. The black smoke spiraled up toward the ceiling and dissipated on contact.

Kieran's shakes returned with a violent intensity.

"She's convulsing," Dina said, grabbing hold of Kieran's legs to try to hold her down.

Merlo shook her head. "I don't think this is a fit." She placed her hands on Kieran's shoulders. The tremors stopped.

"What did you do?"

"I don't know, Dina, but this has happened before when I've

touched her." She ran her hand up Kieran's arm and to her cheek. "Kieran? Can you hear me?"

"Don't let me go back there. Let me stay here, please. I can't...I can't go back there again. Don't let me go. Keep me here. Help me, please, help me. For God's sake, don't let this keep happening to me." Her voice shook with the exertion. Her eyes were wide and wild.

Red still ringed Kieran's eyes around the irises, but the whites were emerging as her eyes changed back to their original shape and form.

Kieran's gaze never wavered from Merlo. "You have to get me out of here. If they see this happening to me, they'll keep me sedated for the rest of my life and I can't live like that. I'll be trapped in that world forever. I can't live like this as it is."

Tears began to trickle down Kieran's face. Merlo caught a few and brushed them aside. The slight movement of taking her hand away for just that brief second was staggering. The red began to seep back into Kieran's eyes and beneath her skin her cheekbones sharpened and hardened.

Dina saw it too. "Do you see what you're doing? You're stopping whatever is happening to her. You're keeping it back. You're keeping it *out* of her."

Merlo placed her hand back on Kieran's cheek, and her eyes began to clear once more.

"That is so freaky." Dina was leaning over Merlo's shoulder to watch the transformation take place.

Kieran calmed enough so that Merlo could question her. "Kieran, what's happening to you? Can you describe it to me?"

"He's coming for us. He has a plan. He's going to kill us all, wipe the planet clean of mankind, but I can't get anyone to listen because they think I'm crazy. I'm not crazy. I'm just the messenger. I can't explain this. Don't let them commit me. It will be a slow death I'll suffer left with this fate. You need to let me go."

Merlo couldn't detect any form of deception in Kieran. She looked haunted by what she'd just experienced. The terror etched itself deep into her eyes and convinced Merlo she wasn't being duped.

"Dina, we need to get her out of here somehow."

"You want to release her in this state?"

"Not exactly. I just want her somewhere safer with people who will care for her and not lock her away." She looked over her shoulder toward the door at the shadow of someone walking past. She waited until she was sure they were gone. "I don't trust her here like this under Cragon's care." She gave Dina a look. "Will you help me?"

Dina nodded. "You're going to need that someone I mentioned if you want to plot an escape from here." She reached for her phone and began typing away. "I'm going to need a recent photo of Cragon," she muttered and tapped on the screen. "Ah, this will do. How fortunate for us he likes to post shots of himself all over the hospital's website. Oh, and video too, that's perfect for what we need." She sent off a series of texts. "Think you can hunt down his itinerary for today if this person can get away?"

Merlo nodded and Dina sent off another message.

"Seems to me, Merlo, we should have let Ms. Lee here escape that time she tried and we foolishly stopped her."

"I didn't realize what we were dealing with then." She flexed her fingers against Kieran's cheeks. "I can't stay glued to her like this all day until we put a plan in action. The staff will get suspicious with us hidden in her room for much longer. I also have appointments I need to cancel if I'm going to devote my time to keeping Kieran in the here and now."

"I'll stay with her."

"Can you keep her calm?"

Dina stepped up to lay her hands where Merlo's had been resting. Kieran's eyes darkened and a wicked smile slashed across her lips. Merlo put her hands back in place to keep Kieran grounded.

"Damn, I seem to be missing the magic you possess. How are we going to work around this, because if she starts acting up again we are screwed."

Merlo hated what she knew she had to do. She just hoped Kieran would understand. "Kieran, do you trust me?"

Kieran nodded. "Against my better judgment for your profession, yes, I do."

"I need to keep you safe while you're like this, and the only way I can is if you're sedated to stop you from drawing attention to yourself and whatever is happening to you."

"No! Don't drug me. It makes the nightmares worse. I lose touch with what little reality I can cling to."

"I know, and I'm really sorry, but I need to do something to keep them away from you." She watched Dina send another text off. "How long until your friend can get here?"

"She's not answered any of my messages yet, but I'm sure, unless she's otherwise detained, she'll head straight here. She's very reliable."

"Good, because we're going to need all the help we can to get Kieran out of here without any questions asked."

"You just get that itinerary, then cancel all your plans for today, and don't forget something to knock Kieran out fast." Dina smiled at her. "May angels grant you Godspeed."

Merlo raised her hands from Kieran's face. "Amen to that." She hurried from the room intent on gathering whatever sedative she could get hold of. After that, she was leaving it in God's hands.

CHAPTER NINE

"Trinity, I swear if you don't get your fucking paw out of my goddamn face I'm going to feed you piece by piece to the dog next door."

Rafe Douglas grumbled out from where she had been buried into her pillow, fast asleep and dreaming, until she'd been rudely awakened.

Trinity's offending paw shifted from where it had been batting Rafe's eyelid. Rafe grunted, snuggled back into her pillow, and tried to go back to sleep. A paw landed right on her mouth, causing Rafe to splutter for breath.

"Goddammit, cat! I'm trying to sleep here." Rafe opened her eyes to scowl at her black cat. Trinity stared back at her with one paw raised in the air ready to bop her again unless Rafe didn't deal with her right away. "What do you want? You were fed before bedtime and your litter box is clean." Trinity lifted her paw a fraction more. "I swear I should have just made Blythe keep your scrawny little furry ass. I should never have fallen for the sob story of you being the last cat in the litter."

Rafe turned her head on the pillow to squint at the clock by her bedside. "Damn it, Trinity, the alarm was going to do its job in a while anyway." She lifted her head a little. A low-pitched noise met her ears—the monotonous sound of a muffled alert pinging to remind the phone's owner they had a message. Rafe stretched a little more to look down where her clothes lay strewn across the carpet. They were reminders of them thrown there in the throes of passion that Rafe had been blissfully recovering from until a Trinity-shaped alarm clock had smacked her hard in the eyeball.

"That had better not be mine or I'm making good on my promise to rip Dean a new asshole."

Detective Dean Jackson was Rafe's partner at the DDU, the Deviant Data Unit. Job or not, he was under strict instructions not to text her unless it was of the utmost importance.

Rafe reached down to tug her jacket off the floor. She grabbed her phone out of the inside pocket. It was silent. She turned over in the bed.

"Ashley…" she called softly, lowering the sheet down from where it was bunched over Ashley Scott's head. "Ashley, wake up."

She pulled the sheet down more and eased it away from Ashley's naked skin. The pale morning light shone through the curtains and lit the intricate artwork Ashley had inked into her skin. Rafe mapped out the tattoo that used Ashley's whole back as its canvas. Two huge wings at rest lay before her as Rafe traced her fingertips over the feathers that looked strikingly real. She pressed a light kiss to the base of Ashley's neck. Then she nuzzled at the short blond hair as she laid a trail of kisses across Ashley's shoulders and up to reach her ear.

"Ashley, darling, you need to wake up," she crooned. "Your phone is ringing and it's pissing off the cat who, in turn, is annoying the shit out of me."

Ashley's shoulders shook with silent laughter. Rafe nipped her on the earlobe in punishment.

"Answer your fucking phone before I go drop it down the toilet."

"Well, good morning to you too, sunshine." Ashley yawned and stretched out a hand to pat around on her bedside table. She came up empty.

"It's still in your coat pocket," Rafe said, not attempting to help and instead petting Trinity behind her ears. She hoped the cat would be lulled into sleep so Rafe could do the same and grab an extra five minutes for herself.

Ashley groaned, running a hand through her hair, causing it to sport little spikes that Rafe always thought were adorable. Ashley then petted Trinity's head too.

"Trinity, go fetch," she said.

Trinity blinked at her with what Rafe called her "patented condescending cat" look and trapped Rafe's fingers between her paws to nip at them.

"Hey, it's not my damn phone that woke you up. Quit biting the hand that feeds you!"

"Rafe…" Ashley drew her name out in a sultry voice. "My sweet Raphael."

Rafe snorted at her. "Oh, there's no way I'm dragging my ass out of bed to pass you your dumb phone now. Calling me by my full name won't get you anything at this hour."

Ashley pouted a little, but then her smile turned seductive. She leaned close to Rafe and kissed her cheek, letting her lips linger. "It got me a hell of a lot last night, though."

Rafe pulled her hands away from where they were being Trinity's chew toys and cupped them over the cat's ears. "Please, impressionable children are present."

Ashley made a big deal of having to get out of bed and deliberately flung the sheets off to cover Rafe and Trinity. Trinity scrambled out and jumped down, but Rafe stayed where she was, laughing.

Ashley bounced back on the bed, rocking Rafe, who pulled the sheets away to see what all the fuss was about on Ashley's phone. She leaned in to peer over Ashley's shoulder.

"What's so desperate that they've left so many texts and messages? Usually if it's something that urgent we get your messenger boy paying us a visit."

Ashley dug an elbow in Rafe's naked side. "Eli is not my messenger boy. He's an angel of high regard. And I'm guessing he doesn't know about whatever this is." Ashley scrolled through the many texts she'd received. She made a humming noise.

"What's up?"

"All of these messages are from someone I haven't heard from in a long time."

"Well, while you're catching up with an old friend, why don't I shower first while you feed the cat, then the bathroom is all yours while I go put the coffee on. Then we can talk about whatever this is while being properly caffeinated and smelling less of sex."

"*I* have to feed her?" Ashley looked up from her phone.

"It was your damn phone that woke her up to play bongos on my eyelids, so yes, you have to feed her." Rafe grinned as another idea struck. "Unless you have time for a quickie before you have to go wherever those texts are calling you away to." She got out of bed and stretched. She let out a satisfied grunt as her spine popped and she could move more freely. "I'd like to think I *come* before the cat in this house."

Ashley chuckled. "You're incorrigible." She sat up in bed and beckoned Rafe closer to her. She tugged Rafe's head down and kissed her. "How busy are you at the DDU today?"

"I'm hoping not very so I can just chill because you fucked my brains out last night."

Ashley held up her phone and pressed play on a video she had paused on the screen. Rafe's mouth dropped open as the video played out.

"No fucking way!" she said looking at Ashley in astonishment. "Will my Spear of Light work on whatever that is?"

Ashley shrugged. "I'm not sure, but I'm gathering from the texts I've just read that we might need to pack more than an overnight bag for this. Seems there's something strange going on in St. Louis."

"So who you gonna call?" Rafe said.

"PI Ashley Scott, Demon Possessions 'R Us." Ashley dipped her head to press her lips against Rafe's breast. "And her main squeeze Detective Rafe Douglas, of the Deviant Data Unit."

With reluctance, Rafe pulled back. "Seems we don't have time for this after all. You'd better call your angel forth and fill him in. I'll go speak to Detective Powell and cook up some story about why I'm leaving my desk." Rafe planted a kiss on Ashley's nose. "Don't forget to get Eli on board for his cat-sitting skills. If we're going on a road trip, someone needs to keep Trinity fed and entertained."

Rafe took another look at the phone. The video had stopped, but the face on the screen was not human. An attack in a back alley with a demon masquerading as a man had brought Rafe into this world where the bizarre had become more and more commonplace. She'd witnessed more than her fair share of demons since coming into contact with Ashley, who brought her own unique connections to the supernatural into the mix. Having Ashley to guide her through this new world had been a miracle for Rafe. Together they fought the demons who used Chicago as their stomping ground.

Now it appeared St. Louis had its own demons to slay.

Ashley went downstairs to feed Trinity, who was warbling loudly.

"We're going to need a lot more than coffee," she muttered and turned off the screen on the phone so she wouldn't have to see that distorted human/demon image any longer. There was no need to remember it. She'd be seeing it soon enough.

❖

"St. Louis?" Eli stood in Rafe's kitchen looking at Ashley's phone while Ashley was cleaning up the breakfast bowls. "How strange that there's been nothing that's come to our attention about such an occurrence."

Rafe snorted at the angel from over her coffee mug. She marveled at how commonplace it was to see this beautiful celestial man, dressed in the purest of white suits, in her home. His huge feather-laden wings lay folded down his back, and he glowed with an unearthly light that no longer blinded her with its intensity.

"Let's face it, Eli. You guys might have the *Almighty* eye in the sky, but not everything pings on your radar until well after the demonic cat has been let out of the bag." Rafe drained her mug and smiled as Ashley took it from her to place in the dishwasher. "I mean, how many calls a day would you guys be getting if every demon possession was reported to a higher source?"

"We do have people on the ground for that kind of thing," Eli agreed. "But no exorcist has had this possession brought before them. I'm wondering why they called Ashley."

Ashley took the phone from Eli and switched it from the video he'd been watching over to the texts she'd received. "Because it's Dina," she said.

Eli's features changed just a fraction from his usual stoic face.

"Oh," he said and began to read the screen.

"So? Do I get to hear just who this mysterious Dina is? I'd hate to be going in blind to a situation where she's one of Ashley's exes and we're going to have to fight over her." Rafe patted at her jacket where the pen Eli had given her was resting. It had the capability of turning into a Spear of Light, a handy weapon that she employed in catching demons. "I'm warning you now. I fight dirty."

Ashley laughed and wrapped her arms about Rafe's neck to

reassure her. "You won't be chasing off any old admirers, sweetheart. For one thing, she's *way* older than me. She's more an informant than anything. It's been years since I last saw her, and that was just for a brief moment for a case I was working on. She had dug up some information I needed." Ashley squeezed Rafe a little more. "She's kind of a go-to gal for knowledge."

"Glad to hear it," Rafe said, slightly mollified. "So we're driving all the way to St. Louis on the word of an old informant who sends you creepy texts?"

"It's getting you out of your office and on a road trip with me," Ashley pointed out as she ruffled Rafe's hair and went to retrieve her phone from Eli. "And there's something more to this than she said. I trust her. She's never failed in any of the information she's furnished any of us with."

"Dina is a much valued source," Eli said. He looked down to where Trinity was weaving her way around his ankles. "You mentioned something about my being required to cat-sit again?" He bent down and Trinity jumped into his arms. She began purring as he cooed to her. Both angel and cat stared at each other. Eli looked away first. "Ashley, I have a feeling you need to take Trinity with you on this trip."

Ashley looked surprised. "Are you serious?"

Eli nodded. "I'm sure there'll be plenty of room for her where you're going and she'll be perfectly safe."

Rafe stared at him. "Did *she* tell you that? Are you hiding some sort of secret Cat Whisperer talent, Eli? What next, she asks for more treats and I come home to find her the size of a Labrador puppy?"

Eli stared back, unfazed by her sarcasm. "I just feel she'll be more at peace with you in St. Louis."

"If you didn't want to bother looking after her you just had to say, Eli."

Eli shook his head at her. "No, Rafe, that's not it at all. I love this cat, as you well know. Except for the hairballs." He paused for a moment in thought. "I'm still trying to work out God's exact purpose in that addition to a cat's repertoire." He held Trinity up to his face and she head-butted him. "This time, she's better off with you. I can feel it."

Ashley shared a look with Rafe. Rafe just shrugged at her. "Guess it's a family trip this time. I'll find her travel cage and then you, Eli, can wrestle her into it for us seeing as you and she have some kind of mystical understanding going on over there." She checked her watch. "Then we'll get this show on the road because from the tone in Dina's texts, time is of the essence."

CHAPTER TEN

Rafe tried to hide a smirk as she watched Ashley get her glamour on to become Dr. Henry Cragon striding through the main doors of the Craven Hope Psychiatric Hospital like a man on a mission. Ashley headed straight for reception and placed her hands spread out across the desk. The nurses began to flutter around "him." Rafe found it fascinating to watch Ashley employ the quirky mannerisms of whoever she had shifted into. Even if that person was a blatant misogynist like this Cragon appeared to be.

Ashley snapped her fingers rudely at one of the receptionists on duty. "I need a visitor's pass for Detective Douglas here. She's come to interrogate a patient."

The receptionist hurried to comply with the order. Within moments, she held out the pass to Ashley and gave "him" a coy little smile.

"Thank you, Mary."

Her eyes widened and she stammered out, "Oh, you're very welcome, Dr. Cragon."

Rafe took the pass from the woman instead. She tried not to smirk at the adoration plastered all over her face for this doctor who was everything Rafe hated in a man. She fastened the pass to her jacket and followed on Ashley's heels as she led her through a set of doors.

"Something tells me he's not big on dishing out the 'please' and 'thank yous' or even knowing a subordinate's name," Rafe said.

"He's the golden boy here. The name that matters to him most is his own on the paycheck, I'll bet." She pointed to the building map on the wall. "The psychiatric unit is this way."

Rafe was exasperated by how many times Ashley was stopped to be fawned over or shown something that only Cragon could possibly deal with on their short walk to the unit. Ashley waved them all away brusquely, too busy to stop and talk.

"How many more times are you going to be stopped so that people can kiss your ass?" Rafe pulled open a door and made a show of ushering Cragon through first. "After you, Your Highness."

Rafe felt her stomach turn as a familiar smell assailed her. A few years ago, she'd spent more than enough time stuck in a hospital after her stabbing. Even having to visit one for something work-related was enough to bring the memories racing back. She had to fight against the desire to turn around and get the hell out of there.

"Christ, I hate these places. When you're in one it feels like there's no way you'll ever escape alive." She rubbed at her nose. "And the goddamn smell clings to your clothes and clogs up your nostrils like days-old kitty litter."

Ashley gave her a sympathetic look before turning back to check off the door numbers. "We're here now. The patient is in room forty-nine."

Rafe swallowed back her nerves about being in an institution that she'd had her own fears about being placed in. Telling the doctors she'd seen a demon before he'd attacked her would have no doubt ensured her a room exactly like this one. "Let's get this over with as soon as possible. These places give me the creeps no matter how clean and well run they appear."

Rafe knocked. A woman stuck her head around the door. Rafe made a disgruntled sound as she saw the shimmering aura surrounding her.

"Dr. Cragon?" The woman almost shut the door again, but then relaxed when she saw Rafe. She ushered them both into the room quickly and made sure the door shut behind them. She looked Cragon over with an exacting eye.

"*You* nearly gave me a heart attack."

Rafe stared at her. "Dr. Blue?"

She shook her head and proffered a hand. "No, I'm Dina. I'm at your service, Detective Douglas."

Rafe scowled as she realized who she was. This woman was in no shape or form *old*. She'd have words with Ashley later on her definition of an older woman when this Dina didn't look much older than Rafe was. "You're the texter who wasn't going to take no for an answer and bombarded us with messages. Nice to meet you at a more civilized hour for communication." Rafe shook Dina's hand. "Now, what kind of a schedule are we on, because I've done some crazy shit in my line of work, but kidnapping a patient from a mental hospital is a first even in my book." She caught sight of the other woman standing beside the bed. She had the palest hair Rafe had ever seen and a shimmer to match. "Oh, for fuck's sake," she muttered. "She's got to be another one of your gang judging by that hair color and the fact she's shining enough to register on my good guys scale."

Merlo smiled at her. "I'm Dr. Merlo Blue. Thank you for coming here so fast. I appreciate it." She nodded toward some papers on the bedside table and looked at Cragon. "I'm going to need your signature on these to release the patient on her own recognizance." She gestured toward the top sheet. "This is what the signature needs to look like."

Before them all, Cragon's form shifted and Ashley's true self flickered into view. Dina and Merlo both stared at the transformation. Rafe was always disappointed that she couldn't see whatever new form Ashley shape-shifted into, especially when she saw other people taken in by the charade. She just saw Ashley covered in a sparkling golden shimmer. The shimmer let Rafe know Ashley's glamour was in place and she had taken on someone else's guise. Judging by the relief on everyone's faces, they were happier to see Ashley than the man she'd been masquerading as.

Ashley started signing the paperwork. "It's a good thing that I have a knack for forging signatures as well."

Rafe edged closer to the bed to look down at Kieran Lee, who was lying there looking terrified.

"Hey, Kieran. How you doing?"

Kieran managed to drag her eyes away from Ashley to stare up at Rafe. "I'm wondering just how delusional I am because I've just watched Cragon disappear before my eyes and this woman appear in his place."

Rafe smiled at her. "You're okay. That's just Ashley's party trick." She noticed that Merlo had her hands clamped on Kieran's shoulders. "Any particular reason why you're holding her down when she's already strapped to the bed like some animal?" Rafe asked.

"Kieran is just waking up from the sedative I had to administer to knock her out until your arrival."

"What's with the laying on of hands, Doc?"

Merlo removed her grasp. Kieran's face shifted into the one Rafe recognized from the video. The change made Rafe take a step back from the bed. Kieran's eyes turned blood red and began to change shape. She spewed forth a litany of unintelligible words and sounds.

"Okay, and the freaky just keeps on a-coming," Rafe said. "Her being strapped to the bed makes perfect sense now." She surreptitiously reached for the pen in her pocket. Ashley's hand stilled Rafe's instinctive reaction.

"The Spear of Light won't work here, Rafe. You can't banish her in this state. She's human. At least, I believe she is."

"I'm only seeing a slight shimmer when she gets her monster face on." She forced herself to relax. "There's more of a shimmer coming off the doctor and Dina here combined."

Merlo smiled at Rafe as she returned her hands to rest on Kieran. "You *are* special, aren't you?"

"Not according to my mother," Rafe muttered and took a step back toward the bed. Kieran had lost the demonic look and was back to looking scared. "Jeez, kid, what have you gotten yourself into?"

Ashley waved the paperwork. "These are all signed and dated. Merlo, what's your plan for getting us out of here?"

"And for moving her where, exactly?" Rafe added. "Because I'm afraid we don't have room at our place for a doctor, her buddy, and Demon Daisy here."

"My home will be sufficient for all we need," Merlo assured her. "We just have to get her out of here before anyone else sees what's happening to her." She turned to Kieran. "Do you think you can keep whatever's got hold of you back long enough for us to get you out of here?"

Kieran shook her head. "I have no control over any of this. But you have to get me out of here before the real Cragon displays me as his pet freak."

"Once we're driving away from here, you'd better keep a firm grip on our patient there. I don't think my squad car is covered for any actuality connected to or resulting from demon possession," Rafe said.

"Don't worry about that. Help me get her in the wheelchair and then we'll just need Cragon to work his magic to get us out," Merlo said. "Detective, can you unfasten the straps please?"

Rafe stared Kieran down. "I have my gun. Don't think I won't use it if you try anything."

Kieran smiled. "If I had the strength to fight, I'd hold you to that, Detective. Anything to be put out of this misery."

Rafe looked up at Merlo in surprise.

"The reason Kieran is in here is because she's a multiple suicide attempter," Merlo said. "A condition probably brought on because of this possession."

"Well, I'm sorry, Kieran, but you're not dying today. Not on my watch. I follow the serve and protect code of conduct." Rafe freed Kieran's hands and took one in her own. "I promise you, I'll do everything in my power to keep you safe, whatever it is we have to fight against. You're not alone anymore." She helped Kieran into the wheelchair, and Merlo kept her hands in place on Kieran's shoulders. Dina tucked a blanket over Kieran's knees and gathered up the few possessions and clothes Kieran had in her room.

Rafe nodded to Ashley. "Okay, Sparky, time to get your glamour on and get us the fuck out of here."

❖

Ashley had come to the conclusion that she didn't like Dr. Cragon one bit. Judging by how everyone reacted to him, she got the distinct impression he was the biggest pompous ass to ever walk these halls. She'd gleaned enough details courtesy of Dina to perfect the air of a man who ran roughshod over his colleagues and staff. She caught sight of herself in one of the windows as she strode down the hall. She could see the man she was masquerading as reflected back at her. Overprivileged, self-righteous, and attractive in his own mind; she knew his sort all too well.

She led the others to the checkout desk and brandished the fraudulent signed forms at the woman behind it.

"We're cutting one loose," she said, knowing the woman could only see and hear Cragon. "Dr. Blue is accompanying the patient to make sure the transfer is complete and then Ms. Lee is someone else's problem." Ashley thrust the papers at the woman with enough force for her to fumble them. She tried to shuffle them back into some semblance of order, which distracted her to the fact Rafe was wheeling Kieran out already. Merlo stuck close by her side as she kept Kieran grounded and less likely to sport her demon face.

Ashley stayed at the desk just long enough to keep everyone's attention on Cragon until she heard the large doors behind her close.

"Now I'll get back to my real work." She turned and made as if Cragon was going back to his office. Once out of sight of the main desk, Ashley slipped into the first empty room she could find and dropped the glamour. She shucked Cragon off like unclean clothes and shifted again. This time she took on the appearance of an ambulance driver. She'd noticed they were in and out of the reception area and never drew any attention by the security staff or the receptionists.

By the time Ashley walked outside, Dina and Merlo had gotten Kieran settled in the back of Rafe's car. She joined them to take the passenger seat while Rafe slid behind the wheel.

"So, where to, Dr. Blue?" Rafe grinned at Ashley, amusing herself with the unintentional rhyme.

Merlo began giving out instructions that Rafe tapped into her navigation system. Rafe drove the car out of the lot, and they were soon on the street.

From the back seat, Kieran spoke for the first time in ages. "Free at last."

Ashley turned in her seat to look at Kieran. "How you doing?"

"I'm hanging in there but that's because the good doctor here is keeping up close and personal." Kieran was squinting. "I'm thankful for the tinted windows in here. The bright sunlight wasn't helping me remain calm."

"You got vampire tendencies to add to that weird-ass list of yours?" Rafe asked, eyeing Kieran suspiciously through the rearview mirror.

"Not that I know of. It's just another in the long line of things I'm oversensitive to in this state. I never used to be." Kieran looked over her shoulder as the hospital disappeared from view. "Thank you for getting me out of there, but I have no idea what you think you're going to do with me now."

"We're going to decipher what's going on with you," Ashley said, "because you don't strike me as disturbed or wired any different mentally. I think you've got something else at work here for your particular madness. But I need you to realize you don't have to do anything we ask of you if you don't want to. We won't force you or take away what bit of control you seem to be clinging to. I think you've suffered enough of that indignity already. All we ask is for you to trust us. We mean you no harm, Kieran. You're among friends here, and all we want is to help you."

Kieran stared at Ashley, then gave Merlo a pointed look. "You're no normal psychiatrist, are you?"

"When my patients are like you?" Merlo shook her head. "No, I'm afraid not."

Kieran looked like she wanted to ask something but was afraid to. Ashley caught her eye and nodded, urging Kieran to speak.

"Did I really see Cragon sign me out or is that another of the delusions my brain conjured up?"

Ashley grinned. "You saw what you needed to see. As did the ones who are now filing the paperwork that got you out of there relatively legal and aboveboard." She coughed a little. "In a manner of speaking." She wasn't about to do a show-and-tell of her shape-shifting abilities in the car.

Kieran seemed to digest this. "What if I'm beyond your help?"

"I have friends in high places whose job it is to work the miracles mere mortals could only wish to witness. Don't worry, we've got you covered."

Kieran's emotions ran free across her face. Fear warred with disbelief in her eyes. Ashley loved skeptics and getting to open their eyes to a much bigger world.

"You know I think you're all certifiably crazy, don't you?" Kieran said, slouching back into the seat and shaking her head at them all.

Ashley grinned. "Then you're in good company, aren't you?"

With Merlo's grounding hands on her, Kieran was able to feel some sense of normality. It wasn't something she was used to, and after all this time, she was having trouble remembering what her life used to be like before. It had changed dramatically once the dreams had started.

Or what she'd thought were just dreams. Her life was no longer her own. Not since she'd started going *somewhere* else in her head.

Kieran was torn between looking out the car window, soaking in the sheer normalcy of everyone else going about their day-to-day lives, or staring at the four women who had, technically, just abducted her. It was curious to realize all of them had more of an idea of what was going on in Kieran's head than she did. She couldn't work out if that was a good thing or not.

"How much trouble are you going to be in for taking me out of the hospital?" Kieran asked Merlo, who was watching the road when not checking on Kieran.

"I didn't sign you out. Cragon did," Merlo said.

"I may not be in my right mind, but even I know Cragon wouldn't allow me to be released. He's pretty much had it in for me since my daring escape plan failed so abysmally." Kieran shot both Merlo and Dina a disgruntled look. "Which would have had a chance of being successful if you and your mysterious partner here hadn't screwed it up for me. This cloak-and-dagger stuff you're pulling now wouldn't have been necessary if you'd let me go in the first place."

"But if you'd have escaped, then what?" Merlo's grip tightened just a little more. "You'd have disappeared and found somewhere else to try to kill yourself."

Kieran didn't react. It wasn't a lie. The unspoken acknowledgment of that left them both just staring at each other.

"So, you took me out of the unit to do what with?"

"Hopefully, more than your trying to break out on your own was going to accomplish." Merlo stared her down.

"You can't keep your hands on me twenty-four hours a day. There's the whole business of bathroom breaks we need to address, for a start. And I'd like an explanation why you alone, Dr. Blue, seem to have the ability to do whatever it is you do when you touch me." Kieran gestured to where Merlo's hands were holding her.

"What does it feel like?" Ashley asked.

"Like breaking the surface of the sea after being held down drowning for so long," Kieran said.

"I promise you I won't keep you in the dark about anything, but let's get you somewhere safe first. This isn't exactly a travel conversation."

Merlo issued a few more directions to Rafe as they left the main road. They drove through a more affluent area where ornamental gardens surrounded the properties and tall walls surrounded them all.

Kieran began to worry if she was exchanging one building that had kept her locked away for another one surrounded by the same high fences. She worked on calming her breathing so it wouldn't give away any signs of her distress. She focused on the weight of Merlo's hands anchoring her to the here and now.

My time will come. She closed her eyes and soothed herself using a few techniques she'd managed to gather together to help herself to just breathe and exist.

My time will come.

After all, they have to sleep sometime.

CHAPTER ELEVEN

Kieran's astonishment at what she saw echoed in Rafe's more colorful phrasing on the first view everyone got of Merlo's home.

"Fuck me," Rafe exclaimed, gawking at the massive building before them. "I sure as hell picked the wrong profession to follow. Who knew there was so much to be made in tightening up people's loose screws?"

Ashley coughed pointedly and Kieran caught the sharp look Ashley directed Rafe's way. Rafe looked at Kieran through the rearview mirror.

"No offense, Kieran," Rafe said.

Kieran had to smile. "None taken, Detective." She had a feeling Rafe had a habit of being brutally blunt in her observations and that malice was never something intended. She wondered if it was a cop thing. To be honest, Kieran found Rafe refreshing after all the double-talk she'd heard from medical professionals.

She shot a brief glance at Merlo. She'd never treated Kieran like a test subject or just another patient to fill her daily quota. What she hadn't expected was for Merlo to live in a mansion that reeked of old money and years-old prestige. Merlo electronically opened the gates using a small remote and they swung wide to allow the car entrance.

"You hiding a secret link to nobility, Merlo?" Rafe pulled the car to a stop on the long driveway and stared out the windshield. "Because this place makes my little home look about the size of a cat bed in comparison."

Kieran craned her neck to take in the immense three-story home. It was painted an immaculate white, with black trimming on the five windows that lined the second-story frontage. On the ground level were another four windows and a huge double door with golden fixtures. Steps led up to the front doors, and Kieran could see that there was a lower level offset in a pale gray brick. She couldn't even imagine how far back the building went.

Yet for all its size and grandeur it looked welcoming, and Kieran felt some of her terror recede. She felt some comfort in the fact that, from the outside at least, it didn't appear to be a high-tech laboratory where unsuspecting Craven Hope patients were taken to be experimented on.

Merlo unfastened her seat belt. "This house has been in my family for generations. I'll admit it's way too big for me living here on my own, but it's home. It's going to be nice having company for a change with you all here." She squeezed Kieran's shoulders. "I hope you'll find it less clinical than your room at the hospital."

Ashley got out first and held open the door for Kieran. Kieran found herself a little restricted by Merlo's hold, but she was soon out with a little pushing from Merlo behind her and Ashley's helping hand in front. Kieran stopped a moment to gather her bearings and to just breathe. Dina opened the front doors and waved at everyone else to follow her in as if it were her home. Kieran mused over Dina's familiarity with both the house *and* Merlo.

Merlo nudged her out of that thought and into moving. Kieran tried to shift her shoulders a little to ease the feeling she was being frog-marched along the driveway and up the steps. "I'm sure you can ease up on the grip there," she grumbled at Merlo, who didn't loosen her grip one inch.

Rafe was carrying bags she'd gotten from the car and overtook them as she bounded up the steps two at a time. "I'll superglue her hands to you myself, Regan MacNeil, till you can rein in your demon face."

Kieran chafed at Rafe's *Exorcist* dig. "I believe the morphing phase doesn't last more than a day after I...go under." Kieran didn't know how best to otherwise describe it. She shrugged. "Or so I was informed by my ex, who had the unfortunate timing of coming over to my apartment and witnessing it all. I know enough to recognize when an episode is about to take place, but my telling her not to come over fell on deaf ears. She thought I was cheating on her. Instead she found me entertaining some*thing* else. That was the first time I had an audience to this Jekyll and Hyde performance. I'd hoped it would be the last."

The mansion's hallway was large and lined with old paintings. An ornate grandfather clock marked every second with a distinct ticking noise that made Kieran flinch. She glared at the clock, hyperaware of every second passing that seemed to beat with the deafening burst of a bass drum. She watched the pendulum swing, and her head filled with the noise of every cog turning. The hands on the clock face moved silently to everyone else, but to Kieran each shift they took to tell the time was like the sound of a hammer striking an anvil. She shook her head, trying to free herself from the overwhelming cacophony.

"Your old clock is way too loud. How do you ever sleep with its constant racket?"

Merlo gave her a curious look. "It's a quieter timepiece than the standard grandfather clocks. You must be incredibly sensitive to noise, Kieran. Try to focus your attention on my voice and the clock will fade into the background. Here, let's go sit in the living room and maybe distance from it will help you tune it out."

Kieran let herself be guided to where Merlo intended for them all to sit and get comfortable. She couldn't help but marvel at the living room that she walked into. Merlo sat Kieran down and settled beside her. It felt as if Merlo deliberately trailed her hand from Kieran's shoulder, down her arm to rest on Kieran's thigh. Merlo slipped her other hand across Kieran's shoulders and again all the way down, this time to rest on Kieran's forearm. Kieran could still feel where Merlo's hands had been. A delightful tingling ran across her skin even through the protection of clothing. She couldn't help but glance over at Merlo to see if she'd felt it too. Merlo's face gave nothing away, so Kieran dropped her gaze. Merlo's hands then caught her attention. Their delicate length belied the strength of grip Merlo could wield.

"You were saying, about your girlfriend?"

"Ex, ex-girlfriend. What more is there to say? She let herself into the house while I was flat out on the floor looking comatose and feverish. She rushed over to administer CPR and came face-to-face with whatever it is my face looks like when *it* takes over. She told me she screamed and sat for an hour cowering in a corner until she could work up the courage to move. I'm estimating I was out for a day before my face was the one I saw in the mirror. But then I never get to see what she said she saw and what you guys witnessed too." Kieran shifted until she was more comfortable on the plush couch cushions. "She made sure to go into extensive detail about what I did and looked like before she called me every kind of freak under the sun and stormed out with her clothing stuffed in a grocery bag. All things considered, though, as breakups go? I'd say that was one of my better ones."

"What did you do next?" Merlo asked.

"I packed up as much of my belongings as possible, loaded them into my car, and hightailed it out of there before she brought the police to my door to arrest me or her whole church in to pray over me."

Ashley laughed as she slipped off her jacket and took a seat opposite them. Kieran noted that she dressed all in black, from her button-down shirt to her jeans and boots. The darkness of her clothing contrasted with her blond hair that was not unlike Kieran's own. Ashley didn't appear to be much taller than Kieran either. She had to admit Ashley made her nervous. Seeing what Ashley had done and that no one had reacted to it at all just made her sense of unease grow. She hated the fact she couldn't meet Ashley's eyes as she was sizing Kieran up.

Rafe's entrance was a relief. It gave Ashley someone else to focus on. Kieran was surprised to see Rafe coming in holding a pet carrier.

"Merlo, thanks again for allowing us to stay here and for letting me bring Trinity. We don't usually bring our cat along for our cases, but someone insisted we should this time." Rafe put the carrier down and started to fiddle with the lock, muttering under her breath. "For some bizarre reason he didn't go into detail as to why. God forbid we should ever have a fucking clue as to what's going on."

Rafe opened the cage door, and a black cat jumped straight into her arms demanding to be petted. If Kieran didn't know better she would have sworn the cat was grumbling at Rafe, but Rafe just cuddled her close and spoke to her.

"Hope none of you are allergic," Ashley said, leaning over to give Trinity her own reassurances as Rafe sat down beside her and Trinity demanded an equal amount of attention from Ashley too.

"I've brought all her food and stuff. She's housetrained better than I am, and as long as someone keeps her entertained, then maybe I won't have to worry about her using any of your fancy-pants furniture as a scratching post." Rafe looked at Merlo over the cat's head. "If you'd rather Trinity and I stay in a motel, neither of us will be offended, honest."

"You'll do no such thing," Merlo said, making coaxing noises to draw Trinity's attention over to her. She hesitated to remove a hand from Kieran's leg, but after searching Kieran's face, she lifted it free. Trinity jumped down off Rafe's lap and was soon rubbing around Merlo's legs. Merlo smiled as she petted the cat. "There hasn't been a pet in this house for more years than I can remember." She cooed and fussed over Trinity, who took it all with a blissful look on her face.

Kieran didn't know which was funnier, Merlo talking in a baby voice to the cat or Trinity closing her eyes and looking smug at all the attention. She was startled when Trinity jumped onto her lap, sat down, and just stared at her.

"What is your cat doing?" Kieran asked, eyeing it warily. She hadn't had any pets growing up and was never quite sure what to do with one.

"She's in your lap. That can mean one of two things," Rafe said. "One, she knows you are the wielder of the can opener and she wants to be fed now. Or two, she's bestowing upon you the honor of petting her. Just be mindful that if you don't start with the fawning over her quick enough, she will start biting." Rafe grinned over at Kieran and settled back in her seat. "I'd go with the petting."

Kieran lifted a hand to stroke Trinity's fur. Trinity never moved. Instead, her large orange eyes stared into Kieran's as if she were seeing something no one else could. It was starting to freak Kieran out.

"Should I be worried she's staring at me?"

There were no purrs, no cat chatter; Trinity just *stared.*

"Do you think she knows there's something wrong with me?" Kieran asked.

"Well, *Constantine*, if you want to hold her little furry face in your hands while we stick your feet in a bowl of water, then go for it. I'm sure Merlo can accommodate you." Rafe laughed.

Kieran grimaced. "Unfortunately, I don't seem to need a cat conduit to see the delights hell has to offer." She found herself hypnotized by Trinity's unblinking stare. "But I am intrigued why it took the four of you to get me out of the hospital. I understand Dr. Blue's role, and maybe Dina's to some extent. What I can't figure out is where you two fit into this. I'm not quite making the connection. I mean, why would you need an out-of-state detective along for this party? And a private investigator too?" She blinked rapidly to break her own staring match with Trinity and looked over at Ashley. "Although you seem to have something else going on that I'm still not sure I saw happen."

"Let's just say that between us we have a unique understanding of what might be happening to you," Ashley said.

"I keep expecting you to announce you're scientists and have you whip out proton packs and traps," Kieran muttered, scratching Trinity behind the ears to see if that broke her spell.

"I wish all you were going to need to do is capture a ghost in a box. Let's be honest, Kieran, you've got to realize you're possessed by something that's mighty powerful. There isn't any trap big enough for that kind of entity," Rafe said.

Kieran shifted her attention back to the cat in her lap. She hesitated to answer. If she told them what she thought was happening, how safe would she be with them? And if she trusted them it still wouldn't change the outcome. Kieran had plans that didn't involve them at all, however well meaning they were. Time and place waited for no woman. And she had very little time and someplace else she needed to be.

"I've been strapped down, drugged, and psychoanalyzed without ever revealing what I think is happening to me. Why should I trust you all with that information?"

"Because unlike the doctors you have seen, we have a clue about what ails you," Ashley said. She knelt before Kieran. "Like I said before, you don't have to do anything or allow anything we ask of you. We're not here to hurt you."

Trinity shifted and turned her head to head-butt Ashley gently. Ashley kissed the top of Trinity's head. "Hey, baby," she crooned as Trinity lay down in Kieran's lap. She placed one paw on Kieran's leg and began to knead and flex while Ashley stroked her other front paw. Only then did Trinity start to purr. Ashley looked into Kieran's eyes.

"I mean you no harm. You're safe here and among friends. You don't have to go back to the hospital. Let *us* try to help you."

"And if I'm not something you can help?" Kieran asked. Her

voice was barely above a whisper as she gazed back into Ashley's oddly familiar eyes.

Ashley smiled at her. "Again, like I told you, I have friends in high places whose job it is to work miracles for the hopeless."

For some crazy reason, Kieran believed her. She'd heard so many promises and platitudes from people saying they could help her, but they'd ended up making matters ten times worse. Looking into Ashley's calm face, Kieran felt a strange frisson of recognition. Something told her she could trust Ashley, and by association, the others too. But to trust her with what, Kieran wasn't entirely sure.

Maybe I can finally tell my side of the story. It would be a relief to get it all out and known before the madness totally takes control and I'm lost forever in it.

❖

Merlo was grateful that Dina had taken over hostess duties and was making sure everyone had tea or coffee. She was too occupied watching Kieran's hands as they stroked over Trinity's black fur. The cat curled up in Kieran's lap basking in the attention.

Ashley had moved back to her seat to have her coffee. Rafe sat beside her with her legs stretched out before her. She looked at ease, but Merlo sensed she was ready to spring into action should the situation arise. Merlo could tell Rafe was a warrior, a fighter who would rush right in, consequences be damned. From what Dina had told her about Ashley, Merlo would wager that Ashley's angelic companion had his work cut out holding Rafe back from a fight. Merlo could feel the energy shimmering around Rafe. It was in marked contrast to the slumped shoulders and defeated air that weighed Kieran down.

Merlo ran her hand up Kieran's arm, unconsciously matching the smooth, steady strokes Kieran was petting Trinity with. She wondered if having the cat to concentrate on was helping Kieran feel more grounded. She was a big advocate of the benefits of pet therapy. Cragon had vetoed her bringing anything with four legs into the hospital for her patients to interact with. She couldn't fathom how someone so unfeeling had entered the caring profession.

"I think I might be safe enough for you to let go of enough to hold your own drink, Dr. Blue." Kieran's gaze never shifted from the cat. "I feel a lot less *conflicted*." She flicked a shy look Merlo's way.

"If you break out your demon face and startle my cat, I swear I'll make you clean her litter tray out the whole time we're here," Rafe said with a stern look that was softened by the humor glinting in her eyes.

Merlo found herself fascinated by the small smile that curved Kieran's lips. It was a rare and beautiful sight.

"I think Trinity is safe from me for now. I believe this is my calm after the storm period." She yawned. "And if you don't mind, before I settle in to tell you all I can gather from what is happening with me, I would really like to take a nap."

As unobtrusively as she could, Merlo slid her hands from Kieran's body. She watched for any sign of the monster that lurked beneath Kieran's skin. All she could see were the dark shadows marking Kieran's cheeks. Kieran shot a baleful look at the grandfather clock in the hallway. Merlo knew its ticking had been grating on Kieran's already raw and exposed nerves. She recognized when some small noise magnified in Kieran's head and became intolerable. Merlo knew that was why Kieran had been concentrating on Trinity, trying to block out the extraneous sounds. It was an old clock that had been in Merlo's home forever. She'd grown accustomed to its melodic ticks and the chimes that announced every quarter of the hour. She cast a glance at the clock face, thankful it was still half an hour before the clock would strike midday and test Kieran's already fraught nerves.

Kieran's head snapped up when she realized Merlo had let her go. She let out a shaky sigh. "See? All madness at bay for another day." She sagged as if all her energy had bled from her. Her hand slipped from Trinity's fur and her eyes closed.

Trinity opened her eyes and stared up at her. She uncurled herself, stood, and rested her paws on Kieran's chest. Merlo smiled as Trinity stretched to bump her head against Kieran's chin.

"Is she asking for more petting?" Merlo asked Rafe, who was watching in silence.

Rafe shook her head. "No. Trinity knows something's not right with Kieran, so she's giving her comfort and love. That consists of head-butting and sometimes cat licks. Which are always extra special if she's had a particularly pungent bag of kitty chow."

"She does that to me when I come home after a hard case," Ashley said. "It's like she knows I need attention for a while. That silent reassurance that everything is okay and I'm home."

Kieran's eyes opened a fraction, her head nodding as Trinity knocked into her. She rubbed her cheek on the top of Trinity's head. "Thank you, Trinity."

"Kieran, I have a room prepared for you upstairs. Let me help you up there and let's get you rested." Merlo got up and waited for Kieran to put Trinity down. She kept a hand on Kieran's elbow from habit as she guided her up the stairs.

"This isn't the kind of place I expected to be brought to, Dr. Blue," Kieran said as she followed Merlo.

"What can I say? It's home. And you might as well start calling me Merlo, Kieran. I think we're way past the doctor/patient constraints now."

Kieran chuckled. "Considering that you broke me out of that place, right, Merlo?" Kieran drawled out Merlo's name using a hint of the accent that Merlo spoke with. "It's a beautiful name. Unusual. A lot like you are."

Merlo hadn't heard anyone speak with her own inflection for a long time. It warmed her to hear her name roll so sensuously from Kieran's tongue. She'd noticed Kieran hadn't done it to mock her barely discernible accent, but instead to honor it. That touched Merlo more than she could explain.

"Will you be all right?" she asked, trying not to be obvious in her study of Kieran's face and actions for any signs of, quite frankly, *anything.*

"I just need a few hours' decent sleep. The unit wasn't a place that was conducive to that."

"I hope you feel safer here."

"You have a wonderful home and I appreciate your kindness. At least while I'm asleep you'll be able to visit with your friends and plot and plan your next course of action you have in mind for me."

Merlo sighed. "To be honest, I'm not at all sure where to even start. I'll defer to Ashley since Dina can't speak highly enough of her."

"There's something about her," Kieran began, but her words trailed off.

"You mean her obvious powers or something else?"

"I didn't dream it, did I? She changed somehow into Cragon. She became him? I did see it, right?"

Merlo rushed to assure her that this time it hadn't been something drug-induced or possession-driven that Kieran had witnessed. "Yes, you saw her shape-shift. Just don't ask me how she does it. I'm hoping to quiz her over supper about it."

"She looks familiar to me," Kieran said. "But I know I've never met her before today. How crazy is that? Would I know her anyway when she can look like other people in the blink of an eye?"

Merlo gestured down the hallway to an open door. "Maybe she looks like someone else and you're seeing the resemblance."

"Maybe," Kieran said. She grinned, surprising Merlo with the genuine delight on her features. It changed her whole appearance. It let Merlo see the *real* Kieran. "Rafe's a class act. I bet Ashley's got her hands full with her."

Merlo had to agree. Rafe's slightly abrasive personality was a marked contrast to Ashley's more laid-back calmness. They balanced each other beautifully to Merlo's trained eyes. "She's made me realize I would like a pet in this old place. It might make it less lonely for me to come home to." Merlo hated that she sounded so pathetic, but she'd been alone for so long now and she was tired of it. She guided Kieran into the bedroom she'd picked out for her.

"Wow," Kieran said, taking in the whole room with wide eyes. "This couldn't be any further from the room I had at Craven Hope."

Bright and airy, the room was decorated in tasteful cool blue tones. A large bed dominated the room, and Kieran made straight for it, sat on the edge, and bounced a little on the mattress.

"No, nothing like the last place."

Merlo went to close the curtains a fraction to darken the room from the sun pouring in. She was nervous about leaving Kieran out of her sight after being "attached" to her for so long. She moved back around the bed and searched Kieran's face. "You look a little better." Merlo noted how much clearer Kieran's eyes looked now that they were once again her own.

"I'm just tired." Kieran kicked off her sneakers and scrambled up on the high mattress to lie on top of the covers.

"When you wake up we'll talk more, okay?" Merlo wanted to

just sit beside Kieran on the bed and stand guard over her until she fell asleep. It was so hard for her to walk away. Kieran was obviously clearer of mind now. Whatever had possessed her had stepped back, and she looked sleepy. Unable to stop herself, Merlo pushed back a piece of hair just to touch Kieran once again.

"Sleep now. You're safe here."

As she started to leave, Kieran leaned up on her elbows and called to her.

"Merlo?"

Merlo paused in the doorway.

"Thank you for all you've done for me, I appreciate it so much. You've done more than anyone else has been bothered to do, and I'll always be grateful."

Merlo smiled at her. "You're welcome. Now let's see if we can help you once and for all. You deserve your life back. You can't live like this."

Kieran nodded. "I know I can't." She lay back down and snuggled into the quilt. "Thank you for getting me out of there. You have no idea how much it means to me to be free of it."

Merlo pulled the door closed just a little, leaving it ajar in case Kieran awoke and needed her. Merlo didn't want Kieran locked in if that made her feel trapped. As she turned around, she was surprised to see Trinity sauntering down the hallway toward her.

"Are you looking for Kieran?"

Trinity just looked at her, so Merlo pushed the door open a little more and Trinity walked in with a flick of her tail.

Merlo went back downstairs wondering what kind of cat she could get to bring home. Would one be enough to bring life back into the place? She ran her hand down the old balustrade worn smooth with use. The house had been subjected to just her presence for long enough.

Merlo stopped for a moment to peer at the grandfather clock. It never had mattered to her how loud the passing of time was ticked out by this antique. It had always been a soothing background noise in her home. The home where she wanted Kieran to feel safe and to find at least some semblance of peace. She sent up a prayer that Kieran could and would because she was long overdue.

May time grant you peace of heart and sleep gift you dreams of the innocent.

The clock chimed and Merlo shushed at it. She looked around, feeling sheepish, and was thankful no one had seen her do that. Maybe she needed to heed her own advice and just relax and try not to remember that she'd just removed a patient from the hospital under false pretenses. Merlo eyed the clock again. She wondered if it was too early for a glass of wine.

CHAPTER TWELVE

Rafe was people watching. It was a part of her job, figuring everyone out by the subtle and not so subtle clues they displayed while in her presence. Merlo was most intriguing to her. Rafe couldn't quite put her finger on what it was about her, but there was something that pinged Rafe's "weird" radar. She wanted to question Ashley to see if she felt the same about the pretty doctor who looked not quite of this world. Rafe consorted with angels, she knew what ethereal looked like, and Merlo was definitely registering on that scale. She had a strange shimmer around her. It was one that Rafe didn't recognize. It was a delicate shade of lilac and pulsed with an unnatural beat. It was driving Rafe crazy having to listen to her and Ashley going over Kieran's history when all she wanted to ask was what on earth Merlo was.

"You'll have to forgive Rafe's staring." Ashley's words broke Rafe from her musing. "She can see auras, and yours is probably driving her insane."

Rafe frowned at Ashley. "It's not a very stable rhythm. It's pulsing in and out like it's broken." She gave Merlo a piercing look. "Your aura's on the fritz." She pointed at Dina, who was sitting beside Merlo. "And you're registering as kind of angelic, but I don't see any wings sprouting from your back."

Dina smiled at her. "I'm a different kind of entity. I'm known as an Oracle."

"Like a font of all knowledge Oracle or a Batgirl in the wheelchair who's a genius with tech kind of Oracle?"

Dina crinkled her nose at Rafe's dry humor. "Well, aren't you the joker of the pack? I'm a keeper of knowledge, past, present, and sometimes the future. I know all, see all."

"Wow, I bet your lovers find that all kinds of annoying." Rafe grinned at her. "I've never met an Oracle before. This part of my job just keeps adding more and more to my list of weird and wonderful things."

"I'd better be on the wonderful side," Dina said, smiling back at her.

"As long as you don't pull the same tricks our newfound friend Kieran does, then you're on the right side." Rafe turned her attention back to Merlo. "Okay, Doc. Ashley here probably knows what your deal is, and Dina's your best buddy and has that 'know-it-all' power, so she's in the know. So tell me, what are you, because you're not—" She stopped when something caught her eye. "*Trinity?*"

Trinity wasn't the kind of feline who ran around the house like a bat out of hell, so Rafe knew something wasn't right. The cat shot into the living room and sprang straight into Rafe's lap. Trinity banged Rafe's face with such force that Rafe swore she saw stars for a moment. She rubbed at her jaw. "Fuck me, Trin, I missed you too, but your affectionate nuzzle needs work. What's bit you in the ass?"

Trinity jumped down and headed back out the door.

Merlo was on her feet in an instant. "I left Trinity with Kieran. I let her in the room to be with her."

Rafe rose too. "Well, let's go see what Lassie here wants." She waved her hand for Ashley to stay where she was. "It's probably a dumb cat thing and she's pissy because Kieran's hogging the blankets. I'll shout if I need help." Rafe began jogging up the stairs. She paused when Merlo froze mid-step behind her.

"Rafe." Merlo's voice was hushed.

"What's wrong?"

"The clock. It's stopped ticking."

Rafe looked back up the stairs to where Trinity stood at the top meowing plaintively at her. "Oh, Christ." She ran up the rest of the stairs with Merlo hard on her heels.

❖

Kieran's room was empty.

"Kieran?" Rafe did a quick search under the bed and in the closet while Merlo flung the curtains open just in case. "Just where in the hell have you disappeared to, Kieran?" Rafe spotted Trinity outside the door. "Trinity, show me. Find Kieran."

Trinity moved a few doors down and Rafe tried the door. It wouldn't budge. She looked over her shoulder at Merlo. "Sorry, I hope this door isn't an antique." She kicked the door open, breaking the lock that had kept them out. She swore at the pain that ricocheted through her knee. *Fuck me! That always looks easier on TV than it actually is.* The room beyond was empty too, but a pair of large doors leading to a balcony were open. Rafe stopped Merlo from rushing forward. "Please," she lowered her voice, "let me do this. I need you to go back downstairs and warn Ashley."

"I'm not going anywhere. This is part of my job too," Merlo said.

"Do you have many of your patients change into demons?"

Merlo stepped back to let Rafe take the lead. Rafe eased aside one of the doors and took a step outside.

Kieran stood on the ledge that framed a wide balcony that stuck out high above the driveway. She was rocking back and forth on the balls of her feet as if caught in a breeze.

"Oh my God." Merlo's voice was muffled but still audible.

Rafe peered back over her shoulder and saw Merlo still framed in the doorway, her hands clasped over her mouth in fright. Rafe warned her with her eyes not to do anything stupid, and then focused her attention back on Kieran. She swallowed hard and began whispering under her breath for Eli to hear her, telling him she was in way too deep and to get Ashley for her. Rafe berated herself for not having Ashley come with her the second Trinity made a fuss. Who knew her cat was a damned demon alarm? But she hadn't been expecting *this*.

"Oh, your angels won't help you now, creature of earth's dust. You are alone and nothing more than a pawn in this much larger game at play."

Rafe didn't recognize the voice that came from Kieran. It had a heavy accent and vibrated with a definite demonic tone. It froze her in her tracks.

Kieran turned around and fixed Rafe with such a piercing look that she flinched as if it had been a physical slap. She'd never been on the receiving end of a look that was the embodiment of hate. Not even when she'd been attacked by the demon who had tried to kill her. Nor the half-human/half-demon serial killer who had plagued Chicago's dark nights. But whatever was inhabiting Kieran was evil personified. Just by what it was doing to Kieran's features, Rafe was certain it wasn't the previous demon Kieran had paid host to.

Just how many cohabitants have you got taking up residence in you, Kieran? Rafe memorized the different features Kieran's face had morphed into. Kieran's skin looked a sickly mottled gray. Her mouth distorted, her face appeared elongated, and her eyes were a solid fire-fueled red.

Rafe jumped when she felt someone press into her from behind. She saw the familiar white wings come around her in protection. She breathed a sigh of relief.

"Fuck, Eli, you nearly gave me a heart attack!"

"So, this is your new charge?" Eli asked. "Something is trying to make its presence known through her."

Kieran stared at them with those flaming red eyes. Her head moved from side to side as if whatever was inside her skull was pushing to make its way out. Her lips stretched into a vulgar, twisted smile.

Rafe took a steadying breath. "Kieran, if you're still in there I need you to get down off the ledge. please. We can talk about this just as well on the balcony floor."

"Talk about what? This pathetic creature has no use. It needs to return to the dust from whence it came. It has no purpose here. Death is the only fitting end. Don't you know it will soon be too late for any living thing to be safe? Not even your angels will save you."

Kieran's mocking demeanor and distorted face disappeared in a split second. She turned around, raised a foot, and stepped off the ledge.

"Oh God, NO!" Rafe didn't know how she moved as fast as she did. All she knew was in one breath she was watching Kieran disappear and in the next she was half hanging over the balcony with one hand gripping Kieran by the collar of her sweatshirt and her other arm wrapped tight across Kieran's chest. Her ears registered Merlo screaming Kieran's name and Ashley calling out Rafe's. The roughness of the brick wall dug into Rafe's belly as she stretched over the ledge. It pressed her belt buckle into her flesh so hard it stung. She felt hands holding her firm from behind, grasping her waist to keep her from toppling over the ledge. Rafe's mind homed in on something else. Kieran wasn't heavy in her grasp. She lifted her head and saw Eli hovering in front of them both, holding Kieran safe in his hands so that she couldn't fall any farther. His wings hardly moved the air as they beat out a steady rhythm to keep him airborne.

"You can let go now, Rafe. I have her. I can take her from you now if your friends would be kind enough to keep a firm grip on you. I don't want you to slip any farther," he said.

Ashley, Dina, and Merlo helped Rafe back over the ledge to firmer ground. Eli flew up and over the ledge with Kieran cradled in his arms. Merlo rushed to his side.

"Is she hurt?" She ran her hands over Kieran's face and torso.

"No, but I believe she is unconscious. Whatever was in her body drained her when it left. She should be fine," Eli said.

Ashley hugged Rafe to her then ran her hands through Rafe's hair. She pressed a rough kiss on her lips. "God, Rafe, you could have gone over the edge with her," she said.

Rafe pressed her face against Ashley's neck and held on to her tight. "Eli had me in his protection the whole time, Ash. I've never felt anything like it. He lent me his wings. I couldn't have caught her on my own. One minute she was there, the next she was gone. And thanks to Eli, I had her in my grip in the blink of an eye."

"Was it the same demon we saw at the hospital?"

"Oh, that one was a charmer compared to the one I've just met. She's either a split personality or she's got two separate entities she's playing host to. And the second one has a very specific agenda."

Merlo appeared by Rafe's side and touched her arm. "Thank you for saving her."

"You need to do what I say when I say it, Dr. Blue. When I tell you to get Ashley, you don't decide not to. I don't know what you are or what your power is, if you even have one, but Ashley is a demon hunter, and when I say I need her you'd damn well better not ignore me again."

Merlo nodded. "I'm sorry. I was so focused on Kieran that I couldn't think of anything else. I promise it won't ever happen again."

"You called us in to help you. None of us can afford not to jump when an order is given to do so." Rafe looked at everyone on the balcony. "And we sure as hell can't afford to leave her unattended at any time now. That second demon? That's the trigger switch in her. That's the one who wants her dead."

Eli cocked his head at Ashley and added, "And not just her, apparently."

Ashley looked to Rafe for more. "It *spoke* to you?"

Rafe nodded. "I'd say it sermonized. Whatever it is has a knowledge of angels. And it had a very cheery line about it being too late for the living."

Ashley's face hardened. "The Preacher?"

"Or one of its apostles, maybe. Whoever it was, it wanted Kieran dead. So I'm wondering just what it is about this particular possessed soul that needs it to be removed from the face of the earth." Rafe shook herself to try to release the tension that had built up in her whole body. "Now, if someone can please go take the first watch with Kieran, I need to go find some treats for Trinity because that beautiful damned cat of mine just saved a life today."

CHAPTER THIRTEEN

Merlo couldn't stop the tremors that made it almost impossible for her to do her task. She'd had Kieran brought to her home to keep her safe, and in less than an hour under her roof Kieran had tried to kill herself. Merlo shook as she tried to close the balcony doors. Locking them was another trial. She'd rummaged in kitchen drawers that had been left untouched for years and managed to find an old padlock that, she hoped, would deter anyone from trying to open the balcony doors again. Merlo shoved the key in her pocket and tried to take a deep, calming breath.

Dina laid a hand on her shoulder. "We couldn't have stopped her, Merlo. It took an angel to save her. She's obviously beyond what we mere creatures can do."

"I can't believe she tried so soon after she seemed so…normal."

"Maybe that's the most dangerous time for her. In the calmness, perhaps that is when the madness is at its peak. And remember, Rafe said Kieran wasn't herself again."

"I know, with *another* entity this time. How many does she have tugging at her from the inside, directing her to do things? What else are they doing to her?" Merlo felt like pulling her hair out. "How damn hard can a simple exorcism be?"

"Honey, there's nothing simple about an exorcism. Especially when it's more involved than it first seems."

Merlo tried hard not to grit her teeth in frustration. "When did you get so wise?"

Dina smiled. "It's part of my job description. It comes with the Oracle mantle."

"So what do we do now? I promised her no more being strapped down. Unless we all take turns to watch her twenty-four/seven, we're offering her no better care than Craven Hope did."

"We'll do some digging. I want to know who we're dealing with. She's the host to two different voices; let's hear what they have to say."

Merlo took a deep breath, trying to calm herself. She'd never get over seeing Kieran cradled in the arms of an angel. She'd looked so pale against his brilliant white suit and his blond hair, as fair as Kieran's own. She'd looked like a child in his care, small and vulnerable.

Merlo made her way back to Kieran's bedroom. She lay on the bed and it looked like she was sleeping. Ashley sat beside her, a frown marring her forehead.

"Ashley?" Merlo kept her voice soft.

Ashley looked up. "There's something about her. I can't quite put my finger on it."

"I just wish I could see inside that head of hers." She was surprised by the look that lit up Ashley's face.

"Merlo, you are a genius. I know just the thing." She patted Merlo's cheek. "You're going to need to get another room ready."

Merlo's heart lightened for a moment. Her loneliness was lifting with every guest that came through her door. She wondered who Ashley seemed so certain could help Kieran this time.

Ashley walked out of the room with her phone already in her hand, so Merlo took the seat beside Kieran. Only then did she look up at the somber-faced angel who stood at the head of the bed.

"Thank you for saving her." Merlo's hands twitched. She wanted so desperately to touch Kieran to make sure she was really there. She feared waking her, and to be honest, Merlo didn't know who or what she would awaken. She contented herself with letting the tips of her fingers touch the palm of Kieran's hand. Kieran shifted in her slumber and seemed to smile.

"Your touch brings her peace, Long Traveled."

"Now that's a name I haven't heard in a very long time."

Eli smiled. "I'd say your journey has brought you right where you need to be." He nodded toward the bed. "She needs you."

"I don't think I can help her alone."

"You're not alone. You're getting everyone you need to support you *and* her."

"She's important, isn't she?" Merlo couldn't believe how at peace Kieran looked when she slept.

"Time will tell," Eli said. "I will watch over her. She won't get a second chance to do what she tried to do."

"I'll stay for a moment more. If only to convince myself she's safe now."

"She's under the watchful eyes of angels."

"Sleeping the sleep of the saved." Merlo couldn't help but think how ironic that statement was.

❖

Ashley found Rafe sitting on the edge of their bed with Trinity curled up on her lap. The cat's rumbling purrs were loud in the silence.

"I think Trinity's been hanging around with your winged friend too much."

Rafe's haunted eyes made Ashley's heart ache. She hadn't seen that look on her face for a long time.

"She knew enough to warn you what was going on." Ashley sat beside them and rested her head on Rafe's shoulder. "How are you feeling? Because I nearly had a coronary seeing your rear end up in the air and the rest of you dangling over the balcony. Thank God Merlo was clinging onto your legs for dear life." She smoothed her hand along Rafe's thigh, more for reassurance for herself than in comfort for Rafe. She'd never forget how close Rafe had come to plunging to her death trying to save Kieran. "How did Eli know to come?" she asked.

"I called for him."

"You *prayed*?" Ashley couldn't help the incredulous tone in her voice. She lifted her head away so she could see Rafe's face better.

"I *called* for him. There's a difference."

Ashley smirked at Rafe's deliberate emphasis on the specific word. Rafe gave her a stern glare in return.

"There's a difference between 'Help me, Father, in my hour of need' and 'Eli, get your winged butt here because we have a jumper who isn't equipped with your kind of accessories'!"

Ashley laughed and wrapped her arm around Rafe's waist to hold her tight. "Have I told you how much I love your irreverence?"

"I'm sure it's come up once or twice."

"So, are you going to tell me how you're feeling?" Ashley bumped Rafe's shoulder. "I'll just keep asking until you cave in."

Rafe sighed. "I've never had much call in my line of duty for talking a jumper off a ledge. People with guns to their heads or to others' heads, yes. Those are a dime a dozen. But someone whose sole purpose is to jump from a height knowing that the landing isn't going to be kind?" She shook her head. "What torment is this kid going through to keep trying this over and over until it sticks?"

"Whatever it is, we've got to try to free her from it before she's successful and we lose her."

"You know, I expected to see my life flash before me like some cheap B movie. If nothing else, I at least hoped to relive that wild night we had on that one stakeout. Remember? Way back when we were still testing the waters in our relationship. You surprised me with your wicked side that night and we tested out just how much wriggle room there was in the back seat of the department's Chevrolet."

Ashley smiled at the memory. She also knew Rafe always had to make light of the darkest times. She was prepared to let her sort out her feelings in whatever way she could.

"You'd brought your handcuffs. What can I say, I was inspired," Ashley said with a grin. She remembered that night too. It had shown her just how much Rafe trusted her and needed her.

"And I was fucked, well and truly." Rafe laughed a little when Ashley nudged her. "One look into those gorgeous eyes and I was yours for life. You're my One, the only one." She shifted so she could cup Ashley's face in her hands. "You know, there was a moment when Kieran was looking at me. It was a split second after the demon let go of her because I saw her face change. For that brief moment, she was someone else. I think it was Kieran herself. All I know is I looked into those eyes and…" Rafe faltered and drew in a shaky breath. "I looked and all I could see was *you* staring back at me."

"You think she looks like me?"

Rafe shrugged. "In that instant she did. Her eyes especially, and maybe here." Rafe drew her finger down the bridge of Ashley's nose. "The hair color's similar too."

"But you *saw* me?"

"I saw something right before her face got this weird look like the power had been cut, and then she just stepped off the ledge. It happened so fucking fast. I'm just thankful Eli was so quick in his reaction. He saved her, Ash. He was her guardian angel today."

Ashley covered Rafe's hands with her own. "Let's go get something to eat. You're still shaking."

"I need more than food. I brought beer. It's still in the car."

Ashley laid a kiss in the palm of Rafe's hand. "I'll bring the beer in and whatever else you brought from home. Then I'll order us all some takeout and we'll start taking turns watching over Kieran every minute of every day."

"I didn't think she'd do anything stupid. She seemed so much better." Rafe rubbed at her forehead. "I should have seen it coming. I'm trained for that kind of thing. You trust no one."

Ashley kissed her again. "You weren't trained for signs of possession, darling. Who knew the time when she looks the most normal is when she's the most dangerous to herself?" She stood and stretched. "I've called in backup for us."

Rafe's eyes finally turned brighter. "The more the merrier if it's who I think you mean."

Ashley nodded. "It'll be just like old times. There's nothing like facing the underworld with your friends by your side."

CHAPTER FOURTEEN

The silence was the first thing Kieran noticed when she awoke. She didn't open her eyes; instead she just listened. Everything was so quiet.

Did I do it? Is this it? Am I finally free?

"You are safe, Kieran. You are being cared for."

Kieran froze at the unfamiliar male voice. Slowly, she became more aware of where she was. She could feel the softness of the quilt beneath her. She started to laugh. It held a bitter tone.

"It's not your time to leave just yet. No matter how hard you try."

"Oh great, they've drafted another do-gooder to keep me safe from myself."

That was met by more silence.

"You can *hear* me?"

Whoever it was sounded astonished. Kieran wondered why.

"Of course I can. You're right beside the bed and you won't shut up." She turned her head on the pillow and opened her eyes to see just who this man was.

What she saw had her scrambling off the bed to land with a loud thud on the other side of it. She tried to scramble to get under the bed, but there wasn't enough space, so she ended up cowering behind it instead. She let out a yell.

"MERLO!"

"I promise you, I mean you no harm." His voice was a little shaky from his own surprise.

Kieran lay curled up on the floor trying to make herself as small as possible. She covered her head with her arms for protection. "What the hell are you?"

"You know exactly what I am, Kieran."

Kieran screwed her eyes shut so tight they ached. She began hyperventilating. "No, no, no, no. You can't be real. This shit isn't happening. You can't come into the real world. I get dragged into yours; you don't get to come into mine." Her chest constricted and Kieran started to gasp for breath. Spots began to swim before her eyes. She barely managed to scream out once more. "MERLO!"

"Please, Kieran," he said, but then hushed at the sound of feet pounding up the stairs.

White noise was clouding Kieran's head, but she managed to recognize the noise of more than one set of feet running down the hallway.

"Merlo," Kieran gasped, so close to passing out in her fear. Her body jolted. It felt as if a bolt of lightning had struck her. Or what she imagined a defibrillator felt like applied to her chest to shock her heart back to life. A strange rush raced through her every cell, sparking tiny explosions in their wake. She'd felt this before, the feeling of something powerful being passed between them when Merlo touched her. The touch this time was electric, a concussive feeling that overwhelmed Kieran like a tidal wave. She was aware of Merlo draped across her back, covering her, protecting her. Kieran's distress calmed and she could drag air back into her lungs to breathe again.

"Kieran, I'm here, I'm here," Merlo comforted her, her hands smoothing up and down Kieran's arms.

"It's in the room. There's one of *them* here. They're supposed to just be in my head, but I can see it now, *here*. It's actually *here*."

"How the hell can she see you?" Ashley's voice was incredulous to Kieran's ears. It also held a small amount of amusement.

"Why the fuck are you all so surprised?" Rafe said in exasperation.

Kieran couldn't understand why they all were so calm. "Can't you see it? It's over by the window." She still was in her duck-and-cover position. Even with everyone in the room with her she still didn't feel safe.

"Kieran, that's Eli. He's a friend. He's been watching over you while you slept," Merlo said.

"You knew that thing was watching me?" Kieran might have felt calmer, but her anger was rising.

"He's a friend. Come, meet him. He's not what you think." Merlo tried to untangle Kieran's arms from where they wrapped around her head. "Get up, it's okay."

Kieran allowed her arms to move, and she opened her eyes. "Do you honestly see him too?"

"Yes," Merlo assured her.

"Like I do?"

"I see a man in a white suit. What do you see?"

"White suit, blond hair, and huge wings on his back." Kieran whispered the last bit, terrified her madness was complete.

Merlo cupped Kieran's chin and turned her face to see her. "I see the wings too."

"Oh God." Kieran let out a shaky breath. "Does that mean my madness is contagious?"

Merlo's eyes softened as she looked at her. "No, I think it means that, courtesy of whatever is going on in that head of yours, your eyes have been opened to a darn sight more than we expected."

Kieran looked up and saw Rafe, Ashley, and Dina all looking down at her with sympathetic eyes. Rafe sat on the floor beside her and ruffled Kieran's hair.

"Welcome to a whole new world, Neo. Someone slipped you the red pill while you weren't looking and now you're trapped outside of the Matrix with all of us."

Merlo was at a total loss what to do. Kieran was still hunkered down by the side of the bed, and poor Eli looked both embarrassed and astonished by the reaction he'd received.

But then Eli hadn't realized Kieran was going to *see* him while he did his angelic inspirational speech. A speech designed to subliminally calm and soothe a human in distress. She'd seen angels before, watched as they comforted the dying and sent them off in peace and love and whole of mind. It was a beautiful thing to witness, but seeing Kieran's reaction to him was anything but.

Kieran was still unwilling to get up. Merlo rubbed at her back soothingly, thankful to note that the shaking had stopped.

"Kieran," Merlo kept her voice low, "what's the worst thing you're thinking at this moment?"

"That if I see him it makes him real, and that means all the other stuff I'm seeing is real too. And I think I'd rather be crazy than acknowledge that all of it really exists."

Merlo peeked over the top of the bed at Eli. "Eli, we've established she can see and hear you. How about a little help here, please."

"I mean you no harm, Kieran."

Merlo felt Kieran flinch under her. Kieran covered her ears with her hands. "I don't want to hear him. I don't want to see him. Make him go away, Merlo. I don't want to hear whatever message he's peddling. I'm not buying it."

Ashley nodded at Eli, and with a grateful look on his face, he just disappeared from the room.

"He's gone. It's just us now." Merlo tapped on Kieran's hand and pulled it away from her head.

"I dreamed it, right? Just another hallucination to join the rest I'm plagued by?" Kieran eased herself upright. She ended up leaning against Rafe, who sat nonchalantly with her hands hanging over her drawn-up knees.

"Eli's not a bad guy once you get to know him. For one thing, he's an excellent cat-sitter."

Kieran gave Rafe such an incredulous look that Merlo had to turn away to hide her amusement.

"How can someone like you believe this?" Kieran asked, frowning at Rafe.

"I got attacked by a demon disguised in human form. He nearly killed me, probably would have if not for the white light that I saw that was my guardian angel that night." She bumped Kieran. "Turns out that was Eli. Then I nearly died by poisoning thanks to that same demon bastard who tried to kill me. I had my other guardian angel look after me that time." She looked up and smiled at Ashley.

Merlo was struck by how much love she could feel between them; it permeated the room like a perfume. Ashley's smile back at Rafe only intensified Merlo's belief that they were bonded. Each had found their

One. She envied them. She'd walked a long lonely path without ever finding her true mate.

"Anyhow, after banishing a shit ton of demons at Ashley's side, it's a blessing knowing that there are angels among us. It kind of evens out how bizarre this all is."

"And are they *really* on our side?"

Rafe's eyebrows rose at Kieran's question. "Why? Have you heard otherwise? Because the last I knew, the guys with the white wings and angelic appearance were the good guys."

Kieran's head lowered, and she seemed to shrink into herself. When she lifted her eyes, Merlo chilled at the look in them.

"Demons talk," Kieran said. Then she seemed to shake herself free of whatever had just gripped her.

"Does that happen often?" Merlo asked.

"I don't know half of what I'm saying or doing most of the time. I'm not usually in social situations when I'm like this for people to remark on it," Kieran said.

"No, you're too busy trying to find a way to kill yourself," Rafe said.

Merlo heard the swift intake of breath from Ashley at Rafe's bluntness. But the words weren't cruel; they were just a matter-of-fact. And Kieran knew it.

"Yeah, there's that too." Kieran sounded tired. "Though I don't know if it's me attempting it or whatever is inside this screwed-up brain of mine pushing me to do it. I never used to be suicidal. In fact, I was rather fond of living."

"Do you think you'd like to get up now? This floor isn't comfortable." Merlo rested her hand on Kieran's shoulder and pushed herself up off her knees to sit on the bed with a grateful sigh.

Cautiously, Kieran peered over the edge of the bed to where Eli had been standing. She looked around the rest of the room to double-check that he was gone.

"I don't care if he's your friend or not. I don't want him near me."

Ashley sighed and pushed herself off the doorframe she'd been leaning against. "Kieran, you're soon going to realize, where Eli and his crew are concerned, you're going to want them on your side."

Kieran ran her hands through her hair. "How can you all be so calm?"

Merlo placed a hand on Kieran's knee. Kieran jumped as if electrocuted.

"And how the hell do you keep doing that?"

"Doing what?" Merlo kept her hand in place, watching as Kieran's anxiety visibly calmed and she grew still.

"*That*. When you put your hands on me it feels like you zap me with a hundred watts and makes me feel…" Kieran speared her fingers through her hair and grabbed handfuls of it.

"Feel what?" Merlo searched Kieran's face as a myriad of expressions, the brightest being *hope*, ran across her features.

"*Me*." Kieran's voice trembled. "It makes me feel like me again."

Kieran looked so lost Merlo did something she never did with her patients. She pulled Kieran to her and hugged her tight.

"I think I'm in more trouble than I realized," Kieran whispered.

The feel of Kieran's breath against her ear made Merlo's chest hitch as her own breath caught.

I know the feeling.

"What makes you say that?" Merlo was amazed her voice came out at all. Kieran had shifted and her lips were so close to the sensitive flesh on Merlo's neck she was having to rein in her shivers of reaction. She turned her head just a fraction and caught the faint chemical fragrance of the hospital's generic shampoo in Kieran's hair.

"I always thought I was going out of my mind with all that I saw." Kieran's grasp tightened around Merlo's shoulders. "But now…"

Merlo soothed a hand down Kieran's spine. "But now what?"

"Now I think I'm stuck *in* it."

CHAPTER FIFTEEN

The well-kept garden that lay behind Merlo's home was as impressive as the house itself. Ashley wondered if Merlo did much of the upkeep herself or drafted specialists to keep everything looking so pristine. Not one branch of greenery was overgrown, and all the flowers bloomed with brilliant colors.

It didn't take her long to find Eli out in the garden, sitting on a bench watching fish swimming in an ornamental pond. Ashley made a mental note to warn Rafe about keeping Trinity well away from that temptation. Ashley didn't want to have to replace what looked to be very expensive pets. Eli's wings spread out behind him, catching the sunlight. The feathers rustled in the light breeze. When she walked around him, she found he had Trinity on her leash and had been training her not to jump in the pond for a snack. The cat instead sat watching them with that distracted air of hers. The one that meant she was interested enough for her attention to be captured, but she couldn't be bothered to do anything. It was her same frame of mind when Rafe tried to tempt her with a new toy. It drove Rafe crazy. Ashley believed Trinity did it deliberately just to wind Rafe up.

"If I didn't know better, I'd say you loved that cat almost as much as Rafe does." Ashley sat beside him and watched as Trinity gave up on fish watching and wandered off to investigate a nearby bush. A leaf blew past her, startling Trinity at first, but she soon pounced on it to make it pay.

"She is one of God's creatures," Eli said, but his smile gave him away. "But I'll admit, she's one of my favorites. We don't spend much time with animals. The humans are our main concern. But this one," he watched as Trinity was now distracted by a bee, "this one is unique." He pulled gently on the leash to divert Trinity's attention elsewhere. "Trinity, please don't do that. You'll regret it if the bee stings you, and Rafe will pull all my feathers out."

Ashley was relieved to see Trinity wander off after something else. She shifted on the bench a little closer to Eli. "Sooo," she drawled, "Kieran's reaction to you has to be a first." She saw his mouth curve down in response. "You're usually a comfort when you give that speech. Admittedly, the recipient isn't supposed to see you unless they're dying. Yet your presence terrified her. What is she seeing to fear angels so much?"

"Her reaction was a little disconcerting, I'll admit." He raised his head to the sky as if taking in the sun's warmth. Ashley knew he didn't need it and wondered if he was instead looking to the heavens for his answers. "I was in the proximity of an atheist once as he was dying. His eyes widened when he saw me, and he swore quite profusely for someone breathing his last. I told him not to fear, for God made humans with the right to exercise free will, even if that meant for them not to look to Him for guidance. I was just there to wish him well on his next journey, on whatever path he chose to take next."

"You know, you drive Rafe insane with your free will speech."

"If you want a strict totalitarian rule, then you'll find that more in your own human governments. You and I both know not to believe everything that has been put to paper about the Creator. So many things get lost in translation over time, and with biased pens rewriting it, the true meaning becomes muddied. And then there's the little matter of it being presided over by *men*, and we all know how one-sided that can get. Even over these thousands of years, prejudice and inequality have a way of sneaking into what were meant to be teachings of love and acceptance for *all*." Eli sighed. "If only mankind could read what had been originally written instead of what was twisted for an elite's ungodly gains."

Ashley conceded that point with a nod. She was quiet for a moment, just enjoying the tranquility of the area that was in stark contrast to where she lived in the city. She leaned into Eli.

"Can you believe I live in a house now just like a regular person?"

Eli's demeanor changed from carrying the weight of the world on his shoulders, and he smiled. "I have learned, where you are concerned, to always expect the unexpected. I'm glad you no longer have to frequent hotels as much. They lacked the warmth of where you live now."

Trinity wandered over to head-butt Ashley's leg, demanding attention.

"I've gained a home, a pet, and the love of my life. Not bad for the child of a demon who feared she'd always be alone."

"You know full well your father was still angelic when he sired you. You make it sound like you don't deserve these things. You do, Ashley, believe me."

Ashley massaged Trinity's fuzzy cheeks and watched as the cat's face took on a look of pure ecstasy. She loved how Trinity's tiny fangs appeared the more blissed out she got. Rafe called her a furry little vampire when she did this. Ashley could only wish for the same peaceful feeling.

"Kieran doesn't deserve what's happening to her, Eli. Something, *two* somethings, are playing with her mind. And the second one wants her dead."

"It *is* curious."

Used to Eli's talent for understatement, Ashley just shook her head and focused her attention on Trinity. She could feel the steady throbbing purr vibrating through her fingertips as the cat relished being touched. She looked into Trinity's eyes. "Hey, pretty girl, what did you see when Kieran looked into your eyes, hmmm? I wish you could tell me."

"If that creature gained a voice all she'd ask for are more Froot Loops. I am forever trying to keep her out of Rafe's cereal box." Eli sounded resigned. "It's an eternal battle we wage whenever I cat-sit."

Ashley ran her fingers over and around Trinity's soft furry ears. "She likes her sweet things, just like her mommy. Speaking of whom..." Ashley turned her attention to Eli. "Thank you for saving her today."

"I saved *Kieran*. Rafe had everything under control."

"You protected her anyway. Don't think I won't forget that."

"She's your One. I'll protect her to the very end."

Ashley considered his choice of words. "*Is* this the end? Because if it turns out that this is the fabled Preacher we were warned about when he was procuring babies for sacrifice, that doesn't bode well. His preaching was very 'end of days.'"

"If it is him, then we need more information so we can banish him deeper than Hell."

"We need to talk to Kieran again."

Eli hesitated. "That might be your job. I need more details about what we can't see happening to her, and I don't think she's ready to face me again just yet."

"Don't take it personal. I think she's just been hanging around with demons in her head a little too much instead of playing with the cooler kids." Ashley placed a gentle kiss on top of Trinity's head. "Eli, I have a really bad feeling about this."

Eli nodded. "I'll see what the eyes above are seeing. There's been a lifted awareness since the Preacher was announced. But you know from your own investigation that whatever he's plotting is being kept in the underworld for now."

"You need to keep a better check of the banished. I don't think they got the memo that they're supposed to be in torment down there and not setting up a prophet of doom to stir up unrest among the demon population. Or to not have it reach above to those already in our world, disturbing the human population."

"Demons were born for discord and mayhem, but their influence on earth is being recognized now more than ever before. You've just got to look at the unrest in the world and at those hoisted into positions of power. Those who use their elected seats to bring misery to their people and undermine any true teachings that this world was once led by. Humans have their own streak of cruelty and malice running through their veins, coloring their choices. Just like they have unlimited goodness and mercy. Whichever influence they look to only enhances their free will to be righteous or to choose that darker path."

"So, do you think Kieran has a regular, garden variety kind of possession or something else?"

"I think she's got something else entirely. Something I have never seen, and I've observed possessed souls on numerous occasions."

Ashley mulled over his answer. "Rafe said that just before Kieran jumped she saw *me*."

"How?"

"I don't know. Reflected in Kieran's face, I guess. She saw similarities in our features. Though I can't see it when I look at her." She gave Eli a stern look. "I'm not going in blind again, Eli. The last time I did that I found a supposed long-dead half brother who was a demonic serial killer with serious daddy issues."

"In Rafe's defense, it was a highly stressful moment."

"Yeah, well, something tells me it's only going to get worse."

"This *feeling* of yours?"

"Tell me you can't feel it too?"

Eli spread his wings and shook them out as if stretching. "I'm an angelic being. I'm *supposed* to dwell on the positive."

Ashley laughed. "So, from that inference I'm getting you're *positive* that there's something hinky going on?"

Eli tried to keep his face expressionless, but Ashley could see through him.

"I'll go check in with the Powers That Be and see if anything 'hinky,' as you so eloquently put it, is showing up from their point of view."

"You do that," Ashley said, holding Trinity up for Eli to pet. "Say bye-bye to Uncle Eli, Trinity."

Trinity just blinked at him while Eli stared at Ashley.

Ashley grinned at his expression. "You know this is the closest you're ever getting to me having a child, Eli. Just roll with it."

He patted the cat and stood.

"I made sure more catnip was packed, just in case," Eli said as he disappeared into thin air.

Ashley draped Trinity over her shoulder and stroked her fur, more for the comfort it provided her than for the cat's enjoyment. She looked over at the house and let out a sigh.

"Let's hope you packed enough for all of us."

Considering the age of Merlo's house, the kitchen was stylish and equipped with every modern appliance. It was light and airy with its clean white surfaces and polished silver trim edging around the doors. There was a red theme in the utensils that stopped the room from being too clinical. Everything from the coffeemaker to the plates and the mugs hanging on the wall was a splash of bright color.

Dina drew a bottle out of the wine rack, perused its label, and then uncorked it. She poured a generous amount into a large round glass and handed it to Merlo. Merlo was tempted to down the whole thing.

"I don't care if it is too early in the day for this; I need it." She took a generous sip and hummed her approval at the rich fruity taste. "I'm going to try to ignore the fact you have just raided a bottle from my good stock to have me use to drown my sorrows, Dina. I'm sure a regular red would have done the job just as well." She licked her lips in appreciation of the slick aftertaste from one of her most expensive vintage wines.

Dina raised her own glass to Merlo. "I thought this situation called for it."

"Would you care to explain how a wine I know full well was hidden in my wine cellar suddenly appeared in my wine rack amid the lesser vintage bottles placed there?"

"You forget, Merlo, I've known you for more years than either of us can recall. I also know the wine cellar as well as you do, having sampled from it on many an occasion. This bottle wasn't kept down there to be uncorked for a celebratory event. This was a bottle deserving to be drunk in honor of the 'oh my gods, what have we gotten ourselves mixed up with' situation we find ourselves in."

Merlo looked deep into her glass and then held it out for a top-up. "I'll drink to that." Dina filled it even higher, and Merlo took a healthy swig from it. "I think I'm in over my head here. I can step into the imaginations of patients and see what torments them. I can help heal them." She swirled the wine in her glass, watching the blood red liquid spin around. For a moment, she lost herself in it. "But Kieran…Kieran is something else completely." She raised her eyes to look at Dina. "And she can feel me just like I can feel her."

"Then at least something's going right."

"What if she tries again?" Merlo couldn't stop the shudder that shook her to her very marrow.

Dina rested a comforting hand on Merlo's arm. "She won't get a second chance to try anything. Eli can watch without being seen if that's what we need to do to keep her safe."

Merlo couldn't help a rueful smile. "He wasn't supposed to be seen this time and yet Kieran surprised us all once again."

"Yeah, well, that just opened up a whole new can of worms, didn't it?" She gave Merlo a sideways glance. "Want me to dig even deeper into Ms. Lee's background?"

Merlo wondered if letting Dina check further into Kieran's past would help shed a light on Kieran's curious ability to see angels. She was tempted but decided to go another route first. "Let me try it my way first to see what I can get from her. If that fails, then I'll let you loose to gather every scrap of information you can lay your hands on. She wasn't aware she could see angels so it's obvious she's never been visited by one before. Which is curious, given that she has that ability in the first place."

"Maybe the demons got there first. We have no way of knowing how long she's been possessed. The demons could have been biding their time before they were 'unlocked,'" Dina said. "Some have that ability, to attach to a human but not manifest until they have purpose. But they can still influence the possessed mind, so I'd imagine they could 'block' the possessed from seeing divine beings. All the better for their control. It isolates the one they have in their hold."

Merlo drained the rest of her wine from the glass. "And this is why I need you here. I have a rudimentary knowledge of angels and demons, but you, my dear, are a font of such knowledge."

Dina gave a small bow. "Comes with the territory. Ashley has called in others to help. They'll be arriving tomorrow. Something about them having just finished a case and needing to report in before they could take off again. I told you she'd be perfect for this. She has the connections we need."

"Now, if I just knew what *this* was."

Dina took Merlo's hand in her own and squeezed it. "How are *you* doing?"

Merlo tried to put into words the jumbled mass of feelings she had racing around her head. "Other than the fact I had to grab a woman I'd just met literally by the seat of her pants and hold on to her for dear life while she kept Kieran from plunging to her death? I'm peachy keen, jelly bean."

Dina laughed. "Gods, I remember the first time you said that. Still tickles me hearing it with that accent of yours."

Merlo bristled. "I do not have an accent. I just sound different because I'm not from around here."

Dina laughed even more. "No truer words have been spoken." She pulled Merlo in for a hug. "It's going to be okay. You don't have to find any of this normal. Even with what you've seen in your lifetime."

With her voice muffled against Dina's shoulder, Merlo let out an unhappy grumble. "I'm here to help people, not be clueless over what is the best treatment for them."

"Forever the doctor, the mender of minds." Dina pressed a kiss into Merlo's hair. "Now, while Ashley is watching over Kieran, I believe you have another room to prepare. Then, when everyone is present, I think it's time Kieran tells us what she knows and we can do the same for her in return."

Merlo raised her head. "*All* we know?"

"I don't think this is the time for things to be kept hidden."

"Is that the Oracle talking?"

"No, it's the friend who can see the look in your eyes every time you remember how close Kieran came to dying today."

Merlo shifted from Dina's grasp. Wrapping her arms about herself, she began to pace. "She's my patient. Of course I'd be upset."

"Yes, you would, but this," Dina placed her hand over Merlo's heart, "this says something more."

Merlo stilled then slapped Dina's hand away. "Stop it. I can't afford to be conflicted."

"But you like her?"

"You know I do because underneath the possession is someone I'd very much like to get to know. There's something about her I'm drawn to. I can feel *her*, deep down under all the madness that has her in its hold."

"Then let's hope when these others arrive we can get closer to finding the answers that set you both free."

CHAPTER SIXTEEN

Craven Hope Psychiatric Hospital's reception was as busy as ever in the early evening visiting hours. Merlo tried to enter as unobtrusively as possible and get lost amid the visitors. She caught sight of Dr. Cragon looming over the desk. His voice rose and the poor receptionist looked terrified. Merlo caught part of his rant and heard her name mentioned. Her hopes of just getting to her office and back out again without interference were dashed when the receptionist's face fell in relief at the sight of her and she pointed in Merlo's direction. Cragon whirled around and saw her.

Damn it. Why couldn't he have been away from the hospital like always when five o'clock rolls around and he's taken his name off the evening schedule yet again?

"Dr. Blue." His voice cut through the noise of the heightened chatter. "I'd like a word with you, if you don't mind?"

Like I have a choice. Merlo followed him out of the reception and into the much quieter corridors beyond. The second the large doors swung shut behind them, he rounded on her, pushing her back against the wall. He was furious, and Merlo regretted coming back.

"You released Kieran Lee," he said, a finger pointing in Merlo's face.

"No, *you* released her. I saw you sign the papers myself."

"It wasn't me. I've just spent God knows how long trying to explain that to the stupid woman on the front desk."

Cragon gritted his teeth so hard Merlo was surprised he didn't crack his expensive veneers. Her own teeth ached in sympathy.

"I gave no such orders to release that damned patient to another hospital."

"Well, it looked like your signature and it was definitely you I saw holding the pen that wrote on the form to let the transfer take place." Merlo lowered his menacing finger away from her face. "Cragon, are you all right? I mean, *really* all right?" He was staring at her, so Merlo continued in a soothing tone, the same one she used on her patients with varying success. "Because you're saying you don't remember doing something when there are multiple witnesses that saw you do it." She tilted her head a fraction to give him her patented concerned look. "I know you carry the burden of running this place on your shoulders alone. There's so much you have to deal with. It's understandable if one task slipped your mind." She smiled at him. "Though you might want to consider taking more time off if the memory loss persists." His shoulders lowered a fraction and his face lost some of its ferocity. He took a deep breath, then raised his eyes at her.

"Are you trying to analyze me, Dr. Blue?" he asked. "Because I warn you I am not in the mood to be condescended to."

"I just want to help you."

Merlo yelped in pain as Cragon grabbed her arm and yanked her toward his office. He threw her through the door before slamming it shut and crowding her up against the wall. He leaned in close, and Merlo fought back a grimace at the smell of stale whiskey on his breath.

"Do not test out your psychobabble on me, Merlo. I am not one of your patients you can analyze and 'cure.'"

"Why are you so angry over that one patient? She wasn't one that you dealt with. She was my patient. You never even had a session with her."

"She embarrassed me in front of the board. That escape of hers fell on my shoulders, not yours. She tried to escape from *my* hospital. This place revolves around me. It made me look bad."

Wow, delusions of grandeur much? She'd known Cragon had to kiss enough ass to rise to his all-expenses paid position, given his mediocre doctoring skills and impatience with mental illness. Add to that she knew all about the management duties he farmed out to others to deal with for him. Merlo had long been aware he was a man in a position of power that he didn't deserve to be in. She knew he had been climbing over bodies to get to the higher ranks, but to *own* the hospital? She wondered how soon her own job would be in jeopardy the second he moved into the big chair.

"She was a patient with a problem, just like all the rest of them we have here. She didn't deliberately set out to inconvenience you. Is that why you transferred her?" Merlo deflected the blame again. She had to keep him off the scent of what had really happened to Kieran. He couldn't know Merlo was the one to blame here.

"I *didn't* transfer her!"

It shocked Merlo how much Cragon's voice boomed as he lost his patience. She flinched at both the noise and the amount of spittle that flew in her face. He was standing way too close for Merlo's comfort, and she could tell he was skirting a fine line before his anger became physical again. That was something she had learned to detect, for her own safety, in her line of therapy.

Cragon stormed over to his desk. He kicked his chair back from the table. Merlo was just grateful he was taking his annoyance out on the furniture and not her.

She began edging her way along the wall toward the door. The professional side of her was fascinated by his reactions. She knew he was a hothead, but this flare-up of temper wasn't what he'd usually let slip out. The other side of Merlo wanted to get out of there, get the painting she'd gone for, and get the hell away from him. Especially before her part in the "transfer" revealed itself.

Cragon was banging through the drawers in his desk. Vulgar words spewed from his lips as he failed to find what he was searching for. He spun around to the filing cabinet beside the window, yanked the drawer open, and then…stopped dead.

Merlo used his distraction to reach for the door handle. She turned it as quietly as she could to not attract his attention.

"How the hell did they get on the grounds?" Cragon said, pointing out the window. "This is not a fucking walk-in center!"

Merlo had just managed to squeeze half of her body out the door when he shot back from the window, obviously startled. He recoiled with such speed he banged his leg on his desk and knocked over his desk caddy, scattering pens and pencils all over the floor.

"What the hell are they?" he asked.

Merlo hesitated in her escape. Something in his voice stopped her. It was pure, unadulterated fear. She cursed herself for her curiosity and took a few cautious steps over to where Cragon was hovering in a nervous crouch under the window ledge. He kept popping his head up to peek through the glass before hunkering down again. When Merlo reached him, he grabbed at her and pulled her down to the ground. Her knees struck the hard flooring and Merlo let out a gasp of pain. Cragon slapped a hand over her mouth.

"Shut up, you stupid bitch. They'll hear you," he hissed at her.

Who will? Merlo was losing her patience and was getting tired of his manhandling her.

Cragon pointed at the window while making sure to keep his head down. Merlo shuffled forward as best she could on her bruised knees and risked a look outside. She wanted to see what had caused Cragon to shift from a seething ball of anger into a simpering, cowering child.

Cragon's office backed onto one of the surrounding fields. It was a nicer view than Merlo's office that afforded her the sprawling vista of the hospital parking lot. She was aware the hospital had problems before with vagrants breaking in trying to steal medication to either take for themselves or to sell on the street. She wondered if someone had decided to be bold and try to do that in daylight instead of waiting for darkness to fall.

Merlo had no trouble finding what had terrified Cragon.

Demons.

Demons in broad daylight and visible. Not ones cloaked in their pseudo human skins; these were blatant in all their demonic glory.

"Dina," Merlo muttered under her breath.

Dina appeared in a split second. "Don't tell me you need my help getting the painting off the wall..." Dina stuttered to a stop when she took in the surroundings she had materialized in. "Okay," she drawled, "this is *not* your office. And why are you hiding in here with him of all people?"

Merlo gestured toward the window. Dina took a step forward to peer outside. Her eyes widened.

"Oh, now that's a problem I didn't foresee." She turned her attention back to Merlo for a second before looking back out the window. "You need to get that painting and we need to get out of here. If there are demons wandering the grounds in their true forms and humans can see them, then that's definitely not a good omen."

Merlo began crawling across the floor toward the door. Cragon tried to grab at her leg and Merlo kicked his hand away.

"Where are you going?"

"I have things to attend to," she told him, standing up and smoothing down her skirt as if there was nothing wrong.

"You can't leave me here with those *things* outside."

"Just keep your head down and your mouth closed and maybe you'll be spared." Merlo grabbed the door handle just as Cragon stood up to impose his authority.

"You need to stay here!"

In the blink of an eye, the demons were up against the window. They pressed against it, and their breath steamed up the glass with a faint brown hue. They were black scaled, with lethal horns twisting out of their foreheads. Cruel barbs littered their bodies like the deadliest thorns on the darkest rose stem. Their eyes were completely black, appearing sightless yet seeing all. Their mouths were huge and elongated, hanging open almost to their chests like gaping wounds. It was like their jaws had dislocated by the sheer weight of the endless sharp teeth that were crammed inside their mouths.

Merlo could never have described the sound of sheer terror that wrenched itself from Cragon's lips. She felt Dina wrap her arms around her.

"Halt."

At Dina's soft command, the air around them seemed to freeze. Merlo could pick out individual dust motes as they hung in the air as, outside of Dina's comforting grasp, time was suspended.

"Reveal," Dina said, and Merlo got to witness what happened while she took a step out of time. Like watching a silent movie reel, Merlo saw the window glass shatter into a million pieces as the demons made their entrance. Every fragment of glass moved through the air as if orchestrated by a silent score, shards flying as the demons crashed through. Merlo almost ducked as some flew toward her face, but she was safe within Dina's sphere, trapped in a time bubble and kept safe from any harm.

Cragon didn't even have a chance to flee. One of the demons

grabbed him by the neck and dug in with its talons. Blood ran from between its misshapen fingers as it picked Cragon up off the ground and squeezed tighter still.

"Where is the Observer?" Its voice rumbled and echoed around the room.

Cragon scrabbled to loosen the demon's hold. The demon lifted Cragon higher to dangle him, helpless and now bleeding profusely. It shook him, chastising him like a dog reprimanding a wayward pup.

"Where is the Observer?"

Gasping for breath, Cragon began struggling again, this time to answer. "I don't know what you—"

"The thing that sees where it should not."

Merlo looked over her shoulder at Dina and mouthed "Kieran?" Dina shrugged a little and mouthed back "Maybe." Dina pressed her lips to Merlo's ear. "If they can sense her here…"

"We have to get back. They're searching for her. It's just a matter of time before they find the trail goes elsewhere."

"Her last 'episode' was here. It must have left a connection open for them to sense her. She's not safe. They're coming for her." Dina closed her eyes. "I hope I can remember how to do this. It's been a while."

A distortion field broke away from the bubble that protected Merlo. It spread out to engulf Cragon and the demons. Blood that dripped down to soak Cragon's pristine white shirt slowed its progression. Everything stilled then stopped, frozen in time.

With an audible pop, Dina pulled Merlo out of the time distortion.

"I am always amazed by how you can do that." Merlo shook herself free from the paralyzing feeling of being frozen in time.

"Go get the painting. I'm going to call friends in to deal with these two. But hurry, I can only hold time still for so long. Then I need you back in here because Cragon can't link you to this. You have to be here when he's released and time restarts."

Nodding, Merlo raced out of the office and was thankful the corridor was clear. She ran to her office, ripped the painting down from the wall, and then leaned it against her desk while she rummaged in her filing cabinet. She grabbed everything she had on file pertaining to Kieran Lee and tucked it away in her purse. She didn't know if demons could read, but she was determined to remove all evidence she could of Kieran's presence at Craven Hope. She would have a word with Rafe to see if she knew anyone who could hack into the computers and erase Kieran's records from there too. To wipe her from existence, just like Kieran had been trying to do physically for so long.

She hoisted the painting up again and balanced its weight with the bag she was carrying. Merlo hurried through the reception area to go hide the painting in her car. Everyone was frozen at their desk, caught in the middle of answering the phones or filing papers. Their predicament didn't even enter Merlo's head; she just ran through and paid them no heed.

She scanned the parking lot for any signs that the two demons inside weren't the only ones deployed in the search for the Observer. She was relieved she couldn't see anything else skulking around the hospital grounds. She'd parked her car in her allocated spot and was thankful she didn't have too far to go. With the painting deposited in the trunk of the car, Merlo finally took a deep breath of the warm air. She steeled herself for having to go back inside and face whatever Dina was about to unleash.

God help us. Merlo ran back toward Cragon's office. *Help me, because this is so out of my usual realm of reality.*

❖

The unearthly tableau of Cragon suspended in midair by a foul-looking demon was so out of place in his office that for a moment Merlo doubted her own sanity at what she was witnessing.

And I've seen a lot of things in my time. She held up a finger to Dina to keep time suspended for just a fraction more while Merlo took out her phone and snapped a few photographs of the demons as a point of reference. She knew Ashley would be disappointed if Merlo went back with just a verbal description of what they had encountered. She cautiously moved closer to take a better shot of the demon's face. She knew her fear was irrational, but she was terrified the creature would spring to life and grab her instead. From close up, Merlo found herself fascinated by its eyes. Trapped in that precise moment in time, it had caught what looked like a flame in its black eyes. It was the burning brightness of a red-hot inferno. She wondered at the rage behind his contorted features. Not human in the least, this was a cruel and twisted creature so very far fallen from grace. There was a part of her that felt compassion for it. It must have shown on her face for Dina to see.

"You can't do anything for them, Merlo. They are beyond redemption." Dina gestured for Merlo to finish up and get back to her side. "Brace yourself because it's not going to be pretty once time resets."

"Have you *seen* it?" Merlo would never fail to be in awe of the powers Dina possessed. The future, the past, and the present, Dina could access it all.

Dina nodded. "This I can see. You will be safe; it's just going to be noisy and a little messy." With that warning, Dina dropped her power over time, and the world came crashing back with a deafening roar.

The demon squeezed Cragon's throat harder still. The punishing hold made Cragon's face turn even redder before it shifted into an alarming shade of purple. Cragon gasped for air as he flailed in the demon's hold. He was asphyxiating as the demon choked out his life as easily as if it was squashing a bug.

"I don't know what you—"

Terror flared in the demon's eyes as its head whipped up to look at the ceiling. He said something that was too low and grating for Merlo to decipher, but the meaning was way too clear.

Something was coming.

The purest white light filled the office. Merlo had to squint to see anything in its glare. The air charged with an energy so physical she could almost feel it pulsing through her. It made the hairs on the back of her neck rise.

Here comes the cavalry. Two celestial beings descended out of nowhere to manifest in the room in all their glory. Huge wings filled the small space with their magnificence, and the white-clothed angels radiated with their own light.

The demons never stood a chance. Cragon was dropped like a stone as they tried to flee. He hit his head on the edge of the table on his descent and fell in an unconscious heap to the floor.

He's going to miss all the fun. Merlo watched in awe as the angels captured the demons. Their Spears of Light pierced through the demons and continued through to pin them to the ground. Trapped as effectively as bugs pinned to a board, the demons howled and clawed, trying to rip themselves free.

The angels nodded toward Dina and Merlo in thanks. Then, as swiftly as they had arrived, they left, taking the screaming demons back to where they belonged.

The sudden silence in the room gave Merlo a moment to take a breath. "So much for me just getting the painting without a fuss," she said wryly.

Dina patted her on the shoulder. "I'll go warn our friends that things have just gotten a little more interesting and leave you to deal with Cragon here."

"Oh sure, leave me with the worse part of all this."

"You're a professional. It's nothing you can't handle, I'm certain." She held out her hand. "Give me your phone so Ashley can start her investigation into what these things are and what we're supposed to do next."

"You'd think as an Oracle you'd already know," Merlo said.

"Ahh, but we both know time is not fixed. It runs in a constant fluid state, so many variables, with so many paths to take. I can only see so much, and just one tiny anomaly in the fabric of time can change the whole course of history." She leaned forward to plant a kiss on Merlo's forehead. "Which is how you came to be, my sweet."

Merlo smiled at the memory, and with an answering grin, Dina vanished from the room.

Merlo let out a sigh. She almost considered leaving Cragon where he was and letting someone else deal with the fallout. But she couldn't leave him, no matter how obnoxious a man and a professional he was, no matter how much she was tempted to flee. He'd seen her there, so she needed to fix it. But how?

Okay, so how is this going to play itself out?

The gashes on his neck weren't as deep as she'd feared when Merlo knelt beside him to check him over. However, they were *very* bloody. She shifted his head to inspect the wound where he'd hit the table. There was a sizeable lump on the back of his head. Merlo pressed on the wound and Cragon groaned. He didn't wake up, though, so Merlo spurred into action.

She lifted his hands to his neck and covered them with his own blood, making sure not to get any on her own hands. She knew that wasn't going to be enough. Grimacing, she angled his fingers so that she could drag his fingernails through the scratches in his flesh. She hoped enough of his torn skin would be found under his nails because she didn't have the stomach to repeat it. Then she left him splayed out on the floor to go crack open the office door and check the corridor. It was clear, but she could hear someone preparing to leave another office. She closed Cragon's door behind her and hurried toward the main doors, then turned around and walked down the corridor as if she'd just entered it from reception.

Dr. Jeffery Eems came out of his office a little farther down the hallway. Merlo knocked on Cragon's door, then paused in the doorway to greet the young doctor. She walked into the office and let out a scream. Eems rushed into the room behind her. *Together* they discovered Cragon on the floor, bloody and bruised.

"Oh my God." Merlo hurried back to Cragon's side. "What happened here?"

Eems knelt beside her and checked for a pulse. He began to examine the gory neck wounds. Merlo tried not to loom over his shoulder to see his reactions.

"It looks like he tried to claw his neck open," she said, drawing Eems's attention to Cragon's blood-soaked hands.

"Why would he do that?" Eems was still pressing around the neck wounds.

"I know he's been under a huge amount of pressure from the board. Maybe it all became too much? He's been a little erratic of late, misplacing files, forgetting what he has requested for patients. I thought it was just the stresses of his job, nothing a cruise to a Caribbean destination wouldn't cure." She'd always envied Cragon's ability to just drop his patients and fly out to laze on a cruise ship for weeks at a time.

Eems's touch finally brought Cragon's eyes open. He began fighting against Eems's hands.

"Get off me! Get off me!" he yelled, struggling to sit up.

Eems tried to calm him down, but Cragon pushed Eems over on his butt. Merlo tried to help Eems back up while Cragon hid behind his desk, curled up into a ball.

"Where are they?" Cragon screamed, searching the room with frightened eyes.

"Where's who?" Eems asked as he edged closer to calm Cragon down, but Cragon was having none of it.

"Stay back! How do I know you're not one of them?"

Eems looked at Merlo. Cragon looked at her too.

"You saw them! You were here! Tell him! Tell him they tried to kill me!"

"Dr. Blue has just arrived, Dr. Cragon. She couldn't have seen anything. We've both just found you like this."

"She saw them!" Cragon screamed, brandishing an accusing finger at Merlo. "She knows exactly what I'm talking about. She was in here with me."

Merlo used her patented patient's voice. "And what do you think you saw, Henry? Tell us please so we can help you."

Cragon's face flamed with anger. "Don't use that tone with me, you bitch! Don't mollify me by using my name as if we're friends! You were here. You saw what they did to me."

"What *did* you see?" Eems asked.

"Monsters. Monsters on the hospital grounds and then they were in my office and they were trying to kill me," Cragon said, his eyes wide and wild looking.

The look Eems traded with Merlo spoke volumes. "Under stress, you said?"

She nodded. "And it appears worse than any of us could have anticipated."

Eems stood up. "We're going to need help." He backed away from Cragon, who was watching them both suspiciously. Eems rested a hand on Merlo's shoulder. "I'll be quick."

Merlo heard the door close, but she didn't take her eyes off Cragon.

"You know what I'm talking about. You were here. You saw it all."

Merlo stood and stared down at him. "You've been in this profession long enough, Cragon, to recognize a psychotic break when one presents itself to you."

He shoved his face into his bloody hands and then screamed into his palms. His face was streaked a ruddy red. It only served to make him look crazier.

"I saw monsters."

"No, I'd say you saw *demons*. That's what people usually say they've seen," Merlo corrected him, watching his brain tick over as he recognized she was acknowledging what he'd seen. He stared at her as if she were insane.

"There's no such thing as demons," he said.

"And yet you claim to have seen them."

"You saw what those things did to me. I'll drag you before the board and have them take your job away. You're deliberately lying to make me sound crazy."

Merlo smiled at him. "Oh, I believe you think you saw something. I have files full of patients just like you who have claimed they saw something unreal. Here at Craven Hope we try to help them the best we can to rid themselves of the demons that plague their lives. Real or imaginary."

"I'm not one of your patients! I saw the fucking things. They nearly ripped my head off my shoulders! They were *real*!"

"The mind can play so many tricks on us. It's such a delicate piece of equipment, especially when we misuse it or the chemical imbalance is knocked out of whack a fraction." She tilted her head a little to catch his eyes. "That's a nasty bump you have on your head. Who knows what damage it caused? The brain just needs a knock to scramble it. After all, didn't you publish a paper describing most people as being just one misfiring neuron away from madness? Something about it all being a mixture of chemicals and temperament?"

Cragon stared at her. "You did not just quote me in order to justify my seeing demons."

"Your opinion only ever seems to be the one that matters to you."

"I'll have you fired for this. I'll have you stripped of your title. I'll make it so you'll never work again with these patients you think are salvageable. You're as crazy as they are!"

"Because *you* saw demons?"

"Because you saw them too," he spat.

Merlo smiled at him, leaned forward, and whispered conspiratorially, "I've always seen them, Cragon. It's you who's been blind to them all these years."

"You're a freak. I knew it."

"But you're the one they're going to think is crazy."

She stepped back as Eems bustled back in along with two orderlies. One of the orderlies was pushing a cart in before him. The glass bottles of medication rattled as he steered it into the room. Merlo ran her fingertips over the vials until she found the one she wanted. She filled a syringe with the dosage she required.

"Please hold him still while I administer this. I don't think he's going to be cooperative."

The orderlies grabbed for Cragon as he began fighting in earnest. They ended up holding him face down across his desk. He kicked and tried to buck them off but eventually they subdued him.

Merlo leaned down to whisper in Cragon's ear while Eems issued more orders to the men. "If this dose is good enough for the patients who try to escape when they are fleeing their demons, then I'd say it's good enough for you." She stuck him with the needle and pushed the plunger down. She could have been kinder in her administration of the drug, but she couldn't forget Kieran's treatment by him. He deserved no less than the same level of care his patients received from him.

"You saw them, you saw them…demons…there were demons…" Cragon's voice tapered off, and he became boneless and much easier to manage.

Merlo stood back as he was carried from his office to a room she knew Eems had waiting for him. She'd heard him mention something about safety first. Merlo hoped that meant padded walls and no windows for a time.

"I hate to say it, Dr. Eems, but I think he's had a psychotic break. He's going to be incapacitated for a long time, as I know he won't be open to any of the help we administer here." She slipped the safety cap back on the needle. "You might want to inform the board of his illness."

"Wouldn't it come better from you, Dr. Blue? You're a senior member of staff here, after all."

"I've got some personal time due that I'm taking advantage of. I will, however, inform the board that in my absence you'd be the perfect candidate to step into Cragon's role here at Craven Hope."

Eems looked taken aback for a moment and then he beamed at her. "Thank you so much, Dr. Blue. Your belief in me means a great deal."

"You're welcome. I've seen your work, Dr. Eems. I think the hospital could do wonderful things with you at the helm. Just always remember, we put the patients first no matter what. We're here to help them and to keep to our oath to 'First, do no harm.'" She peered down the corridor where Cragon had gone. "I'm just sorry none of us saw this coming. Sometimes it's the strongest among us that fall the hardest." Merlo patted Eems's shoulder and gave him a smile. "I know you'll give him all the attention and analysis he deserves."

CHAPTER SEVENTEEN

Ashley, Rafe, and Eli were all huddled over Merlo's phone as Ashley flipped through the photos again.

"I have to say it, those faces are something only a mother could love, and even she'd be hard-pressed not to find them fucking ugly." Rafe stepped away from the group and sat on the couch. Trinity jumped instantly onto her lap. Rafe petted her as she continued. "So what class of demon are we talking here? Because I've banished some mean and nasty-looking hell dwellers in my time, and they weren't even close to how terrifying these ugly bastards look."

Ashley couldn't take her eyes from the screen. She kept flicking the photos back and forth, fixated on what she was seeing. "These are rare. I mean, these never get seen topside at all. They are the so-called *peacekeepers* among the demon horde, so why they've been sent above is very curious. Then there's the fact they didn't even attempt to hide from mortals' eyes and attacked without provocation. That's unheard of. It doesn't make sense."

"Well, we know that they're after the Observer," Rafe said. "Which would stand to reason that the Observer is Kieran because of what she says she's seen. These visions of hers. Right?"

Ashley nodded. "The question now is what do they think she's seen that's got them sending in the heavy squad in broad daylight to attack a human?"

"A human who was in the same hospital Kieran just happened to be staying in before we busted her out." Rafe ruffled Trinity's fur. "Merlo was lucky they targeted Cragon and not her."

"Especially since she has Kieran's scent all over her," Eli added.

To Ashley's amusement, Rafe's eyebrows rose. She waited for the inevitable outburst. She knew Rafe wouldn't let Eli's statement go without comment.

"Eli, I don't think Merlo has gotten that close to Kieran. She's probably still wrestling with the whole doctor/patient shit to even think about fucking Kieran should she be interested." Rafe made a derogatory noise under her breath. "Let's face it, there's no greater romance killer than your possessed girlfriend bringing along her demon buddies for a foursome like no other!"

Ashley stifled her laughter behind her hand so as not to draw Eli's attention to her.

"I didn't mean in that manner, Rafe," Eli said. "There are less salacious explanations."

"Yeah, yeah," Rafe said, waving her hand at him. "But mine are way more fun to imagine."

Ashley sat beside her and nudged her. "Stop antagonizing the celestial being." She held up the phone to Rafe's face to show her the photos again. "Especially with these things roaming around."

Rafe took the phone from her and placed it face down on the arm of the couch. "They look like something out of a horror film. Just look at all those teeth. Their dental plan must be horrendous in Hell."

Ashley leaned into Rafe and rested her head on her shoulder. She felt more than heard the sigh that escaped Rafe's chest.

"So how bad are these things? On a scale of banishable demon to forbearers of the apocalypse?"

Ashley couldn't answer her. She honestly had no idea.

"Fuck," Rafe drawled. "That bad, eh?" She rested her head on top of Ashley's. "How about we quit while we're ahead? Leave the world to sort out this mess on their own while we go to our room, fuck like bunnies, and see out this shit storm together?"

Ashley laughed. She shifted so she could take Rafe's face in her hands and kiss her. "God, I love you."

"I love you too, but I wasn't joking about the bunnies part." Rafe pressed a soft kiss on Ashley's smiling lips. "I guess that's a no, then, and we have to go face this thing, with these things," she tapped the phone, "head-on as always?"

"It's what I was born to do. But you don't—" Ashley was stopped by another kiss.

"I was born to be by your side, so don't even think about suggesting otherwise. I just wish these infestations of demons we keep running into could be dealt with something as simple as a healthy dose of Raid." Rafe looked over at Eli, who was watching them impassively as always. "And I'm worried what little we can do won't be enough one day." She picked up the phone and waved it at Eli. "And judging by the look on this demon's face, I think that day is coming sooner than we'd like."

Dina stepped into the room and halted at the silence that had descended. "Merlo is heading back here with the painting. She shouldn't be long." She beckoned to Ashley. "It's your turn to watch over Kieran."

Ashley got up to follow Dina back up the staircase. "She's still asleep?"

"For now, but she'll wake up soon and want answers."

Ashley wondered just what they could tell Kieran that could possibly help her in the predicament she was in. "How far can you see, Oracle?"

Dina smiled. "I've been waiting for someone to ask. I should have known it would be you, demon hunter. I can see far enough to know that there are many branches of fate opening up ahead of us. The future is set only as long as someone doesn't change their path. Infinite choices, infinite outcomes."

Ashley considered that cryptic message. She knew she shouldn't ask, but she was going to anyway. "Do you see a favorable outcome in all this?"

There was no reply at first. Dina just led Ashley into Kieran's room. She wondered if she'd even hear an answer and worried that Dina felt Ashley was better off not knowing. That unnerved Ashley more than she could admit to.

"You know better than that, Ashley Scott. No one should be told their future."

Ashley nodded, understanding that but chafing at the restrictions. "I'm not asking for myself. I have humans by my side who are in this fight by choice, not by birthright. It's them I fear for, not myself."

Dina gave her a measured look. It was like Dina was looking into her very soul to ascertain how truthful she was being.

"Demons are a variable that shouldn't exist in an earthly timeline.

They're not supposed to be here. They're not *of* here." Dina rubbed at her forehead as if trying to clear her mind. "They are messing with what I see, clouding what I can predict. You were wise to bring in others. I fear this won't be a fight for the few."

"We're going to need to gather an army, aren't we?"

Dina's eyes glazed over, her pupils became opaque. They were unseeing, yet seeing so much more.

"I see tribulations rising, bringing with them an unearthly war. Led by a demon who has amassed great power and prestige in the underworld. One whose lies have corrupted those already corrupt in their diseased hearts." Dina turned her blind eyes on Ashley. "You have allies, the angelic mass." Dina smoothed her hand across the sheets where Kieran lay. "I foresee you're going to need them."

Her mouth dry with fear, Ashley could barely utter a word. "Do you see who is victorious?"

Dina touched Kieran's hand. "Win or lose, you need what she knows. Kieran is the key." She blinked rapidly, and her eyes returned to normal. "We are blessed with time, but it is ever moving like sands through an hourglass. You need to get Kieran on your side. She has to realize the severity of what she's an unwitting party to. She has to reveal what she sees and you need her to know it's *real*. That it's not something her mind has conjured up. It's not dreams or a mental problem." Dina's gaze fell to Kieran's sleeping face. "She's a conduit, being contacted by forces we can't see, and we need to know who it is and why they've chosen her."

"My friend who's coming? She can hopefully help with that. She has...some wild skills I'd never seen before."

"I knew I did right asking for you."

Ashley sat beside the bed to keep her watch over Kieran. "Let's just hope that with all I bring to the table, Kieran here has the answers we need to go forward."

❖

The familiar feel of bed linen under her palms confused Kieran for a moment. She couldn't remember if she was at home. But then she remembered she hadn't had a home for many months now. She let her fingers sink into the fabric. It didn't crinkle so, she wasn't in a hospital either with the familiar plastic coverings. Slowly, her memory returned and Kieran opened her eyes. The fancy stippling on the ceiling clued Kieran in to where she was.

Merlo's home.

Kieran noted it was light out. Her stomach felt empty, and it rumbled with such force it was almost painful. She'd obviously slept through a meal, or maybe two? Kieran knew she was being weaned off the cocktail of medication the hospital had been dosing her with, so she should have been feeling a little more alert.

Then she remembered.

"Oh God, not again," she moaned and flung her arm across her eyes, welcoming the darkness it afforded her.

"Good morning, Kieran. I was just getting ready to wake you so you could come have some breakfast. Judging by the noise your stomach just made, I'd say you're in need of it."

Kieran lifted her arm and saw Ashley seated beside the bed. She had a phone in her hand but didn't seem to be doing anything on it but staring at the screen.

"Another aborted attempt to take my life to add to the previous list of failures, I presume?" Kieran winced as she tried to sit up. Her ribs hurt, and she wrapped her arms around herself.

"You don't remember?"

Kieran frowned as she wracked her brain for anything she could recall. "Did Rafe catch me? I have a vague memory of being high up and then being…stopped?" Kieran rubbed at her temples trying to put together the bits and pieces of a memory that was flashing before her eyes. Her head snapped up. "There was an angel!" She started searching the room for any sign of him.

"He's not here. After your attempt, you saw him as he watched over you, and you made it very clear you didn't want him around." Ashley put her phone aside. "Do you have any idea how you can see angels in the first place?"

Kieran shook her head. "It's never happened before. Is this the next stage of this condition of mine?"

Ashley rose and stretched. "Well, it's going to make life a lot easier, that's for sure." She gestured for Kieran to follow her. "You need to eat and we need to talk. While you were sleeping off your little 'adventure,' Merlo was having one of her own."

Kieran grabbed for Ashley's arm and stopped her before she reached the staircase. "Is she okay?"

"She is. Let's just say you weren't the only one yesterday with a guardian angel keeping a watchful eye over you."

Kieran was almost overwhelmed with the sense of relief that washed over her. "Was it the same angel I saw?"

Another voice cut in. "No, it was a more feminine savior who stepped in to save the day for our illustrious doctor." Dina slipped an arm through Kieran's and steered her toward the kitchen. "We saved you some food. Eat now, then go shower and change into something other than your hospital sweats. We're expecting visitors, so you need to look your best and not like you've just escaped from a hellhole." Dina paused, realized her words, and laughed.

Kieran laughed with her; it felt good. Dina pushed her toward a chair, and a cereal bowl was placed before her. A wide selection of cereal boxes stood lined up for her to choose from.

"Froot Loops?" Kieran picked up the gaudy colored box. "Am I to take that personally?"

Ashley sat down opposite her and began raiding the well-stocked fruit bowl. "No, that would be Rafe's contribution to healthy eating. Just be thankful Trinity is otherwise entertained or you'd have a fight on your hands keeping her head out of your bowl."

Kieran had to force herself not to stuff her face full of the overly sweet cereal. Finally, after gobbling it all down, she spoke around a mouthful. "How long was I out this time?"

"You slept around eighteen hours," Ashley said.

"Trying to kill myself is tiring," Kieran muttered. She reached for the cereal and filled the bowl a second time.

Ashley didn't comment. Kieran had the weird feeling she was waiting for Kieran to continue. She didn't know what Ashley was expecting from her, so she asked the one thing that was going around in her head.

"Why did you all save me? You know how much I want this torment to end. There's obviously a reason why I keep trying. Why delay the inevitable?"

Dina pushed herself away from the cabinet she'd been leaning against. She cupped Kieran's chin in her hand. Kieran looked up and fell into the deep pull from Dina's eyes. They swirled like a star-filled vista set upon the darkness of space. She felt adrift, just one tiny life speck existing in the vast timeless mass of the universe. Kieran blinked and was back in her chair with the cloying taste of cereal thick on her tongue.

"Because it's not your time," Dina said and then walked away.

CHAPTER EIGHTEEN

The GPS's monotone voice announced that they had reached their destination. Detective Daryl Chandler breathed a sigh of relief. She was glad to have the journey over. Between the flight from New York to St. Louis's Lambert Airport and then driving through an unknown city, she was more than ready to grab some quiet time. She was running on fumes courtesy of the last case she had signed off on the previous day.

New York's DDU had been following leads with the Idaho police to catch a predator who had been kidnapping women from women's shelters and trying to create his own harem. They'd finally caught a break and stormed his home, capturing him and releasing all the women he had held there.

On their return flight, Daryl received the text from Ashley. She'd heard Blythe's phone ping with the same message. A different duty was calling them away. So much for a well-earned few days off to go back home to Vermont to visit with her father. She was desperate to relax and clear her mind of the filth she had just witnessed. But Daryl understood that she was needed elsewhere.

Special Agent Blythe Kent sat beside her in the passenger seat. Daryl nudged her, drawing her attention away from the tablet she was working on.

"Are you sure this route planner has us in the right area? This neighborhood looks way too rich to be where we'd usually meet up with Ashley concerning a case."

Blythe raised her head and looked out the windows. "Wow, this is definitely a more upscale area than the last time we met up with them."

"It does have fewer broken windows or burned-out buildings and no visible demon conclaves." Daryl followed the GPS's final instructions and pulled up to a driveway. She leaned out her window and pressed the buzzer on the gate.

"If you're selling subscriptions to some inane religious crap you can fuck off, but if you have Girl Scout cookies get your asses in here!"

Daryl grinned and Blythe burst out laughing. "We're at the right place," Daryl said. She pressed the button to speak. "Hi, Rafe, can you let us in please?"

The gates swung open and Daryl drove up to the house. Blythe peered through the windshield in amazement.

"Oh my God, it looks like something from a film set." She craned her head to try to see it all. "It's beautiful and I'm very thankful I don't have to pay for its upkeep." She began unbuckling her seat belt before Daryl even pulled up. "All I care about is if it has a bathroom because I am desperate to pee."

"Remember I pointed them out in the airport?"

"Yes, but I didn't feel the urge to go then. But you had to go and buy me a caramel Frappuccino grande on our way out."

"Excuse me, ma'am, but I seem to recall it was *you* who told me to do so."

She parked alongside Rafe's familiar car and spotted her standing at the top of the steps. Blythe scrambled out of the car the second it pulled up and took off up the steps two at a time. Rafe just grinned and pushed the front door open wider and must have said something more than just a welcome because Blythe smacked Rafe on her arm as she rushed past her. Daryl heard Rafe shout out something else after Blythe before she headed down the steps laughing.

"Can you believe she slapped me just because I told her she had the bladder capacity of an old lady?" Rafe pretended to look affronted. "I told her if she pees on the carpet I'll rub her nose in it like she said I was supposed to do to Trinity when she was a kitten."

Laughing, Daryl got out of the car after popping the trunk open.

"Hey, Vermont, you might want to hold your horses there a minute and leave your bags put until you hear what kind of mess we're dragging you into this time. You'll probably decide to head back to New York and leave us to it." Rafe gave her a welcoming hug. "I'm glad to see you. You're looking tired, though. Big-city life too much for a farm girl like you?"

Daryl sighed and just squeezed Rafe back. "You know damn well I wasn't raised on a farm, Rafe."

"Countryside, rural areas, all the same to a city dweller like me," Rafe said with a twinkle in her eye. Her face turned serious for a moment as she held Daryl away to get a good look at her. "You okay, though?"

Daryl nodded. "We've had a few rough cases back-to-back. I was looking forward to a few days off watching my father putter around his yard. But we got Ashley's call, and you know Blythe, she was moving mountains to get us to you guys ASAP."

Rafe clapped her on her shoulder. "Let's get you all settled in and then you can sit and put your feet up while we regale you with the tale of Kieran Lee and her demon-fueled death wish."

Daryl frowned at her. "That doesn't sound relaxing."

"Remember that when you hear tell of how I nearly took a header yesterday from right up there." Rafe pointed to a balcony high up on the face of the house.

Daryl did her own perusal of Rafe. "Are *you* okay?"

Rafe just nodded. "Eli was here, thank God." She grinned at her choice of words. "Can't say I want to do it again anytime soon. My hair's back to a normal length now. I don't need it to turn white overnight."

"Ashley didn't give us a great deal of information other than to call us in and give directions to get here. What are we stepping into?"

"Something best described as quicksand mixed with a nest of fire ants."

"Why can't you ever include us in the fun stuff? Like a case with a human-only element? You remember, like in the good old days before everything became demon shaped and twice as ugly." Daryl reached into the trunk and began taking out their luggage.

"Speaking of ugly," Rafe muttered under her breath but didn't elaborate any further as the number of suitcases Daryl was removing from the trunk distracted her. Rafe picked one up, then laid it back down with a grunt. "This has to be one of Blythe's cases. Hell no, I am not carrying that heavy son of a bitch. You sleep with her, you can carry her 'weighs a fucking ton' suitcase." Rafe wriggled her fingers as if trying to ease a cramp. "She's here for a consult, for God's sake, not to move in permanent."

Daryl grinned and held out a smaller one. "This one is mine. Think you can manage that?"

Rafe tested its weight. "See, now that's a proper suitcase weight." She reached into the car and pulled out Daryl's briefcase too.

Carrying the rest of the luggage, Daryl followed Rafe up into the house. "This place is like a museum."

"Yeah, but that didn't stop Trinity from already using one of the antique chairs as a scratching post."

"You brought your cat with you?"

"Eli requested it. I don't know why, but if these demons' biggest weaknesses are hairballs underfoot, then let me tell you, we are armed and dangerous."

Daryl was still laughing at Rafe when she caught sight of Ashley waiting in the living room. She was wearing the happiest smile on her face and her arms were wide open and inviting. Daryl dropped her suitcases to give Ashley a hug that lifted her off her feet.

"I'm so glad you're here," Ashley said with a relieved look. "We are in need of your specific brand of expertise."

"Virgil and I are at your disposal."

There was a noise behind her as Blythe came back and was hugging Rafe until Rafe started protesting.

"Enough, go fling those skinny arms around my girlfriend." Rafe managed to wriggle out of Blythe's grip and pushed her in Ashley's direction.

Blythe gave Ashley a hug. "You called, we're here, what's the story? You gave me just enough to explain our departure to SSA Lake, but not much else to go on. I'm desperate to hear what we're up against this time that warranted such a cryptic call from you." Blythe rubbed her hands together. "And I'm more than ready to hone my demon-tracking skills a little more."

"We're just waiting for our lead *witness* to come downstairs," Ashley said, emphasizing the word. "Then, I promise, all will be revealed."

Daryl looked around the large room. "Do I have time to freshen up before the show-and-tell starts?"

Rafe waved for Daryl to follow her. On the way, she pointed out all the pertinent rooms and then directed Daryl's attention to a broken, boarded-up, and padlocked door.

"Skeletons in that closet?" Daryl asked.

"No. That leads to the balcony I nearly fell from. For safety it's been made inaccessible."

"Good to know," she mumbled.

Rafe opened a door for her. "This is your room. The bathroom is through there," she pointed to the right, "and the walls are pretty damn thick if you and Blythe want to get rowdy in here later on." She smirked at Daryl's face. "Get yourself cleaned up and then come on down. The sooner we start this circus, the better."

"Is this the Preacher making his presence known again?" Daryl asked as she laid the suitcases down to deal with later.

"Oh, it's him *and* all his demonic little buddies. Hope you packed more than one change of clothing. I think we're in for one hell of a storm." Rafe paused at the doorway. "Emphasis on the Hell."

Left on her own, Daryl sat on the bed with a thump. "This wasn't the welcome to St. Louis I'd hoped for."

Kieran tried hard not to fiddle with the collar of the new shirt that Merlo had brought for her that morning. Merlo had been super-efficient taking down all of Kieran's measurements and had come back bearing more suitable attire than the hospital sweats Kieran had been living in. She looked down at her feet in their new Nikes. She hadn't had a woman buy her clothing since she was a child and her mother had begrudgingly clothed her. She had to admit, Merlo had done well. She ran a hand through her newly cut hair. While Merlo had been out after clothes, Dina had sat Kieran down in the kitchen and set to cutting her long-neglected hair into a more stylish shape. Kieran had been thrilled to see something resembling her old self when she looked in the mirror. Dina had shaved the back and sides of Kieran's hair and left the top longer to soften the style.

It's been a long time since I've had this feeling. I feel almost normal again. It was sobering to realize she hadn't felt like that in quite some time.

She sat anxiously in the living room with Merlo beside her, keeping watch as always. The familiar frame of a painting caught Kieran's eyes. She remembered it from Merlo's office and wondered why it was there. She was about to ask when everyone came into the room and found seats. Kieran finally got a chance to see the new arrivals. The tall blonde caught her eye first. Kieran could almost feel a wave of calm energy from her. The dark-haired woman who accompanied her was undoubtedly law enforcement because of her demeanor. Rafe, Ashley, and Dina followed in behind them.

They all looked at Kieran. Kieran, in turn, looked at Merlo. "Why do I get the feeling this is going to be either an intervention or one of your touchy/feely association meetings? The kind where we're all expected to reveal something about ourselves to total strangers?" She began nervously twisting the buttons on her shirtsleeve.

Merlo placed a hand over hers to calm her. "This is more for your benefit than ours."

She swallowed hard and Kieran was surprised to notice that Merlo looked a little shaky herself. *What's that all about?*

"You need to know why each of us is here to help you so that you can trust us."

"Then why are *you* so nervous? I know you more than anyone here." Kieran shifted so that her hand cradled Merlo's. She could feel a definite tremor vibrating through Merlo's body.

"Like I said, we all have a reason for being here. Myself included."

Kieran left her hand where it was but settled back in her seat. "Okay. Let's get the introductions over with and get this thing started."

Everyone in the room looked at each other as if not certain who should start. Rafe cleared her throat. "Why do I feel like I'm being set up on a blind date? You know me already. I'm Detective Rafe Douglas and I work at Chicago's DDU, which stands for the Deviant Data Unit, which deals with the more select undesirables of the criminal world." Her tone then changed deliberately. "I'm a Sagittarius, I'm partial to pizza, and I'm happiest driving my police car very fast with the sirens blaring just so I can go get coffee."

Ashley started chuckling while Blythe shot Rafe a withering look. "You're supposed to be taking this serious," Blythe said.

Rafe rolled her eyes before directing her speech to Kieran. "Anyhow, I was just a regular detective until I was attacked by a demon one night and nearly got killed in the process."

Kieran sat up straighter and stared at Rafe as she continued.

"I was pretty beat up, but when I started to recover I could see things I hadn't seen before. I could see demons, pick them out by the glow of light that shines around them. I thought I was going crazy at first, that the demon who had cracked my skull had maybe scrambled my brains for me too. Then this private investigator with a sideline in the occult and religious practices came into my life and showed me that there was a whole other world my mind was now open to. Since then I've seen plenty of demons up close and personal. I was gifted with a weapon, a Spear of Light, which is an angelic implement that is used in detaining demons for their subsequent banishing. It's a handy weapon given to me by the same angel who was watching over you when you jumped. He was watching over me the night I was attacked and saved me from being killed." Rafe sat back and gestured to Ashley. "Oh, and those coffee breaks? I get to take them with this gorgeous woman here because I'm her sidekick in all things in life, and I count myself heaven blessed for that fact."

Ashley smiled at her but gestured for Blythe to introduce herself next. "Let's start her off easy," she said.

Blythe nodded and Kieran wondered at the significant look Ashley and Blythe traded.

"Kieran, it's nice to meet you at last. I'm Special Agent Blythe Kent from the New York branch of the DDU. I'm able to see both angels and demons in their true forms. It's still a new ability for me, and while it's not one I would have chosen to have, it's saved my life and the lives of my loved ones on many an occasion. I was brought into all this via a case we were working on. Something we thought was a baby-snatching ring ended up having a more sinister involvement. Turned out a demon called the Preacher was calling for a sacrificial lamb to start his reign. We didn't see him, but we met one of his prophets. Thankfully, that she-demon is out of the picture. But there's still too many out there affecting our world." She gestured for Daryl to take over. "Your turn, sweetheart."

Daryl smiled at Kieran and the others. "It's a pleasure to meet you all. I'm Detective Daryl Chandler. I work at the DDU with Blythe, but originally I was a detective in Vermont working with the police there. From a very young age, I became aware that I was different. I could find missing people better than anyone else could. It wasn't something that went unnoticed either, and I had my fair share of suspicion, distrust, and fear poured on me once it became common knowledge I had this ability. I have prophetic dreams at times, usually connected to a case that needs my attention. But mostly I have an intense focus when I look at a map. It pinpoints where I need to search for something either living or dead and helps me bring them home. It wasn't until I met Ashley and Rafe that it was revealed to me that I have an angel, one called an Impressor, and he helps me see exactly where I need to go."

"You have an angel?" Kieran said. She couldn't help herself and began scanning the room for any signs of what she'd seen before.

"Virgil isn't present, but then I'm guessing you know that because you can see angels, whether you want to or not. He's been my constant companion since I was a child, and his gift to me has helped me find many lost souls."

Kieran gave Daryl a wary look. She saw Ashley shift in her seat and wondered what she had to reveal.

"Kieran, I know this all sounds crazier than you've ever been made to feel in your own situation. I can't make it any easier, to be honest. I'm Ashley Scott and I am a private investigator by title but a demon hunter by profession. You've already met my guardian angel Eli. He's been by my side for more years than I can remember. He knew my father." Ashley paused and took a steadying breath. "Okay, let me just say this. I'm the daughter of an angelic being who fell from grace and became a demon. My mother was human, which makes me a hybrid of sorts, an angel/demon/human being. I had a half brother, but he turned out to be a demonic serial killer Rafe and I helped to capture and saw banished. And I can shape-shift, which is what you saw when I impersonated Cragon at the hospital."

Before Ashley could continue, Kieran rounded on Merlo. "Is this some kind of test to see how much I'll believe so that as soon as I fall for it all you'll haul me back to the hospital and throw me in a padded cell?"

Merlo shook her head. "No, Kieran, it's nothing at all like that. We need you to understand who you have by your side."

Dina drew Kieran's attention to her. "I'm Dina. I'm what you would call an Oracle. I can see the future, regale the past in great detail, and am able to manipulate time itself. The fact that you can see me was quite a surprise, for I exist neither in your time nor my own. I *am* time.

In years long past, ancient oracles were the conduits between which God spoke to man. But I am more than that now."

Kieran was silent. She looked at everyone in the room one at a time, then down at her hand still resting on Merlo's. She felt the trembling increase.

"And you, Dr. Blue? What is *your* story?"

Merlo's teeth worried at her bottom lip before she began to speak.

"I am Merloina Bluetralis. I am empowered with empathic skills that I had passed on to me by my mother, as were passed down to her from hers. I utilize it in my job as a doctor of the mind. My father passed on a legacy of his own to me also." She faltered, seeming to change her mind on what she revealed next. "My birthplace was Atlantis. Way back when it was a great civilization, before a great cataclysm befell it and wiped it from the face of the earth."

"*Atlantis*? Did it really sink into the sea?" Ashley asked.

Merlo nodded. "I was evacuated weeks before it sank. When I was eventually able to get back, the island had completely disappeared, along with my family and friends. Entire cities and cultures gone, all swallowed up by the waters. Our leaders were decades beyond their time, with tools and machinery that aren't just confined to the present. They were testing something, some great experiment that would show their mastery of the world. In their ignorance they set off a terrible devastating explosion, taking all remnants of the city of Atlantis to a watery grave."

Kieran slowly moved her hand from Merlo's. "So you're asking us to believe that you're an ancient dweller of some long-lost city when you look, what? Thirty years old at the most?"

Merlo smiled a little. "You're very kind. My title is a *Neverage*. I am long-lived, or long-traveled, as Eli called me when we first met. That was my father's legacy to me—longevity."

"An Immortal," Rafe said in awe. "Wow, that's a first. And believe me, I've seen a lot of crazy shit."

"That title is not exactly true, but I have lived a very long time and I'll continue to do so until death finally arrives for me."

"And you just work at the hospital for what? Kicks? It can't be for the money considering how you live. Or is it to practice your powers on unsuspecting mortals who'll die from old age while you live on to study the next batch that come through the doors?" Kieran stood, fists clenched at her sides. "You know something? My having suicidal tendencies brought on by my supposed possession by demons seems to make me the sanest person in this whole fucking room! At least I know I'm crazy! Take me back to the hospital, please. I'd rather take my chances there than be surrounded by you all who are possibly more certifiable than any of those I shared the unit with!"

Kieran stormed out of the room. She was halfway up the stairs when she heard Rafe's voice.

"Well, I think that went as well as could be expected, don't you?"

Kieran didn't stop until she was in her room. She slammed the door behind her and sank to the floor. With her face pressed into her knees, Kieran fought the need to just scream her head off. Instead, she shook violently from head to toe.

A bump against her leg made her gasp. Trinity meowed at her and bumped her again.

"And what are you? A panther disguised as a harmless housecat? Some kind of shape-shifting creature to join the merry band of X-Men that reside downstairs?" Kieran wrapped her arms around her legs and curled into herself. Trinity laid herself over Kieran's new shoes and settled in to sleep.

Nothing's real anymore. I'm living in a Van Gogh painting where everything is too bright and the world is a series of out-of-control swirls, and I can't even look to the stars for guidance. Make it all stop, please. I'm so tired of it all.

A tear escaped and trickled down her cheek to soak through her chinos. She watched it dispassionately as the wet patch expanded in the pale cream cloth.

Just make it all go away.

CHAPTER NINETEEN

Merlo hesitated before quietly tapping on Kieran's bedroom door. She couldn't begin to imagine what confusing thoughts were running through Kieran's head at the revelations she'd just heard. But she couldn't leave her alone.

"Kieran? Can I come in, please?"

"I'm sitting on the floor right behind the door, so no," Kieran answered in a sulky tone.

"I'd rather be able to speak to you face-to-face than through the door. And you know it's not wise for you to be left alone."

"Merlo, you've got padlocks littered all around this room to stop me from doing everything. Anything I could use as a weapon you have removed. I'm sure you've still got an angel watching over me even though I can't see him. The only way I could kill myself in here now is by being smothered to death by Rafe's damn cat that won't leave me the hell alone. Just like none of you will."

"We're here to help you."

"I don't want your help. I feel like I've been thrown into some crazy hero-filled CW show where everyone has superpowers and I'm supposed to just blend in and think of it as normal. I can't even think of *myself* as normal. But you all seem to think this state of affairs is natural. Business as usual. But it's not." Kieran sighed. "Demon hunters? Cops who can see angels? Not to mention an Oracle, and then there's you, Merloina Bluetralis. Are you even a doctor?"

"I've always been a healer from the very start of my journey."

"Just how old are you?"

Merlo laughed. "Were you ever taught never to ask a woman her age?"

"Do you even know how old you are?"

Merlo closed her eyes at the odd pain that question evoked in her. She knew exactly how long she had lived. She knew it and felt it every single day, the many months, the countless years, and the endless decades that had passed since her family had died. She'd walked a solitary path ever since. The last of her kind, living on to eternity. "I'm not so old that I can't remember things. I might have years of living behind me, but I still have all my faculties working."

"What do you want from me?"

"I need you to come back down and tell everyone your story, and then I want to tell you what happened to me yesterday. You can't hide from this, Kieran. It's too important and you're too vital to it all."

"What could I possibly bring to the table?"

"You are the key to all that these people fight for and against. Your visions are what they need to see."

"You can't just pry open my head and have what I see bleed out. Cragon would have tried it if he could have."

"I'm told they have their own ways to facilitate that in a much more civilized way. I want you to come back and speak with us. We need you."

"And once I've spoken to you all and jumped through your mental hoops, then what? You'll let me go?"

"Do you want to go?" Merlo waited for an answer. She pressed her ear against the door and could hear Kieran talking, but she didn't think it was meant for her ears to hear. Kieran was talking to herself and Trinity.

"I don't know what I want anymore. If left to my own devices, I end up trying to kill myself, and I'm so tired. I want this over and I want to sleep, but…I really want to go back to normal and have my old job back and just…be myself again."

Merlo's chest ached for Kieran. She wished there was more that she could do to help her. She reached out and touched Kieran through their connection. She felt Kieran startle and then unconsciously relax.

"Merlo?"

"Yes, Kieran?"

"Will I ever get to experience normal again?"

"We're going to try our best to help you do that. You know me, Kieran. You know I wouldn't ever harm you. The others are here *for* you, not *against* you." She waited for Kieran to speak again. She heard something else instead.

"Ouch! You damned cat! You're as unpredictable as your owner! Let me guess, you're telling me I should get up and get out of here? Am I to get no peace from anyone?"

"Kieran? Are you okay in there?" She heard a noise behind the door and sat back as the door opened to reveal Kieran with Trinity. The cat hung floppy pawed in Kieran's grasp.

"It's not enough that I have demons in my head and angels watching over my every move. I have this damn fuzzball dogging my every step and biting me when I won't do what she wants."

Merlo stood and smoothed down her skirt. She reached out to tickle Trinity's ears. "Please come tell them what you see. Be sure to bring the cat with you if you must." She grinned at Kieran's huff of displeasure.

"I can't seem to shake her," she grumbled but settled the cat more comfortably in her arms.

"Cats are very intuitive. Maybe she senses you need something."

"Don't I have you for that?"

Kieran's realization of what she had just said caused a red tide to sweep over her cheeks.

"I mean…I just…"

Merlo decided to spare Kieran any more humiliation. Though, to be honest, Merlo was thrilled by Kieran's words. "You do have me, Kieran. I'm here to give you whatever support you need." *And I'd love to be so much more if time grants us that chance.* "Please come talk to us all. And then I need your permission for something."

"Does that painting have anything to do with that request?"

"What makes you ask that?"

"Because it's propped up in the living room instead of its usual place. And besides, it gives off one hell of a creepy vibe that I just can't explain."

"You're more sensitive than I had realized."

"Seems I'm a lot of other things too that I never imagined." Kieran gave Merlo a sheepish look. "Sorry I just walked out on you all. I needed to escape for a moment. It's a lot to take in."

"Unfortunately, this isn't going to go away or get any better for you, Kieran. So please, let us help you in any way we can."

Nodding, Kieran took her place by Merlo's side. She bumped her shoulder. "So, immortal, eh?"

"Long-lived. I will die, eventually."

"How long is eventually?"

"I haven't found out yet," Merlo said.

"Don't we just make quite the pair? I mean, think about it. You're ever-living and I just keep trying to die."

Kieran's sad smile was heart wrenching to witness. It made Merlo want to reach out and hold her close and promise her everything would be all right and a normal life was just waiting for Kieran right around the corner. She couldn't promise anything, though. She had no idea what was coming or how any of them would fare or even survive.

"Just when I think my life couldn't get any crazier." Kieran cuddled Trinity close. "Let's hope Trinity here is a lucky cat, because for the first time in a long time I'm finding myself hoping for something good to happen instead of the bad I always wish for."

From your lips to God's ears.

❖

No one uttered a word when Kieran came back into the room. She'd handed Rafe her cat with a muttered "I think this belongs to you," and then had sat down waiting for whatever came next.

Blythe asked Kieran for her side of the story and documented every word Kieran told them. She was trying so hard not to fall into the interviewing technique she usually employed when talking to a suspect. Blythe knew Kieran was like no one else she'd spoken to and was careful to temper her aggressive form of getting results and was instead letting Kieran tell them her story at her own pace.

"Do you have any idea why all your suicide attempts have failed?" Blythe asked, looking up to gauge Kieran's reaction to her question.

"Apparently, I suck at it." Kieran shrugged. "I can't explain it. That deer on the train tracks was freaky as hell, and the one time I remember driving into a tree, the steering wheel jerked out of my grip as if someone had grabbed it. I know I ended up rolling down the embankment instead. The damn car landed upright and I was somehow able to get out of my seat belt and walk away with just bruises. The car, however, was a total wreck." Kieran rubbed at her face. "I can't explain it no matter how hard I try. I have thrown up so many overdoses that I now gag at the mere sight of pills. I've snapped razor blades when trying to slit my wrists. They have literally fallen to pieces between my fingers. I tried a gun once, but it jammed every time I brought the barrel up to my head. Yet when I aimed it elsewhere, the gun worked. It's unexplainable; no matter what I try, something seems to stop me." She paused a moment. "Though being rescued from a jump by an angel was something new."

"How many times have you tried to kill yourself other than these incidents?"

"Every time I have an 'episode,' as Merlo calls them. It becomes all-consuming. Compulsive. There's nothing else I can focus on except to keep trying until it sticks."

"That must be exhausting."

"It's out of my control. I can't do anything but try. It's like an addict desperately searching for their next fix. The only relief I get is when I am this close," she held up her thumb and forefinger to show just a tiny gap, "to succeeding."

"But it doesn't work," Blythe muttered.

"Obviously," Kieran said.

"How do you feel now?" Blythe could see Kieran looked okay. Her eyes were tired but clear; she seemed calm and coherent.

"Like it's the calm before the storm again. These episodes are speeding up. I can feel it, like something is bubbling inside me getting ready to boil and slip out again."

"The message you carry must be important," Daryl said from her seat at Blyth's side.

"If it is a message," Kieran said. "This could all be for nothing. I could be certified crazy and you've all wasted your time here."

Daryl smiled. "I've seen the recording of your face changing and morphing into something demonic. This isn't nothing."

"What brought you to St. Louis this time?" Blythe flipped through some of the paperwork she'd received from Dina. "You've traveled some distances trying to escape detection after each attempt."

"The bridge suited my needs. Drowning was next on my bucket list of things to try."

"And after that one?"

"Well, I was here by then and the view from the balcony upstairs was incredibly inviting."

"You nearly took Rafe with you," Blythe said with a slight edge to her tone.

"That was never my intention. I've never put anyone else in harm's way when I try to kill myself. It's only me who needs to go."

"That's an odd way to put it."

"I'm the one trying to kill myself. It's not like I need someone to hold my hand to do it. And it's not a sport where I need a partner."

"I get that, but to be the 'only one that needs to go' could point to whatever is driving you to do this specifically targeting *you*. So what do you know about the possessing spirit that needs you to die so you don't reveal it?" Blythe tapped her pen against her bottom lip as she lost herself for a moment in thought. "Intriguing."

Kieran smiled. "But alas, I have no answer for you because I have no idea what or who is possessing me or why. I just know that after I go into that other world and come back from it, I just want to end it all."

"We need to see all that she sees," Blythe told Daryl.

"I know, which is why Virgil and I have been looking into what we need in order to get that ball rolling. He doesn't think he can do it alone, not if we all need to see it, so he's gathering help. Once Kieran starts showing the symptoms that Merlo warned us about, we can step into action."

"So all this rests on me?" Kieran laid her head back against the couch and sighed.

"You're the key to all of this," Daryl said.

"But I don't want to be anything."

"That choice was never yours to begin with," Blythe said. "Now we need to work out why, and as much as I know it's painful for you, we need you to experience another episode."

"They don't exactly come on command."

Blythe felt empathy for her but knew the only way they could solve this was for all the pieces to come into play. She looked over at Daryl, who was studying Kieran with an exacting eye.

"Merlo has great faith in you, Kieran. Both as a doctor and as a friend. I know you trust her too. Hang on to that, please."

Daryl's words made something flicker across Kieran's face. Blythe saw that Daryl had noticed it too. *Ooh, our demon-possessed friend here feels something more than trust for the fair doctor. How is that going to work out considering Merlo is the next best thing to an immortal being?* She could see Daryl shifting in her seat beside her. *And I thought it was hard enough when my love came with an angel attached at her shoulder.* She glanced over at Kieran, who had her eyes closed and was feigning calmness.

What a motley bunch we make. Angels and demons and demigods, oh my! But something is definitely controlling Kieran's fate here. We need to expose what's pulling her strings before she's cut free from them.

❖

As Kieran spoke, Merlo found herself growing more and more enamored of her. To have gone through so much and still be standing and able to tell them about it now without fear of ridicule or disbelief must have been a relief for Kieran. Merlo was just thankful Kieran could finally express herself.

Blythe's interview began to wind down, so Merlo sprang into action. She knew the sooner they got her piece out of the way, the better. Kieran sat running her fingertips over the stitching on her chinos. Merlo recognized the nervous habit as something that calmed Kieran's racing thoughts. Merlo picked up the seascape painting and rested it against the wall within easy view of everyone. She settled a spotlight over the frame and centered it all just so.

"I have a few tricks in my repertoire that are strictly my own and not endorsed by the medical profession. But," she looked over her shoulder at everybody, "what they don't know won't open them up for lawsuits." She gestured to the painting. "This is one of them."

"Paint-by-numbers psychiatry?" Rafe said. "No offense, Doc, but that would drive me loopy too."

"I use this when the patient has a difficult time opening up. That could be because of intense trauma buried so deep in their psyche that they can't bring it forward, or because they literally don't want to tell me what is wrong. This helps me see." She focused her gaze on Kieran.

"This is how I knew you weren't suffering from anything I usually treat. This time I'm asking for your permission. May I use this on you again?"

"I don't recall you using it on me in the first place."

Merlo nodded. "That's why I'm asking this time. You'll come to no harm at all while I employ it, and you won't remember it, just like last time." Merlo turned to Ashley. "Maybe you could record what happens on your phone so that Kieran isn't left in the dark any longer and can see what we will all see?"

Ashley pulled out her phone. "Consider it done."

Merlo brushed her hands together nervously. This was usually a more intimate session, not one with multiple viewers. She found herself experiencing performance anxiety. "Okay, well…I need to ask everyone but Kieran to leave the room for a moment."

"The reason for that being?" Blythe asked.

"I need this to be Kieran's vision. With all of you in the room as Kieran goes under, the painting would end up gathering fragments from all of you too. It needs to be tethered to her mind alone. Dina will usher you back in once we're ready."

Blythe and Daryl left silently but Rafe made a comment to Ashley. "Magic paintings now? I swear my life with you gets more freaking bizarre every second of every day."

Kieran sat immobile, her eyes fixated on the painting. "You say you've done this to me before? Why don't I remember?"

"Because you're not meant to. This was how I realized your problems weren't so much mental as influenced by outside sources." Merlo knelt before Kieran and took her hands in her own. Kieran's hands felt cold. "Everything's going to be all right and you can watch it all afterward. I won't keep anything from you. Full disclosure this time, I promise."

Kieran nodded. "Then let's get this over with."

Merlo patted Kieran's hands and stood. She closed the curtains. The thickness of the old drapes darkened the room, leaving the spotlight as the only light visible. "I want you to focus on the painting. Let your eyes trace across the water…"

The spotlight began to pulse in its steady rhythm, drawing Kieran's eyes to it once again as Merlo's words sent her under.

❖

There was a strange, unnatural feel to the room when Ashley and the others came back in. Ashley faltered in her steps as if something was pressing on her chest, pushing her back out of the doorway, barring her entrance.

Dina's hand came to rest on Ashley's spine. "It's okay, just push past it. It will ease once it realizes it's not you it's reading. Your special physiology calls to it. Magick is drawn to magick."

"I'm not magickal," Ashley whispered.

"You are a being of mystical origins. The painting will recognize that."

"It's *sentient?*"

"It's ancient magick, and magick works in mysterious ways among humans."

"And I'm not exactly human," Ashley said.

"I'd just recommend you try not to think deep thoughts through any of this session and just focus on filming it."

Ashley nodded, but her heart only quit its anxious fluttering when she caught the small smirk on Dina's face. *Pranked by an Oracle, that is so not funny.* Ashley glared at her, not amused in the least.

"Yes, I'm joking. You're just reacting to the magick in the room. It's perfectly safe. Its focus is on Kieran. It won't interact with the rest of your minds. Not even yours, child born of light and dark." She waved everyone to their seats.

Kieran was sitting in a comfortable chair. She looked perfectly normal, much to Ashley's surprise. She hadn't been sure what to expect. She chided herself for being uncharacteristically unnerved before she even saw Merlo's magick in action. Ashley shot a quick glance at Rafe, who mimicked locking her lips to keep quiet. Dina had already warned them all not to speak in case it disrupted the session. That just served to make Ashley even more intrigued. She'd seen hypnotists in action but nothing that involved a magick-imbued painting. This was out of her usual realm of occult knowledge. She wondered if the painting could even be considered an occult relic given its origins in Atlantis?

Eli and Virgil appeared in the room, intent on watching the

performance to see what they were up against. Eli's usual calm demeanor was in contradiction with the worried look visible on his face.

If even the angels are worried, what hope do we have?

Dina closed the living room door and the focal point of the room became more apparent. Ashley stared at the painting. She was trying to see where the foreboding feeling she was getting was emanating from. It just looked like any other seascape in oils.

Rafe nudged her and mimed using her phone. Ashley set it to record and settled in to watch. She could see how easy it could be for Merlo's voice to put someone in a trance. She could hear something else, buried in the tone of Merlo's accented voice. Like a gentle melody playing in the background that soothed the mind. Merlo was utilizing a vocal subliminal message to run like a persuasive undercurrent in every word she uttered. Ashley was impressed; she'd only ever seen angels with the mastery of vocal suggestion. She risked a look back at Rafe and saw her frowning, affected enough for it to be uncomfortable for her. Just what kind of power did Merlo harness as a Neverage?

The painting started to shift. Ashley blinked because she thought it was her vision and the darkness of the room playing tricks, but no, her eyes weren't deceiving her. The painting was *melting*. She focused her camera on what the painting was revealing.

The scene was unfamiliar to Ashley. She watched as farmland replaced the seascape. She spared a glance over her shoulder to where Eli stood. His and Virgil's natural luminescence had dimmed, but they still gave off enough light that Ashley could make out Eli and he could see her. She caught his eye and mouthed "Where?" to him. He shrugged and looked to Virgil. His eyes were tuned toward the painting and nothing else in the room. Ashley knew he was searching for any clue to the location he could find.

The steady progression from beautiful landscape to a ravaged earth chilled Ashley to her core. She felt Rafe shift closer behind her, disturbed too by what the painting was depicting. In front of her, Blythe and Daryl were holding hands. Ashley felt sorry for Blythe; she hadn't been born into this duality of worlds like she and Daryl had. Or drafted into it like Rafe. Watching the painting turn into an ugly portrayal of death and decay, Ashley couldn't help but wonder what not knowing this reality would be like. Utopia, maybe? To be blind to the demonic underbelly reaching out to touch humanity and lead them down a darker path. But that meant being blind to the angelic forces that watched over them and shone the light to illuminate a more peaceful track. Ashley couldn't imagine what kind of life that would be—to not *know*.

Whatever Kieran was seeing and projecting in the magick painting was something Ashley had never dealt with before. Judging by Eli's face, it wasn't something he had much dealing with either. *New territory for all of us, then.*

Nobody moved. All eyes were fixed on the painting, frozen in horror as the canvas poured forth a river of blood, spilling over the frame's edge. The force of the flow threatened to engulf the room.

And then it stilled and the painting reverted back to the calm seascape once more.

Merlo turned to face them all while Dina began letting light back into the room. Numb from it all, Ashley absently remembered to stop her recording.

Rafe was the first one to speak. "Now I understand why no one suggested popcorn for the show. And after seeing that little performance played out in a rural setting, I propose never to set foot out of Chicago again." She stood up. "I think I need some fresh air."

Blythe followed her. "Wait for me."

Eli and Virgil disappeared as soon as Kieran began to regain lucidity. Ashley and Daryl shared a pointed look.

"I guess that's my cue to go hit the maps and find that place. If it even exists," Daryl said.

Ashley remained behind with Merlo and Kieran. Kieran looked around the room.

"Are we going to start this thing or what?" she asked.

Ashley marveled at the power of the painting. A nightmarish vision of death and destruction had grown from the inoffensive seascape. An apocalyptic scenario. Ashley hoped Eli knew someone *higher* up that could explain it all to them.

If that was just the starter for what Kieran had to show them, Ashley feared what the main event would reveal.

CHAPTER TWENTY

The kitchen table had been set for a late lunch and there was a rare moment of normality for everyone. Trinity had found a sun spot to lie in and was flat on her back, legs akimbo, basking in the warmth.

Oh to be that cat. Kieran watched Trinity snooze off a meal of fresh chicken and kibble. Her gaze then fell back to the phone she had grasped in her hand. Ashley's phone. Kieran had watched her session with the painting and couldn't believe what she had seen. No matter how many times she watched it, she was still in denial. It was like something straight out of a nightmare and it had, according to Merlo's expert opinion, come from Kieran's subconscious.

"All I'm saying is I'm glad that piece of art wasn't delving into my head. Especially after the scrambling it got after that damned demon Armitage tried to cave my skull in. I mean, God knows what's rattling around in there." Rafe waved her knife in Merlo's direction. "Is it only the dark side of the brain it shows or can just anything pop up on the canvas?"

"You worried your sexcapades will end up emblazoned in that painting, Rafe?" Blythe asked around a mouthful of salad.

"It would be more entertaining than cable," Ashley said under her breath.

Daryl captured Kieran's attention. "And you have no memory of what happened at all?"

Kieran shook her head. "None whatsoever." She shoved the phone back in Ashley's direction. "And I think I could have done without seeing it at all. My head is screwed up enough as it is without me knowing that kind of vision is in there."

"Dina, you're our resident Seer. What do you make of it?" Daryl asked. "I mean, I have dreams so I know what that particular vision would mean to me, but I'm interested in what's your take on it."

"What do *you* think it's telling us?" Dina asked her.

"I view it as a premonition, a sign of things to come. But it was also very visual, very dramatic, yet not entirely *real*. I take that to mean it was a warning, something like this *could* happen. But it's not set in stone. It can be changed."

Dina nodded. "We saw no people, just a farmhouse, the crops, the lay of the land."

Daryl agreed. "That's what I got. We saw a *location* as much as we saw what happened there. Virgil and I are searching to see if this place exists, but we have a lot of ground to cover."

Kieran watched them all plan their next course of action. She knew what they were waiting for. They needed her to "turn." She didn't know if she could cope with another possession. Every time it happened, she lost another piece of herself in the process. She had so little of her former self left to cling on to.

"You're going to need to see what I see, aren't you? Not the farmland and the end of the world visions, but what I see when I look through that something else's eyes?"

Ashley nodded. "That's exactly what we need to see for ourselves." She sat next to Kieran and squeezed Kieran's knee under the table. "You won't be alone this time. We'll be right there with you, and we make quite a formidable team. You won't ever be alone again in that state."

Kieran noticed that Merlo had been very quiet during their meal. She sat at Kieran's right, so Kieran nudged her foot. "You're very quiet, Dr. Blue."

Merlo jumped and her wandering attention seemed to snap back to the room. "I'm sorry. I am just going over some things in my head."

"Wondering if your hospital has enough rooms to fit us all in?" Rafe said.

Merlo smiled at her. "No. I think I'd need to open an entire new wing to house us all." She turned to Kieran. "I was wondering if we could talk, just you and me."

"Doctor to patient?"

"One friend to another," Merlo amended.

Kieran nodded, wondering what was so important that Merlo

needed to speak to her alone. Merlo's use of the word *friend* made her chest tighten. Not for the first time did Kieran regret that they hadn't met under better circumstances. Kieran caught herself. This was a woman who had lived hundreds, maybe even thousands, of years.

I must look very insignificant to her. After all she must have seen and lived through. And the people she must have met and fallen in love with. What could I bring that would brush all that history aside? She's an empath and a renowned doctor in her field, and I'm a possessed patient with a very noticeable death wish. Not exactly a match made in heaven.

Kieran could see Merlo engaging with Daryl in conversation. All the women at the table had powers, formidable powers, fighting for good against demons. Kieran felt woefully unmatched beside them. She was being watched twenty-four/seven to keep her alive. What use was she ever going to be?

She pushed her plate aside. Merlo turned back to her.

"When you're ready we can go take a walk in the gardens. They're quite pretty this time of year."

"And are probably better viewed from ground level than two stories up like last time," Rafe said.

Kieran let out a laugh. She didn't know who was the more startled—herself, or the rest of the room. It felt good, unfamiliar, but so good.

❖

Her gardens always brought Merlo a sense of peace after a grueling day at the hospital. She steered Kieran toward a small gazebo so they could sit. She breathed in the multitude of scents from all the different flowers and let herself embrace the tranquility. She closed her eyes to center herself.

"God, it must be bad if you're having to psych yourself up to talk to me." Kieran sat back against the bench and stretched her legs out in front of her.

"Kieran, do you trust me?" Merlo asked. She received an odd look in return but Kieran nodded.

"Yes, you know I do. I trusted you in the hospital and I trust you here in your home. I might not have wanted the help you offered me, but I do trust you, Merlo. I trust you with my life more than I trust myself with it. So what do you need to ask or tell me?"

Merlo looked her straight in the eyes. "I need you to meet the angels that are here to help you." She startled when Kieran jumped from her seat and rounded on her.

"No! I won't do it." Kieran started to walk away, but Merlo grabbed at her arm to stop her.

"Why not?"

"Because if I acknowledge their existence, then all the other things I'm seeing are real too." Kieran wouldn't meet Merlo's eyes. "I don't think I'm ready to do that."

"Kieran, you're surrounded by women with extraordinary powers. There's someone who told you that they could navigate time, and I can attest to that because that's how she hid me from the demons in Cragon's office. And I'm a Neverage! I've lived through more wars than you were ever taught about." Merlo ran a hand through her hair. "You can take all that but not the angels? Please tell me why."

"To be honest, the fact that you're the cougar to beat all cougars is astonishing, to say the least." Kieran let Merlo pull her back to her seat. "I've spent so much time trapped in my head seeing these demons. I understand that you think angels are the good guys, but to me they are just as terrifying. Especially how the demons talk about them."

"You need not to listen to demons, as hard as that may be. We don't have the time for me to debate the whole good versus evil thing with you because the second you start to experience your possession, we need to get the angels involved. There's nothing I can do to change that. It's just how it has to be."

Kieran rested her elbows on her knees and hid her face in her hands. "Merlo, I was raised by a mother who told me that angels and demons were never to be trusted. I had it drilled into me every minute of every day. Once I was old enough to understand her, I was certain she was an atheist, but that would have been easier. She believed in a deity; she just cursed Him as much as she cursed my father for leaving us before I was even born."

Kieran had never talked about her family before. "Did your father die?"

Kieran shrugged. "I have no idea. I never met him, and all I knew from my mother was that he left her pregnant with a child she never wanted. She used to describe him, less than favorably, as a handsome devil. She'd get this faraway look and say she could see him in my features sometimes. It was never a compliment and always accompanied by a punishment for something I hadn't even done. She hated him. By the time I was old enough to ask why, she was already bringing an endless stream of men into our home. I learned very quickly to hide in my own room and cover my ears."

"That is not the childhood I'd have wished for you."

"Why she expected so much from him I'll never know. I'm guessing she'd hoped he was more than a one-night stand judging by how much she talked about him. She did say he must have been heading to join a seminary because he kept saying she was his last hope while he was fucking her. Said he kept blaming God, so of course she did too." Kieran shifted in her seat, clearly uncomfortable sharing this. "What will the angels do to me?"

"They'll never harm you, Kieran, and that's a promise. It's just that they'll need your cooperation before you're possessed and not in your right mind. We need to see what you see."

"I realize I have to do this because this was why you got me out of the hospital in the first place, but what will happen to me?"

"Daryl says Virgil has a unique way of sharing information. She didn't go into detail, something about having to see it to believe it. But it's something he shares with her and she doesn't look any worse the wear for it."

Kieran sighed. "None of this is going to go away until I do it, so I guess I have to agree. But I have years of being indoctrinated by a mother who didn't want me; she just wanted the man who got her pregnant with me. To say she was obsessed would be an understatement."

"I'm sorry, Kieran. I wish there was another way to do this that didn't frighten you so much."

"I wish I could say I'd have been happier in ignorance, but that doesn't change the fact that I am seeing these things and something that gets inside me wants me to die. And then, when I look at it another way," Kieran gifted Merlo with a beautiful smile that was so sad it almost broke Merlo's heart, "I wouldn't have met you. And that would have been a dreadful shame. I just wish we could have met before my delusions and this apparent death wish I have hanging over me."

"I'd have liked that too."

"Do you think Dina could find a time for us? One with less demon possession and more wine and fine dining?"

"No amount of time traveling can alter the fact I'm a Neverage," Merlo said. Hers was an age gap that could never be breached.

"Merloina," Kieran said, and Merlo teared up at her trying so hard to get the accents in her name just right, "in the scheme of things, your being a Neverage is the least of my problems." She reached for Merlo's hand tentatively as if fearing Merlo would snatch hers away. Merlo laced her fingers between Kieran's and held on tight. "Promise me you won't leave me alone with them when all this goes down."

"I'll be right by your side. As will all the others."

"I know. But they are here for their own agendas. I think you're the only one truly here for me."

"You are my patient…" Merlo didn't know who she was trying to remind, herself or Kieran.

"I was sprung from the hospital by a band of mad women. I am not your patient anymore."

"The timing for this…" Merlo waved her free hand between them, "*us*, is really awful."

"Yeah, I know. But I'm sure your friend Dina would say that time is precious when you're running on the borrowed kind."

"When all this is over…"

"Do you think I'll be in my right mind by then? Because I can be very smooth when not possessed."

Merlo laughed at Kieran's self-assuredness. Kieran's demeanor changed and grew more somber.

"Or do you think I'll be totally taken over by whatever has a hold on me?"

Merlo couldn't answer her. She had no idea what fate lay in store for any of them, let alone Kieran. She didn't possess Dina's gift for foresight, and Dina was remaining tight-lipped about what she had seen. Everything had to play out according to fate. She knew Kieran was waiting for her to answer, so she chose her words with care.

"I think you're going to be just fine."

Kieran smiled, obviously not believing her for a second. "That's my shrink talking. What do *you* think?"

"I think we're both heading into something neither of us has ever experienced, and believe me, I've experienced a lot."

"Not much call for demon hunting in Atlantis?" Kieran playfully bumped their shoulders.

Merlo was grateful for her trying to lighten the mood. "No. I was too busy studying to be a healer by my mother's side. It was only when I was forced to flee the island that I realized the world was a much larger place than I had envisioned. And filled with more things than I could have imagined. Then my learning began all over again."

"Would you tell me more about Atlantis? I've read speculation and theories. It would be nice to hear it from someone who was actually there."

Merlo squeezed Kieran's fingers. "I'd love to. I'm on night watch tonight with you. We'll consider my tales your bedtime story." She laughed at the disgruntled face Kieran gave her.

"I could sleep by myself. I'm a big girl now." There was an obvious bite to Kieran's comment even though she tried to rein it in.

"Yes, but one with demonic suicidal tendencies. Forgive me for wanting to keep you around for a little while longer."

"Because I'm the key to all this," Kieran grumbled.

"No. Because I believe the world would be a darker place without you in it."

Kieran's lips quirked in a small smile. "That's the nicest thing anyone has said to me in the longest time."

"You've been hanging around with the wrong kinds of people."

"Who knew I needed to get possessed and be surrounded by demon hunters to finally get paid compliments?"

"There has to be an easier way," Merlo said, hating that they had met under these dire circumstances but ever so grateful they had.

"I've never done anything by half." Kieran lifted Merlo's hand to her lips and pressed a kiss on her knuckles. "Go on. Call your angels forth. Let's get this meet and greet over with before I change my mind and chicken out."

Merlo didn't waste a moment. She called out Ashley's name.

"You knew I'd agree?" Kieran leveled a frown at her.

"I know you're amazing and would see sense eventually."

"There's that damned shrink talking again."

"Just be thankful I'm not charging you for all this."

Merlo could tell Kieran forced herself to remain in her seat when all her instincts were telling her to run. She caught sight of Ashley walking toward her with a white-winged angelic being on either side of her. Merlo leaned into Kieran and squeezed her knee just enough to stop Kieran from running.

"Angels," Kieran muttered under her breath. "Angels before me, demons inside me. When do I get to wake up and face reality once more?" Kieran was gripping the edge of the seat so hard Merlo was amazed she didn't shatter the wood.

"What am I supposed to do? Kneel before them? Bow my head in deference? Shake their hand? Can you even touch one?" Kieran's breath started to come out in short, rapid pants.

"Just breathe, Kieran. You're in the presence of the living embodiment of all that is good and pure in the world. There's nothing to fear." She tightened her hold a touch more on Kieran's knee. "Try not to be afraid."

"Oh God, please don't tell me to envision them naked or some other psych trick."

Merlo laughed. "Actually, I was going to point out that Eli is Trinity's designated cat-sitter, if that makes you feel any better."

"He really babysits for the cat? I thought Rafe was joking."

"Not so scary after all, eh?"

"Sure," Kieran said, "what with their huge white wings and the fact they're heavenly bodies sent to earth by God. What's not to be afraid of?" She blew out a tortured breath. "Don't you leave me with them."

"I promise you, Kieran, I'm not leaving your side."

I wouldn't leave you at all if time allowed it.

CHAPTER TWENTY-ONE

Y ou know, usually when we're in a room alone together you're psychoanalyzing me and I'm refusing to talk. I think I like this much better."

Merlo smiled as Kieran stretched like a lazy panther in the large leather chair she'd commandeered in Merlo's private study. Kieran had fallen into a full-bodied stretch of limbs that caused her shirt to rise just a fraction and afford Merlo a tantalizing glimpse of pale skin. She wondered how soft that skin would feel. The pale strip that lay somewhere between the hint of defined abs and the silky softness promised of Kieran's belly mesmerized her. Merlo's need rose like a tidal wave, almost pushing her up and out from behind her desk to go lay her hands on Kieran to find out for herself. She imagined running her tongue over the muscles she could see and tracing it around the belly button that peeked above the waistband of Kieran's chinos.

"Merlo?"

Merlo looked up at the curious tone in Kieran's voice.

"Jeez, you looked like you were a million miles away." Kieran gave her a sly grin. "Or maybe a million *years*?"

"I can assure you, I am not *that* old!" She hoped her own pale skin didn't reveal how turned on she felt just by seeing Kieran's revealed midriff. She held in the groan of disappointment when Kieran sat up straighter in the seat and all tantalizing flesh was hidden from her sight.

"You look a little flushed. I thought it was just me." Kieran fanned at her face. "Can you open a window or something, please?"

Merlo did so, glad of the opportunity to turn her back on Kieran so she couldn't read her needs that were no doubt plastered all over her face. She welcomed the cool evening air as it wafted in through the window, bringing with it the scent of the garden. "Better?"

Kieran nodded. "So, you were going to tell me about Atlantis. Unless this is another ambush to meet more of the heavenly hosts that seem to congregate around most of your visitors here."

"No, I've thrown you in at the angelic deep end enough for today." She sat back behind her desk. "Though you coped very well, considering."

"Considering the last time I came face-to-face with an angel I almost screamed the place down?" Kieran tugged at the seam on her chinos. "I can't tell you how much I wanted to do that again today. They are frightening creatures, Merlo. All huge wings and so white. I can feel the power radiating off them. It's like being touched by an energy blast. I know I shouldn't be frightened by them, but there's something deep within me that says I *have* to be. I can't explain it."

"Like I said, you did very well. Which is a blessing because you're going to have to deal with them as much as their human companions."

"I'd rather stick to dealing with Trinity. She's less nerve-wracking and not a part of this craziness I seem to be embroiled in." Kieran slapped her palms on her knees. "Enough of that. I want to know more about you. You said I'd get a bedtime story. It's almost my bedtime, so come on, Merloina Bluetralis, spill *your* truth."

Merlo unlocked a drawer in her desk and removed a small wooden box from inside. "When I left the island I carried with me just a few belongings. The largest was the painting, rolled up for easier transport back then. This," she held up the box, "held my more personal possessions that I dared not leave behind. I had no idea what would happen to the island. I was always hoping I'd get to go back. Back to my family and back to my life there." She brought the box over to Kieran and took a seat in the chair beside hers. "But I never did get to return home."

"Are you the only one that escaped?"

"I've never come across another like me, another Neverage. But who knows. I'd hate to think that just I escaped while Atlantis was left in the hands of those who couldn't see beyond their own gains."

"You said you went back to where it had been?"

"I did, just the once. I was on a boat that sailed right over the sea where my island had once stood proud. I stood clutching the railing, searching the water for any remnants visible from above, but there was nothing. A part of me wanted to hear the voices from below, calling me back. Like a fool, I put myself at risk to reach my hand over the side of the boat, and I felt the water that covered my home. But no ghostly hands reached back to clutch my fingers to let me know they were safe. All I felt were the cool waters that kept their secrets buried deep beneath them. And from my many years of keeping tabs on deep-sea expeditions to find the 'fabled Atlantis,' there is very little left to show it ever existed. My home is now a myth, lost in time."

And lost to me.

Shaking off the morose thoughts that threatened to pull her under as deep as her island home lay, Merlo lifted out a small stone. She held it out for Kieran to hold.

Kieran cradled it in her palm as she studied it. The stone was a milky white, shot through with red streaks and peppered with golden flakes. "What is this?"

"That was what washed up on our coastline. As a child, I used to collect as many as I could from the shore and rush home to find my grandfather. He was an alchemist and he could pull the jeweled red and gold veins out of the stone and weave it into elaborate jewelry for the elite. It was very fashionable and very decadent." Merlo ran her fingertip over the smooth stone. "He let me keep this one, to always remember the journey it had taken from sea to shore, and how hard he had to work to have it release its treasure. He told me, 'sometimes you have to journey long and hard to reach the place where your true beauty and purpose can be recognized.'" She smiled. "For many years I took that missive to heart and traveled as far and wide as I could to find my own place."

Kieran held the stone up to the light. "Wow. I bet his jewelry was beautiful."

Merlo reached into the box again. This time she pulled out a ring, fashioned from the red and gold and shining like fire. "He made this for me, but it was always too large for my fingers. He'd just wink at me every time I begged him to make it smaller. 'One day it'll be worn,' he'd say, and then he'd go back to his work." She slipped it onto her ring finger, but the jewelry was still too large. She handed it to Kieran, who held it up to the light.

"Can I see leaves and trees fashioned in the strands?" Kieran asked, looking like she was straining her eyes to see closer still.

"Yes, it was a popular pattern back then and my favorite. So I'll never understand why he didn't make the ring to fit me." Merlo laughed. "He was a strange old man, he always had 'reasons.' I never got to find out the reason for this, though."

She pulled out a small leather-bound notebook. "And this is my story."

"You wrote a diary?"

"I wrote all I remembered from being born on the island to the day I was chased off it on a small boat and told to just go, to get as far away as I could, and not come back." She ran her hands over the old familiar binding. "This is the story of Atlantis and what really happened to it."

Kieran stared at the book. "It's not something you could publish without revealing yourself, I'm guessing?" She nodded in understanding when Merlo shook her head. "Can you tell me what happened? Why you were sent away?"

Merlo's eyes never shifted from the cover of her journal. Inside was the truth behind Atlantis's fate. So she shared it for the first time with someone who would eventually age and die and the secret die with her while Merlo lived on.

"Let me share with you my story. Welcome to Atlantis. This," she held up the journal, "and myself are all that remains to tell its tale."

❖

Kieran hung on her every word as Merlo brought the past to life.

The picture Merlo painted was of an advanced island, filled with writers and artists, and people of advanced learning. A genius race, with boundless curiosity of the world they lived in. Artists whose paintings came to life in the presence of empaths. Writers who could capture the fate of the future in weighty tomes but, for some reason, never had revealed to them the cruel fate that would befall Atlantis itself. There were scientists who patented cures and natural remedies for just about any and every human ailment. A civilization that was wiped from the face of the earth, banished from existence, in their quest for knowledge of what lay all around them. Their higher intelligence and mental acuity didn't save them. Their insatiable curiosity proved to be the downfall that killed them all. All but one. Merlo.

"So your parents sent you away weeks before it all went down?"

"Yes, my parents were part of the scientific community, and they had already warned the leaders that what they were allowing to be done was something that was best left untampered with. My parents and a few others could see the dangers of drilling direct into the earth's core, but no one would listen to them. There was this fantastic scientific breakthrough right beneath their feet just begging to be discovered. No one wanted to hear reasons why they might be best to stop their work. All they saw was that the earth was a big mystery waiting to be solved. So why not dig through to its core to see whether the hollow earth theory was a reality? Forget being the first man on the moon. Stepping foot *inside* the earth and populating it was going to be the discovery of all discoveries. Of course, the fact the earth is a giant ball of gasses didn't factor into their calculations. No one knew; it was uncharted territory. But some of the scientists had a healthy fear of how foolhardy it was to drill through the layers of the earth to investigate."

"Wow. No wonder so many people are up in arms over this fracking business all over the world." Kieran suddenly felt uneasy. "Here's hoping history doesn't repeat itself. I just can't get over how your parents stuck you on a boat and pointed you out into the sea. And you were how old?"

"The age you see in my appearance today. I was thirty-three years old. More than old enough to see how foolhardy the scientists were being, but I wasn't of any rank or importance to make them listen. Not even my being an empath was enough to get through to them that I had a bad feeling about what they were proposing to do." Merlo's eyes took on a faraway look. "I begged my parents to come with me, but they chose to remain behind to try to talk sense into the other scientists. I steered my boat away from the island to go search for the help they said I needed to find for them. Or so I thought. But the farther I sailed away, the more I realized this wasn't a rescue mission. Especially when I found a month's worth of food and clothing hidden in the boat and a note from my parents telling me not to return, no matter how safe the island appeared."

Kieran couldn't imagine what that felt like. Banished from your home, sent away by the people you loved, and not knowing why you couldn't return or if you even could. She wiped a hand across her forehead. She felt hot, and sweat was starting to bead on her skin. She looked outside at the darkening sky. Surely it should be getting cooler by now? She turned her attention back to Merlo, desperate not to miss a thing.

"I found land miles away, after weeks of sailing alone. I remember landing at a small dock and being met by the people, all welcoming me into their homes. I was an adventurer, and they wanted to hear of my travels across the great seas from lands unknown. I'd soon found a place to stay and a job to do among them. Then one night something compelled me to take a walk. I climbed up the highest ridge and waited for the dawn to rise. The sea was a beautiful tableau of pinks and oranges as the sun rose to greet the day. And then I felt it. The ground shook beneath my feet and seemed to take hold of the whole area. From my vantage point, I could see for miles across the ocean, and my heart stopped as I witnessed an enormous black cloud begin to rise from over the horizon. It spewed upward as if a volcano had erupted, but I knew there was nothing volcanic where that smoke was coming from. It spread across the horizon like a blanket, cutting off the daylight as it stretched into the sky. In that instant, I felt my home blink out of existence. Gone. Silenced. Nothing but an inky black plume that sparked and crackled like it was filled with lightning that rose ever upward as if seeking divine assistance from the heavens." Merlo looked up and smiled sadly at Kieran. "But no one was listening."

Kieran reached over to clamp Merlo's hand in sympathy. "I'm so sorry."

Merlo brushed away a tear that had escaped. "It was a *very* long time ago."

"True, but it must still be very lonely for you. Being the last of that race and never really knowing what happened in the end. Kind of puts my complaining about demons in my head into perspective." She winked at Merlo, hoping to cheer her up a little.

Merlo took a deep breath and seemed to calm herself. "Well, I can't get Atlantis back, but I promise to do everything in my power to make sure you get some peace of mind back in your life."

Kieran ran her thumb over the ring she still held on to. "I'd like that. I wouldn't know what to do with it after this length of time, but it would be nice to have the choice given back to me." She held out the ring and Merlo placed it and the stone reverently back inside the box. Kieran felt hot and bothered all of a sudden. She caught at her breath. "Where did that breeze go? I'm stifling."

Merlo pointed to the curtains moving. "It's still here and getting cooler by the minute." She examined Kieran closely and placed her hand on Kieran's forehead. "You're burning up."

Oh no, not again. "It's too soon for me to go again. It's barely been days since my last episode."

"You said they were quickening."

"What if you can't see what I see? What if this time the urge to kill myself works? You'll never know what all this means in here." She rapped her knuckles on her skull. "Blythe says I'm a key. What if I can't open the door for you all?"

Merlo grabbed Kieran's face to sooth her babbling. "Shhh, it's going to be okay. You're among friends this time and you have everyone on your side now. You can do this."

"But do what?" Kieran asked. She knew she had a purpose, but once she was possessed she wasn't even present.

"Just let it happen. Let them come. You're not alone. We'll be waiting right by your side. For we are legion too."

CHAPTER TWENTY-TWO

There was something odd about the silence Kieran woke up to. The room was still dark, and she had no idea why she had roused from what had been a deep sleep. Her eyes grew accustomed to the room so she could pick out the shadows of the furniture through the slither of moonlight that peeked through the drapes. She tensed as she listened for the usual sound of breathing beside her from whoever had drawn the short straw to sit with her through the night. There was none. Kieran turned her head on her pillow to look toward the designated babysitting chair. There was no one in it. Kieran's eyes narrowed.

"I know you're there. I can feel you. Show yourself, please, so I don't add talking to myself to my crazy list."

Slowly, a shimmering ball of light appeared. It flickered almost tentatively in revealing itself. It grew until it coalesced into the body of a man. A man with huge white wings. He was sitting in the chair, one leg resting over the other leg's knee. He smiled and nodded to her. His glow lit up the room so Kieran could see as clearly as if it were daytime. She was amused to see the light around him dim as he toned down his brightness for her squinting eyes.

"Hi, Virgil. We didn't get a chance to talk earlier since Eli and Ashley dominated the conversation. You're Daryl's angel, right?"

Virgil nodded and touched his lips.

"Are you telling me to shut up and go back to sleep or that you don't speak?"

He just nodded, so Kieran guessed he meant her second question. She signed to him and made sure to speak clearly in case he could lip-read. She'd learned sign language for her deaf clients at the practice.

"Do you use sign language?"

He shook his head. Kieran dropped her hands.

"So how do you communicate? Or are you the strong and silent type?"

He made as if to rise, checked himself, and looked politely at Kieran for permission. She nodded. Virgil leaned down very slowly so as not to spook her. Kieran froze as his face moved closer to hers. He rested his forehead to her own, and Kieran gasped as her head filled with sound. It was a low chorus of a million voices all singing out in harmony.

One voice rang out loud and clear above it all.

I mean you no harm.

He withdrew, and Kieran missed the comforting voices that had filled her head and shut out her own thoughts.

"I remember now. Daryl said you were an Impressor, and that you didn't exactly speak, but you…" Kieran racked her tired mind for the answer, "you could sometimes draw on the conscious collective and have them form your words for you if you need them to? That's very cool and thank you for sharing it with me."

His smile was beatific and Kieran couldn't help but return it. "You're the one who's going to help them see what I see." She considered him. "Not sure how you're going to do that, and I don't think I want to know." She sat up against the headboard and wrapped her arms around her knees. "Do you think you can take this away from me? Whatever is inside me?"

Virgil seesawed his hand. Kieran puffed out an annoyed breath.

"Oh, that's so reassuring, thank you." She looked at the clock on her bedside table and was surprised she'd only slept two hours. "Do your directives in watching over me allow me to go to the kitchen because I have a raging headache and would kill for a cup of that herbal tea Merlo has in stock."

Virgil gestured for her to get up. Kieran tiptoed down the hallway trying not to wake anyone else up. She made her way down the stairs and into the kitchen. She gestured to Virgil to see if he wanted a cup, but he shook his head. Trying to be as quiet as possible, Kieran began searching the cabinets for any sign of headache pills. She came up empty-handed.

"Why do I get the feeling Merlo has cleared the house of any kind of medication in case I find it and use it for an attempt?" she muttered.

The kettle boiled, and Kieran shut it off. She poured the hot water over the tea bag and watched the leaves color the water. She rubbed at her temples, then sat at the table to stir her tea. Her head felt full of pressure, like something was squeezing her from the inside. The irony of that didn't escape her for all the pain she was in. Virgil moved a little closer. He held up his hands and mimicked rubbing his head.

"You want to massage my head?" Kieran couldn't help how incredulous she sounded. "Is this an angel thing? Do you all come preprogrammed with healing hands?"

Virgil gave her a disgruntled look and, much to her amazement, pretended to be a robot. Kieran didn't know which was more freakish, the fact she had an angel offering to ease her headache or the fact he was tottering around like he was a white-winged version of C-3PO. Kieran had to chuckle. "Okay, I apologize. You know I'm nervous around you guys, don't you?"

He stopped and nodded at her somberly.

"I'm already touched by demons. Are you sure you want to touch *me*?"

He flexed his hands and gestured for Kieran to turn in her seat and face him. He stood before her, magnificent in his pristine white suit. Close up, his radiance was almost blinding, so Kieran closed her eyes against the light. She still jumped when she felt his touch on her. It wasn't like being touched by human hands. She felt a tingling like static that brushed against her skin. It penetrated into her head and was as painful as the headache itself.

She willed herself to relax, remembering all that Merlo had told her. He began to massage in small concentric circles, and the tension in her shoulders dropped. She lost herself in the peace that flowed in and around her through his fingertips. She fought to open her eyes, but she'd been fighting so long that the utter bliss of having no pain made her inexplicably drowsy. Her tea untouched, Kieran felt herself slip into a light doze. She was awake just enough to be aware of what was happening. Strong arms lifted her up and cradled her gently. Virgil carried her upstairs and laid her back in bed like a sleepy child.

"Thank you," she said.

He pressed his forehead one more time to hers, and the multitude of voices lulled her once again. The heavenly choir's soothing presence accompanied her into a much deeper sleep, for once feeling safe under the protective gaze of an angel.

❖

The swiftness of Kieran's possession surprised everyone. The delirium fell upon her within hours and they got to see just how much Kieran suffered. All had been distressed at how much of Kieran was lost as the madness clouded her mind.

"Isn't there anything we can do for her?" Ashley asked, leaning against the doorframe of Kieran's bedroom, where she was for her own safety.

Merlo shook her head. "Medication won't touch this. Even though my touch can ease some of it, we need her to go through this. We need your team and the angels to get your answers from her. Then we have to try to rid her of these demons." She looked toward the bed and lowered her voice. "If they will even leave her. This is unlike anything I have seen before."

"It's a first for me too, but Eli is bringing us some of his friends who are more knowledgeable. I hunt demons in their earthly shapes, not when they infest someone with their evil via transference."

"At least she's a little less terrified of your angel companion now."

"Yes, and I'm told she has quite the rapport with Virgil. Eli told me she was talking with him last night."

Merlo looked relieved. "Oh, that's good news. I wonder if it's because he doesn't speak. I can't imagine what it's like for her, to have demons trapped in her head and to have angels manifest before her."

"How long do you think before she's ready for us to..." Ashley hesitated, searching for the right words. "What are we going to do to her? Invade her consciousness, see into her head, seek out her dreams? It's so out of my realm of demonology."

"From what I've been told from Daryl, we are going to be observers. I can't begin to imagine what that entails. And I gather Virgil is somehow involved."

Ashley grinned a little and Merlo narrowed her eyes at her. "What? What does that face mean? Do you know something I don't know?"

Ashley nodded. "I know what he does for Daryl. I just don't know how he's going to include the rest of us. Guess we're all in for a surprise when he starts."

Merlo moved closer to Kieran's bedside. Kieran had curled into as small a ball as she could physically make herself. She had tucked herself underneath the blankets, totally hidden from sight. Every so often, a strange low rumbling escaped.

"The growling is demonic," Ashley said. "From my studies of possession, the vocal cords are part of the first stages of the takeover. The facial distortions are a later stage. We're going to have to get her out from under there soon so we can prepare her the second she is taken. I'm going to call in Eli and Virgil. They might be able to pinpoint the moment she 'leaves.'"

Ashley had never had much to do with demon possession. She'd always been too busy hunting down the physical demons that walked the earth. She was intrigued that this was a multiple possession and couldn't help but wonder what that meant in terms of getting both out of Kieran.

Kieran was unique in so many fascinating ways. The lump in the bed seemed to be trying to burrow through the mattress. She wondered what was going on in Kieran's mind. Or if Kieran was even there anymore. Watching Kieran struggle with the pain and gasping for breath, Ashley hadn't been able to watch her as an impassive observer. It had torn at her soul to watch Kieran fight so hard to keep the tenuous hold on her sanity for just a few more minutes before her eyes had glowed as she'd slipped further away. Merlo had turned pleading eyes to them all and begged for them to help her. Ashley had assured her they'd do their best. She just hoped their best was good enough.

A deep growl rumbled from the bed. The bed seemed to shake with a tremor that grew in intensity.

Rafe appeared by Ashley's side and whispered in her ear. "If her head starts spinning like Linda Blair's you guys can exorcise her on your own. I've just had this suit dry-cleaned. I'm not being vomited on." She moved a little more into the room and watched as the bed shook. "Eli and Silent Bob are downstairs. They want to talk to you before they wrangle Kieran down to the living room."

Ashley nodded, then gestured for Rafe to stay with Merlo. She hurried downstairs to seek out the angels. Eli wasted no time the minute he saw her.

"It's time. Kieran needs to be secured quickly."

Another angel appeared by his side. This one was in similar attire to Eli and Virgil, but his forehead was way more pronounced. It lent an odd shape to his otherwise handsome features. Ashley was sure she could see his veins pulsing under the skin. Bright, split-second flashes of light danced across his skin as if he were emitting electricity. More angels appeared in the living room from out of thin air. Ashley seldom got to see so many. Her usual dealings with the angels were exclusive to Eli. She bowed to them, honored to be in their presence.

"Child, you need to bring the other to us now," an angel instructed.

Ashley looked at Eli. "I might need your help to wrestle her out from under the covers. The last time this happened to her, the hospital orderlies had her restrained to the bed rails. I know she's no bigger than I am, but she's got the strength of demons inside her."

Eli and Virgil fell into step with Ashley as she led the way back upstairs. The sounds from under the covers were continuous now. It reminded Ashley of the deep growling of a rabid dog, snarling and sending out a warning to stay back. She was cautious as she approached the bed. Ashley wanted to damn Rafe for putting scenes from *The Exorcist* in her head. She feared the bed was going to lift off the floor when she got near.

"Kieran? We need to move you now." Ashley grabbed a handful of the sheets and peeled them back.

What met Ashley's eyes wasn't Kieran.

Ashley gasped at the contorted features that revealed the demon inside her. "Oh God, Kieran," Ashley whispered. She reached out a hand to touch, but Kieran rounded on her like a wounded animal. She screamed when she saw the angels and unfolded herself from her cramped position. Her hands clenched so tight into fists that her nails had broken through the skin on her palms. The blood began to drip down her hands and fell to the white sheets beneath her. Her head thrashed back and forth as if something inside was searching for an escape. Her eyes turned to Merlo, and for a second, Kieran's face fought for dominance over the demons inside. Her voice rang out, loud and clear.

"Merlo! Help me!"

The plea hung in the air as her face hardened and lengthened. Her bones cracked as a new form molded her features into its own image.

Eli and Virgil grabbed her and carried her down the stairs. Kieran kicked and howled all the way down. The noise was unnatural—the amalgamation of every evil tongue that had a voice. The demonic screams blended with the fading remnants of Kieran's last pitiful calls for help.

Merlo started to sob. Ashley gathered her into her arms. They didn't have a moment to lose. "She's going to be all right. After this, we're going to fight to get her back. She's seen enough."

They placed Kieran in the center of the living room. All the furniture had been pushed back to create a large free space currently filled by the angels. The angels formed a circle around Kieran. Rafe, Blythe, Daryl, and Dina were all standing with an angel at their backs. Ashley guided Merlo to her spot, and then Ashley took her own place in front of Eli. She looked over her shoulder at him.

"Something new for us to try." She tried not to sound quite as nervous as she was feeling.

He just smiled. "Indeed."

The only noise in the room was the furious growling rising from Kieran's chest. She snarled and bit at the angels holding her in place. Her face was still contorting. Eli let out a curious sound that had Ashley turn to look at him. He never acknowledged her; he just stared at Kieran. By the look on his face, something had spooked him beyond the demon rising.

Virgil moved away from Daryl, leaving another angel to take his place. Ashley noticed Eli did the same.

"What…?" she asked before the realization struck her. *Oh fuck, no!*

Virgil took his place behind Kieran and then *impressed* himself into Kieran's skull. There was something incredibly disturbing about watching his head sink into the back of Kieran's. Kieran's eyes sparkled for a moment as his connection was made. Virgil held out his hands and the angels on each side took hold. All the angels linked hands, and Ashley had a horrible feeling this was about to get even more unsettling. She caught the look Rafe tossed her way and read her lips.

No fucking way!

Ashley didn't get a chance to say anything back. The angel with the high forehead gestured for the other angels to step forward and repeat what Virgil had done on the rest of the humans. Ashley felt Rafe's hand seek out her own, and they squeezed each other tight.

Ashley didn't know what she was going to feel and braced herself. She'd hoped that Daryl and Virgil would have been the only ones *impressed* and that there'd have been some magical way to have the visions "broadcast" to the rest of them. She hadn't expected what was about to happen. She took one last look around as, one by one, the other Impressors leaned forward and pressed their heads into Blythe, then Daryl, Dina, and Merlo. Ashley couldn't turn her head to see it happen to Rafe because she felt something touch the back of her head and then her senses were no longer her own. It wasn't so much painful as just uncomfortable, but suddenly, her sight was a hundred times sharper. She could see everything in the minutest detail. Dust motes floated by and looked as if they were the size of a pool ball. Ashley felt overwhelmed by how much larger the world seemed. Her respect for Daryl grew knowing that she'd lived with this since childhood.

Her eyes were directed to the angel with the high forehead. His head was vibrating and sparking brighter than ever. He leaned forward and Impressed into Virgil's skull.

Kieran's eyes closed and her screaming died down. The lead Impressor spread out his arms, and light beams flew from his fingertips, striking each of the angels' heads in turn, linking them all to what he was directing.

Ashley felt a jolt go through her like a savage blow from a steel bar. She felt her head reel with the pain, and then…she was falling so fast, down and down to God knows where. She knew she was no longer in her own mind.

She was in *Kieran's*.

It was a long, tortuous journey down into Kieran's madness, and this time she was taking everyone with her to witness it all.

Chapter Twenty-Three

K ieran screamed as the nightmare she couldn't escape began again. Trapped, with no form of her own, Kieran railed against the endless black void.

Get me out get me out get me out get me out!

It didn't matter how many times she was put through this, death would be a mercy over the feeling of existing, and yet, *not*. If this was heaven or hell, she wanted none of it.

Just let me die! End this now!

She screamed, but there was no sound from nonexistent lips. Then she felt something. A presence. Maybe more than one. She tried to look, but she had no control here. But for the first time, she heard something in the dark, whispering to her.

"Time has no hold on me, Kieran."

Kieran knew that voice. *Dina?* She had a strange feeling, more a sense, of hands reaching out to touch her. She couldn't feel them or see them, but she knew they were there. *Merlo.* She could *feel* Merlo.

"You're not alone this time. We're here," Dina assured her.

Kieran strained to hear more, but there was only silence.

Don't leave me here! Kieran shouted as loud as she imagined she could yell.

"Not in this lifetime, nor the next."

Kieran wasn't sure if she'd heard what was said or felt it in her heart. *Merlo?* She was certain that had been Merlo's voice. Kieran struggled to find her to no avail. Comforted by the knowledge her friends were close, Kieran let the void wash over her. She relaxed into it and waited for all that was to happen to just play out. It was out of her hands anyway. But this time she wasn't going to fight.

See it. Prove to me I'm not crazy. See through my eyes. Because if this is the last time I'm here, then I need someone to bear witness to Hell and its plans. Then maybe my life won't have been in vain.

"Hold on, Kieran. I'm with you."

Kieran felt Merlo's message just as light began to bleed through once more and Hell welcomed her back.

❖

"Come forth, Lucian, the one who will help me bring my light to the world. Come, sit beside me before I go back up to walk among the vermin." The voice of the Preacher left Kieran with no doubt where she was.

The Preacher's hand was firm against Lucian's shoulder. Kieran could feel it pressing Lucian to where he wanted him to go. She shuddered at the sight of the Preacher. His was the awful face that followed her into her nightmares. But Lucian? At last, Kieran could put a name to the demon whose body she was trapped in.

"How much longer will you walk the earth, Master?"

"My time is nearly here. I have sown the seeds of discord around the earth. I've maneuvered the pitiful nations into their positions against each other. They just need the fuse lit and they will blow each other apart for me. I've nurtured tyrants and funded dictators and watched their armies grow. I've set my plans in motion and waited centuries for it to come to fruition, all while moving the unsuspecting players like pieces on a game board. All I have predicted has come true. The human race is weak. They follow the loudest voice and listen not to peaceful prayers. And all the time they build their weapons and amass their monies and buy the silence of the elite while they crush the pathetic masses under their feet. And there I sit, whispering in their ears, forging them on *my* path to *my* glory. Disease, pestilence, poverty, hatred, my fingerprints are all over this world. They listen to falsehoods and elect idiots to positions of power and bring about their own destruction."

The Preacher stopped his grandiose postulating and grinned. From under the shadow of his hood, his teeth glinted in the light like those of a shark moving in for the kill. "They are like children, so easily led. So I will lead them…right into the paths of my demons. For it has been prophesied. I have seen it all come to pass. In fiery visions I have seen the slaughter I have brought above. I am the bringer of death to the human population that festers like a cancer on the earth. I have seen a glorious future for all my demons. We shall take back our birthright, for we were fashioned first, in His image."

The Preacher laughed and threw back his hood, bringing his hands up to his face. "Which our banishment altered and took away our beauty and instead fashioned us with this horrific image. Which is a beauty all of its own. I shall make us all in *my* image, and the world shall reflect our glory."

Kieran cowered at the terrifying demon that faced her. He was the embodiment of all that was evil. The Preacher was huge, at least seven feet tall. Huge black wings hung half-open on his back as if prepared for flight. They were ragged and battle worn. They had a leathery sheen, as black as crude oil. The edges were lined with sharp spikes that looked like teeth ripped from his fallen enemies. His thin skin was every shade of gray, as if he'd been fashioned from clay and was drying out in the heat of Hell. It made him appear mottled, like he was still in the process of being formed. The robe covered most of his torso but what could be seen was all sinew. His pale gray skin was almost translucent; it revealed the muscle and bones beneath. The pulse of blood through his veins was discernible. He was a living, breathing, walking x-ray. His legs were covered in fine gray hair, and huge cloven feet held him upright.

But it was his face that set him apart as the most demonic of all the demons. His head was large and misshapen, blunt cut and angular. His cheekbones were razor sharp and protruded from his face. His eyes were a fiery red, set deep into his bony eye sockets. Flames burned deep within them like an inferno. His nose was little more than nostrils that only emphasized his skeletal features more. His mouth was wide and crudely shaped; it split the lower half of his face as if added as an afterthought. When he smiled his lips pulled back to reveal teeth rotten and pitted like aged tombstones. A black tongue poked out from behind, thin and snake-like, dripping with saliva.

Two massive horns protruded from his forehead, black in color and ridged. They appeared to have been twisted and molded until fashioned to a deadly point. The Preacher was malevolence personified, his ancient body rotting, yet very much alive.

The Preacher swung around and pushed aside the rags that served as doors to his temple. It was a crude area, laid open to the elements. Above lay the fierce red sky, below was the burning heat of a ground trampled by cloven hooves.

Kieran had seen this place before. It was the Preacher's seat of power. A ramshackle dwelling elevated high in the rock mass, with a flat podium from where he could preach to the masses. Kieran followed the Preacher out to look over the landscape. The carnage terrified her. It looked like something left from a nuclear war. Broken buildings, scorched earth, destruction as far as the eye could see. The air burned her lungs, though she had no body to breathe it in. She stifled in the heat of a burning Hell. Plumes of dirty smoke rose to where lightning streaked across a sky full of blood red clouds. The clouds spilled acid rain that caused the ground to hiss as each drop landed.

The Preacher walked out onto his stage, and the demon Lucian that Kieran found herself confined in walked beside him like a faithful pet.

"Look at my army."

Kieran was able to see the seething mass of demonic forms inhabiting Hell. There were beasts with large scaled wings that circled above their heads like vultures searching for carrion. Demons that walked on all fours, skittering like lethal spiders, Death's-head patterns emblazoned on their backs, cut out into their flesh.

"My children," the Preacher said proudly. "From the shape-shifters to the beasts. *Mine.*"

"All will serve you to the death, Master," Lucian said. "For you are one of the famed."

The Preacher's smile was cruel. He stretched his wings out in a show of power. "Banished for availing ourselves of human flesh." His eyes turned sly. "We only fucked them; it's not like we ate them. Yet we were cursed for all eternity for taking what was ours to start with, for we were the masters over those pathetic creatures." His wings cracked like a thunderbolt as he flexed them. "And I was a god. The Nephilim were my children and we were going to seed the earth and make it our own. But in His wisdom He sent forth the flood and wiped out my progeny."

"So you waited."

"Yes. I lost my children and found myself consigned to Hell. Tormented, tortured, and all while above the humans got to start again and squander the gifts they've been given. But I found a way to reach them. If I couldn't have my seed walking above then I'd plant anew."

"You seeded their dreams. You reached in to their hearts and minds."

"I may have been banished for all time, but I still possess the angelic qualities of being able to heed the humans' call. I chose to ignore the prayers for peace and instead focused my energy on cultivating the ones with their dark hearts crying out for war." He barked out an evil laugh. "And so many wars have I instigated. So many leaders and warlords who bowed their heads to my will and influence. The humans may have been created in His image, but He made the mistake of allowing them free will. Mindless automatons would have been easier to command, but the human race is so easy to corrupt. They really do have an angel and a devil seated on each shoulder. I pride myself on being the louder voice whispering in their ear."

"Your reach has been far and wide, Master. No one has been able to stop you from spreading your message."

"And then I found I could slip through the cracks here. Escape from Hell and walk above, and then all I prophesized came true. We will take back the earth for we, as the first born, are the rightful heirs." The Preacher turned and placed his hand on Lucian's shoulder. "Angels keep falling, Lucian. Temptation is something built into us because if humans aspire to be holy in thought, then why can't angels covet the basest of nature from the human race? Are we not born from the same father?"

"Weren't we supposed to be better?"

The Preacher whirled on him, fire in his eyes and his face a mask of fury. "We *were* better. We were *angels*. And now we are something far superior. We are demons, Lucian, born again of fire and brimstone, and look at us." He gestured again to the mass of demons below. "We are many and our time is coming. I have foreseen it. I will bring forth Hell on earth and take my rightful place as king over them all. This was to be my legacy from the start. My destiny."

The Preacher threw up his hands, and a loud clap of thunder struck high above their heads. A swirling black portal began forming in the sky above them. It opened, and a clear blue sky became visible.

"My power has grown, as has my hatred. I was a child of God and am owed that respect. If I can't sit by His side, then I will do everything in my power to destroy His beloved human race. They are nothing more than a failed experiment. The earth will be mine." The Preacher beat his wings and he began to rise off the ground. "And then, I shall turn my eyes to the heavens and take back what was stolen from me there. I shall wage war on heaven itself and leave white wings weeping in my wake."

The Preacher flew higher and higher until he reached the portal and was sucked through it with a deafening boom. The sky returned to its usual blood red hues. No remnant of what had been there was visible.

Hell was left to its own devices. Its king had gone to spread his havoc across the earth.

❖

Kieran's view was still on looking upward for a long moment until Lucian finally lowered his head. She wondered if he'd been making sure that the Preacher had gone. Lucian burst into action. He broke into a run and jumped off the edge of the rock. Had Kieran possessed a stomach, it would have flipped and rolled with nausea as he dove down at a breakneck speed then swooped upward, heading toward the clouds. Borne aloft on huge wings, Kieran was able to see the landscape below her. She marveled as she flew through the remnants of the destroyed buildings and brimstone covered fields.

He flew farther and farther until they left the ruins far behind to fly over a crumbling coastline that met Hell's version of a sea. It wasn't clear blue waters that flowed beneath them. It was a river of congealed blood. The stench was putrid and the liquid bubbled as it boiled from underneath. Kieran could see Lucian's shadow rippling across the surface. Huge wings reflected, a thick heavy torso, and a large head tipped with two massive curled horns like that of a ram. Kieran guessed this demon was much larger than any man she'd seen, in both height and bulk. A giant of a beast, just like the Preacher. She was curious what his face looked like. If he'd be hideous, skeletal like his master, or resemble the animal-like demons she'd seen so many times through Lucian's eyes.

Lucian landed on a rocky outcrop of an island far out in the sea. He stopped for a moment and seemed to scan the sea and air for something. Then he turned and walked around the rock until he came to where a large round stone was propped up against the rock base. With a few pushes and pulls, he managed to maneuver the stone aside to reveal a cave entrance. He stepped inside, making sure to roll the stone back to hide the cave's opening but leaving just enough of a crack so he could get back out. It afforded Kieran a fraction of light to illuminate their way. Deeper into the cave he went. There was an odd scraping noise that Kieran realized was the sound of his wings catching against the loose shale of the cave's ceiling. They broke off fragments in the cramped confines, showering Lucian with tiny pebbles that fell under his feet, pulverized to dust by his hooves.

There was the noise of rock striking rock, and a fire was alight before her eyes. The misshapen torch blazed and lit up the cave walls. Shadows danced upon the rough jagged walls that were so narrow they just let Lucian scrape through.

He stepped into a large dug-out cave area, so roughly hewn it looked as if it had been clawed out of the rock by hand. He held out the torch to light the room they now stood in.

On the walls were drawings. Not hieroglyphs of ages long since lost in time, instead these were intricate renderings almost inked into the smoothed-out rock. Someone had made sure that they could paint on these walls. It must have been a painstaking task. And what detailed artwork they had left behind in the cave.

Lucian lit up each piece and lingered, as if making sure every detail from each panel wasn't overlooked.

Kieran could see everything. The first drawing was undoubtedly angels falling from heaven and going straight to Hell. It showed them losing their white wings and being cursed with the black ones, scaled and barbed, as their forms changed from man-like to beast. Lucian waited a while, then moved to the next one. This depicted the rise of the Preacher. Kieran marveled at how his fall from grace had been depicted. He'd obviously been an angel of high rank and privilege, but hubris had been his downfall. Kieran had to admire the artwork that showed the pride-filled angelic being who had seduced human females to his bed with his handsome features and boastful lips. He was drawn as a king, surrounded by fawning subjects bowing down at his feet, gold and jewels around him, and women at his command. Images of Hell unfolded in the next piece, and the Preacher was standing higher than all the other demons, already taking his place as their master.

The next drawing was the Preacher working his magic to open portals from the underworld to grant him entrance on the earth. It featured demons let out to wreak havoc among mankind. Then the next was an endless display of demons whispering in the ears of politicians and military men as they built ever more powerful weapons. It showed the Preacher with his lips to the ears of the religious leaders seated on grandiose thrones while their feet rested on the backs of women and children cowering in fear behind them.

Another depicted earth's inhabitants in constant conflict with each other and the Preacher washing his hands in the blood that flowed upon the battlefields. What followed that was the first scene that depicted him as something other than triumphant. Kieran was astounded by its inclusion and by what it meant. It showed angels carrying off a child from out of the Preacher's reach. The knife in his hand and the altar he stood behind spoke of a sacrifice he had intended to make. The rage on his face was so expertly drawn Kieran could almost feel it.

Then she remembered. Daryl and Blythe had rescued a baby stolen by a demon. She searched the drawing again but found no depiction of any humans involved. Just the outcome that had thwarted the Preacher's intentions. Kieran had another thought.

That wasn't long ago.

The artist was keeping up to date with what was occurring in the life of the Preacher. Kieran was desperate to see the last piece drawn into the rock.

She saw a familiar scene, one that looked out of place among the rest of the artwork. A windmill was prominent in place in the foreground. Behind it a farmhouse stood, one well-tended, and intact. Cattle grazed across the pasture and wheat grew healthily on sturdy stalks.

That's the same farm that was revealed in Merlo's painting. The one that's supposed to be in my head.

Kieran searched it thoroughly, looking for anything that might pinpoint an actual location. She felt her sight blur for a second, and then the artwork loomed closer before her, like someone had placed it under a microscope and every inked line was now sharper and more distinct. Kieran had never known a vision to employ that kind of trick, so she wondered if this was Virgil's ability at play. She scanned the drawing for any small detail that they had missed before. There was a mailbox on the edge of the property. Now, with Virgil's Impressor capability at work, Kieran could make out a name. She hoped everyone else could too.

Schmidt.

How hard could it be to find a Schmidt somewhere out in the vast fields of wherever this farmhouse was situated?

A clawed hand pointed to the farmhouse. Kieran was surprised. Lucian had never interacted with her before. *Never.* She'd always wondered if the demon who inhabited her was ever conscious that she was inside him. It appeared he had known all along and was making sure she recognized the importance of this last drawing.

Thanks, Lucian. For whatever it is you're doing.

She felt her eyesight begin to fade. Her connection was failing, and Kieran could only pray this would be the last time she had to endure this claustrophobic possession. Surely she was done now? Hadn't she suffered enough?

Kieran felt her consciousness yanked out of Lucian's body. It was as brutal as if she'd been strapped in an ejector seat jettisoning from a crashing plane. Kieran tried to gather her bearings as the darkness returned and she was adrift once more. She felt a grasp that somehow managed to pull her forward, like someone had grabbed her by the shirt collar.

Merlo?

It wasn't a friend.

The white skeletal face of the Preacher appeared, his terrifying face pressed so close to Kieran that, had she possessed a face, they would have been nose to nose. He was all and everything she could see. Kieran screamed.

"Oh no, dear Observer, no one can hear your screams here. You're cast adrift in the tantalizing space between possession and death. And you just won't die, will you?" He pushed his face closer still until Kieran could feel the heat from the endless fire in his eyes. His teeth were bared, his rage tangible. She thought she could smell his foul breath, and she dry heaved. She *could* smell him. Kieran realized she could feel too. She became aware of his massive clawed hands as he fastened them around her throat and tightened. Kieran tried to grab hold with her own hands to wrench his off, but she wasn't strong enough. His hold tightened on her neck.

"You have been watching for far too long. I don't know what you are seeing or who you are seeing it through, but I will end you now. You are not welcome in my domain, pathetic vermin, and I forbid you to see what glory I am to bring when I take my power. From dust you were made and to dust you shall return." His claws tightened even more and Kieran gasped for air as the pressure on her throat grew. She struggled to breathe, but his stranglehold was growing. Kieran started to slip into unconsciousness. White flashing lights began to spark and ignite in her vision as he crushed her windpipe and stopped her from catching her breath.

Kieran could hear voices screaming for her to hold on, but the darkness was all-consuming and death beckoned her closer.

"See you in Hell," the Preacher said as Kieran's heart started to fade and she felt the warm embrace of death welcoming her home.

CHAPTER TWENTY-FOUR

Merlo was still screaming as she felt the Impressor angel remove his presence from behind her and she was free to move. She stumbled forward, desperate to get to Kieran, who was still held upright by the angels and Virgil. The lead Impressor had pulled back, and Virgil was in the process of doing the same. Kieran was turning a violent shade of purple as she struggled to take in one last breath. Livid handprints were visible all around her neck. Her eyes, wide open but unseeing, looked to be bloodshot and were clouding over. The angels laid Kieran to the ground and stepped back.

Eli's voice rang out like a clarion call. "Exorcise her now! We've seen enough!"

In a flash, another angel descended into the room. She had skin the color of polished ebony and dark hair cut close to her skull. She wore a white dress, fashioned like an ancient Grecian robe. Her wings were magnificent. They were the purest gold, each feather shimmering and rippling as if they were a living entity all of their own.

"An archangel," Dina gasped, bowing her head in deference.

Merlo understood the hierarchy of the angelic system, but her attention focused on Kieran lying on the floor, thrashing and trying to dig her own nails into her wrists to slit them open. She took a step forward, but the female angel forestalled her with just one finger held up in warning.

"Wait," she commanded.

Merlo had no choice but to heed her. She literally couldn't move, held back by the angel's words.

The archangel knelt beside Kieran and placed her palm on Kieran's forehead. There was a dreadful hissing sound as if Kieran's skin was boiling and the angel's hand had been a blast of cold water. Steam rose from Kieran's face, and her writhing grew more ferocious.

Merlo fought to take another step, but this time human arms held her back. She struggled against Ashley, whose arms had wrapped tightly around her waist.

"Let her do her job," Ashley said as she pulled Merlo back against her chest.

"I promised I wouldn't leave her alone." Merlo made one last futile attempt to break free, then went limp in Ashley's grasp. "She shouldn't be alone," she whispered. "Not like that."

"She's not alone. She knows you're here. She knows we're all here for her. And she has the best exorcist with her. Archangel Kasumba is renowned for her skills at casting out demons. Kieran couldn't be in better hands."

Merlo took comfort from Ashley's arms that were holding her upright. She felt everyone else crowd in around her, offering their silent support as they watched Kieran fight.

"A black female archangel," Rafe said. "Won't that be a bite in the ass for all those so-called Christians who can't rid themselves of their hateful racism when they should just be loving their neighbor regardless of gender or race?"

"She's beautiful," Blythe said, "but she needs to hurry because whatever is inside Kieran is trying very hard to get her to rip open a vein."

Kasumba ordered the other angels to hold Kieran down to keep her from ripping herself apart in her frenzied attack. Kasumba's words poured over Kieran. She incited the demon forth using an ancient language that Merlo had studied long ago when she had been a child. An old language, long lost in time. She couldn't translate much of it now, but she remembered the cadence of the words and how it sounded like singing. Kasumba's voice was lyrical, her performance powerful as she commanded the demons inside Kieran to leave her. Kieran shook and snarled; whatever was inside was not going to go quietly. A litany of unintelligible words spewed from Kieran's lips, and Kasumba's eyes widened just a fraction in surprise. She spared a look toward Eli, who nodded back at her.

"Well, something significant just passed between Kasumba and Eli," Rafe said to Ashley. "How intriguing."

Ashley nodded. "I have no idea what it was about, but I'll be sure to grill Eli once this is all over."

Watching Kieran fight and rage while Kasumba dragged the demons out of her broke Merlo's heart. She began sobbing when, amid the snarls and unintelligible words forced from Kieran's lips, the recognizable sound of Kieran's own voice burst through. Merlo collapsed in Ashley's arms, falling to her knees as her legs gave way. She took Ashley with her, and they both huddled on the floor, Merlo keening as she heard her name being called out amid the demonic vitriol.

Kasumba began reciting an incantation, a prayer that was full of the energy of God Himself, to drive the demonic forces out from the one possessed. While the demons inside Kieran made their voices louder to try to drown out her words, Kasumba never faltered, and the energy in the room began to change as she called forth powers from the heavens. Kieran's movements slowed, the voices quieted, and then her chest heaved as she took in a cleansing breath. The prayer ended and there was a cracking sound as Kieran's rib cage snapped in two as the demons broke free. The sound was unnaturally loud and reverberated off the walls.

Kieran.

Kasumba called Eli forward. He knelt beside her and placed his hands on Kieran's chest. Healing light poured from his hands. The discolored bruises that stained Kieran's neck began to fade away, the blood spilled from her wrists erased and the torn skin mended. Kieran lay motionless, being healed inside and out by Eli's touch. Finally, he drew back his hands and he and Kasumba rose.

"Why isn't she waking?" Merlo asked. She rushed to Kieran's side. She was startled by how much younger Kieran looked now that the demons had been removed. *So this is what the real Kieran looks like. She is so beautiful.* She stared up at Kasumba and Eli. "Why isn't she awake now?"

Dina's voice drew Merlo's attention. "Maybe you need to do *your* thing, Dr. Bluetralis."

Merlo frowned then reached out to place her hands on Kieran's shoulders. Kieran jerked beneath her as if shocked. Her mouth opened in a silent gasp. Kieran's eyes fluttered then opened. Small lines creased their corners as she smiled up at Merlo.

"Merloina, I'm sure I heard you calling to me in the darkness."

A sob caught in Merlo's throat and she flung herself around Kieran, gripping her tight, hugging her close. She nestled her head in the crook of Kieran's neck and she breathed in Kieran's scent. *Home. She smells like home.* Merlo lifted her head just a fraction to brush her lips against Kieran's ear. "I told you I wouldn't let you be alone this time." She looked over her shoulder at the angels watching them with indulgent smiles. "Thank you."

Kasumba bowed her head to her. "It would appear you have some mystical powers of your own, Neverage. Usually a body sleeps after an exorcism. Your touch on this one seems to work miracles of your own."

Merlo felt her face begin to heat under the gentle knowing smile of the archangel. She helped Kieran to sit up, amused by the awe on Kieran's face when she got her first look at Kasumba.

"You got rid of the demons inside me?" Kieran ran her hands over her arms and her wrists, looking amazed that there was no sign of the trauma she had inflicted on herself. Kasumba nodded gracefully at her. "How can I ever thank you enough?"

"I think we should be thanking you," Eli said.

"Did you get what you needed to see?"

"Thanks to you, Kieran, we saw more than we could ever have imagined. We are in your debt."

Kieran shook her head. "No, if that's what I needed to go through to get those things out of my head for good, then I'm forever in your debt for bringing me through it."

"And your fear of angels?" Eli asked with a twinkle in his eye.

"Growing less by the minute and being replaced instead with a healthy respect and admiration." Kieran ran her hand over her neck, touching where the death grip had held her so tight. "I thought he was going to kill me."

Merlo studied Kieran's face. "How do you feel now?"

Kieran grinned at her, looking almost giddy. "Like dying is the last thing on my mind."

❖

Daryl and Virgil had disappeared from the room while everyone else was concentrating on Kieran. When she returned, Daryl strode to Ashley and held up the directions she would need to find the farm.

"You found it."

Daryl nodded. "It's so much easier to look for missing people than it is to find a vague piece of farmland somewhere on the planet." She went to hand Ashley the paper but paused, eyeing Ashley curiously. "But you already know where this is. I can see it on your face."

"The name on the mailbox triggered a very old memory. One I'd tried to forget. But I'll still need this to get there." She took the paperwork from Daryl.

"Guess I had the easy job. Now you get to work out what its true purpose is in all of this. I'll expect to hear all when you're ready to brief us." Daryl squeezed Ashley's shoulder and hurried over to where the celebration was happening.

Ashley looked over the paper and felt the blood chill in her veins. *Goddammit.* She recognized the roads on the map. There was no denying it now.

Ashley went to speak with Eli.

"The crack that had been sealed, it's open again, isn't it?" she said. Eli nodded back at her.

"It would appear so. You recognized the name on the mailbox as well, I take it?"

"How could I not? I fought the demons that poured forth from that fissure when I first started on my journey with you. I thought a seal was in place on that derelict farm? I was told it was benign. Closed for business."

"The Preacher appears to have ways and means to open an angelic seal."

Ashley blew out an agitated breath at how calmly Eli was taking all this. "That means he's more powerful and more dangerous than any of us could have imagined."

"True, he will prove to be formidable, but we have faced evil before."

Ashley stared at him. "This is a goddamn fallen angel, Eli. You've just seen the same vision we all got to witness. He's huge, he's demonically powerful, and he's fucking insane! And he's got plans to bring his war party up from Hell to decimate the entire human population here on earth. This isn't going to be an easy banishment this time, Eli. This is *Armageddon*." She folded her arms. "And it's in *Kansas*! I told you I never wanted to go back there."

"I'll start our preparations," he said.

Ashley grumbled. "Yeah yeah, whatever. You do what you need to do and I'll try to explain to my girlfriend why I'm going to the one place I told her never to ask about."

"It will be pretty this time of year," Eli said. Ashley just stared at him. "That was just an observation," he added, nonplussed.

"I don't suppose there's any chance I can go it alone?"

"Do you really think Rafe will leave your side? And the others are loyal to you and their following. You have a team, Ashley. Like it or not."

"And what about Kieran? Hasn't she done enough? Can't she be safe now?" Ashley knew the minute those words left her mouth they had been the wrong thing to ask. "Fuck. She's not going to be safe until the Preacher is gone, is she?"

Eli shook his head. "You'll need to remember to get more travel treats for Trinity."

"Sure, because when you're running into an end-of-the-world situation, you need to make sure your cat is well taken care of."

"Exactly," Eli said, completely sincere. "I will be back shortly. I need to speak with Kasumba and the other angels on another matter."

"Anything to do with whatever came out of Kieran's mouth at some point?" She felt a measure of smugness at the surprised look Eli gave her. "I don't know every angelic/demonic turn of phrase, Eli, but I recognized enough to know that something was said that startled you both."

"We'll talk of that later," Eli said. "For now you need to welcome Kieran back. She fought well and brought us a great deal of information."

"Yes, she did. And by the way, is anyone going to mention that she can *still* see angels even though she's been exorcised?" Ashley was not surprised when Eli just disappeared before her. "We *will* talk later, Eli. Don't think that we won't," she called after him, annoyed by him making a swift departure before she could question him further about what was bothering her. Still fuming, she felt the comforting feel of

Rafe wrapping her arms around her from behind. Ashley melted back into her.

"Angel companion pissing you off again? Want me to glue his wings together? I would, just for you."

Ashley shook her head. "One of these days they're going to smite you, just for the hell of it."

Rafe nuzzled Ashley's neck, laying soft kisses over her pulse. "No, they won't. They think I'm funny, they're just too tight-assed to let it show." She planted one last kiss on Ashley's neck and drew back. "What's got you looking like you want to start throwing things? Because Merlo has a lot of really cool breakables in here and I've just managed to keep Trinity away from most of them. I don't need to start keeping watch so that you don't start smashing vases too. So give, what's chafing your butt?"

"Remember when I told you not to ask about Kansas?"

Rafe frowned, obviously racking her brain to recall that particular conversation. "Hmm, maybe? That was probably a discussion many demons under the bridge ago." Her frown deepened as she tried again to remember and then her eyes widened.

Bingo.

"The farm in the painting and in the demon's cave? That's in Kansas? The Kansas I forgot you won't ever talk about because we haven't ever talked about it?"

"One and the same."

"Am I right in thinking we're going to talk about it now?"

"We're going to have to."

"Damn it, and I forgot to pack my red shoes."

Ashley felt some of the heaviness lift off her shoulders at Rafe's wicked wit. "You're an asshole, Rafe Douglas."

Rafe turned Ashley around in her arms and smiled at her. "True, but I'm yours anyway, and if you're going to Kansas, I'm going to Kansas. Because you're my safe place, Ashley Scott, and I've made my home with you."

"You're trying to work out how to get 'there's no place like home' in a comment, aren't you?"

"You know me too well." She nodded toward where the others were eyeing them both. "Do you want to break it to the other friends of Dorothy over there?"

"No. I want to welcome Kieran back from Hell, eat copious amounts of pizza, and hold you tight all night before the angels return and tell us what our next move is. They'll want to be in charge of this."

"Sounds like a plan to me. So, take the night off, Ashley. The angels will be calling us forth soon enough."

CHAPTER TWENTY-FIVE

There was something disconcerting about being alone for the first time in weeks. Kieran felt almost lost without a permanent shadow by her side, watching over her, keeping her from being reckless. She knew she wouldn't be alone for too long, but there was something she needed to do. She climbed up the staircase and headed for Merlo's bedroom. The large mirror that had hung in Kieran's room had been removed, leaving an obvious empty spot by the wardrobe. The mirror in the bathroom had also been unscrewed from the wall. Kieran understood the precaution, but she needed to see herself right now.

Merlo's room was more personable than the rest of the house. It was all shades of cream with soft tones of pink and blue. It looked lived in, and Kieran felt comfortable in there. Kieran headed straight for the full-length mirror and scrutinized herself. She had forgotten that her eyes were that shade of blue after seeing them bloodshot and bruised looking for so long. She ran her hand through her hair, pleased with the style Dina had given her. She looked over her shoulder and listened in case she was going to be interrupted. It was quiet; not even Trinity was following at her heels.

Kieran unbuttoned her shirt, revealing the new bra underneath. There had been something strange about having to give Merlo all her measurements for the new clothes, but for now that was the last thing on Kieran's mind. She pushed the shirt aside and looked at her chest. She ran her fingertips down from under her bra to the top of her stomach. There was nothing there. No mark, no bruises. But her bones ached like she'd been kicked by a mule. Her ribs were hurting, yet were not tender to her touch. Kieran couldn't understand it. She ran her fingers over her skin again, searching for any noticeable sign of why they throbbed. She was at a loss to explain the pain she was *sensing* more than *feeling*.

"Not that I'm complaining, but is there a reason why I'm finding you half undressed in my bedroom?" Merlo asked from behind her.

"Yours was the only room I felt comfortable in. I needed to find a mirror, seeing as you never trusted me with one in the room I use." Kieran watched Merlo through the mirror's reflection. "I have to admit, it's nice to stand before a mirror without wanting to smash it to pieces and pick up a shard to slit open my wrists with."

Merlo moved closer. "I'm very glad to hear that. If you're searching for scars you won't find any." She peered over Kieran's shoulder to face her in the mirror. "The demons broke your ribs as a parting gift as they were cast out. But you were healed."

Kieran looked down again but found no sign of that trauma anywhere on her flesh. "Healed? Who by?"

"Eli healed you."

"Then it's a good thing I stopped yelling at him, isn't it?" She jumped a little when Merlo moved closer and slipped her hand under Kieran's to rest upon her skin. Kieran could feel the heat from Merlo's fingers warming her skin. Kieran pressed Merlo's hand closer, relishing the feel of her touch. Kieran closed her eyes and sighed.

"Forgive me, but I find myself aching to reassure myself that you're all right." Merlo's head lay on Kieran's shoulder. "How are you feeling?"

Kieran laughed. "You've asked me multiple variations of that question ever since I awoke."

"You have no idea how frightening it was watching you being exorcised." Merlo shuddered behind her and crowded in closer for comfort. "I shouldn't be thinking of you as anything other than a patient, but you've been more than that since the start."

"A patient for what? I've been cured, or so I've been reassured. Exorcised of my demons and back, alone, in my own mind. I have no reason to be a patient now, and you have no reason to use that as an excuse anymore to try to deny what has been building between us from the moment we met." Kieran laid her head against Merlo's as they eyed each other through the mirror. "So, are we going to talk about the undeniable spark that's between us? The one that makes me react to you like no one else I have ever encountered?"

Merlo made to remove her hand, but Kieran held on even firmer.

"You've pulled me from the depths of a demon possession and brought me back to consciousness from the exorcism. Your touch calms and soothes me, both me and the savage beast that was inside me." Kieran shifted until she was facing Merlo, still wrapped in her arms. "Tell me I'm crazy for thinking that there's something rare to whatever this is between us."

"Even in my time, back in Atlantis, there were stories about how two people could meet and their lives would change in an instant. Call it what you will, true love, kismet, soul sharers, kindred spirits, life bonded, the One," Merlo reeled off her list and then grinned impishly, "the U-Haul."

Kieran laughed. "Seriously? I'm betting you didn't have that on Atlantis."

"Whatever we call it, it's that precious moment in time when the universe recognizes two lonely souls reaching out to connect and lets them make magic together."

Kieran smiled. "I like the sound of that." She pressed her forehead to Merlo's. "So, are we going to make magic?"

"Most definitely."

At the first soft press of Kieran's lips on hers, Merlo choked down a sob of relief. *Finally.* Strong arms pulled her closer and they fit together perfectly. She lost herself in the heady rapture of Kieran's tongue tasting and teasing her before deepening the kiss. It made Merlo almost giddy. She clutched at Kieran's shoulders to keep herself anchored. Merlo was swept away by Kieran's ardor. She was rendered powerless to resist her and a fool for ever thinking she could.

Merlo swept her hands down Kieran's spine before slipping them under Kieran's loose shirt and discovering the softness of her bare skin. She felt Kieran's stomach muscles tighten as she brushed her fingers over Kieran's chest and then lower still. She trailed fingertips and a taunting trail of nails along the waistband of Kieran's chinos. When she started tugging at the belt buckle, Kieran gasped into Merlo's mouth and pulled back from their kisses.

"Point of no return, Merlo," she said.

Merlo slipped the belt free from around Kieran's waist and let it fall to the floor. "I think we're way past that now." Merlo reached up to grasp Kieran's head and pull her close for another kiss, this time instigated by her, yet no less passion filled. She took extreme pleasure in noting how Kieran melted into her. How Kieran let Merlo take her and let the passion flow between them. When the need for air grew too much, Merlo drew back. Kieran's eyes were still closed, her mouth slightly bruised. She looked like she was waiting. Merlo kissed her again, softer this time, gentle, continuous pecks because now that she'd tasted her she wouldn't ever want to stop. She rested her forehead against Kieran's. "You wreck me. I haven't felt like this in more years than I can remember."

"From the moment I saw you I was drawn to you." Kieran nuzzled her nose against Merlo's, then pressed tiny kisses across her cheek, down her jaw, then back to her waiting lips. "If nothing good ever comes from my being possessed, at least it led me to you."

"I'd rather we'd have met under less demon-filled circumstances," Merlo admitted.

"Me too, but we're here now and I want you."

Kieran's kiss this time was urgent, possessive. It made Merlo's heart pound with the fire of sensuality that poured from Kieran's lips to hers. It engulfed her, igniting her own flame that burned deep and bright inside. She tore herself from Kieran's arms, hearing Kieran's groan of disappointment behind her as she hurried over to shut the bedroom door. She leaned against it and saw understanding dawn in Kieran's eyes.

"I'm not sharing you with anyone else tonight." Merlo pushed herself off the door and took her time walking back across the room, unbuttoning her silk blouse as she went and revealing the lacy bra underneath. She smiled as Kieran's eyes grew dark as she took her in. Playing to her captive audience, Merlo ran a finger over the swell of her breasts.

"Don't tease," Kieran said, shrugging off her own shirt. She let it fall where it landed. "You'll arouse a very different beast inside me that's all *me*."

Merlo shivered at the look of intent that burned across Kieran's face.

They undressed, neither of them looking away from every inch of flesh the other revealed. Merlo barely had time to step out of her heels before Kieran engulfed her in her arms. They both groaned as their bodies touched.

"God, you're so soft," Kieran whispered, burying her head in Merlo's neck and running her hands down her back to cup Merlo's buttocks. Kieran lifted her up.

Merlo wrapped her legs around Kieran's waist. She could feel the muscles in Kieran's stomach pressed against her wet and wanting flesh. She couldn't resist rubbing herself against Kieran, smearing her arousal on her. Her clit ached at the pressure that wasn't enough to satisfy her need but was tantalizing and made her want more.

Kieran kissed her again. Merlo knew she'd never get enough of those thin lips pressed against hers, owning her, surrendering to her, driving her to the brink of pleasure and then teasing her back down again with an indolent flick of her tongue.

"I've waited a lifetime for you," Merlo said when Kieran pulled back to look at her. Merlo saw the surprise spark in Kieran's expressive blue eyes.

"I'm sorry I kept you waiting." Kieran smiled softly. "I'm here now and I've been waiting for you too."

Their lips locked as tears escaped Merlo's eyes. Kieran kissed them all away tenderly. She laid Merlo down on the bed and climbed up beside her to settle above her. "I'd really like to do this slow and romantic-like, but I'm one breath away from coming all over you after you rubbed yourself on me. You turn me on so much, and your kisses are driving me insane." Kieran grinned down at her. "And I know from insane."

"Just take me. We can save the hearts and flowers for another time." Merlo pulled Kieran down on top of her and delighted in the feel of Kieran's body keeping her pinned to the mattress. "I foresee lots of other times in our future."

Kieran started to rock on Merlo, letting her feel the friction as their nipples caught and dragged on each other's skin. Merlo's legs were still wrapped around Kieran's waist, opening her up so that Kieran could press her mound against Merlo's clit and lazily roll her hips. Merlo dug her nails into Kieran's shoulders as she felt sparks of pleasure radiate from her sex and tingle down to her toes. Kieran continued to move, but she trailed her lips and tongue down Merlo's chest. Kieran began to shiver, and Merlo cried out at the loss of motion when Kieran shifted to break their intimate twining.

"I want to last at least a little longer," Kieran said as she reluctantly sat up. "You're like a lit fuse to my dynamite, Merlo. You're going to make me explode with very little coaxing." Kieran ran her hands over Merlo's hips and thighs, leaving them wrapped around her waist. She leaned forward and began cupping and molding Merlo's breasts with firm hands. Kieran tugged on Merlo's erect nipples and brushed a thumb around the areola to make it pebble and harden further. She bowed her head and sucked a nipple into her mouth, lashing it with her tongue before moving to do the same on Merlo's other breast.

Merlo couldn't still her restless movements. She tried desperately to rub herself on Kieran's body, but Kieran had positioned herself so that Merlo would get no relief. When Merlo began almost whimpering, Kieran slipped lower still from where she was laying kisses on Merlo's chest and pushed her way down to between Merlo's spread legs. Kieran draped Merlo's thighs over her shoulders, and Merlo finally had Kieran right where she wanted her.

Just fuck me, Merlo's head screamed. Her nipples ached in a deliciously pleasurable way, and Merlo rolled them between her fingers to keep the feeling going while Kieran directed her attentions elsewhere.

"Oh, you are beautiful," Kieran said, kissing the silky soft flesh of Merlo's thigh before nuzzling her cheek against the hair that framed Merlo's sex.

"I need you to fuck me so hard," Merlo rasped. Her hips twitched as she tried to feel more of the hot breath that Kieran was whispering over her swollen folds. She almost screamed when Kieran's fingers began tracing a lazy pattern through her wetness.

Kieran lifted her head for a minute. "I bet that wasn't a word you heard on Atlantis."

"Well, I know it now and I need it! You're driving me crazy! Please put your—" Merlo groaned when Kieran pushed two fingers deep inside her with no preamble. Her back bowed and she gasped as she felt Kieran reach deeper still and fill her up. "Oh God, yes."

Kieran withdrew just a fraction then pushed in again. The short, sharp, rough strokes made Merlo want to swoon. She had no idea how soundproof her walls were, and given *why* she had visitors in her house meant that any screaming would surely send them running in her direction. Merlo slapped her hand over her mouth and stifled her moans as best as she could.

"Feel good?" Kieran asked before adding her tongue to Merlo's clit.

Merlo's answer wasn't muffled this time. Her whole body was concentrated on the feel of Kieran's fingers pushing inside her and taking her with enough force that it rocked Merlo's whole body on the bed and she loved it. The alternating licks and flicks on her clit made her writhe and beg for more. She could feel her inner muscles clench almost painfully as her orgasm fought for release. When it hit fast and hard, Merlo's back arched from the bed, and she hung for a moment, her hips pushing back at Kieran to draw her in even farther. A second wave of pleasure followed and wrenched a soundless cry from her lips. She fell back down, shivering and shaking with the aftershocks. Kieran continued to push inside her, gently now, easing Merlo through every pleasurable pulse. She finally pulled out, and Merlo moaned at the feeling of loss. Kieran's tongue took over instead and licked and suckled at Merlo's folds and lips, drinking her in, soothing her ravished flesh.

Merlo lay boneless, blissed out and satiated. She felt Kieran kiss her one last time on her clit then move up to lie beside her. Her warm, wet hand spread out on Merlo's stomach and Kieran nuzzled into Merlo's neck.

"You okay?"

Merlo fumbled to pull Kieran closer so she could hug her. "Oh my God, all the times I could have had you on the big couch in my office," she said. She'd been fucked to within an inch of her life and she felt fantastic. She just didn't know if she would ever move again.

Kieran laughed. "With the demons inside me, it would have made for a very bizarre ménage à trois!"

"You're an excellent lover. I knew you would be." Merlo gasped when Kieran lay back and pulled Merlo on top of her to snuggle into her. "Oh, that's much better." She gloried in the feel of Kieran beneath her.

Slowly regaining her senses, Merlo explored Kieran's body. She felt Kieran tense when her fingers brushed over an erect nipple. So Merlo did it again. Kieran's arms tightened around her. Merlo smiled against Kieran's chest and shifted just enough to take one sturdy nipple into her mouth while she plucked and tugged on the other.

"What do you like?" she asked, noting how Kieran's breath hitched when Merlo sucked rather than licked. She tested it again, and Kieran shuddered beneath her. A red flush bloomed across Kieran's chest as her arousal built and Merlo delighted at the sight.

"I'm going to shoot off like a rocket if you keep playing with my nipples. I need quick and fast because I'm so ready." Kieran shifted to spread her legs wide and guided Merlo's hand directly on her clit. "Feel how hard I am for you already. You do this to me."

Merlo eased her fingers on either side of Kieran's clit and squeezed. Kieran's hand on hers pushed her closer still as Merlo fondled around the hooded flesh and then smoothed across the hard nub that peeked out. At her first stroke, Kieran jolted and her raised leg fell aside, opening herself even more to Merlo's touch.

Merlo sucked on Kieran's breast, pulling the nipple deep between her lips.

"Yes, just like that. So good, that's so good," Kieran moaned, her hips twitching in rhythm to every pull on her nipple. Merlo slipped her fingers into Kieran's wetness and smoothed it liberally over her swollen clit. She rubbed gently at first, then with increasing pressure. Kieran's gasps grew muffled as she buried her face in Merlo's hair.

"Harder, please, Merlo, touch me harder." Kieran's breath caught when Merlo complied, and Kieran curled herself even closer around Merlo. "Yes, just like that. Fuck, I'm so close."

Merlo ran her thumb in circles, and the gasps of *yes* from Kieran's lips intensified. Sucking harder on Kieran's straining nipple and thrumming out a harsh rhythm on Kieran's clit, Merlo knew exactly when Kieran was about to come. She felt Kieran's muscles tense and her body still for a fraction before a harsh exclamation burst from her lips as she crested and climaxed. Merlo continued her rough fingering until Kieran's hand stilled hers. As Kieran gasped for breath, Merlo pressed her palm against Kieran's soaked sex and felt the pulses rolling through her, spilling her juices all over Merlo's fingers. Kieran's hips jerked again and again until she lay spent in Merlo's hold.

"Fuck me," she groaned.

Merlo let Kieran's nipple pop out from between her lips. She was proud of how red and raw it looked. "I believe I just did." She pressed a tender kiss to Kieran's cheek.

"You knew exactly how I like to be touched." Kieran rested her hand over Merlo's where it pressed tightly to her sex. "God, you made me see stars." She moved, rubbing herself against Merlo's hand. Then she removed it, cradled it in her own hand, and kissed Merlo's knuckles reverently. "Where have you been all my life?"

"Waiting for you." Merlo could feel tears leak from her eyes again. Not wanting Kieran to see them, Merlo cuddled in close and buried her face in Kieran's neck, clinging to her.

"I've never felt this." Kieran sounded thoughtful. "I've been with a few women, not many since I always put my work first and no one really understood that commitment. But no one ever made me feel like you've just done. I could feel your touch everywhere, all around me. It just felt so different from anything I've experienced before."

Merlo knew what she meant. She steeled herself for her own confession. "It's been a long time since I took a lover. It's hard for me to be with anyone for long without my secret being revealed. I never age, but my lovers would, and I found too soon that I just couldn't stay as they grew older and frailer and I *didn't*. Falling in love wasn't something I could allow myself to do. It only served to make things harder when the time came for me to leave." She gripped Kieran tighter. "And fleeting romances are hard on the soul and not what I needed either."

"How very lonely you must have been. All this time, always alone."

Merlo's heart clenched at the mournful tone in Kieran's voice, echoing the same one in her soul. It was clear she understood Merlo's lonely existence, as she lived a long, full life, but one that was loveless since Merlo was always destined to outlive anyone she grew close to.

"It was easier in some eras. I lived through the many times when homosexuality became frowned upon and vilified. I became the eternal spinster and learned to harden my heart. The time we're in now is at least freer, but I still tried to hide in my work and not let anyone in." She felt another tear escape unbidden. "Until you."

"I'm glad you let me in." Kieran kissed Merlo's head and pulled her closer still.

Merlo closed her eyes tight and breathed in Kieran's unique scent. She smelled like a plant that had bloomed on Atlantis's coastline. A heady musk was derived from its leaves and, once synthesized, was used by the male inhabitants as a cologne. It reminded her of her father's office where she'd hide as a child, reading her books. It was the scent of home, safety, and love. It comforted Merlo as much as it distressed her.

Because for all we share now, I'll still be left mourning you for an eternity. I'll be left to live on with only my memories of these precious moments. Knowing just how much I loved you, no matter how hard I tried to fight it.

Because you are my One.

I've known it from the very first touch we shared. And you can't ever know because a lifetime is never enough to a heart that knows that one day it will cease beating. And it's even crueler on a heart that will never age.

CHAPTER TWENTY-SIX

A loud crash brought Kieran awake with a start. She found Merlo still in her arms, as they had fallen asleep tangled up in each other.

"What the hell was that?" Merlo asked groggily, rubbing at her eyes and brushing her hair back from her face.

"I have no idea." Kieran looked up at the ceiling trying to gauge if it was going to come crashing in. The noise had seemed to come from right above their heads. Kieran was shaking from being startled from her sleep.

Another crash, twice as loud this time, seemed to shake the very foundations of the house. Items on Merlo's makeup table fell over with the quake that followed.

"That's not thunder," Merlo said.

"It's not an earthquake either," Kieran said.

Dina burst through the bedroom door.

"Merlo, you have to—oh!" She turned around, flustered by the sight of Kieran and Merlo naked on the bed. "I didn't realize—I am so sorry!"

Kieran grinned as Merlo reached for the tangled sheets at their feet.

"What's going on, Dina?" Merlo made sure that they were both covered up sufficiently.

"You need to get dressed, both of you. Ashley says we have to get out of here fast. She says we're under attack."

"What?" Kieran could hear the voices of the others outside in the hallway. "Attack by what?"

"Judging by the fact we have something hitting the roof, I'm guessing something big and with massive wings," Dina said.

"They found us? How?" Merlo scrambled from the bed and began pulling out clean clothes from the drawers.

"Your guess is as good as mine. I'm sure Eli and the others will have some explanation for what's happening. For now we need to pack and go. Gather what you can quickly and meet us downstairs." Dina risked a look over her shoulder at Kieran, who was still in the bed. "Glad to see you've recovered, Kieran. You might want to find something to cover that sizeable hickey you're sporting on your neck. Our new friends might not be as discreet as I am concerning it." She winked at Kieran and gave her a quick thumbs-up. "I'll leave you to get dressed, but hurry, please. I think we're evacuating before whatever is above brings the whole house down with us in it."

Merlo had already put on clean underwear and was pulling on a pair of jeans. Once Dina left, Kieran jumped out of the bed and began scrambling to pick up the clothes she'd thrown all over the floor just hours previous. She threw on her wrinkled trousers and shirt, not bothering to fasten either properly.

"I'll go get clean clothing from my room and then I'll meet you downstairs." She kissed Merlo. "This wasn't at all how I envisioned us waking up together."

Kieran kissed her again and then hurried out of the room to get to her clothes. She redressed in clean underwear and picked a checkered shirt to tuck into a new pair of black jeans. She grabbed the bomber jacket Merlo had gotten for her that was black with white piping. Kieran loved it and wasn't leaving it behind. She took off down the stairs, taking the steps two at a time. She had nothing else to bring. As always, she traveled light.

Everyone congregated in the hallway. Rafe had Trinity's carrier in her hand. She was rocking back and forth on her heels, obviously anxious to leave.

"Okay, we're all here now, so let's get the hell out of here." Rafe drew her gun.

"What's happening?" Merlo asked, lacing her fingers through Kieran's to keep her near.

Ashley drew her own gun. "Unclassified BMF demon, as Rafe likes to call them."

"Big mother of a winged demon right above us. Roughly the size of a lion with huge fucking wings. He's dive-bombing the roof trying to get in." Rafe led the way to the front door. "So we need to go."

"I don't think my insurance covers any of that," Merlo mumbled under her breath. Kieran squeezed her hand in sympathy.

"The angels are going to distract it while we all get out. Dina," Ashley said, looking around until she found her, "we need your time distortion to grant us enough cover to get us away from here without being spotted. We can't afford them following us. We're splitting between two cars. The majority of us in ours while Blythe and Daryl will follow behind. Do you think you can hide us both?"

Dina nodded. "I've covered bigger. Believe me, it will be no problem."

"Okay, looks like we've got to do the brief for this shit storm en route." Rafe turned to Kieran, Merlo, and Dina. "Sorry, you three. I was hoping your part in all this was over and that we could leave you behind to get on with your lives. But it seems for your own safety you're going to have to come with us for now."

"Do you think they're here because of me?" Kieran was horrified by that thought. *What if it's all my fault these people are in even more danger because of things I can't control? Even when I'm not possessed.* "Is it *all* my fault?"

"Not intentionally. Maybe when you were exorcised they saw through your eyes like you saw through one of theirs. Who knows? It doesn't matter; we just need to go." Rafe looked over to where Eli stood stone-faced. "Eli, call in the other angels. We're on the move."

Tugged along by the hard grip Merlo had on her hand, Kieran ran out of the house. She saw a veil descend around them, and though they moved with speed, everything outside appeared to have slowed. She risked a look skyward.

High above Merlo's house, a winged demon was paused in mid-flight. His mouth was wide open in a roar, his eyes blazed a bright orange, and his claws extended as he reached out to inflict damage on the ones flying toward him. Spears poised in attack, five angels were challenging the demon. Their white wings stood out against the blackness of the night. Kieran thought it looked like a painting, the battle drawn out against the night sky. She stumbled as Merlo pulled on her to bundle them into the back of the car.

"Rafe, wait," Blythe called to her from the back of her car. The trunk was open and she half hid behind it. "If we're going to do what I think we're going to do, then you'll need these."

Rafe pushed the cat carrier at Kieran and headed off toward Blythe. Kieran looked out the rear window to see what was happening. She was surprised to see the impressive pieces of weaponry Blythe handed over.

"Blythe, this is why you're my best friend." Rafe kissed Blythe's cheek and then brought the weapons back to the car. She looked like a kid whose Christmases had come all at once. She handed the weapons over to Ashley. "Sparky, Blythe has given us a gift. Just make sure you have them pointed away from me while I drive."

"What am I supposed to do with something this size?" Ashley shifted the heavy automatic rifles awkwardly onto her lap. "They're almost bigger than I am."

"Just point and shoot. These are guaranteed to either kill or slow a demon until they can be banished." Rafe started the car and shot off down the drive. An accompanying squeal of tires assured that Blythe and Daryl were right behind them.

Kieran was at a loss as to what she was supposed to do. She couldn't shoot; her aborted attempts at suicide by bullet had proved that. She wasn't much of a fighter; her strength lay in using words to put the bad guys away when she was a lawyer. *What use am I going to be on this trip?* She looked at the carrier where Trinity lay looking back out at her. *I've got to be able to do more than watch over the cat.* "Rafe? Where are we going?"

"We're looking for I-70, which is doubling this fine morning as the yellow brick road."

Kansas? "What the hell is in Kansas?" she asked.

Ashley laughed humorlessly from her front seat. "Funny you should put it that way…"

❖

The time field around them dropped as soon as they received word they were in the clear. The roads were all pretty much deserted. It was barely past two in the morning. So far all they'd passed were a few trucks lit up like Christmas trees, their colorful lights adorning the windshields and cabs.

Kieran had spent most of the drive looking out every available window, searching the skies for any sign of something following them. She was tired and in danger of being lulled to sleep by the motion of the car. She hadn't gotten much sleep before the rude awakening because she and Merlo had spent as much time as possible exploring each other's bodies until they were exhausted but only slightly sated. The conversations that were going on in the car kept her alert.

Ashley had set Rafe's phone up on a stand and had called Blythe's so now both cars were in contact. She also had her own phone in reach, for when Eli called. Ashley had said she was waiting for a call to finalize their plans.

Since when do angels needs phones? Kieran listened as Ashley took the lead in whatever they were doing. She spared Trinity a look. The cat was fast asleep, curled up in a ball. Kieran could only wish for half her luck. She had a question she wanted to ask but was afraid to hear the answer to. She decided to ask it anyway.

"Are all demons going to be as big as that thing that was trying to bring Merlo's house down? I mean, it was..." She gestured wildly with her hands.

"Not exactly the size of moths, are they?" Rafe said.

"I've only ever seen them in my visions. I didn't know how true to life that was. This was..." Kieran couldn't begin to describe what she'd seen. "And the angels were *fighting*! With *weapons*!"

Rafe smiled wryly at her. "What? Did you expect them to just beat things to death with their wings?"

Kieran shrugged at her. "I just thought angels were supposed to be all about peace and love."

Rafe laughed even harder and side-eyed Ashley. "See? This is what happens when you keep portraying cherubs as cute little babies with itty-bitty wings and baby bows and arrows tipped with hearts. The fact that angels are badass keepers of all that is great and good gets forgotten. They are God's Army, Kieran. They are all-powerful and imbued with God's Holy Spirit to wage war on the unrighteous."

They all jumped when Ashley's phone rang. She answered it swiftly.

"And they always know when you are talking about them," Rafe added with a grin.

Ashley listened for a moment and then frowned. "Are you sure?

Okay. No, we'll work something out." She listened and then shot a look over her shoulder at Dina. "*Really*? Ooookay. I'll do that. Yes, we'll see you soon. Yes, we'll be careful, I promise."

Ashley finished her call and seemed to draw upon something deep inside to center herself before speaking to the rest of them. Kieran didn't see that as a good sign at all.

"Eli says we're in the clear and that nothing is following us, so our plan is to keep heading to Kansas and he'll meet us there." She shifted in her seat. "We have a problem, though."

Kieran stiffened because Ashley was looking at her.

"Seems the demon dive-bombing the house was a blabber jaws. When the angels captured him he told them he'd been sent to retrieve the Observer."

Fear made Kieran's chest constrict, and her breathing stopped altogether. She registered Merlo's hand tightening on her own, but her vision narrowed to a single point on Ashley's concerned face. She became aware of a firm hand on her shoulder shaking her. In a rush, air slammed back into her lungs and she let out a loud gasp as her need to breathe overwhelmed her. She looked blindly at Dina, who shook her until Kieran got a hold back on reality and recognized her surroundings. It took Kieran another moment to gather her wits about her.

She was so sick of being scared all the time.

"But I can't see them now. You got the demons out of me so that I'm not a threat anymore, to them or myself. My link to their world has been broken."

"Well, you've made the top of the Preacher's shit list, so the fact we were going to find someplace safe to drop you and Merlo off to lay low has had to be abandoned. You need angelic protection, Kieran, at least until we can deal with this bounty on your head. And all angelic forces are concentrated on Kansas, which is where we're heading too. So, as much as it wasn't what I originally intended for you, you're going to need to stay with us. It's the only chance you have to be safe."

Kieran felt an old familiar feeling make its voice heard in her head. This time it was whispering without the help of the Preacher pushing his agenda to shut her up.

For everyone's sake, I'd be better off dead.

It must have shown on her face because Merlo reached for her chin and pulled her around to face her.

"Don't you even dare let your mind go to that place I know it's just gone. You are worthy of living. You did not ask for any of this. It was all just dumped in your lap without your consent."

Kieran watched the fierceness spark and flame in Merlo's eyes. It lent a wholly inappropriate sexy sternness to Merlo's face that made Kieran catch her breath. Merlo's eyes darkened even more as she looked at Kieran. Kieran tried to dampen the sudden rush of need that roiled through her. *God, I am such a mess.* She closed her eyes to try to shut everything out for one precious moment until she could gather her thoughts. She tried to quieten the insidious voice that told her she wasn't worthy of anything if she put her friends in danger like she was doing.

Ashley looked over at Dina. "I'm going to need you to keep them in a *time-out* while we deal with the portal."

Dina chuckled at Ashley's deliberate choice of words and nodded.

"I'm quite adept at handling a gun," Merlo said. All eyes turned to her. "I had plenty of time to learn how to defend myself over the years. I'm also proficient in the longbow."

"Well, Robin Hood, I'll be sure to pass that on to the appropriate channels and see if we can't get you set up with a weapon of some sort," Rafe said. "What about you, Kieran? Any weapons you can use that you haven't already tried to kill yourself with?"

Kieran couldn't imagine how Ashley dealt with Rafe's razor-sharp tongue on a daily basis. The sting was taken out of her words, though, as Rafe was watching her through the mirror with a playful gaze.

"Potato peeler," Kieran answered, deadpan.

Rafe snorted. "Oh yeah, we're so keeping you off the field of play trapped in a time bubble." Her eyes narrowed slightly. "It's just a shame we couldn't leave you two lovebirds back at Merlo's, feathering your own nest—"

"Lovebirds?" Merlo squeaked out her exclamation. She turned on Dina.

Dina held up her hands in surrender. "I never said a word."

Ashley looked back over the seat. "You two are glowing, and most of us here can see auras anyway. Besides, we were all still in the routine of watching over Kieran, so when I found her bedroom empty last night I might have panicked a little and gone searching. Then I heard voices from your room, Merlo, and figured you had everything in hand."

Rafe sniggered. "Yeah, I'll just bet she did."

Kieran could hear Blythe and Daryl laughing over the phone along with everyone else. Merlo was smiling but had turned a subtle shade of scarlet.

"As delightful as it is to tease these two newly bonded sweethearts about their post-exorcism sexcapades," Rafe said, "I want to know more about this damn farm in Kansas that seems to hold all the answers to why we are all here and why the hell we're heading toward it."

"Ashley, do you think the farm from Kieran's vision and from the cave art is the same as the one you helped close an escape hatch from Hell on?" Daryl's voice came through loud and clear over the phone.

"The vision was definitely a more stylized version. When I was there, the farm was derelict and the land was a total wasteland. No one had lived there for years, which made it perfect for demons to pop in and out of the portal without detection."

"Are there many portals?" Daryl asked.

"The last official count was seven, worldwide. Seven places where the demons are banished into Hell from. Trouble is, that means there are seven places demons can use to escape from damnation to run riot on the earth. They *are* closed, but evil will always find a way through. Whether it's by their own accord or by being summoned by people. And that's where I come in, and others like me all over the world. It's always been my job to clean up whatever gets out here. Demons are notorious for being sneaky. They all have their own agendas, so the fact they can escape from Hell to run amok up here is not that much of a surprise. I mean, you have to remember some of the demons are like the Preacher himself. They were once mighty angels thrown out of heaven. They're not all stupid."

"The stupid ones are just easier to spot and capture," Rafe added.

"But the fact that it's the Kansas portal reopened is a huge worry. The Preacher has to possess an incredible power to break the seal that the angels placed upon it. If they've somehow managed to create a fissure in it, then that's how the Preacher and the most recent batch of demons have been bleeding through. It *has* to be closed again," Ashley said.

"Why can't the angels just seal it now and be done with it? Save us the trip?" Blythe asked.

Ashley didn't answer but looked at Dina. "I'm told *you* know the answer to that, Dina."

"Because in every timeline I have witnessed there is but one constant. You *all* need to be there for the Gathering before the portal can be closed."

"*The Gathering?*" Blythe asked.

"Where Heaven and Earth and Hell collide, and there is a final reckoning," Dina said.

Kieran stared at them all in shock. They were going to have to *fight* there? Against the demons? Hadn't they all seen what the vision portrayed? It didn't end well for *anything*.

"Of course we'd all have to be there because what fun is a looming apocalypse without your handy-dandy demon hunting humans in attendance?" Rafe sounded weary. "What exactly are we supposed to do at this shindig?"

"Save the world," Dina said.

Everyone was silent for a moment.

"So no pressure there at all, then," Rafe muttered. "Just another day at the office."

CHAPTER TWENTY-SEVEN

K ieran's steady, rhythmical breathing while sleeping was soothing to Merlo's ear. Kieran had succumbed to exhaustion partway through Missouri, and Merlo was hoping she'd stay asleep until they reached Kansas. She knew Kieran's sleep patterns had been sporadic at best for way too long. Any rest she could get would be beneficial for her. When Kieran had given in to her fatigue, Merlo had managed to get Kieran to lay her head on her shoulder so she could brush her fingers through Kieran's hair. It served to soothe them both.

Dina sat beside her with a faraway look in her eyes. Merlo recognized it and waited for Dina to finish divining the future. It wasn't until Dina released a small sigh that Merlo seized her chance.

"Our presence is still required at the farm, isn't it?" Merlo had no idea what they were expected to do; she could only guess that whatever was to happen needed all of their input. They had to be important players in the mix because no matter how many times Dina looked into the timelines, they were still there.

Dina nodded and let out a much bigger sigh, this time of frustration. "So many paths to be taken, so many outcomes, but always you all have to be there right in the center of it."

"You've always told me everything has a reason. I've lived a long time and have seen fate weave its threads through many a point in history. In my own life, fate has intervened. First, to get me off the island. It lent wind to my sails to take me far enough away that I wasn't still in the blast radius when Atlantis blew up. It moved me like a chess piece across the board of time, steering me clear of death by plague, war, and famine. Fate has let me live a long life. A life that now, in this exact moment in the timeline, has brought Kieran to me. What are the chances of that if it wasn't all preordained and meant to be?"

"Of all the bridges in all the world she had to choose from." Dina's smile was faint.

"She just washed up on the banks of St. Louis and was brought to my hospital for me to treat."

"And for you to find that she's your One."

Merlo stilled her hand and just let herself feel Kieran there with her at that precise moment. Merlo nodded. "I've been waiting for her, Dina. And now that I've found her I'll fight to keep us together for as long as we are blessed with."

Dina's smiled wavered. Merlo didn't miss it.

"You see us at the farm. I know and you know we are heading into a fight there. The vision foretold it. Lucian pointed toward it in the cave. You are not breaking any time laws by telling me we're going to have to prepare for an unholy war." Merlo swallowed hard to push back the fear she felt at the anguish she could see coloring Dina's expressive eyes. Merlo had a horrible feeling she knew what Dina had foreseen.

"What *do* you see ahead for us, Dina?"

Dina shook her head and refused to meet Merlo's gaze. "I can't reveal it. It could alter the timeline you're destined to make."

"I've known you for centuries, Dina. Not once have I asked of my own future from you."

Dina nodded. "I know, and I'm hoping you won't ask this time either." Dina took Merlo's face in her hands. "Trust me as your faithful companion through time and as your Oracle."

Merlo nodded to put Dina's obvious fears to rest, and Dina let her go. She'd known Dina longer than anyone else in her lifetime. In her heart, she already knew what Dina had seen. In every scenario, in every timeline that Dina had used her powers to foresee, every action, reaction, decision, or choice, fate was already sealed. Merlo knew, in that moment, whatever happened at the farm in Kansas, it would be life-changing.

I've lived a long and productive life. Maybe this is finally my time's end.

She looked at Kieran still fast asleep at her side.

I've lived more than a lifetime's worth of experiences, but Kieran simply desires her life back. Back to how it was when it was demon free and she could help people. Such a giving soul for one who had her life taken from her by the demons who possessed her. I'd do anything in my power to see she gets to live that life again.

She looked to the front of the car at Rafe and Ashley, both calm and determined and so professional in the face of what they had to know they were heading into. She had seen the same looks on the faces of Blythe and Daryl. All of them had seen the vision, the destruction of the farm foretold. She wondered if, by some unspoken agreement, they were prepared to sacrifice themselves for whatever the Gathering was to bring forth. Would so few be the sacrifice for the many? Merlo hoped it wouldn't come to that. But she'd seen the strain on Dina's face.

Time will tell.

Merlo closed her eyes and remembered home. *Atlantis.* Long consigned to a watery grave because of humanity's inability to stop playing God. She knew it wouldn't be the first time, and it certainly hadn't been the last. The increasing technology that had been amassed in the world to date, the intensity of the bombs built, and the plundering of the planet day by day had proved this to her over and over again.

But still I am grateful for every day I get to walk this earth. To see the beauty and the goodness and the love that still resides here.

Kieran muttered something under her breath, and Merlo soothed her back to sleep. She wanted a lifetime with this woman. She wanted to learn everything there was to know about her. To share her own life with her. To keep this feeling of love close in her heart for the truly precious gift it was. She'd spent long enough with Dina by her side to know that everything had a reason and its own moment in time.

I just want more time with Kieran.

She brushed her fingers through Kieran's short hair again. She didn't look up but spoke for Dina's ears alone, her voice soft and low.

"You won't leave us, will you?"

"I'll be right by your side until the end of time," Dina said earnestly.

With that promise made, Merlo took a deep breath and sent up a prayer.

Let me live just one more day, walking by Kieran's side. Please don't let this be all the time we have to share. She turned to ghost a light kiss on Kieran's head. *Let our love be endless.*

❖

Kieran startled out of a vivid dream of a farmhouse on fire, woken up by Blythe screaming, "Watch out!" She hardly had time to open her eyes before the car was hit with such force that it pushed them off the road and almost into a wheat field. The resounding slam against the side of the car shook everyone inside. Kieran watched in horror as the door nearest to her buckled and bowed in, fashioning itself into a crude head-shaped lump that appeared to have horns. The glass cracked into a spider web of a million tiny fractures.

Thank God for bulletproof glass in the DDU's cars. Kieran threw an arm up to cover her face just in case the glass didn't hold.

"Hold on!" Rafe yelled as she tried to keep control of the vehicle. Kieran felt the car tip, and it must have been teetering on just two wheels before it slammed back down with a bone-shaking thud. Her teeth clashed together, and she was thankful her tongue hadn't caught between them. Trinity's cat carrier banged against her leg from where it had been resting on the floor. That was going to leave one hell of a bruise. Kieran figured it was the least of their problems.

The screeching of brakes sounded somewhere behind them and Kieran had just managed to get her bearings when Rafe's car was hit again, this time by Blythe's. The impact shoved the car farther into the field where it came to a jarring stop.

"Is everyone okay?" Rafe asked, reaching over to run her hand over Ashley to make sure she was all right. She then reached for her gun and began searching their surroundings. "What the fuck hit us?"

Everyone said they were all alive, just banged and bruised and with no idea what the hell had just happened. Kieran couldn't take her eyes off the damaged door. It was so pushed in it encroached where Kieran would have been sitting had Merlo not grabbed her.

"Blythe? Daryl?" Rafe called out and cursed when she saw her phone had fallen to the floor and there was a massive crack across the screen. Rafe fumbled with her seat belt, intent on getting out of the car. Ashley grabbed at her.

"No, don't get out. I think it was a demon that hit us."

Rafe looked out the window but they were in the middle of tall stalks of wheat that obscured their view. She shook her head.

"Whatever it was it just came out of nowhere. Damn near shook my damn brains out." She stretched her neck and grimaced at the popping sound it made.

Ashley's phone rang from inside her jacket. She answered it and turned on the speaker.

"Sorry we ran into you. You spun into our path before we had a chance to even stop." Blythe's voice shook. "It was a demon. A hellhound, short and squat and built like a tank. It just appeared out of the wheat field on the left and plowed right into you. We nearly hit it, but we smashed into you instead. Can you see it at all?"

Kieran tried to see anything past the tall wheat stalks. She was surprised to see it was light out and checked her watch. It was seven a.m. and she was surrounded by wheat. "By that welcome I'm guessing we're in Kansas," she muttered.

"Everyone stay very quiet," Ashley said and lowered her window. She picked up one of the large automatic rifles and flipped off the safety. She positioned it out the window as proficiently as any sniper. "Glimmer trail incoming, three o'clock."

In the distance, the wheat started swaying, heralding something big was plowing its way through at great speed. Ashley readied her weapon, and as the demon burst through the wheat at them, Ashley squeezed off a shot. It hit the demon right between the eyes, blowing the back of his head wide open and propelling him backward some length to land with a thud on the ground.

Kieran's jaw dropped. "My God, that was awesome."

Rafe got out of the car. "Sweetheart, remind me never to piss you off. Let me make sure the thing is dead before we call in the angels to get rid of the body. Don't want to give some poor unsuspecting farmer a heart attack now, do we?" She got out of the car and groaned when she tried to straighten up. "Goddamn crash has put a kink in my back." She stretched and groaned again. "I'm getting too old for this shit."

Daryl met Rafe on the other side of the car and they walked into the wheat, both armed and on alert.

Kieran watched them disappear. She started to tremble.

"Kieran?" Merlo's voice was tentative behind her.

"I can't stop shaking," Kieran said, holding up a hand to her face. The tremor in it was visible and nonstop.

"Are you just frightened?" Dina leaned around Merlo and took Kieran's hand in her own. "Kieran, you're burning up."

Kieran stared at her hand in Dina's, then looked up at Merlo. She opened her mouth to speak, but her mind just went...blank. All thought disappeared, all sense of self too. But she heard a voice speak with a familiar guttural growl.

"You are wasting time. The seventh seal is a trap you need to trigger. Hurry, before all is lost."

Kieran felt herself snap back into her body. All sights and sounds came rushing in. Her thoughts were screaming at the brutal intrusion.

Lucian again? Will I never be free of this madness?

"I thought we'd gotten rid of his presence?" Merlo said.

"Could this get any worse?" Ashley said, leaning out the window and screaming for Rafe and Daryl to get back to the cars. "Because the question now is, was that a chance attack by a lone demon or do they *all* know we're coming?"

Wind turbines lined the horizon like huge sentinels keeping watch over the landscape. Kieran was anxious as she watched the road ahead. She couldn't roll down the window in its cracked state, so there wasn't enough air for her to cool her heated skin. The air conditioner just wasn't touching it. The trembling was not abating, and Kieran was terrified she'd be possessed again with another dire warning.

"Kieran?"

Kieran didn't register Merlo's voice from beside her. She hadn't even felt Merlo's hand come to rest on her shoulder.

"Kieran, can you hear me?"

Kieran nodded. "It's so hot inside me."

Merlo and Ashley traded looks. "She was supposed to be free from this," Merlo said.

"She was exorcised. I have no idea what is happening now," Ashley said.

"Is it some kind of residual connection, perhaps?" Dina asked. "It's not unheard of for demons to leave a little reminder behind. A calling card, if you like."

"Like what? Damn fingerprints left on her soul marking her as his territory? Like some demon version of a tenancy agreement? He's not in at the moment, but he reserves the right to occupy later?" Rafe looked at Ashley. "Can the bastards even do that after an exorcism?"

Dina answered for her. "Who knows? Let's face it, Kieran's whole possession has been an unusual one from the start."

"Kieran, do you know much about your father?" Rafe asked.

Kieran shook her head. "He was gone long before I was even born."

"Detective, what are you detecting?" Ashley asked.

"You and I both know that fallen angels aren't consigned to just ancient biblical times. Those with lust in their hearts for mortal women still fall to this day."

"Like my own father, for one," Ashley said.

"So, I'm just wondering if young Kieran here is a product of such a union. It wouldn't be the first time, Sparky. It would go a long way to explaining something still linking her to what's happening."

Merlo squeezed Kieran's shoulder tighter. It felt like Merlo was the one thing grounding her, but this time it couldn't quite break the link between Kieran and whatever was inside her head.

"Kieran, what were you told about your father?" Ashley asked.

"That he did a disappearing act on my mom before I was born. That he was religious and heading to a seminary, at least according to my mother. I can't vouch to the truth behind it."

"A seminary?" Ashley frowned. "He was a priest?"

"Well, Mother always said he called her his 'last hope' while they were conceiving me, though I never understood him being religious, when with the next breath she said he was cursing God. You have to realize, my mother wasn't the most reliable of women. She didn't have a good word to say about him leaving her with me, and by extension, me for being the child she was saddled with. She had the impression he left to go do God's will." Ashley and Rafe traded significant looks. "Does this mean I'm never going to be demon free?"

Ashley hoisted up one of the rifles. The big gun looked incongruous in her small hands. "One way or another, Kieran, we're getting you free from all of this." She was distracted by something on the road. "Rafe, pull over for a minute."

Rafe pulled the car over and Kieran saw that the car behind followed suit.

Ashley turned to face everyone. "Okay, we're in Hays now and are just a few miles from Catherine, where the farm is situated." She turned to Dina. "I know you've foreseen all of us as a group at the farm in your divinations. However, I'm offering everyone here the chance to stand down and leave if you want to go. No one has to go anywhere they don't want to, whether it's been predicted or not."

"We're not leaving you," Daryl spoke for her and Blythe.

Dina smiled at Ashley. "There's nowhere else for me to be at this time," she said.

Merlo dipped her head to look at Kieran, who was staring into the cat carrier as if it held all the secrets of the universe. "Kieran?"

"I think I have to be there. I don't think I *can't* not be there. Everything I have experienced has been leading me to this point in time, for whatever lies ahead on that damn farm. I had one day free from whatever hold Lucian has on me. So I think I *need* to be there. This has to stop."

Merlo nodded, then looked at Ashley. "Where she goes, I go."

Ashley turned back around.

"I suppose I get no choice?" Rafe said, starting the engine. "Because, honestly, I'd rather be back at home, watching Trinity sprawled out in front of the fire, while I eat my Froot Loops and listen to rain falling." She eyed Ashley and pouted. "Kansas is too fucking hot, Ashley."

Ashley patted her thigh. "The fact Kansas has a portal to Hell in it has a lot to do with that. It helps heat the whole area, especially when it's allowing inhabitants from Hell to escape."

The drive was quiet for a while before Kieran spoke. "What do you think we're heading into?"

Ashley hesitated before answering. "At the last report, angels had been sent out to watch over all seven of the seals. Eli says that the other six appear to be secure, but they're leaving watchers in place just in case."

Daryl's voice came through the phone. "You think all Hell's going to break loose all over the farmstead?"

Even though Daryl couldn't see her, Ashley nodded. "I fear we're going to get front row seats to whatever the Preacher has been working on for centuries."

"Hell on Earth," Kieran said, her voice not her own. "Time is running out." She looked up at everyone, her face her own, but her voice colored by something else entirely.

"And he's coming to take what is his."

Chapter Twenty-Eight

The farm was in an even worse state than the last time Ashley had seen it. The walls of the old farmhouse were cracked and the roof was half missing. Kieran wondered if a rogue tornado had ripped it off. The house was still standing and sturdy enough for someone to shelter in. The front door had long since been broken off its hinges and now stood precariously propped up to bar entrance to the building. Ashley lifted it aside and ushered everyone inside.

"Merlo, Kieran, Dina, I'd like you all to stay here so you're protected. Dina, can you work your magic from in here?"

Dina nodded. "Walls are no boundaries for me."

"Great, then I need you to cloak yourselves and keep hidden and safe. The rest of us are going to look around outside."

Ashley left to go find Rafe. She was surprised to notice that the skies looked empty above her.

Covert operations it is, then.

She soon found Rafe, Blythe, and Daryl huddled around the trunk of Blythe's car.

"Ash." Rafe beckoned her over. "Come look at all the goodies Blythe appropriated from the DDU for us to play with."

"I figured that if the necessity arose, then we'd need something more powerful than our sidearms." Blythe was packing her pockets with ammunition. Both she and Daryl had on Kevlar vests.

Daryl held out vests for Rafe and Ashley. "We didn't think you had time to even consider bringing your gear into this fight."

Rafe snorted. "We weren't expecting a goddamn fight at all. It was supposed to be a possession, pure and simple." She helped Ashley get into her vest, making sure all the tabs were tight and secure. She ran her eyes over Ashley with unashamed appreciation. "My my, Ms. Scott, don't you look dapper in your armored attire? We'll make a DDU officer of you yet." She began filling her pockets with everything Blythe handed her. She grinned at the large serrated knife. "This is more like what I take off the gangs in Chicago. Not exactly DDU fare, Agent Kent."

"You know how to use it. I want us prepared for any eventuality. Even though I don't really know what we're preparing for." Blythe began handing over the same to Ashley. "Hope your demon hunting skills stretch to using these weapons, Ashley."

"I've handled a knife a few times in my career," Ashley admitted, looking the blade over before sliding it into her boot. "I'm hoping we're just bystanders to this, though."

"What are the chances of this being anticlimactic and the angels just sealing the thing up and we all get to go grab breakfast?" Daryl asked.

Ashley and Rafe exchanged a glance in silence. Rafe loaded a full round of ammo into her assault rifle and flipped off the safety.

"You have much to learn, young Padawan. Where angels and demons are concerned, everything has to be a show of biblical proportions. But I promise, if we get out of this alive? The pancakes at IHOP are on me."

The sound of a trumpet blasted from the heavens, shaking the ground beneath them.

"Oh fuck me," Rafe said. "I wasn't expecting that." She whirled on Ashley. "This is way more serious than a seal if they're blowing trumpets, Ashley."

"What? Why?" Blythe asked, searching the skies.

"Did you never read your Bible?" Ashley motioned for them all to take shelter behind the cars.

"Revelations? The Last Days? The opening of the seventh seal?" Rafe's eyes grew wide. "The seventh seal? *The Seventh Seal*? Oh my God." She drew in a shaky breath. "Jeez, literally!" She grabbed for Ashley's hand. "Is this the Apocalypse? *The* Apocalypse? The Great War? Judgment Day? The 'We're all seriously fucking screwed' Apocalypse?"

Ashley shrugged. "I have no idea. Please calm down, sweetheart. You'll give yourself an aneurism."

"Are we in deeper than we thought?" Daryl asked, looking concerned at Rafe freaking out.

Ashley shrugged again. She was in the dark as much as they all were. She breathed a sigh of relief when Eli appeared beside her. "Eli, thank God. What's with the horns?"

"A clarion call for the Gathering." He looked up as the sky lit up with an unusual array of stars, more than were ever seen in the early hours of the morning.

"So it's not Judgment Day?" Rafe said. "Because I'm not emotionally equipped today to deal with Armageddon."

Eli gave her a strange look. Ashley had never seen him try to pull off a condescending look before, but he was faring quite admirably.

"Rafe, do you not know that no one knows either the day or the hour of that event? Not even the angels."

"It's not very reassuring that you don't have the inside track on that, Eli," Rafe grumbled. "It would be nice to get a warning before-hand."

"Rest assured the trumpet you've just heard was for the angels worldwide to hear and those of you blessed with the power to see us."

Rafe took a deep breath and calmed herself. "Okay, fine then. Something to expect for another day, *if* we survive whatever this day brings." She ran a hand through her hair, muttering, "Damn angels and their flair for the dramatic."

Ashley just laughed at her and asked Eli, "Is Trinity safe?"

"She's well out of harm's way."

"Lucky little fur ball." Rafe gave Eli a nod of thanks. "So, the gang's all here. You've got an army of angels above us and you have gathered a motley crew of an Oracle, a Neverage, an exorcised yet apparently still possessed woman, and an assortment of the DDU's finest. Oh, and best of all, the most beautiful of all your demon hunters. I'm not seeing a coincidence here, Eli. I'm seeing fate and destiny gathering, so where the fuck is our free will in all this?"

"Some things are inevitable." Eli gestured to the stars above shifting in the pale light of morning. "It would appear this fight is as much yours as it is ours."

"So our being brought in because of Kieran was all predestined?" Daryl looked over to where Virgil stood watching. "This isn't our usual kind of case. I don't understand why we're here."

"All will be revealed in time, I should imagine. Not all the angels are privy to every event God sets in motion," Eli said.

Ashley laid a hand on Eli's arm. "Kieran still has a piece of Lucian in her. He's been using her to relay messages to us."

"Lucian seems to be playing both sides in this war." Eli looked out across the fields. "No doubt we'll see where his true loyalties lie when the time comes for him to reveal himself. Also, I came to tell you this. The seal on this farm is *not* broken. The Preacher must have opened another portal somewhere else on the farm. He's that powerful now."

The implications of that sank into Ashley's brain. The angels hadn't resealed the seal beforehand because it didn't need to be. That was why they weren't revealing themselves. They were lying in wait for the new portal to open so they could see where it lay from their vantage point and then swoop in. The portal could be anywhere on the farm and its surrounding land. They weren't going to get the jump on the demons; the demons still held the element of surprise.

Ashley looked back toward the homestead. "The farmhouse. It's the first thing wrecked in the vision. I left Kieran and the others in there. We've got to get them out of there and fast."

Before anyone could move, the ground beneath their feet began to shudder.

"Seriously?" Rafe rolled her eyes. "Now is not the time for there to be a freak earthquake rolling its way through here. Can't your angels control the weather or something, Eli?"

Eli seemed to be hearing something other than Rafe's voice. "It's no earthquake."

Ashley took off running toward the farmhouse with Rafe on her heels. Ashley screamed all the way there.

"Everyone, get out of the house! Get out! GET OUT NOW!"

❖

Merlo grabbed Kieran's and Dina's hands and dragged them with her as she took off out of the farmhouse. She spotted Ashley as she and Rafe were running toward them. They stopped and waved for Merlo and the others to follow them as they switched directions and started back across the field toward their cars.

Merlo felt the earth crack and break up beneath her. She almost fell, but Kieran grabbed her and kept her upright and moving. The earth slipped out from under them, and Merlo felt Dina's hand start to slide from her own.

"Dina, no!"

"Just keep running!" Dina yelled, trying to keep up with them.

Merlo almost balked, but she kept going, trying desperately to catch up with Rafe and Ashley who were now some distance ahead. By the looks on their faces, whatever they were running from was terrifying. Lungs burning from the exertion, Merlo felt the ground move from under her feet again, and then there was no ground at all. She heard Kieran yell as she fell. Dirt flew up around them and then over them like a tsunami that threatened to engulf them both. Merlo feared she was about to be buried alive. She risked a look behind her. The farmhouse had been wrenched from its foundations. It was perched atop a massive mound of earth that grew and grew to mountainous proportions. The farmhouse cracked and crumbled, then disintegrated right before Merlo's eyes.

The mound grew larger and larger. From it came the hideous sound of buzzing, like a million angry wasps trapped beneath the dirt were fighting to break free. It filled the air with a static noise that rose in pitch the higher the mound expanded. Then an ear-shattering boom turned everything white in a blinding flash. Merlo felt the concussive force from the explosion slam into her body. It lifted her into the air, then slammed her back down. She lost her grip on Kieran. Her vision was hampered from the flash and flying dirt that choked the air. Merlo never saw what hit her; she just felt like she'd rammed into a brick wall. The air escaped from her chest as she lay on solid ground trying desperately to breathe.

Hands grabbed for her. Merlo realized it was Rafe picking her up and running with her. Merlo tried to speak, but she choked on the dirt coating her tongue.

"Ashley's got Kieran," Rafe said.

"Dina?" Merlo gasped.

"She's with the angels."

Merlo's whole body stiffened in shock.

"No, no, not like that," Rafe hastily amended. "The angels grabbed her and got her to safety after she fell."

Merlo let out a sob of relief to know her oldest and dearest friend was okay.

Rafe deposited Merlo behind her car. A bottle of water was pushed into her hand to wash her mouth out with. She used some of it to wash away the dirt from her eyes too. Merlo felt more than saw the arrival of Kieran beside her. She wiped at her face and then set to cleaning Kieran off so they could see each other.

"Are you frightened?" Kieran asked, huddling into Merlo.

Merlo nodded. "Terrified."

"Thank God, I was hoping it wasn't just me." Kieran gave her a weak smile. "My time at the hospital seems like a lifetime ago. Maybe I should have stayed there and let them drug me to death because this reality is *really* crazy."

The ground was still shaking. Merlo was relieved to spy Dina on the other side of the field they were hiding in. Dina was forming the biggest time distortion field Merlo had ever seen her do. It fell over the entire farm for as far as the eye could see and reached up high into the heavens. Angels flanked her, keeping her safe, until Dina just winked from sight.

Oh God, what the hell is going to happen here if she's having to do that?

Eli appeared behind the car with them. "Dina has put up a barrier between us and the rest of the inhabited farms. No one outside of it will ever know what happens here." He looked out across the fields then back at Merlo and Kieran. "Unfortunately, that means she's not here to protect you as we'd intended."

Merlo nodded. "Then someone had better hand me a gun."

Before anyone could do anything, the ear-shattering sound of the earth being ripped open caused everything to shudder. A dark mass of demons spewed forth from the top of the newly formed mountain. They burst free like a swarm of locust, escaping from Hell and swarming out on both land and into the air.

The Preacher emerged, flying high among them. His hood was drawn back so his pale skull shone bright in the rays of the early morning sun. His laughter filled the air. He hung suspended in midflight, wings and arms outstretched as he called forth his demons to populate the earth and sky.

"Father," his voice projected to every corner of the land. "Behold, your prodigal son has returned to take what is rightfully his." His wings carried him higher above the farmland, king to all he surveyed. He smiled down at the demons spilling out of the portal.

"And the forsaken have returned to take the rest."

CHAPTER TWENTY-NINE

Crouched behind the car, Ashley leaned back into Rafe and shouted in her ear over the commotion. "Next time I say 'hey, let's go to Kansas,' tell me no fucking way like only you can, sweetheart."

Rafe nodded, but her eyes weren't on Ashley. They were trained skyward. Her mouth dropped open, and Ashley turned to see what held Rafe's attention.

A host of heavenly beings were descending from the heavens. Their white wings shone in the sun, while their white robes were as pure as snow. Armed with bows and arrows, this first wave flew down and began firing at the demons. Ashley was satisfied to see the arrows strike home every time. There'd be no more banishment for these beasts. They had lost the right to eternal damnation.

"We're going to need lots more like those," Rafe said. "The odds aren't in the good guys' favor if that's all they are sending to fight."

"Oh, there'll be more, never fear." Ashley laid her gun over the hood of the car. "But let's help even the odds a little." She began shooting.

Blythe and Rafe followed suit. The sound of their gunfire was lost amid the demons' roars. Daryl snuck to the back of the car to get more rifles and handed them to Merlo and Kieran. Merlo started firing, but Kieran looked at her rifle, clueless. Ashley flicked the safety off for her.

"My mother never allowed guns in the house, and I never bothered to get acquainted with firearms once I left," Kieran said.

Ashley noticed that she held the gun awkwardly and was thankful Kieran didn't knock her teeth out when she pulled the trigger for the first time. The shot went wild, but Ashley commended her for trying. "Just aim low so you don't hit an angel by mistake."

"Can you tell me why we're killing them instead of you banishing them back to hell?"

"They were banished for their sins. Nowhere did it say that when they got tired of being in Hell they could come back above and meddle once again in the affairs of humans. It's kind of a two strikes rule." She looked up at Rafe's hoot of delight, wondering what had her cheering.

A flock of golden-winged angels were teeming down from the heavens, armed with Spears of Light. A beautiful mixture of winged beings with skin of all colors, brandishing golden swords and shields, flew in behind them.

"Now we're talking," Rafe said. She executed headshot after headshot on any demon that turned his attention from the fight with the angels and tried to head toward the humans instead.

Ashley forced herself to keep loading her weapon. She wasn't used to handling such a large rifle. She always carried a smaller gun for protection when she was doing her PI work. But she traveled with an angel; that was more than enough backup she could ever need.

"Ashley Scott! Show your face, you goddamn whore!"

Ashley looked up at the unexpected callout. Rafe scanned the field, searching for the culprit.

"Who the fuck is that?" she said, then spotted something. "Oh my God. You have got to be kidding me. Didn't we banish that asshole once already?" Rafe dipped back down. "Of all the hellholes in all the world, your demonic bastard of a half brother has to escape from this one."

The demonized voice of Lucas Thorpe was just discernible over the sound of the fighting going on. He was nearby and getting closer.

"Hey, bitch! Come out here and face me! You owe me that much!"

Rafe prepared to stand up. "Oh, that's it. I'm going to bust his balls!"

Ashley pulled her back down before Rafe vaulted over the car and got herself killed. "No!"

"You can't talk him down this time unless you let him get close enough that I can spear him again. Which," Rafe grumbled, "I happen to think is not what he deserves."

"Please don't kill him." Ashley knew it was a crazy thing to beg for, but she couldn't help herself.

"Ash," Rafe began to argue.

"He's still my brother."

"No, he's a psychopathic, serial-killing demon with a daddy complex. *That's* what he is."

"He's still my half brother, demon or not. He got the wrong end of the same genes we share. That could have been me out there."

Rafe stared at her, blew out an irritated breath, and then gestured to Blythe to do something. "Please talk some sense into her. I'd still like to sleep with her after all this mess, so for once I'm going to keep my mouth shut." She shot a baleful look in Ashley's direction. "Even though it kills me to do so."

"Ashley, you don't need me to tell you he's calling you out on the battlefield as a diversionary tactic to weaken our defense here."

Rafe waved an enthusiastic hand in a "See? What she said!" gesture.

Ashley looked over at Eli. "Did Dina tell you any of the outcomes of our actions here?"

Eli looked caught. He nodded.

"Then we're damned if we do, damned if we don't no matter what we do." She looked over the field at the angels on the ground, fighting toe to hoof with the demons. Ashley gasped as a massive demon knocked an angel to the ground. Other demons piled on and white wings were lost amid the rabble of black. She saw a flying demon snag an angel in mid-flight and rip his wings off his back. The demon threw the bloodied wings to the ground where waiting beasts shredded them. She couldn't stomach the demon's raucous celebrations as he dropped the wounded angel into the baying crowd. The spoils of an unearthly war.

"He's going to draw unwanted attention to us all if he doesn't shut up. I need to stop him. But I can't just kill my brother. He's still my family. We could at least try to capture him again before I have to even consider shooting him." She caught Rafe's gaze. "However much we know he deserves it. And yes, I know I'm being called out and no doubt am being set up, but I can't see what else to do. So, please, I beg of you, if he gets closer just wing him, slow him down. No kill shots from either of you sharpshooters." She pointed out Blythe and Daryl with a stern look. She looked out again to see Lucas targeting angels' wings with his talons, scoring them wide open and leaving them bloodied and torn.

I have no choice. I don't want his death on my conscience. I want him banished to pay for what he did, as befits the demon he became. I know too well what kind of life he came from.

"Eli, if he breaks through, you're with me," she said. "I'll move to draw his attention away from here and from what he's trying to do to the other angels. If I draw him out, we can capture him. I doubt he's grown any smarter in his time consigned to Hell."

"*We* will draw him out," Rafe said firmly. "I have the Spear of Light, after all. Let me pin the goddamn pest to the earth until he stops wriggling." Rafe drew out the pen from her pocket and triggered it. The spear appeared in her palm in all its glory.

"Virgil, protect these, please." Ashley gestured to the others. She knew the ammunition wasn't going to last forever and they were seriously outnumbered.

Virgil stepped forward and spread his wings to encompass them all.

"If we don't…" Ashley began but found she couldn't get the rest of her words out.

"You go get your brother sorted and we'll regroup soon. You're getting ten minutes, Ashley, and then we come for you. No one is being left behind." Blythe gave Rafe a hug. "And you, no damn fool heroics. Your skull has finally mended after the last altercation you got yourself into with a demon. Besides, I don't want to be left with your cat. You've spoiled her too much, and I could never live up to the level of pampering that she's accustomed to."

Rafe nodded and then joined Ashley hidden under Eli's wings. "Let's go see what your brother wants," she said, holding the rifle in one hand and her Spear of Light in the other.

"I have a horrible feeling this day isn't going to get any better soon," Ashley whispered to herself as they set off across the field.

And I don't need an Oracle telling me this is not going to end well.

❖

Moving closer to where the battle was raging wasn't something that Ashley had wanted to do, but Lucas was drawing attention to himself calling out for her like a naughty child. She was reluctant to leave the safety and invisibility of Eli's wings and the protection he afforded her.

"You can change your mind," Rafe said. "Just give me the word and I'll deal with him for you."

Ashley shook her head. "My half brother, my battle." But she was so tired of having to deal with his petulance and endless contempt. She'd banished a lot of demons in her time and was despised by many of them for it. But Lucas was a living vendetta wrapped in demon form. She wasn't stupid. He *frightened* her.

She kissed Rafe. "Watch over me, Raphael." She smiled as Rafe rolled her eyes at the use of her full name.

"I'll always have your back, never fear. Just create enough of a distraction so Eli and I can get behind him. He's always so focused on you that maybe he'll fall for the same trick we pulled last time."

"Here's praying." Ashley slipped out from under Eli's wings. She was now visible to the field. A lone human standing out like a sore thumb. She took a deep breath to steady her nerves.

"Lucas Thorpe! Get your whiny ass here right now," Ashley called. She heard the distinct sound of hooves, and then there he was, his demonic transformation complete. His eyes burned with fire and his fury centered on Ashley. She tried not to let her fear show.

God help me. My little brother got so big.

"I'm back! I'm back on your earth and my new family is going to kill you all! But you're going to be mine because this is all your fault."

"How is it my fault, Lucas? You're the one who let their demon side take over. You're the one who killed those women. You're the one who chose to give in to those impulses and turn evil. That's not on me. *You* let your anger twist your soul, and it's made you exactly what you are today."

"I know. Isn't it wonderful? I am beautiful in this body! No one could ever ignore me in this form. I am powerful, and look what I have now." He flexed his muscles and a pair of newly forming wings spread out from his back. "I have my own wings growing, and soon they will be big enough for me to fly. Choke on that, big sister! I have the real deal. You just have poor tattooed imitations on your back. *I* am the true heir to our father's legacy. I'm as great a demon as he is."

Ashley could see Rafe and Eli moving into position, but she

needed to keep Lucas's eyes on her. He was antsy, as if waiting for an attack. She did the one thing she could think of to distract him. She drew back her fist and punched him in the jaw.

He staggered back a few steps, more in surprise at her audacity than from the blow itself. He didn't get very far. Rafe ran him through with the Spear of Light. Lucas wailed at his capture. His cries rang through the field like those of an unruly child denied candy. But no one came to his aid.

Ashley cradled her aching fist in her other hand. *I guess not even the other demons can stand him.*

"Daddy! Daddy! Help me!"

Ashley looked around for who he was calling out to. Was her father here? Somewhere out on the field attacking the angels? Maybe he was one of the demons they'd shot at? Was his body already littering the field somewhere where she could walk past him and never even recognize him?

Two angels flew down, but Ashley lifted a hand to stay them before they could take him away. She couldn't kill him, but she could do something much worse. Retribution for the innocent lives he'd taken and never once showed remorse for. She owed him that for what he'd done and blamed her for.

Ashley removed the knife from her boot and held it up so Lucas could see it. Then, staying well out of the way of his flailing arms, she walked behind him. "Eli, hide us, please."

Eli's wings spread and hid them from view. Rafe stepped aside as Ashley took hold of one of Lucas's wings and stretched it to its full length. It flapped weakly as Lucas tried to escape her grasp. The wings were still growing; they were soft and as yet missing the muscle needed to aid flight. The knife's serrated edge tore through the membrane and the thin bones. Blood began to pour from the wounds as Ashley kept cutting.

"Natalie Gray," Ashley said as she sliced right through his wing and rent it in two. She started again from the top, leaving the bony edge intact but shredding the soft flesh of the wing. "Andrea Mason…" Ashley dragged the knife down again, naming each one of the four women that Lucas had killed. When the one wing was ruined, Ashley took hold of the other and meted out the same punishment.

When she was finished, all that remained were the bloodied stumps sticking out from his shoulders. His majestic black wings were ripped to ribbons. They hung like bloody streamers from his back.

Ashley stood back, her hands covered in blood, sweat beading on her forehead. She nodded at the angels to take him away. They trapped him in a ball of silver light and started to lift him into the sky.

"Enjoy your last flight, Lucas," Ashley called after him.

"I hate you, Ashley!" Lucas screamed, struggling against the angels who held him firm. "I hope the Preacher fucking slaughters you all!"

Ashley watched until he disappeared. She caught sight of Rafe staring at her, dumbfounded.

"Do you think less of me?" she asked, fearful of Rafe's reply.

"I didn't think I could love you any more than I already do," Rafe said, reaching out to take the blood-soaked knife from Ashley's hand. "But then you go and pull that kind of badass move and I couldn't be more proud of you." She made a face. "Or oddly turned on. Which is rather disturbing, but I'm enjoying the buzz." She returned her spear back to a pen and draped her arm around Ashley's shoulders. "Just remind me never to piss you off more than usual when we're in the kitchen and you're armed with a butter knife."

❖

"Can you see what's happening down there?" Blythe asked Daryl as she watched angels carry something into the sky.

Daryl was watching through the telescopic lens on her gun. "If I've just seen right, I think Ashley cut her brother's wings off." She turned to Blythe. "Wow. Well, that explains how she can handle Rafe. She's got ovaries of steel!"

"Considering all the years of torment that demon put her through he's lucky she didn't just kill him."

Blythe wondered what she would have done in the same position. She didn't have Ashley's angelic blood running through her veins so she knew, deep down, given the chance to mete out some vengeance, she wouldn't have stopped at his wings. Did that make her a bad person? Blythe wasn't sure, but she'd worked for the DDU and in the realm of demons long enough to know that there were varying degrees of badness, and sometimes retribution was the only way to quell the tide.

"I'd have been tempted to slit his throat," Daryl said. "I'm surprised Rafe didn't use her own knife to remove his tongue."

Blythe had to agree. One demon down, hundreds more to go. She looked over her shoulder at Virgil.

"Virgil, your friends need to find a way to plug that portal. For every demon we incapacitate there's at least another hundred that take its place."

"Blythe?" Daryl's voice was low and urgent. "We're outnumbered here and I can't help but wonder why we haven't retreated to a safer position. The demons are killing angels. What chance do we have against them with nothing but bullets when they have the power to murder angels?"

Blythe was wondering that too. She'd watched with a grim satisfaction every time the angels' arrows or blades struck down a demon. Yet she'd also watched angels dragged from the sky and smashed into the earth, their wings ripped apart and the feathers left floating in the air.

"I'm going to be annoyed if we're sacrificial lambs in this ungodly war," Daryl said.

"Can you get a shot at the Preacher?" Blythe knew how good a shot Daryl was. Who knew the mild-mannered country detective was a closet expert sniper?

"No, not while he's so high in the air keeping watch over the proceedings. I don't want to bring him down on us. Do you see that other demon glued to his side?"

"Are you thinking that's Lucian?"

"Could be. I'd imagine that's where he'd be." Daryl nodded in the Preacher's direction. "And weren't Kieran's visions always where Lucian was by the Preacher's side?"

"The angels aren't challenging him. I find that curious."

"The angels have enough to contend with. And anyone who has dared to get near him Lucian has chased off or maimed. That demon is the Preacher's guard dog, chained to his side to do his bidding. Besides, I think we're watching a heavenly power play in motion. You and I know everything happens for a reason. We are but pieces on a divine chessboard, moving only where we are placed. The Preacher's time will come once his demons have been culled down to a more manageable rabble."

"Can you see a way out of this? An ending that doesn't leave us dead in this field?"

Daryl took Blythe's face in her hands. "I can't see the future with Virgil's help, only what is missing. You were missing from my life. And then I found you. Whatever happens today, we're together and we'll go forward together. You're my One and that means forever, whatever the outcome."

"You know you're going to have to marry me, don't you?" Blythe said, never loving Daryl more than in this moment.

"You're seriously proposing to me during an apocalypse?" Daryl's eyes were shining with unshed tears.

Blythe held up her hand and flashed the ring she still wore from their very first case. Neither had removed their "wedding rings" once the case was over. They'd been in love by then, and the rings were a symbol of that. "It's not like we haven't just been waiting for the right moment to do this. Our job keeps getting in the way. Well, I'm tired of waiting."

"And you chose *now*?" Daryl shook her head in amusement. "You know I'm just going to say yes, don't you? Over and over, always yes."

They kissed to seal the deal, mindless to everything around them but each other. They both jumped when Virgil's hands alighted on their heads, his smile radiant and joyous.

Blythe shook her head at them both. "Great. Now we have the added pressure of not dying here so we can plan a wedding."

"Rafe is never going to let you live it down that you asked for my hand here."

"Maybe it will push her into marrying her own One. Everyone deserves a happy ending, my love." She nodded toward Merlo and Kieran. "Especially these two, don't you agree?"

Daryl nodded. "Love has to triumph over evil, right?"

"From your lips to God's ears."

CHAPTER THIRTY

Behold the discord I bring to the earth. Humans will perish at the hands of my demons, and we shall take our rightful place in this paradise that should have been ours from creation." The Preacher's voice carried across the fields. "My work here is nearly done. I have poisoned the minds of the politicians into thinking they are in charge, while all the time they have been my puppets invictus. Peace and security? This earth shall know neither while humans walk on its face. *I've* seen to that. It's so easy to manipulate those tiny brains of theirs. They may have been born in God's image, but their souls are as corrupt as my demons and just as easily led. The pious with so much hate in their hearts? They're praying to a god, but *I'm* the one answering their prayers. Oh, Heavenly Father, you stupidly gave humans free will, so I impressed upon them *mine*."

Kieran curled into herself while the Preacher spouted his message of self-indulgence and hate. She clapped her hands over her ears but could still hear his insidious voice worming its way into her brain as it broadcast over the entire area for his demons to hear and cheer to. He was preaching to the masses, to his already loyal followers and the angels who were fighting to bring order back on the earth. She could feel her body shaking with an uncontrollable rage.

The trouble was, she didn't know if it was hers or Lucian's.

All Kieran knew was that the self-serving contempt the Preacher was preaching was driving her as insane as it had when she'd been out of her body and she'd had to see him in Hell. Kieran wanted to scream, to drown out his voice and fill the air with a white noise to bring her some semblance of quiet.

"Kieran? Kieran? What's happening to you?" Merlo clutched at Kieran's shoulders.

"He's in my head again," Kieran gritted out. "I can't stand it."

Merlo hugged Kieran to her, rocking her. "Hold on, baby, hold on."

I don't think I can. I don't think it's my choice anymore.

Kieran was overloading with violent thoughts and sensations. The proximity of so many demons and Lucian and the Preacher's force of presence was playing havoc with her mind.

I thought I was free from this.

Kieran felt like she was suffering some sort of psychotic breakdown. The pressure in her head was growing to an exploding point. It made the previous possessions seem almost inconsequential and trite. Something was pulling her toward the field. She had the horrible feeling the Preacher knew where she was. She could sense it, sense *him.* It felt like she was being drawn out of her hiding place. And if he knew where she was, then that would lead him straight to the others. Kieran couldn't live with that thought.

She broke free from Merlo's grip but grabbed for Merlo's shoulders. She felt like she was having to push past walls and barriers just to get some kind of control in her whirling head. "I have to go."

"What?"

For a moment, the chaos in Kieran's brain fell aside and she could see in crystal clear clarity. "I love you, Merloina Bluetralis, with all I am and all I ever will be."

"Kieran, what are you…?"

Kieran kissed her with the most gentle, passionate, soul-destroying kiss that poured out all her love for Merlo. She pulled back reluctantly, enjoying the dazed look in Merlo's eyes.

"Forever, Merlo. I'm yours forever." With that, Kieran stood and began walking away from the car.

"*Kieran!*"

Kieran heard Merlo scream her name, but she wasn't in control of her feet. She wasn't in control at all, and resigned to it. Resigned too to her fate and that it was no longer her choice. She ran toward the field.

"Kieran? What the hell are you doing?"

Rafe's voice called out to her, but Kieran just kept going. She stopped just a few yards from where the fighting was and raised her head to the sky.

"Hey! Mr. Monologue! How about you save the speeches for someone who actually gives a fuck what you think?" she screamed. Her voice carried unnaturally over the heads of the demons, and they stilled. There was a resounding timbre to her voice, resonating, commanding. She spoke with an authority that stopped demons in their tracks.

Kieran knew it wasn't her voice.

A strange hush fell over the field as the demons turned to her like a pack of dogs called to heel by a soundless whistle. That gave the angels their chance. They started bringing the demons down in droves.

Above them, the Preacher descended out of the sky like a huge majestic bird.

"Well, if it isn't the Observer. So good of you to show yourself at last." He flew closer until Kieran could make out his terrifying features. "I have to say I expected someone more..." His voice dripped with condescension. "Just *more*. You're just a human. A female one too. You're of little consequence." He flicked his wrist, and three demons came rushing off the field toward her.

Kieran closed her eyes, bracing herself for death that was about to befall her, but...nothing happened. She opened an eye and saw the white wings that were forming a barrier all around her. Kieran looked up into the face of an angel she didn't recognize.

"Thank you," she whispered. She had no idea where he had come from. "Have you been with me all along?"

He nodded. "We all have." He opened his wings and she saw three more angels, armed with swords, standing in a circle around her.

"You travel with angels." The Preacher descended to hang over Kieran's head. She had to crane her neck to look at him. His shadow darkened the ground beneath her. "I have my own honor guard too." He gestured to the very large demon behind him. The demon unfurled his wings to their fullest extent and moved from behind the Preacher to reveal himself.

Kieran felt her stomach drop. This demon was massive and lethal looking from his cloven hooves to the sharp points on his wings.

So this is Lucian. The Preacher's shadow that brings forth his light.

The Preacher smiled. "Lucian, be a dear. Deal with them."

Kieran had never seen anything move so fast in her life. In the blink of an eye, Lucian had flown down and grabbed one of the angels and knocked him to the ground. All Kieran saw was a black blur and red spraying into the air as he attacked the other angels, showing them little mercy. The angels fell at his feet, all unconscious and bleeding. Kieran looked at their battered bodies and resigned herself to the same fate.

"I command you to come before me," the Preacher said.

Kieran forced herself to stand firm. She felt rigid and frozen in place, but her insides were whirling like a leaf in a hurricane.

"All my followers heed my voice," he warned her.

"I am not one of your followers." Kieran just managed to speak from behind her gritted teeth.

The Preacher lowered himself to the ground, and Kieran finally got to be face-to-face with him. He was even more terrifying in reality. He drew in close and sniffed at her.

"No, you're not one of mine," he said, his eyes flaring. "But something inside you is. It's faint now, but I can still detect it. You couldn't exorcise it all away. It calls you to me." He leaned in closer and Kieran gagged on his putrid breath. It smelled of burned flesh and ages old decay. "It's in your blood," he said. "How intriguing." He sniffed at her again, running what was left of his nose down her neck.

"Lucian, if I didn't know better I'd almost wonder if this wasn't one of your detestable human spawnings. But I can see your first-born bitch with her precious guardian angel. And your bastard son was too stupid to just go ahead and kill her and got himself captured again. You really were a slave to your basest desires to go forth and multiply. Was there no human female you didn't rut with?" He ran his tongue up Kieran's cheek like a dog. "If she's indeed yours, I will deal with you later."

He continued to inspect her like she was a specimen under a microscope. Then he shot a glance over his shoulder at Lucian, who loomed at his back watching his every move. "But for now, she's mine," he said, kicking Kieran in the chest with such force she felt her ribs cave in from his cloven hoof. The blow sent her flying across the field to land with a thump in the dirt.

Kieran knew her friends were screaming for her as she rolled on the ground in agony. No angel came to her rescue this time. Lucian kept them all at bay, as did the demons. She spat out blood and struggled to rise, rocking drunkenly to her feet.

"So, you're abusive to women too," she said, deciding that she was at least going to go down fighting in this painfully one-sided match.

"I'm abusive to everyone, child." The Preacher walked over to her as if he was taking an afternoon stroll. "It's in my nature."

"Let me guess, *Daddy* didn't show you enough attention?" Kieran said, knowing exactly who his father was, and she watched with great satisfaction as his face darkened with rage.

"I would have made an excellent Savior. One less self-sacrificing and more the warrior than a peacekeeper."

"Wow." Kieran wiped at the blood trickling from her lips and tried to breathe through the pain from her chest. "There wouldn't have been a stake big enough to nail your ego on, would there?"

The Preacher sneered at her. "Don't you mean a cross?"

"Interpretations differ, but I'd reckon you had a hand in that as well. Changing the Word of God to fit the ruler of the time, altering words so they fit better to further your propaganda. Adding your own prejudices to cause men to keep women under their subjugation, to have gays branded as unnatural when they are still God's children. To treat anyone of color as a lesser being when they are equal and a damn sight better than the white man who looks down on everything in judgment from his misappropriated privileged pedestal you have set him on. Is there nothing you haven't tried to bring ruin to your father's creation?"

He shook his head at her. "No, not really. You are a worthless plague infesting my inheritance. I'll wipe you out, one by one, if I have to." He smiled at her. It wasn't a pretty sight. "Starting with you who saw too much and then tipped the angels off to my plans. There's a special place in Hell for you, my dear. Let me help you get to it."

The second kick knocked Kieran into the middle of the demon horde who descended like jackals upon her. Their hooves kicked and stomped all over her defenseless body. Kieran almost blacked out from the ferocity of the assault. All around her, she could see demons fighting off the angels that were trying to reach her.

"Now, now, brethren. Be sure to leave something for me to play with." The Preacher walked forward, and the demons parted like the Red Sea for Moses.

Kieran rolled into a ball, sobbing out in pain. Breathing was hard now. She feared they'd punctured her lung. She couldn't stand. The bones in her legs were shattered.

The Preacher nudged her with his hoof. "Hmm, it's been a long time since I've worn the flesh of my enemy, but I think I might have to make an exception with you. Your skull will make quite the addition to my trophy wall." He bent over her. "I'll have your dead eyes staring out at nothing because I think you've seen enough, haven't you? Yet how you managed to see is still a mystery. You're not psychic. You carry no special powers. You're just the vessel for another who has been working against me." He turned to address the fields. "There is a traitor in my house. Someone who found a way to let other eyes see what was long planned for our redemption."

The Preacher looked around. By the smile Kieran could see on his face, he was happy to see his demons fighting to the death with the angels. He never gave pause to the bodies of his demonic army littering the ground, beaten by the angelic forces. He walked over them without a care. He dragged Kieran along behind him, hauling her over the dead from both sides.

Lucian strode behind them. Kieran just stared at him, wondering why he still had his master's back in all this. She blinked to clear the blood from her eyes. Then she blinked again because, for a moment, she could have sworn she saw an angel walking behind her in Lucian's place. When she looked again it was just the demon who loomed large and ugly.

Kieran couldn't see where she was going, but she couldn't get a footing with her shattered limbs so resigned herself to being dragged. She managed to snag an arrow from a demon's chest as she was hauled over him. She hid it up the sleeve of her jacket, wincing as the sharpened tip pierced her palm. Kieran didn't care. She used the new pain to try to center her thoughts.

She could still hear her friends yelling; they sounded closer now. She could hear Ashley issuing orders and threatening to call on someone higher if the angels didn't stop the Preacher and make him hand Kieran over.

The Preacher ignored it all. He dragged Kieran up a steep incline and she could finally get her bearings.

The portal.

"Your eyes have seen too much, little one. You were privy to Hell in all its glories. I can't help but wonder what else you saw." He stopped and let her drop with a thump on the dirt. His large black wings crackled like old leather as he knelt to face her. His hand brushed at her cheek, and Kieran pulled away, repulsed by his touch and the look on his face.

"Do you know whose eyes you saw through, child? Did you hear his name mentioned while you watched unnoticed by us all? Did he call you to him? Did you feel his hands upon you when the possession set in and he controlled your very being?" He ran his clawed hands over Kieran's body. She squirmed at the intrusive touches. "Did he use your body to fuck his way through unsuspecting women?" His grin was wicked. "I can smell that on you, lover of women. Shall I let you in on a little secret? Contrary to belief, your kind don't get sent to Hell. I have had so much fun twisting the minds of bigots to spread the word that you will all burn for your perversion. They seemed more than happy to spread the lies instead of speaking of truth and love." He laughed. "Isn't the human race just delightful?"

"Love is not a perversion," Kieran said. She was flirting with passing out, the pain was so bad now. She knew she stood on the edge of death. She'd been there numerous times before, teetering on the precipice to fall into its blissful release. She could hear it calling to her.

"Ahh, *love*. My Father's greatest gift to mankind and yet the easiest thing to corrupt and turn to hate." He drew closer, staring into Kieran's eyes. "Shall I whisper to you in the insidious tongue of death, girl? I've done it before. Once I'd found you, mind wide open in the possession of another, and I whispered to you to kill yourself. And you tried so hard," he crooned. "But you just won't die. Why is that, do you think?"

Kieran forced herself to think of Merlo and to fight. Possessed or not, under the Preacher's influence or not, Kieran knew she had to live. Merlo had lost enough already.

But time was running out.

He stood and picked Kieran up to hold her by her jacket, dangling her from his fist. "Tell me, who is the traitor among my demons?"

Kieran looked behind him at Lucian. Lucian stared back at her. He closed his eyes and turned his head skyward as if seeking help there. Kieran had a horrible feeling it was of no use for either of them.

She could hear Merlo screaming for her. Kieran prayed she was making the right choice.

"I never saw his face. I just got to see too much of yours." She spat at him, gratified to see him flinch as she struck him with bloodied phlegm.

The Preacher wiped the spittle from his face. "He left something in you. I wonder if I can find it?" He raised a clawed hand and slashed open Kieran's stomach. Then he lifted her up to peer into the gaping wound while she screamed. "No, nothing there after all." He lowered Kieran back down to meet her eyes. "You saw Hell through the traitor's gaze." He walked closer to the mouth of the portal. "I think it's time you see it with your own eyes."

Merlo broke free from her hiding place and clambered over the multitude of dead bodies that lay scattered at the base of the mound. Golden arrows stuck out from demon bodies at all angles. She was horrified to find an equal number of dead angels among the pile. The sight tore at her heart, and she couldn't hold back her tears when she saw the angels' magnificent wings ripped and broken under the bodies of monsters. She spotted something half hidden underneath the broken wing of one angel. Merlo tugged at the bow and pulled it free. She then began picking her way over the bodies, removing arrows until she had too many to carry.

She knew in her heart what the Preacher's intention was and she needed to stop him. Merlo had one thought in her head. To get to Kieran before it was too late. She was so intent on reaching the top of the mound she barely manage to stop herself from tumbling over it. She could see the Preacher holding Kieran up by her neck. Her body was dangling helplessly in the air as he flew above the center of the portal's swirling opening.

Merlo couldn't see Kieran's face, but she could see her fumbling for something at her sleeve. The Preacher was laughing at her struggles and tightened his grip more.

"You want to see Hell? So be it."

The Preacher's eyes widened and his mouth dropped open in shock. It was then Merlo spotted the glint of gold from an arrow Kieran had shoved through his soft underjaw and rammed up into his brain. He roared out in pain. Merlo fought to keep her footing as the earth shifted beneath her as everything trembled.

The Preacher struggled to pull the arrow free. Flames began to lick out from his eye sockets.

"Go to hell," he said and let go of Kieran to clutch at his wound.

Kieran fell.

Merlo screamed out but knew she couldn't save her. She grabbed her bow and aimed an arrow at the Preacher. The first shot hit him in the eye. The arrow pierced his skull and stuck out the back. She shot another arrow into the other eye, then continued to shoot one arrow after another. The lethal tips pierced his skin and ripped through his wings.

She realized Lucian was holding the Preacher in place to stop him from escaping.

Merlo heard the unmistakable sounds of bullets firing. She didn't need to look behind her to know that Daryl and Blythe had moved into position and were taking him out with her. All head shots. Lucian had ducked enough to use the Preacher's body as a shield. Merlo continued shooting until she couldn't feel her fingers. She shot until they were raw and bloodied. She didn't stop firing until she reached for another arrow only to come up empty-handed. It dawned on her how time had seemed to stand still for everything in the portal. She could see the dead Preacher still held aloft by an unmoving Lucian.

Merlo looked down into the portal. Kieran hung suspended in mid-tumble.

There was still time.

The Preacher's body was limp and unrecognizable in its shattered state. Time returned to normal, and Lucian let go of him. He then stretched out his wings but hesitated, deferring to Eli, who was flying toward him.

Eli spoke. "I can't use the portal. So you'd better go rescue your daughter, Lucian, before your other one jumps in after her."

Merlo turned to see Ashley frantically climbing up the mound. When she looked back, Lucian was diving into the swirling portal, disappearing into its light.

Merlo laid her bow down. She brushed at her forehead, streaking blood across her face from her torn fingertips. She leaned forward a fraction, just enough to look into the portal where Kieran had fallen. It was a long way down.

Merlo felt numb. She knew now how Kieran had felt, wishing for death to swallow her whole.

I could just fall right in. My journey would be over and I could rest at last with her.

She leaned a little farther hoping she could see something, anything, that pointed to Kieran still being alive. Before she could look any further, two strong arms jerked her back from the precipice. Dina dragged Merlo away from the edge and grasped her tighter, refusing to let her go.

"No, my friend. Please believe me. That's not where your future ends."

CHAPTER THIRTY-ONE

The steady thrum of wings beating drew Merlo's head from Dina's shoulder. Lucian appeared out of the mouth of the portal with Kieran in his arms.

"Oh my God," Merlo whispered, trying to see if she could detect any signs of life. "Dina, is she breathing? Tell me you can see her breathing."

The demons were in an uproar. They had just witnessed their leader killed before them, and Lucian had been an accomplice to his death. They snarled and hissed at him, baying for his blood when he reappeared from the portal. They surged forward as a mass, with the hive mind fixed on bringing Lucian down. Angels be damned; they wanted Lucian to pay.

A trumpet call sounded from the heavens. Then another and another in swift succession, each sounding louder, more strident, and ominous. The sky above turned from morning blue to a dark gray heralding the storm coming. Black clouds formed, lightning crackled and lit the sky with angry flashes. The fields were plunged into darkness. Then a huge swath of white light burst through the clouds, blinding in its intensity. It struck the whole of the farmlands like a spotlight, focused on angels and demons alike. The massive silhouette of an angelic being stepped in the brilliance and, accompanied by a loud crack of thunder, unfurled his gigantic wings to reveal himself.

"ENOUGH!" His voice boomed. His giant furious face pushed through the clouds as he leaned his upper body right out of the light to look down upon them all. He was like a Titan, looming over the earth, blotting out the sun and directing his wrath down on the battlefield below.

All hell broke loose among the demons. Torn between fighting or saving their own skins, they chose to run. Like rats leaving a sinking ship, they scattered, pushing aside the angels in their haste, all racing for the same destination. They ran toward the mound where the portal remained open, choosing to return to Hell rather than stay above and face whatever divine retribution they were about to incur.

Merlo slid down that same mound on her backside, ignoring the scrapes and cuts she was acquiring as she fled from the stampede heading her way. Dina was right behind her, trying to keep up. Lucian swooped down to their vehicles. He laid Kieran on top of the hood of Rafe's car, then flew back into the sky. He circled above with a menacing air.

He's protecting them. Merlo watched as he grabbed hold of any demon that flew at him, tossing them away as if they were nothing more than gnats he was swatting aside.

She slid to the ground and broke into a sprint toward the cars and Kieran. She was shaken by how much Kieran looked like she'd been laid to rest on the hood of the car. As lifeless as a statue carved on an old tombstone that depicted a fallen warrior.

Merlo refused to believe this was how it ended for Kieran, not after all she'd been through and suffered.

Merlo ran straight to the car and reached out to touch Kieran. She wasn't moving. Merlo couldn't even see her breathing. She checked the pulse in Kieran's neck and was relieved to find it beating against her fingers. The beat was sluggish, but Kieran was still alive. She was terrified to touch Kieran anywhere else. The injuries she could see were horrific, and Merlo couldn't hold back the tears at how much damage the Preacher had inflicted. Kieran's clothing was soaked a deep crimson with her blood, her skin was torn open, exposing her insides. Merlo couldn't even begin to look at what was left of Kieran's legs. Kieran was bruised, bloodied, and broken.

What the hell can I do? Merlo stared at her own hands resting on Kieran's arm, powerless to help her love.

Eli flew toward them. "Please," she begged him, "help her."

"We're going to." Ashley took a place opposite Merlo and laid her hands on Kieran. "Stand back, Merlo. We're going to heal her."

Kieran's body jerked as it reacted to the power that flowed from Ashley's hands. A low groan escaped her bloodied lips, and Merlo's tears fell even faster. She began praying for a miracle as she watched Eli join Ashley in the laying on of hands.

"Heal, my darling, please," Merlo pleaded, never taking her eyes from Kieran's face.

Ashley brushed aside the tattered remains of Kieran's shirt, revealing the true extent of the damage the Preacher had wrought. Even Ashley paled at the sight.

"Okay, this might take longer than I thought," Ashley muttered to Eli and began smoothing her hand over the jagged and torn flesh on Kieran's stomach.

Merlo had to turn away for a moment. She looked up into the light at the luminescent being whose presence had terrified the demons so much. "Is that really...?"

"Humans aren't the only ones susceptible to trickery," Eli answered.

Merlo could see and hear the demons still fighting each other to get up the mound and into the portal. "They're terrified."

"With good reason," Eli said, never taking his attention from his healing. "They have felt God's judgment before. Thinking He's coming to unleash His wrath on them has literally put the fear of God in them."

"So if that's not God, who is it?" Whoever *he* was, he was magnificent. She watched as he began to withdraw back into the fading light to watch from the clouds.

"That's probably Gabriel playing the big guy," Rafe said from behind Ashley where she stood with her gun poised, guarding her. "He's got the wings for it."

Daryl and Blythe came behind Merlo and hugged her close.

"That was some pretty amazing bowmanship you displayed," Daryl said. "We're talking Amazons of Themyscira levels of proficiency here. I'm going to beg you for lessons."

Merlo knew they were talking to keep her mind off what was happening to Kieran. She played along with them for her own sanity. She couldn't bear to see how injured Kieran was. And she still wasn't waking up. Merlo wondered if that was a good thing considering all that Ashley and Eli were doing to her.

"I'll trade bow lessons for sniper ones. You never once hit Lucian as you blew the Preacher's head apart." She couldn't hide her relief at that, however awful it had been to see close up.

"We owed him," Blythe said. "He was attempting to sacrifice children when we were brought into all this. He ruined so many families trying to further his own sick agenda. He didn't even need them; it was just his cruelty at play. Besides, it helped having Dina freeze him in place so we had a clear line of vision. Stopped us from taking out the demon behind him as well."

Dina lowered the time shield from around the farmlands and was now concentrating it around the mound to keep the demons contained as they poured down the portal. Merlo could see how crushed together they all were, pushing and jostling, fighting each other in their getaway. They had trampled over each other in their panic to escape. Dying demons were strewn in their wake, trodden into the ground by the multitude of hooves that had stormed over them. A grisly trail of dead and injured lay in their tracks.

Merlo paid them no more heed. She stared at Ashley who was wiping the sweat from her brow on her sleeve as she poured her energies into healing Kieran. Eli looked unruffled as always, but she could see the strain even in his eyes.

Something was wrong.

A shadow fell over her, and she flinched. Lucian landed beside the car and edged over to stand at Eli's side.

"Can she be saved?" he asked.

Ashley didn't look at him, but her anger was plain to see. "It's too soon to tell. Your Preacher did a lot of damage, and your demons didn't help either using her as a soccer ball. She was already weak because of your damned possession, Lucian. We appreciate all you've done to warn us of this impending demon-led apocalypse, but did you need to drive her to the brink of madness *and* leave her open to the Preacher's influence? He had her try to kill herself. Not just once but multiple times." She drew in a deep breath. "Why her? What did she do that was deserving of that fate?"

"She was the only one I could reach out to and influence and *trust* with this knowledge. She is of my blood, conceived while I had the very last vestiges of any angelic goodness inside of me to pass on to her. It left her as the perfect conduit."

"Damned Fallen. How much easier it would be if you'd all

practiced safe sex and used protection to protect us from *you*," Ashley said.

"But then you wouldn't have been born, my child, and I know the earth has been a much better place with you walking it."

Ashley's head whipped up at his gentle voice.

"I was an angel led by love. Thrown out of heaven because I desired a woman so much. I gave up everything for her, and we created the most beautiful child that I can never regret fathering. But I was imperfect, losing my goodness with every day that I remained on earth. I lost my love and selfishly sought comfort in others because I knew I was living on borrowed time. I was to be banished; my demon soul was rising." He moved in closer. "This one was created unintentionally, but I can see how much she is loved." He glanced over at Merlo. "I have no excuses. I did what I did without honor or thought for anyone other than myself, and she is suffering for my mistakes. But she was the one who answered my call when I reached out to find someone to warn the world."

"You used her," Merlo said, hatred boiling inside her as he tried to justify Kieran's very existence as something to fulfill his purpose alone.

He nodded. "Needs must when the devil drives you. Isn't that how the saying goes?"

Merlo wished she had her bow at hand. Her hands twitched for the weapon so she could use it. She pointed at Kieran, her body twitching and jerking as Ashley and Eli healed her. "Was *this* worth it?"

"She's just saved the world."

"Only because she didn't manage to kill herself before she got to me and I was able to see that there was more to her than madness. But this time, *this* time she might not survive, and that's on *you*." Merlo felt someone hold her back to keep her from pounding her frustration out on Lucian.

"*I* made her fail those attempts. Do you think I wanted my daughter to die?"

"You didn't even know about her!" Merlo yelled at him.

"Once I did know I knew she would be a wonder. After all," Lucian looked over at Ashley, "my firstborn turned out to be extraordinary."

Ashley stared wide-eyed at him. "*Dad?*" She began shaking. "*Lucian?*"

"I went as Luke on earth. I never used my full name. Marion

named Lucas after me, but unfortunately, that apple didn't fall very far from the demonic tree." He gave Ashley a considering look. "With all he did, you still didn't kill him. I'm curious why."

"Because even though he was despicable, he was still my brother and all I had left of you." Ashley looked down at Kieran. "Or so I thought." She spun around to Rafe. "You said you saw me in her that time. Did you think she was my sister?"

Rafe shrugged. "Stranger things have happened. Let's face it, your daddy here is the epitome of the randy little devil. There could be a whole tribe of Scotts out there. With this family's history, you're already just one call away from being guests on a Jerry Springer show." She shot him a look of disgust before turning back to Ashley. "Sweetheart, you're starting to go pale. You and Eli together are struggling to heal her. Call in another healer angel." She gestured upward. "It's not like we don't have enough on hand to help out."

Ashley leaned back into Rafe. "We've done all we can. She's lost way too much blood, though." She raised her hands from Kieran's body.

Merlo saw the newly healed skin across Kieran's abdomen. She was still covered in gore, but the bruises were healed and the blood had congealed. She looked expectantly at Kieran's face.

"Why isn't she waking up?"

Lucian moved forward and reached out to Kieran. Before he could touch her, Merlo slapped his hand away. She winced. That had probably hurt her more than it had him.

"You don't get to touch her," she said. "You've brought her nothing but bad."

Lucian's hand hovered in the air. "I need to see if it's my fault she's still not reacting."

"Why would it be your fault?"

"Because everything is." He looked at Merlo poignantly.

Merlo nodded and tried not to get too antsy when he laid his clawed hand on Kieran's forehead, then down over her heart.

"The Preacher has drained her of her life force. He must have been doing it every time he possessed her and pushed her to suicide. Every attempt was a deliberate drain. It's weakened her. Then when he slashed her open he was able to spill even more out."

Blythe frowned. "Are you saying the life force is in her blood? In *all* our blood?"

Eli nodded. "Part of what sets humans apart in creation is what you know as your soul, your spirit, that spark of life that makes you sentient and eternal. You are knowing, *aware*. Conscious there is *more*. Your blood carries that within it."

Lucian held out his arm. "Take mine from me. My taking responsibility for her is long overdue. I owe her more than blood to gain her forgiveness."

Eli placed his hand on Lucian's scaled arm. He shook his head. "Your blood would kill her. In the end, it's what helped drive her mad. Surrounded by demons, she was called forth. Your blood's neither angelic nor human anymore. She wouldn't survive with pure demon blood in her veins."

Ashley began rolling up her sleeve. "Then if she needs blood, take mine. We're siblings, and I have both the angelic *and* human types flowing through my veins. That has to be a plus."

Eli laid his palm on Kieran's arm, covering the veins just visible under the blood she had shed and closed his eyes. His face grew somber. He shook his head at Ashley. "It won't be enough to save her."

Merlo slapped a hand over her mouth to hold back the screams desperate to make themselves heard.

NO! Not now, not now I've finally found her.

Merlo placed her hands on Kieran's chest, waiting for the telltale jolt of recognition they had always shared. Kieran didn't move. Merlo tried again. Still, Kieran didn't react. Merlo caught Eli's shake of his head to Ashley.

No, she can't die. It's not fair.

Eli placed a hand on Kieran's forehead and nodded as if deciding he needed to do something, however unpalatable it appeared. "I can grant you but a moment." Eli bent to whisper in Kieran's ear, "Wake up, child," then drew back, waiting.

Kieran's eyelids flickered and then, ever so slowly, she opened her eyes.

"Is it over?" she asked, sounding tired.

"The Preacher is dead," Eli told her.

"Merlo?" Kieran began to search for her.

Merlo crowded to Kieran's side as Kieran turned her head toward her.

"I didn't mean to nearly die again. I just knew I needed him to stop. I needed it all to stop."

Merlo nodded. "I understand. It's over now. You're safe, we all are. The demons have sent themselves back to Hell."

Kieran's eyebrows raised. "Now that's a story for later." Her eyelids began to droop as if they were too heavy to keep open. "I feel kind of strange."

"Ashley and Eli healed you. You're going to be okay," Merlo said, knowing in her heart it wasn't the truth but desperately needing it to be. *Don't you dare leave me.*

Kieran's brow crinkled. "No, I don't think so." She paused as if gathering her thoughts. "I think I'm dying."

Merlo's heart seized in her chest. "No, Kieran, no. You're going to be fine. Just fight it, please."

Kieran looked at Merlo. "I've been close to death so many times, it's never felt quite like this. I can *feel* it." She held up a hand and searched for Merlo's. She gripped it as tight as she could. Her eyes slipped closed again. "It's not painful; it's not really anything. It just feels inevitable."

"Please hold on. I've waited a lifetime for you. You can't just leave now that we've finally met and I love you. I love you, Kieran, and I don't want you to go. Please don't leave me. Don't make me spend another long and lonely day without you."

Kieran opened her eyes again even though it looked painful for her to do so. "I love you too, Merloina." She took a slow breath in. "Funny how, after all the times I wished I could die, now that it's happening I don't want to go. I don't want to die, Merlo. I don't want to die and leave you alone."

Merlo brushed at the tear that escaped from Kieran's eye. She brushed her hand tenderly over Kieran's cheek, memorizing the shape of her jaw, the color of her eyes looking at her so plaintively, and the shape of her lips that were curved into a melancholy smile. *So beautiful. She is just so very beautiful.*

"Stay with me," she begged, leaning down to press soft kisses all over Kieran's face.

Kieran smiled at the tender touches. Merlo drew back and rested her cheek on Kieran's forehead, loathe to let her go.

"Is that light for me?" Kieran asked, staring into the distance.

Merlo followed her line of sight. Kieran wasn't looking toward the bright light shining from the heavens; she was looking somewhere else entirely.

"I promise I'll wait for you," Kieran whispered, "Even if it takes an eternity for you to reach me. I'll be there, waiting to take you in my arms and welcome you home."

Merlo kissed Kieran's lips again, this time less gentle and sobbed as she felt the pressure from Kieran's kiss back start to fade.

"Kieran? KIERAN!" Merlo shook her head angrily and looked up at the sky above her. "No! I've waited long enough for love to find me." She ripped her shirtsleeve open. "I've been cursed to walk alone for too long. I won't take another step without her by my side." She looked around wildly and then bent to snatch up the knife tucked inside Blythe's boot. Merlo held it at her wrist.

Everyone yelled at her to stop, frozen in horror as Merlo prepared to slit open her wrist.

"Take my blood and give it her," she ordered Eli. "Give her *my* life. She doesn't deserve to die. I've lived more than long enough as it is. I give my life gladly in exchange for hers so at least my immortality will have had meaning and I will live on in her."

Eli reached over to still the knife on Merlo's flesh. It was already cutting into her skin; a slow trickle of blood was pooling under the sharp blade. He took the knife out of Merlo's shaking hand.

Merlo cried desperately. "Please, no, Eli. Don't let her die…"

Eli soothed her with a look. "I won't need the knife to transfer your blood to her. But are you sure, Neverage? Are you certain you want to do this? It's unheard of. It might not even be possible."

"My life without her would be no life at all." Merlo held out her arm. "Give her my life."

Eli took hold of Merlo's arm, placed one finger to a vein, and then found a corresponding one on Kieran's arm. A thin beam of light connected them as he formed a conduit.

Blood began to drip through, then flowed.

"May the Spirit bring forth life," Eli prayed.

❖

The last thing Kieran remembered was plummeting toward the circling kaleidoscope of colors that made up the portal's opening. It had pulled her toward it like a piece of flotsam helplessly drawn into the depths of a maelstrom. Time had slowed then stopped, and Kieran had just existed, trapped immobile right above the portal's mouth. It was too much for her to bear. It was too much like her possessions by Lucian, and what was left of Kieran's mind rebelled and refused to suffer that claustrophobic state anymore. Wounded, almost blinded by pain, Kieran blacked out.

Flashes of more intense pain brought her to the brink of consciousness before she slid back under to the blessed peace of oblivion. In those brief moments, Kieran flirted with the idea that at some point Merlo had been beside her and Kieran had managed to tell her how she felt before losing consciousness again. She wondered how much of a dream that had been because she couldn't tell the difference between reality and this endless sleep. Closing her eyes and having to leave Merlo behind had been the hardest thing she'd ever had to do, but her body had dictated the rules.

Kieran realized she was dying. *My timing totally sucks.*

It felt like a second had passed, or maybe it had been eons, but Kieran's fading consciousness could see a bright sparkling light. She watched it form, growing larger and larger, brighter, stronger, almost pulsating in its intensity. She felt her body react, like it was preparing itself for war. Rebuilding, reconstructing, being *reborn*. The light engulfed Kieran's mind, blinding her senses until finally, her lungs filled to capacity and she let out a breath of air. It was followed by a burst of light that triggered in her brain.

Kieran could feel something solid beneath her back. She moved a fingertip to touch it. It felt like metal. And it was hot.

Was this Hell? Was she staked out on a grill being roasted for her sins? She could hear voices now. Angry voices. Who knew Hell was so noisy? She squinted and saw gray clouds above drifting away to reveal a bright sunny day.

Welcome back to Kansas.

"Why are you stopping? I told you to give her it all."

"I'm a healer. It's not in my nature to kill."

Kieran opened her eyes and saw Merlo squaring off with Eli.

"I told you her life comes first, over my own. Drain me, goddammit! My life in exchange for hers."

Kieran shifted a little and that drew everyone's eyes to her. She smiled. "I'd rather no one died, if my opinion counts."

Merlo looked down at her in shock. "Kieran?" She flung her untethered arm around Kieran and clutched at her. She sobbed into Kieran's neck.

Kieran held on just as tight, burying her face in Merlo's hair and finding comfort in its familiar scent. She felt light and giddy and inexplicably happy. "What's happened?" Kieran asked because her wrist was aching when the rest of her body felt untouched. Kieran had a feeling she had missed something important but had no idea what.

"You needed a blood transfusion." Merlo's answer was muffled against Kieran's neck. She wrapped her other arm about her the second Eli dissolved the transfusion line between them.

"Oh." Kieran peeked over Merlo's shoulder at everyone watching them. The strain on their faces told a much more detailed story. "So many to choose from. Was it Demon Daddy or my newly discovered sister who had to pop open a vein for me?"

Rafe snorted at Kieran's impudence. "I like this kid a lot. She's going to be fun at family get-togethers. She's already great with the cat, so that's a major plus in her favor too."

Kieran laughed, but the look of exasperation on Ashley's face held something more now when she looked at Kieran.

"It wasn't us," Ashley told her, stepping forward to rest a hand on Kieran's knee. "We couldn't have saved you."

Saved. Kieran mulled that word over for a moment. Things had been worse than she'd imagined. She drew back from Merlo's tight hold and lifted Merlo's chin so she could meet her eyes. "*You?*"

Merlo nodded and said, "I love you."

Kieran ran a hand over her chest. Her ribs seemed to be miraculously intact. In fact, she felt hardly any pain at all except for the niggling tenderness on her wrist. There was no sign of any needle mark on her skin. "I'm guessing the transfusion wasn't exactly normal?"

Merlo's eyes widened. Kieran frowned at the flinch that Merlo couldn't hide from her. What was she missing here?

"I meant no needles unless the DDU have that kind of equipment tucked alongside their big guns." She bumped Merlo gently. "Do I at least get a cookie? I always get a cookie and orange juice when I donate."

"You might have gotten more than you bargained for, Kieran," Ashley said.

Kieran looked to Merlo for an explanation. "You can tell me. It's okay."

"Merlo wanted to trade her life for yours. She intended to have me infuse you with her blood to bring you back to life while she died in your place." Eli's voice was as harsh as Kieran had ever heard it.

Back to life… Kieran digested the implications of that statement. No wonder Merlo was clinging to her. Another near-death experience to add to her tally. A near-death experience for *both* of them, according to Eli.

"Why would I need all of it?" Kieran asked.

"Because yours had been spilled all over this farm and you were dying," Rafe answered.

Kieran tightened her hold on Merlo. "Okay, that's a little more than I can remember. I'm guessing, seeing as we're both alive, that you didn't drain her completely, Eli."

"No, I merely took what was necessary to even the score a little."

Merlo pulled back and wiped at her eyes. "What did you do, Eli?"

"Transfused enough of your immortality to bring Kieran back from the brink and added just enough to make sure it wasn't for nothing."

Kieran and Merlo shared a look between them. "Care to enlighten us, Eli?" Kieran said.

If an angel could look proud of himself, then Eli was it. "Let's just say, as far as I can tell, you're going to live a long and happy life *together*."

The hug Merlo gave her made Kieran's head spin. It bordered on desperation, but it was comforting and made Kieran feel surrounded by her love. Merlo drew back, her face wreathed with the biggest grin Kieran had ever seen her wear. Merlo pulled out of Kieran's arms and rushed over to Eli to hug him too. Rafe laughed at the startled look on his face, but Eli took it well and patted at Merlo's back.

"You're welcome," he said. "Just don't waste a second. Life is precious, however long it lasts."

It took Kieran a little longer to realize what everyone else seemed to already know.

"Wait…if I've been given blood from a Neverage, do *I* become a Neverage too?"

Merlo shrugged nervously. "I wasn't entirely sure, but I guess we'll have more than enough time to find out. You had your life taken from you with the possession, Kieran. I think it's only fair you get it back with interest."

Kieran's head swam with all the implications such a blessing or a curse that could be. She caught sight of Merlo's nervous face. *She did this for me. She literally saved my life.* Kieran ran a hand over her chin, considering all the consequences. "Soooo," she drawled, "I'm always going to look this good?"

Everyone laughed, and it shattered the tense moment and lightened the air. Kieran knew it was going to take some getting used to, but for now she was just happy to be alive. She looked around at her new friends and newfound family. She froze on Lucian, whose features were altering right before her eyes. She pointed a finger at him. "Am I still seeing things or is something happening to him?"

Lucian's horns were shrinking down to nothing until they disappeared, leaving behind a high forehead no longer covered in dark scales. Paler skin revealed itself, and a more human face started to emerge. He shrank a little and his bulk diminished. The huge black wings dissolved and turned into ashes on his back. The demon was being wiped away to leave in its stead the familiar sight of an angelic being.

Kieran stared at the blond-haired man that now stood before them. He was clothed in the ubiquitous white suit that most of the angels that consorted with mankind wore. The look on his renewed face was priceless as he stared down at his hands that were no longer clawed or misshapen.

"Dad!" Ashley gasped. She tugged on Rafe's arm. *"That's* my dad!" She bolted toward him, and he opened his arms to pull her in close.

"Ashley." He laid his head on top of hers and began to cry. "My girl. My sweet, sweet girl."

After a moment, Eli stepped forward. He and Lucian clasped forearms. "Welcome back, Brother," Eli said.

Lucian looked at him. "Thank you for always looking after her."

"It's my pleasure. I told you I would always watch over her in your stead."

Lucian raised his hand again and twisted it around in the sunlight. "I don't understand."

"It's because you sent out a warning when you could have just sat back and let the chaos unfold. Or because you dived into the portal to rescue Kieran and then offered your own life to save hers. Acts of unselfishness from a demon who had been banished for his sins. You didn't think of yourself this time. You thought only of humanity and of her." Eli nodded toward Kieran.

Lucian looked at Kieran. "I think you and I have some catching up to do."

"As long as it doesn't entail possession or telepathy this time," Kieran said.

Kieran looked at Ashley held tight in her father's arms. She didn't feel any envy. She didn't really feel anything where Lucian was concerned except for a lingering animosity that wouldn't die down. It was going to take her some time to separate the madness she equated with his presence to what she now saw before her. She'd never had a father figure in her life. She wasn't sure she needed one now. Especially one who had used her nearly to the point of death. She couldn't help but wonder how much of a mediator Merlo would be sitting in on *those* father/daughter sessions.

So Mom slept with a demon who is now a reinstated angel. She's probably turning in her grave screaming about heaven screwing her over in more ways than one. Kieran sought to clear her mind of both of them. *I am not the sum of my parents. I am my own person and I have been gifted a second chance on life.* Kieran slid off the car before the heat from the sun melted her onto the hood. She ran her hands over her filthy and tattered clothing, mourning the loss of her new shirt and her treasured jacket. *So much blood.* The dried blood had baked into the fabric by the fierce Kansas heat. *No wonder I needed to be saved. I doubt there's any trace of my own blood left inside me now.* She welcomed Merlo back by her side and wrapped an arm across her shoulders.

She gave me my life back. I'm not going to waste another second. And I'm never taking her sacrifice for granted.

Lucian was still marveling at his own transformation. "But I don't have any wings," he said.

Eli shook his head. "Of course not. You of all people should know that you have to earn those back. For now, you have to learn once more to walk in His footsteps to regain your place at His side."

"I won't let Him down again," Lucian promised.

Kieran held Merlo closer to her and marveled at the second chances she and Lucian were blessed with. Lucian was to walk again in the presence of God, whereas Kieran was free to walk at Merlo's side. Kieran offered up a silent prayer of thanks for all that had transpired that day. Out of the trials and tribulations had come Kieran's redemption. She had been *saved*.

She now had a lifetime to dedicate her heart first to Merlo, then in the helping of others. Second chances didn't come around very often. Kieran was determined not to let hers go to waste.

CHAPTER THIRTY-TWO

The landscape was littered with bodies for as far as the eye could see. Angels were walking among the dead and dying, mourning the loss of their own, and carrying them back to the heavens. The last of the demons had disappeared down the portal and Hell's inhabitants had closed it from their side. Now the farm was silent. The scars from the battle cut deep into the ground. Blood from the slain demons seeped into the dirt, poisoning it. Nothing would ever grow there again. The bodies of the demons were dealt with in a much different manner. An angel, wearing a heavy cowl drawn over his face, carried what looked to be an incense burner swinging from a chain. He walked by each demon, uttered a few words, and then swept the burner over them. The bodies evaporated and he moved on to the next one and repeated the gesture time and time again.

Kieran was staring at the sky. The face of God, or whoever, *whatever*, that had been, had dissolved back into the clouds. Kieran could still make out a pair of eyes staring down at the fields from the now clear blue sky. She was glad she had been out of it when all of that had happened. Blythe was still shaking from it. Done merely for effect or not, it had had the desired result. It had sent the demons scurrying back to Hell in terror. A timely reminder that He did watch over them all, good and bad alike.

She looked out at the fields and the bodies left lying in the dirt. *I should have been one of those.* Kieran didn't know quite how she should be feeling. She'd returned back from the brink of death again, but this time with the added bonus of the gift of never aging. *A kind of immortality with an eventual expiry date. So much longer than the life span I'd been expecting to live out my days with.* It still hadn't sunk in. In the short space of time she'd been conscious again, she'd gained a larger lease on life. She'd also gained a half sister that she'd never dreamed of having. One that was some kind of angel/demon hybrid who hunted demons for a living. Then there was the half brother who had been a serial killer before taking on his full demonic form and ending up banished for his sins *twice.* Kieran decided to save any thoughts of him for another time. And she'd finally met the sperm donor her mother had hated so much for impregnating her with Kieran. She'd seen angels and demons warring with each other and had almost met her demise by being thrown into Hell.

There wasn't a large enough dosage of medication on the planet for the level of crazy she felt she had reached and come out the other side of.

Kieran watched Lucian as he followed a healer angel who was tending to the injured angels on the field. Lucian was apologizing to the angels he had attacked, helping them to their feet, and bowing his head to them in shame.

"He could have killed them," Eli said, appearing at Kieran's side. "He didn't, though. He had already chosen his side when he started communicating with you in the visions."

"Yeah, well, good for him. He gets to start over with a clean slate. Maybe he'll even get his wings if he doesn't fall from grace a second time because of some woman he just can't keep his eyes off again."

"Time will tell," Eli said. "You've been avoiding him."

Kieran wasn't surprised someone was calling her out on rebuffing Lucian's overtures to engage her in conversation.

"I've just escaped the jaws of death for the umpteenth time. Playing happy families isn't high on my list of priorities right now. Especially with someone who never acknowledged me until I was useful to him. He's Ashley's father, Eli. He's never been mine. She was brought up by him, cared for by him, loved by him. I never knew him as anything but the detestable being who screwed my mother and left her to make my life a misery because of it." She tried to keep her temper in check, but it was hard work not to just rage it all out.

"Then when he does reach out to me he brings me to the edge of madness with visions of Hell and demons and damnation. He opened me up to the Preacher's persuasive whispers that told me over and over again to kill myself. I tried to *kill* myself, Eli, not just once but many times. He drove me crazy. Yes, it was to save the world and I'm glad it had a reason, one that in the end I was able to help stop from coming true. But it's hard to have familial feelings for someone who used me as much as a pawn in his game as the Preacher did to his blind followers here on earth. I will always associate Lucian with the madness I suffered and the horrors I have seen. I can't help how I feel toward him." She took a deep breath, trying to calm her racing heart.

"I understand," Eli said.

"He wasn't some great and beautiful angel that came to rescue me. He was a demon using me to further his own desires while he force-fed me the visions over and over again." Kieran kicked at the dirt beneath her feet. "I'm not sure if I'll ever be ready to talk to him to try to get to know him. But thanks to Merlo and you, I've got a long time to think about it and maybe one day I'll reconsider."

Eli smiled at her. "But the same doesn't apply to your sister, I hope."

Kieran shook her head, looking over her shoulder where she could see Ashley fussing over Rafe, who held her in her arms and appeared to be slow dancing with her. "No, I liked Ashley from the moment I met her. I'm happy to call her a friend and would love to get to know her as a sister. I want to learn more about her and that force of nature partner she has."

"Rafe knew you two were related before even I saw it."

"She's a detective. She's trained to spot the tiniest of details."

"*I* should have seen it. When you first mentioned the demon's name I should have questioned it then, but there are a great many angels in the heavens and demons down in Hell. Lucian is not an uncommon name amongst my winged brethren nor, I imagine, among the banished." Eli shook his head. "I doubted myself again when I saw his face appear in yours when you were under his possession. It was so fleeting, a flash amid the changes your face was shifting through as the possession took hold. But Kasumba and I both heard his voice in the dying throes of your exorcism." He smiled sadly. "But demons are notorious for being tricksters. It took me seeing him to believe it was my long-lost brother stepping back toward the light. You brought him home, Kieran, back to his father's side."

A flock of angels flying down from the heavens was a grateful distraction for Kieran from that line of thought. They were carrying a large golden disc.

Eli hummed. "The eighth seal. No one will be escaping from that portal again."

"But they'll keep finding other ways out."

"No doubt, and there will be ones waiting to banish them again. Though I think the demon hordes might lay low a while once word of what happened to their self-professed messiah gets out." He cocked his head toward where Ashley, Rafe, Blythe, and Daryl stood. "They've made it their life's work to keep this world free of demonic influences. We are blessed by their presence at our side."

"Yet still mankind falls foul of lies and false prophets."

"Free will, Kieran. It was built into the human condition once it became clear that they desired knowledge above blind obedience."

"Why didn't God just wipe us out and start all over again? Or did the great flood not take well enough the first time?"

Eli stared at her a moment. "You and Rafe will get along just fine," he muttered. "There is no restart button to press because how will anyone of us, of Heaven or earth, learn from that? Better to keep the plan going and see what the outcome is than to keep erasing mankind when it doesn't play by the rules. They seem to do that well enough without heavenly interference."

Kieran thought about that for a minute. "Well, now that I've got more time on my hands than I could ever have imagined, maybe I'll be around to see that final reckoning." She cast a sly eye in his direction. "Whenever that is."

"Indeed."

Kieran laughed at Eli's noncommittal answer. "So, what happens now? The dead demons are removed from the farm and life just goes back to normal for the rest of the world?"

"Yes. They'll never have any knowledge of this occurrence. Only those of you who witnessed it from inside Dina's time shield will ever know what happened."

"And life goes on."

"As it always does. Humans are very resilient. You possess an amazing strength to pick yourselves up and start over. It's inspirational to watch."

Kieran could see Virgil standing near Daryl.

"Has there ever been someone watching over me, Eli?" Kieran had wondered this since she'd found out the truth. Ashley had Eli as her guardian; Daryl had an angel at her shoulder aiding her in her work.

Who's been watching over me all this time?

"I believe so," Eli said. His gaze followed Lucian around the field. "In the most unconventional of ways, I think you had a guardian demon. One who pulled you back from the edge of every suicide attempt you made. Maybe he was the one who pushed you out of the way of that train in the guise of a deer. Perhaps he took the wheel from your hand when you were driving straight for the tree. Like it or not, he *is* your father. He has a great deal to atone for. Maybe while he's proving his worth and loyalty, he can show you his true face this time."

"I'll speak to him before we leave," she grumbled good-naturedly at Eli's gentle coaxing. "I'm not promising anything. I've had to grow up taking care of myself. I can't see that changing just because he thinks he has a parental right to butt in now."

"I'm sure he'll respect your wishes. Besides, you have your whole life anew. I understand there's been mention of a job in the legal department of the DDU that might just be a perfect fit for you?"

"You don't miss much, do you? Yes, Blythe has been hinting there might be a need for a lawyer who could deal with the more 'unusual' cases she and Daryl sometimes handle. But they are just hints at the moment, nothing concrete. I'm still trying to wrap my head around almost being cast into Hell by a demon whose intention was to take over the world."

"All in good time, then." Eli placed his palm on her head. "Blessings be upon you, Kieran Lee. Because without you, we'd never have known what was coming or been prepared for the fight."

"Doesn't *He*," Kieran looked skyward, "know everything?"

"He does. But it's left to us to show Him how well we can cope together in a crisis."

"Free will, eh?"

"Humanity asked for it."

"Yeah." Kieran shook her head. "We're crazy like that." She felt a familiar touch ghost across her cheek and turned around. She caught sight of Merlo waving to her from over by Ashley and smiled.

"Go to her. She's waiting for you."

"Do you know she's the one person in my life who has ever

accepted me and loved me for all that I am? Even when I was at my worst and off my head in the possession."

"Rafe would say she's a 'keeper.'"

Kieran couldn't disagree with that. "But you'd call her my One?"

Eli nodded. "The One that completes you."

"She's the one I want to spend the rest of my life with. Even an eternity won't be long enough, but it's going to be a great place to start."

❖

They returned to Merlo's home and traipsed off to their respective beds exhausted and glad to have left Kansas far behind them.

Breakfast the next morning was a celebratory meal of the long-awaited pancakes Rafe had promised them, and Dina arrived back with Trinity in her care. The house was again filled with noise and discussion and the feeling of relief that they'd all survived something they'd never imagined they'd have to go through.

By the afternoon, Merlo's home was devoid of all its guests, and Kieran was able to collapse on the couch to curl up beside Merlo to just chill out. An hour earlier, they had waved Blythe and Daryl off with promises of a wedding invitation in the mail. Rafe and Ashley had lingered a little longer. Ashley had been reluctant to leave her newfound half sister behind. Kieran was still reeling at the fact she was now the middle child of the three siblings when she'd been the unwanted only child for so long. Rafe and Ashley had left once Ashley had received numerous assurances that Kieran and Merlo would drive to Chicago to stay for a weekend very soon.

Kieran was still thinking about the huge hug Ashley had given her before she left. Maybe being part of a family that genuinely cared for her wouldn't be quite so bad after all.

"What were you and Rafe whispering about before she got in the car?" Merlo asked.

"Nothing much."

"Keeping secrets from me already, Kieran? That doesn't bode well for our future together." Merlo poked her fingers into Kieran's side.

Kieran yelped as Merlo found a ticklish spot. "Hey! Hey! Quit it! Tickling is a form of torture and you're above that!" She managed to grab Merlo's hands and stop them from attacking her any more while she tried to catch her breath. "What happened to you trying to get secrets out of me using your psych skills?"

"We both know it takes forever to get you to reveal anything that way. And I speak from experience dealing with you in a professional capacity."

"I was a pain in the ass, right?" Kieran pressed a kiss on Merlo's knuckles hoping she was looking suitably contrite.

"You were an obstructive patient, yes. It took all my skills to get you to open up to me."

"Oh, darling, you have so many more skills at your disposal that can be used to have me open up to you without any argument." She leaned in to kiss the look of surprise off Merlo's face. She smiled when she drew back and Merlo's lips were left waiting for more.

Merlo opened her eyes and smiled. "Tell me what you two were plotting before I withhold those skills and leave you hanging."

Kieran tugged Merlo close. "So this is how it starts, eh?" She wrapped her arms around Merlo, loving the feel of her. "It's supposed to be a surprise."

"I've had my fill of surprises for a lifetime, even *my* lifetime, thank you very much. I thought I saw the face of God in the heavens, Kieran. I nearly took off running like the demons did. It was awe-inspiring and terrifying all at the same time."

"It's a nice surprise. Nothing bad, I promise."

"Then tell me."

"When we go to Chicago to stay with them, Rafe's going to take you to pick out a kitten or two." She laughed as Merlo let out an excited sound and twisted round in her arms. "I take it you approve?"

Merlo kissed her long and hard. Kieran forgot everything about cats in that moment and focused on Merlo and what she was doing with her teasing tongue. "Wow," she said, feeling a little dazed when Merlo stopped. "I should have led with that straight away. I see that now."

"What was it that made you laugh?"

"Rafe being Rafe. She warned me that I needed to find, and I quote, 'a shit ton of chair leg protectors or you'll have none of your fancy-ass furniture left,' unquote."

"I'll look into it, but furniture is replaceable and maybe it's time to update the house. Perhaps get you to stamp your seal on it, as I'm hoping you might consider moving in with me?"

Kieran nodded. "I'd like that a lot. I think Dina brought my backpack from the hospital when you guys broke me out, so that's all my worldly belongings here already."

Merlo contented herself with leaning back against Kieran and playing with her fingers. "So, you and Ashley. Not what I was expecting when Dina called her in to help you."

"Which part? The sister part or that it led to me finding out my father was a fallen angel who became a demon and is now an angel again?"

"That last bit alone boggles my mind, so I can't begin to imagine what it's doing to yours."

"I like the Ashley part. She said she's finally lucked out because the only other sibling she had was a psychopath, whereas I was merely possessed."

"You're going to miss Virgil too, aren't you?"

"He's very calming for some reason. I think it was right Daryl got him because she's so thoughtful and zen-like. He'd never stand a chance if he was Ashley's angel where Rafe is concerned."

"And what about Lucian? Is he going to be *your* angel now?"

Kieran stiffened at the thought. "I hope not. I've had my fill of not being left alone by invisible forces. If he wants to contact me he can do it the usual way. He can come knock on the door and ask if I'm in."

Merlo chuckled. "He's an angel, not a door-to-door evangelist."

"Well then, he needs to make an appointment because he's still on top of my shit list and I need some time away from him now that he's finally out of my head."

"I understand, sweetheart. Don't worry. I won't let any of the angels press you into anything you don't want to do."

"Thank you." Kieran heard a noise in the kitchen. "Dina?" she called and waited for Dina to wander through from the hall.

"Hey, you two. I was just helping myself to one of Merlo's bottles of wine because, after the last few weeks, I am going to go find a quiet spot out of time and drink myself into oblivion."

Merlo waved a hand at her. "Take as many as you like. Just remember where I keep the headache medicine when you come staggering back here with a hangover." She sat up a little. "Tell me something, old friend, what *did* you see? At the end there, when the angels and demons were fighting."

Dina drew in a deep breath. "I saw many things but always the same outcome. Death. Death for the angels, death for the demons that fought them. I saw your friends fighting as hard as they could to help." Dina raised her eyes to Merlo. "And I saw you kill the Preacher."

"And for Kieran?" Merlo asked.

Dina tilted her head to consider Kieran. "Death. Always death. No matter what timeline I saw, whatever the future revealed, Kieran was never to leave that farm alive."

Kieran felt her blood run cold. No, not her blood anymore, *Merlo's* blood.

"But the alternate futures I saw never counted on an immortal who dared to challenge it all because of something as simple as love." Dina smiled. "Either that or I'm losing my touch." She waved the bottle of wine at them. "I'll ponder that particular quandary too as I drain my cups." She waved Kieran and Merlo up from their sprawl. "Come, give me hugs because I am so thankful that what I saw didn't happen. You two were made for each other, and one thing I do see now very clearly?" She squeezed them both tight, then rested her hands on their shoulders. "I see a long life, with you bonded together in life *and* death. I couldn't have wished more for you, my oldest friend." She kissed Merlo on her cheek. "And you, young Kieran, you have your whole life ahead of you now. You're going to love it." She kissed Kieran's cheek too. Then she saluted them with the bottle of wine as she sauntered out of the room, shouting over her shoulder as she went. "You have all the time in the world, young lovers, enjoy it!"

Merlo tugged on Kieran's hand and Kieran followed behind her. She was surprised and disappointed when Merlo directed her into the study instead of up the stairs.

Merlo let go of Kieran's hand, went to her desk drawer, and pulled out the aged box that held her treasures. Kieran's breath caught when Merlo held up the red/gold ring she'd kept safely tucked away.

"My grandfather was a wise old man. I see now this ring was never meant to be mine to wear. I think he fashioned it for the one, in time, I would come to love more than my own life." She held out her hand to take Kieran's.

Merlo slid the ornate piece onto Kieran's ring finger with ease. It fit perfectly.

"Are you sure you want me to have this?" Kieran asked, astounded at the priceless gift she was being given.

"I do. It was made for you, like you were made for me." Merlo pressed her lips to the ring, then kissed Kieran. "We have a lot to talk about," she said between kisses that were increasing in fervor.

Kieran kissed her back just as desperately. "Such as what?"

"About how we'll have to leave this home at some point to move elsewhere when our neighbors and work colleagues start to age but we don't. I have homes dotted around the country that we can move into and start our lives over again in a new town."

Kieran hadn't thought about the perils of what immortality could entail, especially when surrounded by people not blessed with the same condition. "Okay," she said, a little nonplussed. "That's something we're going to have to discuss." Kieran had a sobering thought. "I'm going to outlive Ashley, aren't I?"

"You're going to outlive everyone except for me and Dina," Merlo said. "Days will pass, loved ones will age and die, and we'll be left behind to watch it all."

"You'll guide me through it, though, won't you?"

"I'll be by your side every step of the way," Merlo promised.

"And we can help people? I want to do something that helps people again. I miss that from the life I had before. I had purpose and I changed lives."

"Then we'll endeavor to do that together. We'll find what we enjoy doing the most and what effects the most changes for the better. We can do anything you want, Kieran. As Dina said, we have all the time in the world."

Kieran nodded, trying not to let her mind get bogged down with all this new information clamoring for her attention. There was a lot to take in. But she had more important needs on her mind. She pulled on Merlo's hand, guiding her from the study and up the stairs.

"Then let's not waste a moment of it, starting with you and me and that big bed in your bedroom."

"A lifetime of kisses ahead of us," Merlo said. "I waited forever for you to come bestow them on me."

"I'm sorry I kept you waiting. But I'm here now." Kieran bumped the bedroom door open with her hip and led Merlo toward the bed. "Forever might not be long enough for me to show you how much I love you, but I'm going to do my damnedest to try." She lay Merlo down and lowered herself beside her, tucking into her side to hold her close. "You are beyond beautiful." She kissed her softly, relishing every touch of Merlo's skin against her lips. "After all I've been through, you, my love, truly make life worth living."

About the Author

Lesley Davis lives in the West Midlands of England. She is a diehard science fiction/fantasy fan in all its forms and an extremely passionate gamer. When her game controller is out of her grasp, Lesley can be found on her laptop writing.

Her book *Dark Wings Descending* was a Lambda Literary award finalist for Best Lesbian Romance.

Visit her online at www.lesleydavisauthor.co.uk.

Books Available From Bold Strokes Books

Breakthrough by Kris Bryant. Falling for a sexy ranger is one thing, but is the possibility of love worth giving up the career Kennedy Wells has always dreamed of? (978-1-63555-179-2)

Certain Requirements by Elinor Zimmerman. Phoenix has always kept her love of kinky submission strictly behind the bedroom door and inside the bounds of romantic relationships, until she meets Kris Andersen. (978-1-63555-195-2)

Dark Euphoria by Ronica Black. When a high-profile case drops in Detective Maria Diaz's lap, she forges ahead only to discover this case, and her main suspect, aren't like any other. (978-1-63555-141-9)

Fore Play by Julie Cannon. Executive Leigh Marshall falls hard for Peyton Broader, her golf pro…and an ex-con. Will she risk sabotaging her career for love? (978-1-63555-102-0)

Love Came Calling by C. A. Popovich. Can a romantic looking for a long-term, committed relationship and a jaded cynic too busy for love conquer life's struggles and find their way to what matters most? (978-1-63555-205-8)

Outside the Law by Carsen Taite. Former sweethearts Tanner Cohen and Sydney Braswell must work together on a federal task force to see justice served, but will they choose to embrace their second chance at love? (978-1-63555-039-9)

The Princess Deception by Nell Stark. When journalist Missy Duke realizes Prince Sebastian is really his twin sister Viola in disguise, she plays along, but when sparks flare between them, will the double deception doom their fairy-tale romance? (978-1-62639-979-2)

The Smell of Rain by Cameron MacElvee. Reyha Arslan, a wise and elegant woman with a tragic past, shows Chrys that there's still beauty to embrace and reason to hope despite the world's cruelty. (978-1-63555-166-2)

The Talebearer by Sheri Lewis Wohl. Liz's visions show her the faces of the lost and the killers who took their lives. As one by one, the murdered are found, a stranger works to stop Liz before the serial killer is brought to justice. (978-1-635550-126-6)

White Wings Weeping by Lesley Davis. The world is full of discord and hatred, but how much of it is just human nature when an evil with sinister intent is invading people's hearts? (978-1-63555-191-4)

A Call Away by KC Richardson. Can a businesswoman from a big city find the answers she's looking for, and possibly love, on a small-town farm? (978-1-63555-025-2)

Berlin Hungers by Justine Saracen. Can the love between an RAF woman and the wife of a Luftwaffe pilot, former enemies, survive in besieged Berlin during the aftermath of World War II? (978-1-63555-116-7)

Blend by Georgia Beers. Lindsay and Piper are like night and day. Working together won't be easy, but not falling in love might prove the hardest job of all. (978-1-63555-189-1)

Hunger for You by Jenny Frame. Principe of an ancient vampire clan Byron Debrek must save her one true love from falling into the hands of her enemies and into the middle of a vampire war. (978-1-63555-168-6)

Mercy by Michelle Larkin. FBI Special Agent Mercy Parker and psychic ex-profiler Piper Vasey learn to love again as they race to stop a man with supernatural gifts who's bent on annihilating humankind. (978-1-63555-202-7)

Pride and Porters by Charlotte Greene. Will pride and prejudice prevent these modern-day lovers from living happily ever after? (978-1-63555-158-7)

Rocks and Stars by Sam Ledel. Kyle's struggle to own who she is and what she really wants may end up landing her on the bench and without the woman of her dreams. (978-1-63555-156-3)

The Boss of Her: Office Romance Novellas by Julie Cannon, Aurora Rey, and M. Ullrich. Going to work never felt so good. Three office romance novellas from talented writers Julie Cannon, Aurora Rey, and M. Ullrich. (978-1-63555-145-7)

The Deep End by Ellie Hart. When family ties become entangled in murder and deception, it's time to find a way out... (978-1-63555-288-1)

A Country Girl's Heart by Dena Blake. When Kat Jackson gets a second chance at love, following her heart will prove the hardest decision of all. (978-1-63555-134-1)

Dangerous Waters by Radclyffe. Life, death, and war on the home front. Two women join forces against a powerful opponent, nature itself. (978-1-63555-233-1)

Fury's Death by Brey Willows. When all we hold sacred fails, who will be there to save us? (978-1-63555-063-4)

It's Not a Date by Heather Blackmore. Kade's desire to keep things with Jen on a professional level is in Jen's best interest. Yet what's in Kade's best interest...is Jen. (978-1-63555-149-5)

Killer Winter by Kay Bigelow. Just when she thought things could get no worse, homicide Lieutenant Leah Samuels learns the woman she loves has betrayed her in devastating ways. (978-1-63555-177-8)

Score by MJ Williamz. Will an addiction to pain pills destroy Ronda's chance with the woman she loves, or will she come out on top and score a happily ever after? (978-1-62639-807-8)

Spring's Wake by Aurora Rey. When wanderer Willa Lange falls for Provincetown B&B owner Nora Calhoun, will past hurts and a fifteen-year age gap keep them from finding love? (978-1-63555-035-1)

The Northwoods by Jane Hoppen. When Evelyn Bauer, disguised as her dead husband, George, travels to a Northwoods logging camp to work, she and the camp cook Sarah Bell forge a friendship fraught with both tenderness and turmoil. (978-1-63555-143-3)

Truth or Dare by C. Spencer. For a group of six lesbian friends, life changes course after one long snow-filled weekend. (978-1-63555-148-8)

Children of the Healer by Barbara Ann Wright. Life becomes desperate for ex-soldier Cordelia Ross when the indigenous aliens of her planet are drawn into a civil war and old enemies linger in the shadows. Book Three of the Godfall Series. (978-1-63555-031-3)

A Heart to Call Home by Jeannie Levig. When Jessie Weldon returns to her hometown after thirty years, can she and her childhood crush Dakota Scott heal the tragic past that links them? (978-1-63555-059-7)

Hearts Like Hers by Melissa Brayden. Coffee shop owner Autumn Primm is ready to cut loose and live a little, but is the baggage that comes with out-of-towner Kate Carpenter too heavy for anything long term? (978-1-63555-014-6)

Love at Cooper's Creek by Missouri Vaun. Shaw Daily flees corporate life to find solace in the rural Blue Ridge Mountains, but escapism eludes her when her attentions are captured by small town beauty Kate Elkins. (978-1-62639-960-0)

Twice in a Lifetime by PJ Trebelhorn. Detective Callie Burke can't deny the growing attraction to her late friend's widow, Taylor Fletcher, who also happens to own the bar where Callie's sister works. (978-1-63555-033-7)

Undiscovered Affinity by Jane Hardee. Will a no-strings-attached affair be enough to break Olivia's control and convince Cardic that love does exist? (978-1-63555-061-0)

Between Sand and Stardust by Tina Michele. Are the lifelong bonds of love strong enough to conquer time, distance, and heartache when Haven Thorne and Willa Bennette are given another chance at forever? (978-1-62639-940-2)

Charming the Vicar by Jenny Frame. When magician and atheist Finn Kane seeks refuge in an English village after a spiritual crisis, can local vicar Bridget Claremont restore her faith in life and love? (978-1-63555-029-0)

Data Capture by Jesse J. Thoma. Lola Walker is undercover on the hunt for cybercriminals while trying not to notice the woman who might be perfectly wrong for her for all the right reasons. (978-1-62639-985-3)